NO TURNING BACK

NO TURNING BACK

LIDIA FALCÓN

TRANSLATED BY
JESSICA KNAUSS, PHD

Loose Leaves Publishing
www.looseleavespublishing.com

Paperback ISBN: 978-1-62432-002-6
eBook ISBN: 978-1-62432-003-3

BISAC Subject Headings:
FIC044000 FICTION / Contemporary Women
FIC037000 FICTION / Political
FIC056000 FICTION / Hispanic & Latino
FIC019000 FICTION / Literary

Cover design by Megan Eichenlaub

Please address all correspondence to:
Loose Leaves Publishing, LLC
5158 S. Lavender Moon Way
Tucson, AZ 85746
Or visit our website at:
www.LooseLeavesPublishing.com

To Anna and Andreu
who lived this book

To everyone who tries to
change the world, from
all their eccentric points of view

Introduction

Imagine the terror of being imprisoned in an isolated cell in the State Security Headquarters of a dictatorship and being dragged off for interrogation by sadistic guards. Imagine the trauma of reliving years later the unnerving clanking of the guard's keys against the cell. So begins Lidia Falcón's historical novel, *No Turning Back* (*Camino sin retorno*, 1992), and her dramatic account of Elisa Vilaró's personal and political struggle in the final years of the Franco regime and the post-Franco era. With the combined skill of a novelist and social historian, Falcón joins the ranks of Ernest Hemingway and George Orwell in presenting her readers with a compelling narrative of more than a decade in Spanish history—1973-1986—and the events that leave a permanent mark on her protagonist, Elisa, as well as on the other characters of the work.

The last years of the thirty-six-year dictatorship of Francisco Franco (1939-1975) were characterized by harsh persecution of radical left-wing parties intent on waging an armed revolution that Santiago Carrillo's clandestine Spanish Communist Party had long since abandoned. Falcón describes in elaborate detail the inner workings of one such political party of which Elisa Vilaró is a member, the Marxist-Leninist faction of the Communist Party (PC-ML), and its relationship to the political landscape of the Franco and post-Franco period. *No Turning Back*, however, is not just a vivid narration of political resistance during this period of Spanish history. It is also a complex portrait of the sexual politics engrained in the fabric of left-wing affairs of state, and the not so surprising similarities between the patriarchal values of traditional institutions of Spanish society and leaders of the Left. Falcón gives life to these diverse spheres of power through the framing event of the novel that takes place in 1986: the five-hour-long conversation between Elisa and her ex-husband, Arnau, who asks for her help in testifying in support of a PC-ML party leader accused of terrorism.

This lengthy conversation, which has only one goal for Arnau, becomes for Elisa an opportunity to relive twenty years of her life, and most particularly the events that transpired between 1973, when she was arrested, and the present moment. As she moves back and forth between past and present, and the personal and the political, Falcón provides her readers with numerous insights into the intricate relationship between these two realms. *No Turning Back* is a compelling portrait of power — how it is used and abused by political parties, institutions and individuals, and how it infiltrates the psyche of those who have it, those who desire it, and those who are marginalized from it. George Orwell dissected with the skill of a journalist and humanist the struggle for power among leftist parties during the 1936-1939 Spanish Civil War in his classic *Homage to Catalonia.* Falcón performs a similar and much needed role in *No Turning Back* as she focuses on the struggle for power in the final years of the Franco dictatorship, the transition to democracy, and democracy itself, considered by some to officially begin in 1982, the year of the electoral victory of the Spanish Socialist Workers Party (PSOE). Her novel unveils the opportunistic political strategies agreed upon by the Left and the Right and their concerted attempts to annul the past and with it, the atrocities of the Civil War and the thirty-six-year Franco regime.

Elisa's act of remembering the past, as opposed to Arnau's attempt to forget it and steer the conversation in the direction of the present, becomes emblematic of a broader debate in Spanish society in the 1980s, and of Falcón's salient role as novelist. *No Turning Back* — a work that resonates with the belief in passionate commitment to social change — suggests that the past needs to be reckoned with in order to create forward movement. The 1977 Amnesty Law in Spain, agreed upon by parties of the Right and the Left, granted immunity to those who committed crimes of a political nature prior to 1977, thus assuring that abuses against Republicans would not be prosecuted. Lidia Falcón, as witness and voice of history, is ever conscious of the contributions of those who fought for the Republic and engaged in clandestine resistance during the Franco dictatorship. She narrates Spanish history from the perspective of a critical insider who has lived up close and personal the struggles of being a communist, a member of a communist splinter group, a political prisoner, a lawyer involved in defending members of radical political groups, and the leader of the modern feminist movement in Spain. Her essays, *The Feminist Reason* among others, reflect her conviction that the only political movement and ideology that can transform society is feminism. Her novels capture the journey that her female protagonists take as they shed countless layers of patriarchal values learned at home, in Catholic schools, love relationships, and left-wing political parties. For them, as for Elisa Vilaró, there is simply no turning back.

Readers and students of Spanish history will be fascinated by the historical events Falcón places before them in moving detail: the militant actions of FRAP (People's Revolutionary Anti-Fascist Front), the armed wing of the PC-ML, between 1973 and 1975; the September 13, 1975 military tribunal which condemned to death three members of this group as well as two members of the Basque nationalist movement, ETA (Freedom for the Basque Country); the political amnesties that followed Franco's death and the continued use of torture during the transition to democracy; the political pacts and sell-outs in the post Franco period and the maneuverings of the Spanish Communist Party; the attempted coup initiated by reactionary members of the Army in 1981; and the anti-NATO campaign of 1986. History leaps from the pages of the novel, dramatically framed by "herstory," the rendition of a female perspective or "historicity that moves across and against 'his story'," as critic Diana Fuss theorizes. This narration of a complex "herstory" is without a doubt one of the most compelling and moving aspects of *No Turning Back*.

As Elisa engages in the process of fusing personal and communal memory, Falcón captures the varied experiences of a member of the Catalan bourgeoisie educated at the elite Sacred Heart school who "converts" from Catholicism to atheism and radical leftist politics through her relationship with Arnau, and who finds herself treated as a second class citizen by the leadership of the PC-ML. Consigned to the subordinate and domestic role of taking care of Arnau while he engages in the party's mission of destabilizing the Franco regime, she is arrested following a political meeting and spends two years in Yeserías prison, the same prison where Falcón was incarcerated for nine months in 1974-1975. Falcón's moving 1977 memoir, "In Hell: To Be a Woman in the Jails of Spain," resonates throughout *No Turning Back*. Elisa recalls the many acts of resistance the thirty-four political prisoners engaged in to survive, acts of resistance which capture in a markedly female light Michel Foucault's theory about the way power creates resistance to power.

Elisa portrays herself and her sister prisoners locked up in jail and unable to communicate effectively or at all with imprisoned male companions. Privy to information smuggled in and out of prison, they face dire issues that require immediate decisions. They arrange for an inmate's abortion, procure from the prison infirmary the antibiotics needed to cure her infection, suffer torture and silence rather than betray their lovers, salute their executed comrades, and console each other in the face of death and torture. While the party's male leadership praises their stoicism, they also criticize their decision to arrange for the abortion, highlighting the devaluation of the female body in the hierarchy of leftist politics. Spanish writer Jorge Semprún denounced the blind obedience to dogma demanded by both leftist parties and the Church in his novel, *Autobiography of Federico Sánchez and the Communist Underground in Spain*. Falcón's relentless denunciation of the "Marxist-Leninist catechism" in *No Turning Back* presents a unique feminist perspective to this critique of leftist ideology.

During her imprisonment, Elisa focuses on surviving and sorting out her increasing doubts about the violent strategies employed by the armed wing of the PC-ML, FRAP. Upon release from prison, however, she and her sister comrades begin the difficult work of analyzing their decisions made in jail. The experiences they narrate are an important and much needed chapter in testimonies about political prisoners, and a tribute to the resilience of women in Franco's jails. *No Turning Back* does not provide, however, an easy path from leftist politics to feminist awareness. Falcón is too adept a novelist to give her readers and her protagonist a ride devoid of bumps and detours. Her body of fiction demonstrates in moving and complex fashion the odyssey her female protagonists traverse as they come to terms with patriarchy and its reach into hidden corners of leftist ideology.

Readers enticed by historical fiction and by a soul-searching view of love, relationships, and betrayal will find in *No Turning Back* a treasure trove of experiences. Elisa's gradual awareness of the manipulations of the Left does not protect her from falling prey to

Arnau's persistent manipulation of their relationship. Political awareness, while not quite the booby prize, does not translate into the personal realm, and Elisa's struggle during the entire novel is to understand what went wrong in her marriage with Arnau, whom she still loves and whom she refuses to blame for the break-up of their life together. She involves herself in feminism following her release from jail in January of 1976—the year of the explosion of feminist activity in Spain that Falcón herself spearheaded—but experiences a radical disconnect between feminist theory and feminist ethics. She cannot seem to find in feminism the same sense of commitment she felt in leftist politics. Devastated after the end of her marriage when Arnau divorces her to marry a colleague, she has an affair with his brother and is convinced a false pregnancy is real.

Falcón surrounds Elisa with a chorus of female friends whose alternately savvy advice, involvement in feminism, and concerted analysis of their subordinate role in leftist politics inspire her to find a way out of emotional despair and to take responsibility for her life. Several of these characters, most notably Isabel and Elisenda, appeared before in Falcón's 1983 novel, *El juego de la piel* ("Skin Games"), an uncompromising critique of a commune in London populated by disaffected Spaniards during the final months of the Franco regime and its aftermath. They join other characters in *No Turning Back*—Octubre, Pilar, and Juana—whose noble acts of heroism are part of the female epic that Falcón creates. Their words resonate in Elisa's ears and fortify her as she cites them to a skeptical Arnau who, not surprisingly, reveals little interest in feminism during their five-hour conversation.

Falcón has an extraordinary ability to seamlessly merge her different roles as novelist, feminist, social historian, and courageous iconoclast. She is a writer whose characters not only grow up under Francoist ideology but actually "spit it" out during the course of the novel, as Elisenda recommends. Elisa is acutely aware that they are all "Franco's children and grandchildren," socialists and communists alike. To this end, her mission is "to find that woman who wasn't allowed to develop, weighted down under tons of lies and repression." The end of the novel and Elisa's five-hour conversation with Arnau provides movement toward that quest. Readers will be rooting for Elisa's self-assertion, and while not giving away the novel's punch line, I will tell you that you will not be disappointed.

v

Jessica Knauss's masterful translation of Lidia Falcón's novel does justice to this important work. Followers of contemporary Spanish history who are familiar with Javier Cercas's dramatic rendition of the 1981 attempted coup in *Anatomy of a Moment* (*Anatomía de un instante*, 2009) will now have the opportunity to understand some of the complex factors that led to this historic event through Falcón's unswerving critical appraisal of Spanish politics. If Elisa poignantly declares, "We're simply a pious memory for the scholars in the libraries," Knauss's agile and eloquent translation guarantees that the memory of clandestine resistance is no longer consigned to the past or to scholars. It is readily available to a wide reading public eager to discover compelling and insightful voices from Spain. Lidia Falcón's voice is simply one not to be missed.

Linda Gould Levine

Acronyms in the Novel

ABC: Long-time bestselling national newspaper in Spain, with a conservative standpoint.

CCOO: Comisiones Obreras "Worker's Commissions" The largest and most powerful union organization in Spain.

ETA: Euzkadi ta Askatasuna "Freedom for the Basque Country" The famous organization still terrorizing Spain for Basque autonomy.

FRAP: Frente Revolucionario Antifranquista Popular "People's Revolutionary Anti-Franco Front" Terrorist action branch of the PC-ML.

GRAPO: Grupo Revolucionario Armado Primero de Octubre "Armed Revolutionary Group of the First of October" Communist terrorist organization.

HOAC: Hermandad Obrera de Acción Católica "Worker's Brotherhood of Catholic Action" see ORT below.

LCR: Liga Comunista Revolucionaria "Revolutionary Communist League"

MCE: Movimiento Comunista de España "Communist Movement of Spain"

ORT: Organización Revolucionaria de Trabajadores "Revolutionary Organization of Workers" Maoist group originating in Catholic worker's groups, like HOAC, created by the Jesuits.

PCC: Partido Comunista de Cataluña "Communist Party of Catalonia"

PCE: Partido Comunista de España "Communist Party of Spain" Headed by Carrillo and known by the PC-ML as "Carrillo's splinter group."

PCI: Partido Comunista Internacional "International Communist Party"

PC-ML: Partido Comunista Marxista-Leninista "Marxist-Leninist Communist Party" Elisa and Arnau's organization, which tried to stick to the original ideals when the PCE appeared to get off track.

PCPE: Partido Comunista de los Pueblos de España "Communist Party of the Spanish Peoples"

PSOE: Partido Socialista Obrero Español "Spanish Socialist Labor Party" This party held power in Spain from 1982 until 1996, with Felipe González as Prime Minister.

PSUC: Partit Socialista Unificat de Catalunya "Unified Socialist Party of Catalonia" Another Catalan communist party, in which Lidia Falcón was active during the years 1959 - 1966.

PTE: Partido de los Trabajadores de España "Party of the Workers of Spain" Originated in the PCI.

TOP: Tribunal de Orden Público "Tribunal of Public Order"

UGT: Unión General de Trabajadores "General Worker's Union"

USO: Unión Sindical Obrera "Unionist Worker's Union"

Chapter 1

The clanking resounded off the walls. It echoed in the twisting passageways of those catacombs, repeated in the corners of the cells, and multiplied, becoming more terrifying. The guard swung keys hanging from an enormous iron ring like an artifact from the Middle Ages. When he passed in front of the grille that marked off each of the cells from the corridor, he beat the keys against the bars. Sometimes the clanking meant the prisoner was summoned. Other times, the guard paused a few seconds in front of the door, pretending he was hesitating to call its tenant. Then he continued on his way. During that brief moment the prisoner's heart rate tripled, and the guard knew it. He didn't do it at every cell. Some were empty, others contained uninteresting prisoners. The ones chosen for his game were the cells of the political prisoners. Even better if they were women, who must be more frightened. Sometimes he walked the entire length of the passage underneath the Puerta del Sol without summoning anyone. He had to do something to pass the endless time between sunrise and nightfall when he was on duty. In the end, he too was imprisoned twelve hours a day in the maze of dungeons. He had to wait for retirement to be freed, while the prisoners came and went as rhythmically as flowing water, leaving him there with the keys his only company. The authority he possessed over the prisoners rested only in those keys he would strike once in a while against the iron bars. The metallic clanking reminded the prisoners who held power there — underground.

The guard could see only the stripes of sun that entered through the skylights at the unreachable height of the ceiling, and all he knew of his companions who worked outside were their feet raising dust in the parking lot. He could barely hear the distant, harsh, and always irritated voices of the officers at the entrance, but at least he had the keys to the underground cells, and their clanking against the bars compensated for so many other situations in which he was powerless.

The guard's steps became erratic. They quickened, they hesitated, suddenly they stopped. He knocked the keys against the bars of the cell door in front of him. The profound silence that followed hinted at the tense and crouching wait of the bodies that still breathed in that mausoleum. The prisoners strained their ears to perceive clothes swishing, hands brushing together, the guard's breathing, the hoarseness of his throat, and the stretching of his lips into a smile. As the silence became prolonged, everyone knew that the summons was imminent. The silence began to deteriorate. Muscles, fatigued by contraction, began to release. Suddenly, unexpectedly, the steps began again, and, with them, a whole world of lively murmurs: bodies moving on mattresses, quickened breathing, moans, muffled sobs, bare feet moving on the cement.

The clanking began again, with no rhythm, in no order. It clashed the bars. It came closer in the turns of the passageway, resounding louder each time. Suddenly, it stopped right by her side, and this time not one second passed before the call echoed through the basement.

"Elisa Vilaró!"

His voice sounded hoarse, as if just awakened from a deep, necessary sleep. Now sounds could clearly be heard: coughs, quilts and blankets moving, the deep sigh of relief of the prisoners who for hours had been fearing the sound of their own names.

The clanking of the keys against the bars of her cell didn't stop. It kept ringing off the walls, in her ears, in her head, an unstoppable drum. Like the question that was screamed again and again, spewed out from Twistface's throat.

"Why did you come to Madrid? Eh? Your family is from" — here he pronounced something unintelligible that the Catalan name of her town became in his mouth — "and you were born there. You studied in Barcelona. Why the hell did you come here?"

And the clanking on the bars began again right away, like the screaming and the question.

"Why did you come to Madrid? Why? Why?"

She hardly recognized her own voice as she repeated in turn: "To take care of my husband. To take care of my husband. To take care of…"

Now the clanking against the bars echoed around the office where Twistface insisted on the same question for hours, as if he didn't feel the same urges as other human beings: fatigue, hunger, boredom, dejection. Twistface's screaming and the clanking keys against the bars filled up the entire space. Elisa felt unable to react, to answer, to argue. She heard herself responding.

"To take care of my husband…, my husband. To take care of…"

Suddenly the shouting grew fainter and disappeared, and the twisted face of her interrogator became smaller and smaller, blurred. She heard only the clanking that sounded closer and closer, as if it were ringing off an iron bar on the top of her head.

She awoke, covered in sweat, to the sound of the garden gate resonating with a visitor's clanking knocks. With the same painful effort she had had to make every time she got up from the mattress in prison, Elisa sat up in bed and looked through the window. She hadn't put on her glasses, and the noisy visitor was a blurry figure beyond the sycamores in the garden. She threw on a robe and looked for her glasses. The man's way of standing, with his head tilted and one foot in front of the other, was all too familiar to her. She began to shiver from the sharp contrast between the temperature in the bed and in the room, and her sweat quickly began to dry. She would have turned on the space heater if the rhythmic clanking against the grate hadn't been so urgent. She opened the door in front of her and, only a few feet away, leaning against the entryway frame, was Arnau. And she began to sweat again in distress.

When she opened the door, Arnau was unable to come up with a satisfactory greeting. Leaning toward her without daring to kiss her cheek, and brushing against her hand, but not grasping it, he said, "You still sleep like a rock, as always…" And even while he was saying it, he regretted such an idiotic start to the meeting.

Elisa didn't take note of the words. She merely said, "I went to bed late last night. I was correcting exams until morning… When you started knocking on the gate I dreamed I was at State Security Headquarters…"

"Come on. After so long? You still haven't forgotten?"

"I never forget anything," she responded bitterly, and right away they were both sorry to have uttered those sentences that had such an uncomfortable double meaning.

"I'm going to wash my face, I'm not awake yet."

Elisa leaned over the sink and turned on the cold water. Why would he come to her house at this hour? What for, after two months? He seemed worried, despite his everlasting expression of self-satisfaction. Elisa tried to remember the last time they had seen each other. They had had lunch at a bar next to the newspaper offices, and she listened to him in silence, as she had so many other times, trying not to choke on her food. Afterward they said goodbye hurriedly so each could run off to work, and for two months they hadn't seen each other again. *Because I haven't called him.* Whenever a friend asked about him, she always explained that they saw each other often, that they were close friends, that they had still work and interests in common, and in this way she silenced their assumptions and her own grief. That was why it was always she who called and suggested the lunch dates. Until the last time, after Christmas, when, during the routine conversation — the anecdotes from work at the newspaper and the latest news — Elisa understood that the connection that had brought them together no longer existed.

The memory of the relationship they had had for so many years caused her renewed pain. She closed her eyes so she couldn't see herself in the mirror and angrily scrubbed her teeth and gums until they bled. Spitting blood and water into the sink, she was reminded of herself crouching over that hole in the floor where she puked up that disgusting grub she had tasted only a little while before the interrogation. An armed guard impassively watched her from the toilet room door. She was dizzy, and to keep herself from falling she had to hold herself up with one hand on the wall, leaning over the dark hole, filled with remains of shit and blood belonging to all the arrested people who had concluded their interrogations there. Elisa was still not finished. She had been at the State Security Headquarters three days and had barely said a thing. She repeated the same story time and again. She explained that they had been in Madrid since the previous year, how she had followed her studies, Arnau's work and little else, because when she would monotonously begin the same story again, the screaming would also start anew.

Her stomach felt calmer and the nausea stopped. She stood up, supporting herself against the walls. The guard was impatient. He turned around and started toward the cell. He opened the door and waited for Elisa to take off her shoes with her clumsy hands, and closed the grate with the customary creak. When she lay down on the mattress, every bone in her body screamed its protest. She hadn't slept in three days.

And that was only the beginning, she thought as she spit out the last mouthful of water and dried her face with a towel.

She didn't want to think about what happened later. She didn't want to remember anything. She wanted to run away from space and time, to levitate like the great mystics she had worked so hard to imitate in grade school. When she had wanted to be a saint. And that memory made her smile in spite of the pain. But before her muscles had relaxed into the mattress, and rest had begun the healing process, she again heard that chilling call.

"Elisa Vilaró!"

She decided not to get up that time. Let them drag her if they wanted. She could no longer straighten herself out on the mattress on her own. With a mechanical gesture she raised the blanket to her eyes to shut out the light from the bulb in the hallway, and then, remembering the prohibition, lowered it again. She heard the voice again, sharper, more alert, outside her cell bars.

"Elisa Vilaró, to questioning!"

Elisa opened her eyes, and with terror and amazement she contemplated the figure of the guard who was opening the lock on the bars and sternly signaling her to get up.

"Are you deaf? To questioning, I said!" The man whipped away the blanket that covered her and tugged at her arm so hard her shoulder was nearly dislocated. Elisa loosed a shriek that didn't seem to interest him and sat up on the mattress. She motioned to the guard that she would get up by herself. She put on her sandals and stumbled through the hallway behind him.

Whenever she passed by the cells, she tried to identify the bodies lying on the mattresses. Their faces became blurred in the darkness. Only one cell was directly across from the light bulb fixed in the hallway, and in it was a man Elisa didn't know. Arnau wasn't in any of the cells in that part of the corridor. She wanted to believe he was somewhere close by, in the corner right next to her cell, but in all that time she had never heard his name shouted in the underground hallways, not once.

The isolation and darkness of the cell had made her profoundly confused and disoriented. She made an effort to concentrate on the ground she was covering with the guard, but she became faint. The guard had to hold her up by the arm, and he looked at her with concern. Again she forced herself to walk upright and in a straight line. She felt a discomfort in her stomach she could not identify and her knees shook. She suddenly remembered the way her legs had fallen asleep after the Benediction every Wednesday night in the school chapel, and almost smiled when she remembered those supplications asking the Lord for strength in the hour of need. She felt sad, suddenly, to not have that consolation.

In the long days and nights of her detention, the prayers that had consumed her childhood and adolescence would have helped her pass the time. She was startled to realize suddenly that she didn't know how many days had gone by since the arrest. Perhaps she had suffered one of the mental lapses which, as a little girl, she had confused with the ecstasy she so often asked of the Lord as a sign of his grace.

A sudden brightness jolted her. She was outside. The surprise made her stumble over the curb and the guard held her up again. She could tell he was disgusted by the job. When she stood up, Elisa found that they were in a large parking lot full of cars right next to the street. There, twenty feet away, people were walking along Correo Street, not bothering to glance at the well-known lot where the police vehicles parked. No one must have known that beaten prisoners with bruised faces and bloody lips were sent through that lot without precaution.

The guard pushed her toward a nearby door. When she staggered from the blow, her handcuffs slipped and she had to hold them up because they were falling off her wrists. The guard looked at her, and an expression she could have taken for tenderness passed fleetingly over his face. They went through the doorway and got into an elevator that left them on a landing across from a hallway. Elisa didn't recognize the office from a few hours earlier, but the same interrogators were waiting for her there.

Elisa vigorously shook her head to drive out the memories and decisively entered the bedroom to get dressed. With every movement she expelled more of the deadly air her memory had called up again after ten years. No, she hadn't gone ten years without remembering. From time to time, every two or three months, though less often lately, all the details of that period of her life revisited her.

The therapist explained that it was better that way. That way, she was analyzing and working through the events. She wasn't letting them fester in her subconscious the way others did, only to be driven insane by them years later.

Better this way, she repeated with determination as she finished putting on her pants. *But my muddled mind refuses to sort out the details in any recognizable order.* She hated the river of memories flooding her on precisely the morning Arnau had come to visit her, after two months of no lunches or calls.

Why had he come? She thought she had noticed a different look on his face. The way he lightly brushed against her hand and leaned forward to kiss her were no longer usual in their relationship. He hadn't shaved and he looked tired. He acted less stiffly, more naturally than he had lately, when they met only when she called him and they always spoke of business matters. She felt a prick of unease. She didn't want to put what she was thinking into words, but the desire to do just that kept getting stronger. She suddenly remembered some of the latest news Isabel had told her and shook her head again. It was better not to second-guess Arnau's motives in coming here. He himself would explain them in a few minutes. Elisa adjusted her belt violently and slammed the door as she left the bedroom. In the dining room she bumped into Arnau, who was coming at just that moment with coffee and some toast on a tray.

"Damn, when you get up, you really get going."

He was trying to be playful, but to Elisa he seemed more pathetic than ever. She smiled and gushed over his culinary attentions. It was better to make light of the situation and ignore all references to the past. And suddenly Arnau, as he poured the coffee, said in the same way one would comment on the weather, "This dining room reminds me of the one at the Deputation offices, don't you think?"

Only a man could say that. The sound of Isabel's voice startled her as if she were sitting right next to her. She feigned indifference and nodded with a half smile. But that was a mistake, because he kept talking about it.

"I've never been here before. It's really nice. How much does it run you?"

"I share it with Isabel. We pay fifty thousand pesetas a month, but heat is included and since these places get so cold in the winter, it seemed worth it. What they do is turn it on in November and turn it back off in March, and it's still awfully cold to not have any kind of heating, so I got some space heaters…"

Elisa heard herself talking in a voice that was too loud, too happy, too casual.

"Isn't it hard to go to Barcelona every day from here?"

"You get used to it. The express trains leave from San Cugat often, and if not that, I take the car…"

She was getting impatient. She didn't understand his strange visit, the apparent calm with which he was eating his breakfast, the insubstantial conversation they seemed to have had a hundred times before. Her desire became mixed with distrust. It didn't make sense that he should have appeared that morning at her door. He should have called her at school. They could have had lunch or dinner. Something was happening, something new and important, and he didn't dare tell her.

"We're thinking about renting a house outside the city, here or in Valldoreix. But I just can't make up my mind to do it. I'm not sure about staying in Barcelona."

"No?" She was genuinely surprised. "Is the agency moving you to another city?"

"No… Well, I don't know. If I asked, maybe…" Now he seemed sorry to have said so much. "How about you?" For a moment Elisa thought he was asking whether she was considering moving to another city, but before she could say no, he added, "What are you doing for Easter? Are you going out of town? Do you get any time off?"

"Yes, I do."

"I'm going out of town, too, but to work. I'll be in Israel for a few days covering the aftermath of the Libyan attack and the American response. I won't have a vacation until April. Since I'm leaving in two days, I thought I'd come by here."

Finally, he was getting around to the real reason for his visit.

"I couldn't wait until I got back, and the telephone would have been imprudent…"

Elisa jumped. Again, the forgotten rites returned, as stale as old actors made up for a performance that existed nowhere but in their own minds. She stared at him without comment, waiting for an explanation. She observed him carefully, trying to guess before he explained, how much of it was true and how much paranoia. Arnau was uncomfortable despite his famous ability to take control of any situation.

"You see, Elisa, we need you… I need you," he added hastily to correct the blunder.

Elisa didn't bat an eye. She just waited, avidly eating a biscuit spread with jam that would have repulsed her only minutes earlier. Arnau continued with visible effort.

"There's a comrade in trouble and we need your help."

There was a long silence between them that Arnau could not overcome. For an instant, Elisa felt the satisfaction of revenge, remembering how he always seemed so in control. Finally, without bothering to hide the sarcasm in her voice, she said, "So you need me. This must be the first time."

Arnau's look made her ashamed. Then she felt silly and that made her angry. Again he looked confident and at the same time, like the victim of her bad mood.

"Come on, Elisa. You're better than that. You know perfectly well that I appreciate what you're worth, and you're worth a lot more than me. I've told you so many times, and I've always treated you accordingly."

"Who is it?"

For once, Elisa was satisfied with her action. Arnau became disconcerted by her emotionless tone. And then she regretted it. Her face was tense and she compulsively pressed a crumb between her fingers. Her anger wasn't provoked by the news that one of those obsessed members of the party, about whom she never even thought any more, had gotten into a mess again. She tried to relax, and put on a slight smile which was out of place and caused Arnau more distress. Feeling used by the party had nothing to do with it anymore. The painful part of the situation was Arnau's presence there, having breakfast with her, talking about things no one cared about, pretending he was happy to see her, tricking her once again. Or not. Perhaps he had never tricked her. She had imagined it, or he changed. It wasn't that, either. It was she who had changed over the last few years. She realized that Arnau was looking at her tensely, waiting for a reaction. He had said something she hadn't heard. She arched her eyebrows and asked him with her look. In a louder voice, which poorly hid the throbs of anguish that underlay his tone, he repeated, "Antonio Cherta. The comrade in trouble is Antonio Cherta."

And suddenly, to Arnau's surprise, Elisa began to laugh out loud, so much that she choked on her last biscuit crumbs and had to get up to spit in the sink.

Chapter 2

Comrade Ramiro didn't reply. He folded his hands over his knees and waited. His hands were large and angular, with remains of the calluses that had formed in the shipyards of Vigo when he was fourteen. Whenever Elisa talked, she felt like he wasn't listening. Ramiro waited for her reply, more indifferently than patiently. With an absent expression, his square, solid face looked as if it were carved from wood. *A chip off the old Marxist-Leninist block,* Elisa thought angrily, and she loudly blew her nose to show her fury more ostensibly. Her tears only confirmed Ramiro's opinion that women didn't serve the interests of the party.

Elisa never understood Antonio Cherta, known as Ramiro within the party, nor any of the other male comrades in the party, especially the leaders. Their responses, their behavior, always indifferent to the reasoning and requests of the comrades at the bases, disturbed her, and she preferred not to participate in meetings or answer questions.

"You'd rather just stay out of it, right?" Arnau reproached her bitterly. "Meanwhile, those of us who protest and demand the party's legalization are the bad guys, the separatists, right?" But his complaint quickly became meaningless because Arnau, in spite of the different crises he went through over the course of his active party life, was still an important part of the leadership. He was almost the only one, except for the general secretary and two or three others, who had been there since the early days. Elisa, on the other hand, fell out of favor with the party almost immediately afterward, precisely because of that first meeting with Ramiro.

"Well, Comrade Antonia" — Cherta, always stuck to the rules, addressed Elisa by her party alias — "you already know the reasons that brought our Central Committee to this decision. What's your final response? Do I have to report back to our political bureau that you refuse to follow orders?"

In Ramiro's light brown eyes, there shone a strange light that Octubre explained by saying that the party leaders always kept their gaze fixed on Albania. Octubre would later be Elisa's cellmate in prison, and according to her, that gaze was essential when it came to fulfilling a responsible role within the party: carrying out the outrageous orders of the Central Committee with Ramiro's imperturbability, talking to her the way he did on that occasion.

Elisa remembered that when she left prison she was afraid Arnau would someday have the same look.

"I don't know. I still don't know."

Comrade Ramiro now adopted an understanding tone. "Comrade Antonia, you must be tired. The trip has been hard and you're not in any condition to think it over calmly. Let's rest a little while and reconvene in three hours. We're all tired and overexcited. A little rest would do us good. I'll report on the secretariat's decision later."

In the hallway, Elisa took María aside. "Do you agree with them?"

María looked at her with surprise and fear. Cherta's wife, María was small, slight, and seemed to be in a permanent state of panic. Elisa believed she could have better shown her natural intelligence if it hadn't been for her extreme adoration for her husband.

"What are you talking about?"

"María, please, you know exactly what I'm talking about. They brought us here, hundreds of kilometers from our homes just to cook for our husbands. Is that okay with you?"

María blinked convulsively, and Elisa noticed her arm trembling under her hand.

"You can't say that, Antonia. We're here, at the party's request, to put together the organization in Madrid."

"Manuel, Jorge and Antonio are, but not us. Didn't you hear what Ramiro said? Or don't you remember? We're here to take care of them. The party isn't giving us any specific task. It was made very clear."

María's innocent blue eyes reflected her incomprehension of Elisa's anger.

"But that's fine. Antonio needs someone to take care of him. How would he eat? If he were alone he'd get sick within a week and his work for the party carries a lot of responsibility."

"But don't you want to do anything else? Don't you think you could be useful to the party in some other way?"

"How?"

Elisa looked at María's thin, pallid face for a few moments and sighed. She let go of María's arm and went down the hall to her room without saying anything more.

Lying on the bed, Elisa came face to face with the evidence of her failure. In this instance, Lenin's instructions were of no use to her. Lenin never took the militancy of his comrades' wives into account. Not Lenin, nor Ramiro, nor Antonio, nor Jorge, none of them took any interest in the hopes and dreams Elisa had invested in what she had taken for a promotion when they asked her to move to Madrid. She saw herself in that miserable apartment in Vallecas, waiting every noon and night for Arnau to come back from his daily outings, taking part in the fundamental work of rebuilding the debilitated party organization, and it made her feel like handing in her resignation. But the prospect of returning, alone, to Barcelona, distressed her even more. Arnau's resignation was unthinkable. He wouldn't follow her, and he wouldn't even consider it for an instant.

He had dedicated ten years of his life to activism, become estranged from his mother, whom he loved very much, quit the studies that interested him, left behind his homeland and his language and set aside all his professional goals for the revolution. It would not be love for Elisa that would persuade him to leave the party. Particularly when it seemed he was successfully carrying out the most difficult mission they had ever charged him with: rebuilding the organization in Madrid, which was almost totally destroyed as a result of the repression the party had suffered since May first, 1973.

Elisa lay on the bed in the dark with her eyes open, dry and stinging, until the meeting reconvened. Ramiro knew her, or did he? How could he know her if he had never seen her before? More likely, he knew the impossibility of choosing in a situation like the one she found herself in. Elisa didn't cry. She had hardly cried ever since the time she had decided to become a saint at seven years of age and had begun her training in suffering silently for the love of God. When the meeting began again, she gloomily said, "I agree," and stared at the wall to avoid María's satisfied smile.

Ramiro didn't even answer, "Fine," or anything of the kind. He simply made a brief note in his schedule and they continued speaking about the agenda for the day, which consisted solely of reading them a summary of the latest communiqué from the Central Committee, whose entire text María and Antonia had to turn in to their husbands.

Elisa politely took her leave of Ramiro, but when María carefully approached her to talk about the meeting, Elisa avoided her.

"Your feelings should be known only to God. Do not let your rage show the weakness of your character to your enemy. Do not permit your thoughts and feelings to show on your face or in your words. Your enemies will take advantage of them to wound you to the heart. Impassiveness in the face of humiliation and suffering is a talent attained only with the grace of God." Elisa had always listened attentively to her spiritual advisor, absorbed the words, meditated on them for days on end, and remembered them constantly so that she would not forget a single one. Being a saint implied complete serenity, emotional control, impassiveness, an absence of anger, rage and grief. How to attain this level of spiritual superiority? With God's help, and she petitioned for it constantly.

That was why Elisenda got bored with her in the end. She accused Elisa of being a sanctimonious wet blanket, and in the last years of school they hardly paid any attention to each other in spite of having been such good friends. Elisa recognized at that moment that in a certain way, Elisenda had been the smart one.

While she cleared her throat, after spitting out the crumbs she had choked on, she surprised herself thinking of Elisenda and school, so far removed from her present interests. As she dried her hands, she wondered what her present interests really were. *The impassivity of a saint...* and she smiled tenderly at the adolescent she had been, willing and responsible, struggling so hard to achieve sainthood. It was because of her willingness and responsibility that she finished her degree after so many years of militancy and prison, and got that job at the school, and made a good living, and had her own car and house and an independent life... without Arnau.

When she returned to the dining room and had to face Arnau's anxious, expectant look, she was overcome with indifference. If only she didn't have to keep talking, explaining, if only Arnau wouldn't ask... but he was already saying, "What happened?"

"Nothing. I just thought it was funny it was Antonio Cherta who needed my help."

"I see."

Arnau hadn't forgotten the difficult relations Elisa had always had with Cherta. He felt no more like discussing it now than he had that afternoon in Madrid when Elisa returned from the Valencia meeting.

"You must be pleased, huh? They've brought me out here just to take care of you."

"No, I'm not pleased. I've always been very concerned about it."

Then she understood that he had known about the party's plans for some time. It was yet another one of the absurdities they said clandestineness required.

"You already knew what Ramiro was going to propose. You knew and you agree with him, don't you?"

Arnau nodded his head hesitantly. "Yes, I knew, but I didn't entirely agree. The worst part of all this is that nothing else can be done. I'm responsible for the organizational work, and right now you don't have any specific responsibility. Since you're not at the University, we can't give you an assignment. But soon that won't matter. We'll rebuild the departments and then you can get back into it."

"That isn't what Ramiro said..."

But she wanted to believe it and he looked at her with his most convincing expression, exploiting all the magic of his dark gaze, his obvious influence over her, to quiet her protests. *But not totally*, Elisa told herself obstinately. *I never forgot that episode, I never forgave them for treating me like Arnau's maid. I never forgot and I never will.*

Arnau looked at her in surprise after she recalled that old conversation. "You never talked about it again. You seemed to understand and agree with the reasons…"

Elisa looked at him with her lips pursed and her eyebrows furrowed. She hadn't let her rage show her weakness of character to her enemies and her strength of spirit had won. For five years she hadn't mentioned the episode. Until she left prison and seriously considered the other alternative, and then, one fine day, to Arnau's dismay, Elisa had made him sit through all the reproaches she had accumulated over those five years. In chronological order, by order of importance, and in a detailed account from the least to the most influential events in her life. Arnau, amazed, admitted that he had never imagined she was capable of harboring so much rage in silence.

"But then, why didn't you leave the party? How could you keep working in it so long, and in prison and everything?"

"I loved you and didn't want to lose you."

It was the only confession she hadn't wanted to keep silent. But the honesty had worked only to surrender her to him in all her weakness. Her confessor had been right. The only one who triumphs is he who remains impassive and indifferent. That was why Elisa now waited calmly for Arnau to ask and explain.

"Well, what do you say?"

Elisa arched her eyebrows and asked in turn, "About what? You still haven't told me what's going on and why you need me."

"Yes, that's true, but you know… I'd like to be able to count on you before I explain the details. If you're disposed toward us we can talk about it, but if you don't want to help us by any means, then there's no need to bore you with this story."

Elisa wasn't bored by the story. That morning at the end of March 1986, perhaps she was going to finally get some closure to the years of militancy that consumed most of her youth. Perhaps she would find in Arnau's words the key to what had happened years before. Finally, after so long, he and she were going to talk about people and events that affected them personally. Finally – and she had had to wait two years to reach that "finally" – Arnau was going to tell her about the things that were much more important to her than the Iran-Iraq war, or the United States' attack on Libya. She had to convince him to tell the whole story. It would be best, then, to let him think he could count on her help.

"If it's serious, you already know that you've always been able to rely on me…"

Arnau nodded, but the look of distrust which had been manifest in his large, dark eyes since he had arrived that morning didn't disappear.

"It all goes back to July '73. When we were arrested, you know. What they call 'the fall of the leaders.'"

The date summoned the endless inquiries for Elisa again. The interrogation office had changed, because daylight was coming in through one of the balconies. It was impossible to believe that the open street existed only a few meters away from them. Twistface was chain-smoking and his shirt was stained with coffee and tobacco. The senior officer was still sitting in the big chair, but now she could see him by the light of day, and Elisa was surprised that he had a symmetrical face. The third was still waiting for a declaration to write on his ancient typewriter.

"What was your husband doing in Madrid? And you? How many are there on the executive committee other than the ones who were with you?"

But they didn't hit her. Her interrogation was routine. They knew her role in the project led by Ramiro and his comrades had been secondary.

Days later, when she was able to discuss the detention with other prisoners, she realized she had been very lucky. In the end, she should've thanked comrade Ramiro for keeping her out of the important business of the party. In spite of being Arnau's wife or perhaps for exactly that reason. But it wasn't easy to explain that she had been sent to Madrid all the way from Barcelona to make her husband dinner and look after him while he dedicated himself to the most important organizational activities in the party. And it wasn't because the police thought a woman was adequate for executive responsibility, but, on the contrary, because they had always known that the communists defined themselves with equality between men and women, for making use of women in jobs inappropriate to their sex, for the degeneration of morals and manners in the bosom of the family, and, as such, it wasn't so improbable that Elisa or any other of those aberrant communists, including that dunce María, might have actively participated in the directive functions of the party.

Yes, in the end she should be grateful to Ramiro that he hadn't made more use of her in the struggle, though it was the party itself which should receive her gratitude, since Elisa's interrogation brought nothing new to the investigation.

She tried to make out the city streets in the blackness of that dawn from the truck in which they were moving her to Yeserías Prison. Seventeen days buried in the police station basement, in the torture offices. An entire era — afterward, nothing would ever be the same — in seventeen days. Some lights revealed deserted streets and avenues. The watch they had returned to her showed three o'clock, but it was the three o'clock in the afternoon of seventeen days before, when they had dragged, pushed, and shoved her into the police car after she left that attic on Olmo Street, in the center of Madrid, where they'd held the meeting. She thought of asking the driver or the guard sitting next to him what time it was, but she didn't have the strength. She thought it must be four or five in the morning, and then she fell asleep. They had to wake her up when they got to Yeserías. The driver said to his companion in surprise, "That's the first time a prisoner's ever fallen asleep on me."

Elisa didn't usually talk about the detention with anyone. She had to put her ideas in order. If the police hadn't believed her, she would have been seriously beaten. Maybe they believed her because everyone else told them the same thing. It was a true story, even within the party.

"The police have never really believed us, and even though they gave us amnesty later, we always remained on file, and even years after legalization, they still connect the party to terrorism."

Chapter 3

The blows resounded off the walls. They echoed in her ears at the same time that they dug into her stomach and her liver. That split between the sound and the impact on her flesh gave her a strange sensation. She could not tell whether it increased or diminished the pain. She couldn't understand it, but she was seeing and passing judgments on herself from the outside, as if she were not a participant in the situation. In spite of the pain. In spite of her nerves being near the limit of what they could bear. She would lose consciousness in just a few moments, and nevertheless she kept coldly analyzing her sensations. Her torturer had one eye higher than the other, and with a twisted nose and a frenetic expression, he was the perfect image of a villain, just like in the movies. But he was real, as real as that dirty office furnished with what seemed to be the remains of a fifty-year-old trash heap. As real as the four officers who played out their roles with the clumsiness and enthusiasm of amateur actors.

The one with the crooked eyes shouted questions at her as he hit her, time and again, in rhythm. Another, whose face she could not make out because of the shadows produced by a flexible lamp with a 25-watt bulb, waited, bored, in front of a nineteenth-century Underwood typewriter, for her to produce a declaration he could scrupulously copy. Another officer, higher up on the salary scale, she thought, was behind them all, his face in shadows, observing them, not participating. A fourth chorused Twistface's shouting. The scene was lasting an interminable length of time. A clock on the wall always showed the same time. At first she thought it had stopped, but the second hand was moving. The blows kept time with the seconds, and the torture never ended, but time wasn't passing.

The question was always the same. Later she could not remember whether they had interrogated her about anything else. Like an obsessive drumbeat, Twistface inserted the question between the blows: "Why did you make that secret cabinet in your house?" Afterward, the blows and screaming were repeated for a few minutes. Then a pause, and again the question, "Why did you make that secret cabinet?"

She didn't say anything any more. For three days she had attempted to convince the officers of the truth. Now, it wasn't worth the trouble. She had learned that they didn't listen. They knew everything they wanted or needed to know. They had reconstructed all her activities from Vitia's accusation and the other prisoners' declarations. They knew it all, or they tried to. They needed no response, but the blows continued and so did the question.

"Why did you make that secret cabinet?"

"To hold my papers…"

Her voice sounded muffled, as if as if she were speaking under water. Her mouth tasted salty and disgusting. She spit out a mouthful of blood and took another blow to the liver.

"Why did you make… Why did you make…?"

"To hold my papers… papers, just papers… to hold…"

The voice echoed through the small room, and her mouth continued to taste like rotten blood. The blows continued, and the torture never ended. The blows repeated, and time wasn't passing.

Elisa leaned over Octubre's bed and touched her. "What's wrong?"

Octubre was sweating and moaning weakly. It was hard for Elisa to wake her up. Finally, her dark eyes shone in her pale face.

"Sorry, I must have been dreaming."

"About the detention?"

Octubre nodded as she sat up in the bed and dried the saliva that escaped from the corners of her mouth with the corner of the sheet. "Yes, of course. The torture doesn't end with the detention. It comes back again and again to torment its victim."

She got up and washed her face at the sink. Looking at herself in the mirror, she furrowed her brow.

"What do you know, they left me my beauty."

"You always look beautiful."

Octubre was going to respond with a polite thank you, but she noticed the sincerity in Elisa's look.

"You're the beautiful one. So young, so innocent…"

"Stop complimenting me like that. You'll end up calling me dumb."

There was no bitterness in Elisa's tone, but Octubre was startled.

"How can you think innocence is the same as stupidity? It has to do with purity of heart, the best in a human being."

"Argh! Don't talk to me like the nuns, please!"

Octubre couldn't help but smile. "Sorry, I wasn't trying to conjure up your ghosts. I was never at a Catholic school, so I don't have that unpleasant aftertaste."

"Then, why do you talk about purity of heart?" Elisa asked, surprised.

"Because it's a good thing to have. Those who have it —"

"Will be called the 'children of God,'" Elisa droned.

"Yes, I know that's what Christian hagiography says. But what's important is not what they're called, but what they're able to do. For example, making this lousy world a place worth living in."

Elisa looked disconcerted. Octubre was using language that was uncommon in the world of communist parties.

"What do you mean?"

Octubre was almost always smiling, and now she looked at Elisa tenderly. "I'm talking about the revolution. But the one only the pure of heart can carry out."

Elisa began to sulk. Even though she herself didn't know why, she replied, "Pure hearts don't exist."

Octubre smiled once more and declared, "You have one."

Elisa remembered how strange Octubre was. Arnau had once insultingly referred to her as "mystical," but Elisa didn't think that was exactly it. She had a pleasant temperament, but at the same time, a bad temper. And when she got enthusiastic about something, her passion was completely human.

That was the way she explained the conspiracy against her between the police, the military tribunal, and her friends, who were terrorists, though she didn't know it.

"They slandered me because it was convenient for them. In spite of the beatings, the police know full well that I had nothing to do with those lunatics' plotting. They dragged me into it because that way the case would be more convincing. They wear themselves out saying, 'the masses' without ever having seen more than three people together. Without ever listening to a shopkeeper or a housewife. Without ever really working, as they should, organizing the people. Then they make a firecracker, put it somewhere, in a coffee shop, and when they kill twelve civilians with it, they accuse them of having been police informers, and it's all taken care of…"

"Are you in the PCE?" Elisa asked.

Now Octubre was about to laugh. "That's not something you just ask, my dear. Can you see how innocent you are? But I'll answer you. Why not! The police know everything. No, I left the party quite a few years ago, in '66. When I was fed up with all those dimwits with their national reconciliation and peace accords. They were like priests, but worse, because now there are quite a few communist priests and they're less wishy-washy and conciliatory than the party leaders. And Ormazábal singing the praises of the army in '62 at the military tribunal where they sentenced him to twenty years, and hundreds of things just like that. You know what my father said to me after the congress of 1956 when they approved national reconciliation? He was in the pen in Burgos then, with a death sentence, and reprieved. He was there twenty years, twenty years all together. Do you have any idea what that is? I was ten when he went in, and the next time I hugged him I was thirty. He was a captain in the Republican army, and he went through the same thing they all did, the way out through La Junquera — the concentration camp — and, when they set him free, the guerrilla fighting in France, and then he went to the Pyrenees… My father had been receiving a pension from the French government since 1945, and from that year to 1965 Franco kept him in prison… Well, as I was saying, my father told me, when he got out, that the hardest thing was to convince the imprisoned comrades to accept national reconciliation. Do you know what it meant to say to one of those guys who had been there twenty years that he should forgive the judge who condemned him to death? Yes, make that face, it's the same face I made. And lots of other things. The leaders are blockheads, all of them, not just the ones from my ex-party, no, yours, too, why not? They live on another planet. They only come into contact with each other, and of course they have a body of followers, they're kinglets of nothing. Governors of Barataria Isle, with even less common sense than Sancho Panza. So, now those shits have turned their backs on me. Don't let me near them! A terrorist!"

Octubre grasped her right arm and moaned, her face contracted with pain. "Those bastards have destroyed my shoulder."

Elisa looked at her wide-eyed. She had met Octubre a few days earlier, upon her arrival in the penitentiary hospital, because when she appeared in that condition at the prison they wouldn't take her. She was feeling better now, but she was still weak.

The doctor who released Octubre from the hospital seemed to harbor the sentiment that obliging him to treat her had been a waste of his time. Three broken ribs, a few bruises, and a so-so inflammation of the liver didn't require a week at the hospital. In jail she would heal just as well by resting, and what else was there to do in prison?

The doctor looked at her mockingly as he held out the form. "Do you have any complaints to report? Mistreatment, diseases, wounds?"

Octubre felt the swelling on her cheek and eye, and the sharp pain in the right side of her thorax. Though there were no mirrors, she knew that she must look disheveled and lifeless. The doctor continued to smile, holding out the form.

Octubre shook her head and reached for the paper. The movement made her wince. Her shoulder seemed ready to fall off her body with every gesture, and always surprised her with the pain. With great difficulty, she traced her name under the printed declaration which reported her release from the State Security Headquarters in a state of perfect health, and that the treatment she received from the inspectors had been appropriate at all times.

"The worst of it, I think, was getting up from the mattress when they called you to interrogation. I don't know if it was because you knew what came next… After you got up and walked, the beating didn't hurt anymore. Your muscles got warmed up again… I still dream about it. I guess it's better that way, it's a relief. I read somewhere that in Sweden they did studies on the effects of torture, observing Nazi concentration camp survivors and Latin American torture victims, and they've shown that many of them have lived ten, twenty, thirty years after as if they had completely overcome everything from that time in their lives. And suddenly, in old age, they started to suffer from nightmares that woke them up screaming at night, in which their tortures were replayed minute by minute. Well, I hope if it makes me dream and moan and all that now, I'll have gotten it out of my system for the rest of my life. I'm sorry to trouble you, but of course you understand. You must have done the same thing when you first got here, right?"

Elisa shook her head slightly. "No, not exactly. They didn't hit me."

Octubre looked surprised. "They didn't? How odd. I wonder why?"

"They knew everything when they arrested me. I was of no importance to the party."

Octubre observed Elisa's bitterness. "I too was nothing more than a baby bird fallen into the nest from God-knows-where. My wonderful friends, when they came to my house to make me a cabinet for holding my papers, were throwing me in with those crazy terrorists with the submachine guns. All a big adventure. Just to sell me off at the first sign of trouble. They didn't even have time to get all the way down the stairs of the State Security Headquarters before they'd told them everything. A big trial, yes, sir. But they still broke me a little. Like everyone else, more or less. I guess it's a tradition. I was interrogated by some guy with one eye higher than the other and his mouth twisted upward…"

Elisa jumped in enthusiastically. "I called him 'Twistface!'"

"Like a movie villain!"

"Yeah! That's what I thought."

"He's so ugly, he really couldn't be anything but a torturer. He hit me in the head like it was routine. I wasn't going to tell them anything they didn't know."

The blows kept coming. They hit Octubre's head and echoed in her ears. Suddenly the pain was so sharp her ears started ringing and a stream of blood escaped from her mouth. Then, luckily, she fainted. When she woke up, a man was manipulating her dislocated shoulder. It was the pain that woke her, but her screams didn't appear to affect the character who was fastening a tension device to her upper arm.

"She's fine, perfectly fine. Give her some coffee, in any case."

"I guess he was a doctor. He didn't seem like one, did he?" Octubre commented.

Elisa agreed, but at that moment she wasn't interested in commenting on the ethical conduct of the doctors who worked for the police, using their knowledge to prolong the torture of the accused. She was fascinated by the critique of the party leaders Octubre had begun.

"You were saying that the party leaders don't have common sense. You're making that criticism because you're not ideologically firm enough."

She meant to provoke her, but she was worried when she saw how upset Octubre was.

Her chin trembled as she replied, almost shouting, "A person can be full of ideological garbage. Just like a barrel in the street running over with rusted cans, rotten food and shitty toilet paper. That's what I feel like. Like a big receptacle made to be filled with worthless things. Verbal rubbish. The obscenity and vulgarity of the spokespeople of the world fill me to bursting. A party member used to say that the leaders had their intestines in their heads. Instead of thinking they digest, and instead of uttering ideas they defecate."

Elisa was startled. She was panic stricken, though there was no one else in the cell but her and Octubre. The prisoners were sure there was a complex network of microphones hidden in all the walls that allowed the warden to record their conversations. Though Elisa never completely shared this belief, and was less tense about it than her companions, it still kept her constantly vigilant. It obliged the political prisoners to hold their conversations in almost inaudible tones, to express their ideas in a code that was updated every day, even in the visiting room where they met with their lawyers. It made conversation tedious. One current tactic was to write what they really wanted to say and put the paper up to the glass pane that separated lawyer from client, so the lawyer could read it, but at the same time continuing to talk so that the tape would not register suspicious silences. After the meetings Elisa would be exhausted.

Octubre was the only one who took no precaution when she talked with her companions in the cells or the dining hall or the TV room. She always shouted that that stuff about the microphones was ridiculous and that young people watch too many American spy movies, that in Spanish prisons they couldn't even dream of such sophisticated devices.

"I mean, they don't even have torture instruments! They just knock you around like in caveman times, and they get their electric shocks from a lamp cord… Hidden microphones!" And she would laugh out loud, giving vent to her immense vitality.

Now Octubre grumbled in a half-whisper, more afraid that the other prisoners would hear through the thin partitions than of the prison officers, whom she never took into account. Elisa was panic stricken that Octubre's shrill voice might reach the other women in the next cells. Nevertheless, what Octubre was saying was fundamental to her. Perhaps her future depended on it. She insisted in a whisper, "Careful, now, they might hear you." But she could not give up on finding out. "Are you talking about the leaders of our party?"

"About the leaders of all parties."

Octubre seemed to be thinking of something else, looking out the window at the ball game five inmates were playing.

Elisa waited impatiently for Octubre to continue. She knew that in talking with her it would be impossible to avoid digressions like that, but she had already learned to appreciate the lucidity of her room mate, who at forty years of age had been militant for twenty-five, getting her start during the most sinister years of the dictatorship. "I don't deserve all the credit," she would add. Daughter of militant communists, granddaughter of anarchists, her mother had been imprisoned in Ventas throughout her childhood, which she had spent, in the care of a grandmother, endlessly visiting the prisons of Yeserías and Ventas to console with her presence those two poor people who grew old during their sentences with no hope of reaching the ideals for which they had struggled so hard. "Irony of dictatorship ironies that thirty years later I'm locked up in the same prison where my mother rotted. I don't deserve all the credit," she would say, "I suckled democracy at my mother's breast and used the Manifesto as a primer. I understand your torture," she said ironically, "that you all had to pull away from so much ideological crap your families and schools must have stuffed into your craniums."

On one occasion, an oversensitive comrade replied with hostility, "You're just like the priests, too, you're always bragging about your purity. Well, yeah, we're all sinners, repentant and all that, and I think we deserve more credit than you, since you've never been contaminated and don't know what the struggle against temptation really is…"

Octubre took the dispute good-naturedly, and merely replied, "If I didn't know already what kind of education you've had, I would guess right now, from those suggestive religious images you've explained the problem with. You might be right, but the truth is, if you hadn't said so, I would never have noticed the similarity between purity and sin and having a conservative or liberal family…"

The argument ended with that. Elisa observed, with pleasure, the bewilderment of Octubre's adversary, who could never figure out whether or not she was joking.

"What Rosa said didn't bother me, because I understand that she feels extremely uncomfortable being the daughter of a civil guard, which on the contrary says a lot in her favor, that she must have had to fight tooth and nail with her family because of her communist activity. But I've heard similar objections on the lips of some petty bourgeois who found my very existence objectionable. You know, besides having been the children of the winning side, with all the advantages that implied in the postwar years — food, good schools, comfortable homes, elegant clothes, vacations, et cetera, et cetera — now, when it's not so fashionable to openly belong to Franco's side, it still bothers them to be compared with those of us who were children of the defeated. After going hungry and miserable throughout our childhood and youth, after years of waiting in lines in prison courtyards to visit our parents in the cold of winter in Burgos or Madrid or Ocaña or El Dueso, after having worn clothes and shoes full of holes, and, worst of all, fearing every night and every morning that our parents in prison would be executed or die, or that they were going to take away our old grandmothers who could hardly see anymore, they would like us to just forget such a sinister past. We were silenced before, terrorized by the police, censorship, denouncements by police or neighbors, the imprecations of the priests at school; and silenced today out of consideration for the last-minute democrat privileged assholes, sons of fascists who massacred and terrorized us, just so we won't prick their conscience."

It was true, as Octubre said, that in 1975 it was no longer stylish to be fascist. The most conspicuous of them, after years of disappointment with the regime, had begun to gradually erase their old connections to the party. The PCE had also decided to forget the quarrels that had divided them, as concerned not only the newly penitent, who as such should be accepted without reservation, but also those who had expressed no such sentiment, or who in everyday practice acted differently from the way they should have, if that stuff about forgetting old hatreds which had separated the two contending factions in the civil war was to be taken seriously.

"National reconciliation killed me. When it was approved at the Party's fifth congress in 1956, I didn't understand because I was too young. At eighteen I wasn't mature enough to understand certain things. Besides, on the inside we took a long time to get to know the approved theses, and not in their entirety. Little by little, when it was necessary to put the Congress's plan into practice and it turned out that I had to make friends with the judges who had condemned my father to death and my mother to twenty years in prison, or with the jailers who had slowly murdered both of them — my father lasted all of six months after getting out of prison — my blood simply rebelled. And former comrades from my parents' generation told me the same thing, that there was no way they could forgive the judges who had sentenced them. Because there was no single objective fact that could defend such a position. The judges continued to condemn communists and unionists and all kinds of people who believe in democracy, to dozens of years in jail, as we know all too well. So what good is national reconciliation? So Carrillo could be well-received by Ruiz-Giménez, who, to make matters worse, has always refused to see him, and when this is all over, have his own ministry, right? Well, you know what I say? Screw them all!"

These and other considerations had led Octubre to abandon, or to be expelled from — the situation remained unclear, as they usually did in the confusing years of clandestineness — the party her parents had belonged to, and in which she had been active for twenty years. She always declared that she didn't give a fig, because she had been dying of boredom when she had to sit through her superior's speeches, but it was obvious how much the decision had frustrated and embittered her. "Just as it did so many others," she would quickly add. "There are already more of us on the outside than in."

Elisa thought, for a moment, that Octubre never knew how close she was to the truth then. Ten more years would have to pass before the weakness of the party's activity and the persecutions among its members, which had fatally wounded the organization, became public knowledge; the disappointment and frustration experienced by thousands of sincere militants who were kicked out of the party as though they had the plague, by that sectarian leadership whose members now, as if they were reenacting the myth of Chronos, were devouring each other in turn.

"Like all political parties, Elisa, though you won't believe it. Sectarianism, to fanatic extremes, dominates the leadership of all parties. Just look at your own leaders, whom you trust the way you do the Bible. Those maniacs are ready to sacrifice themselves on a martyr's altar, and I maintain that it must have to do with their religious education, these ultra radical Marxist-Leninist leaders. A convert is always the worst."

Octubre was ranting about the strategy recently approved by the political bureau of Elisa's party, the PCE-ML, and the details, published in *The Worker's Vanguard*, had just come to them in one of the packages the inmates regularly received from their families.

"Revolutionary violence! Revolutionary violence! Damn it all! What the hell kind of revolutionary war do those beasts think the workers and masses of Spain want today? They're all doing fine in Geneva or Paris or Tirana and to hell with everyone here!"

And when she saw the panic in Elisa's wide eyes, she added, "You shouldn't hope to find God in a party leader who sends you to plant Molotov cocktails everywhere, as you hoped for from the priest or nuns at your school. Those who do are headed inevitably toward fanaticism or suicide."

"So, for you, no one is good?"

Juana Parroto was watching them from the doorway, her brows furrowed. The aggressive tone she used was in itself a provocation. Elisa looked at Octubre, dreading her response. Juana was much younger than Octubre and it made no sense to strike up a futile discussion with her. *Prison's making us hysterical,* Elisa thought, and she could not concentrate on the first words of Octubre's reply, which was coming out much more calmly than Elisa had expected.

"But what do you mean by 'good' or 'bad'? It's all about the revolution, right? So, only the political leaders who bring it about will be good. That's the only criterion a revolutionary should use to judge his party and his leaders."

"Our party is the only one that follows the proper Marxist-Leninist line!" Juana's voice rose in a pointless shriek. "Only through armed struggle can power be taken and the dictatorship of the proletariat be implemented!"

"And that's why the party has given the order to go shooting civil guards on every corner?"

Octubre remained calm and sarcastic while Juana was overcome with rage.

"All struggles begin one day, and for Spain that day is today! Victory is near, that's what you can't see!"

"When you organize the first revolutionary government, don't forget all the times I gave you something to eat in jail and save a ministry for me, please…"

Elisa was powerfully fascinated by the conversation, most of all by Octubre's strange attitude. She sat down on the bed and held up her hand to stop the angry reply Juana was preparing for her.

"And if that's what you think, why are you here?"

Octubre twisted her face into a smile that didn't cover her bitterness or her caustic tone. "I'm here because some tattletales ratted on me. I was working with the people in the neighborhood association and I had some equipment I used for printing a bulletin. Nothing more, nothing less. Have you ever heard of ideological strength?"

Elisa took a few seconds to understand the irony, but she didn't pursue it. She was interested in discussing the matter seriously.

"But, what are you hoping for? What are you fighting for?"

Octubre's face quickly took on a sad expression. "I still believe in the revolution. My problem, which must be the same as yours, is that we don't know how to carry it out. We probably don't really want it, just like the Spanish people don't want it, either. That's what we should consider if we were a little more sensible and less fanatic."

Elisa stopped paying attention to the discussion Juana and Octubre had started. She knew Juana's arguments and was fed up with them. On the other hand, Octubre's words had had tremendous impact. An unidentifiable anguish tightened her chest. If Octubre was capable of showing so much skepticism, so little trust in all the communist parties' lines and tactics, how could she speak of ideological strength? And if Octubre could be so skeptical, after having devoted her whole life to the struggle, what was to become of Elisa? Did she truly have enough ideological strength? Had she devoted all her enthusiasm, her hopes and her ambitions to the party?

On that hard prison bed, covering her face with the sheet so as not to see or hear the two women shouting both at the same time, she submerged herself in thoughts she had never considered before. She suddenly saw herself in the town plaza, taking her walk with her school friends, the only ones she was permitted to go out with on Sunday afternoons, and who, like her, were trying to earn enough merit points to be welcomed at the Communion of the Saints in heaven.

That spring afternoon was soft, smooth, and golden. The almond and cherry trees in bloom in the nearby groves filled the air with enervating light and fragrance, but she didn't know why she was so distracted, uncomfortable, unable to pay attention to what Anita Pedreguell and Mar Font were saying about the mandatory fasting on those days of Lent. Neither did she know why she felt so upset when her neighbors' son, whom she'd known since they were both children, approached them, and didn't understand how he was able to separate the friends' linked arms, or how she ended up sitting on a bench in the plaza alone with Arnau.

Was that the problem, then? The emotional dependency that kept her tied to Arnau? Elisa stirred under the sheet, trying to escape the anguish of her reflections. Arnau looked at her provocatively and told her about the farm his father ran, about his brother's progress in the seminary, about the charity work some boys from school were doing, but Elisa hardly listened. Between her eyes and Arnau's a dialogue had been opened, which repeated every Sunday afternoon on a bench under the trees in the plaza, while their mouths talked about the catechist and apostolic work Arnau wanted to win her over to.

"The victory was all his," Elisa murmured, and for a moment Octubre and Juana interrupted their dispute to look at her in surprise. His conquest began by talking about catechesis and became, in a couple of years, the organization of a group of Christians for the socialist cause. Almost immediately afterward, she found herself an active member of the Marxist-Leninist Communist Party. She did all these things, always loving him. She jumped. Only for love? She didn't want to think it, but the question was there, pricking her like a needle. Had she joined the party, worked clandestinely for ten years, enduring the fear, the continuous and lurking fear of every day, just for love? Had she endured comrade Ramiro's and Pepe's lack of appreciation and the marginalization they had submitted her to, and gone through the detention at the police station without saying even the little she knew, and was she disposed to remaining faithful to the party's directives, despite the latest terrible news, just for love? Just for love of Arnau? Was he her only connection to reality? He had been the one who had saved her from schizophrenia when she was devoting her seventeen-year-old body to fasting and hairshirts and endless meditations on death and Hell. He was the first to show her that God's grace could be found in pleasure, in the enjoyment of being alive, and he definitively saved her from mental breakdown when he taught her to make love and to want to live for herself and not just for God.

It surprised Elisa to realize that her real concern at that moment was her own fate, instead of the party's problems and the struggle in the difficult times that were drawing near. Becoming responsible for her own sins and not for the others'. She became so fretful that she had to turn over in bed. The words of the confessor who directed every moment of her childhood and adolescence now came back to bewilder her. If the political reflections she was sifting through got mixed up with religious memories, it would be impossible to overcome her confusion. Where had she heard that the ideological power of the bourgeoisie consisted precisely in convincing people that their problems were individual rather than collective? But if Octubre complained about her treatment by the party, was she making a political problem personal? Or, perhaps, would resolving her complaints improve her political work? And what political work could she do now that the party had given the signal for armed struggle? Would she be able to kill someone if the party ordered her to? She imagined Ramiro holding out a gun to her and giving her detailed instructions to kill the police officers at a bank. She knew that if Arnau approved, she would comply.

Arnau looked at her with anxiety he no longer bothered to hide. "What are you thinking about?"

"I was remembering those times…"

"Hmm… we were in jail and we weren't sure why they'd decided to begin the armed offensive of spring and summer of '75, remember? But for whatever reason, now they've found out what Cherta did during those times. You know that the accusation can't prove responsibility for the attacks, but then the judges had no guarantees…"

Elisa looked at Arnau, but she didn't see him. At least not as he was at that moment. Over his present image appeared the young man who had looked at her adoringly, while he waved his hands behind the bars in the visiting room of the Carabanchel men's prison, where they had taken her to see her husband. He shook his hands and repeated smiling, "Look! I still have the same hands! Do you still love me?"

And she had hardly been able to speak because she didn't want to cry, and the tears closed her mouth.

"Don't worry, sweetheart, everything will be fine, you'll see. We're about to take power, you know."

"But you didn't really believe it, did you?"

Arnau looked at her with renewed worry. "What are you talking about?"

"You never believed, then, that the party was coming into power, right?"

Arnau looked annoyed. "Why are you asking me that?"

"It just occurred to me. Did you really think the party was going to take power?"

Elisa was surprised at Arnau's unease. She stared at him and again the image of Arnau at twenty, thin, dark, fit, and cheerful, superimposed itself over the present day figure.

"He's really handsome. You'll see, mama, he'll blow you away. No one knows how this old bore here caught herself the best looking guy in town."

And Gemma ran through the hallway, laughing at her sister, who ran after her angrily, ready to die of embarrassment. Angrily and vainly, she remembered, and a smile, which Arnau hadn't seen all morning, lit up her face, pallid from nights awake correcting exams and mornings sleeping in the dark of the bedroom, tangled up in sheets damp with sweat.

All her school friends, all the townswomen, spoke jealously and indignantly about how that insignificant goody-two-shoes had caught the attention of the most elegant, fun-loving, available bachelor in the region. What did Arnau see in her? Elisa wondered the same thing every day of the years she lived with him, and his explanations never completely convinced her.

"You have the bluest, most limpid, most innocent eyes in the world," he repeated, and she thought that didn't mean they were beautiful or big, and she knew quite well that they were not. "Your hair is silky; your waist, the smallest in Catalonia; your feet, like those of your father's lambs, and your small face reminds me of the pre-Raphaelite virgins," he recited, imitating the Song of Songs. But she knew very well that the description could be translated, with less lyricism and more malice, into a description of a skinny, pale-faced girl, with colorless eyes and a tuft of light brown hair. What else?

"Your goodness, your intelligence, your loyalty, your courage… Isn't that enough?"

Elisa accepted that some of those qualities belonged to her, but didn't allow herself to think she truly brought together such a group of exaggerated virtues, so she would not fall into the sin of pride. But weren't many of her other classmates just as good, loyal, or brave as she was, and much more? At that point in the lover's dialogue, Arnau would get angry and shout that he must be mistaken, that she was right, she was obviously much more foolish than he had thought up to then. Because who, who, was as brave, as intelligent, as loyal as she and much more beautiful? The presumptuous, idiotic Mari Carmen Oliveras? Or the sanctimonious Anita Pedreguell, and Mar Font, who would have sold their own parents for a plate of figs? Not even Elisenda Verdiell, who was so beautiful, could compare with Elisa, because Elisa was much more responsible and conscientious. The proof of that was in the strange things her friend was doing then, living with a gang of good-for-nothing hippies in London, not caring at all about the social and political situation of her own country, while they were there, risking their lives to change it.

That was Arnau then. Puzzled, she looked at this new Arnau sitting before her. "That was the reason, wasn't it? Because you molded and guided me and made me what you wanted me to be…"

Arnau was more and more worried. "What's wrong now, if you don't mind telling me?"

"That's why you loved me, that's why you married me…"

"What the devil! Why are you talking about that now?"

"Oh, no reason. I was thinking about the past. The party is your whole life. If I hadn't followed you in your devotion to it no matter what, you wouldn't have married me, would you?"

Arnau made an effort to hide his bad mood and decided to participate in the conversation along the lines Elisa was laying out. It was necessary to convince her; he could not leave until he knew she would help.

"Yes, of course. I could never have married a conservative woman, like that idiot Gerardo Iglesias says. You understood my struggle immediately, you got involved in it, accepted the way it changed your life…"

"Surely, any wife would've done the same."

"Out of obedience to her husband, but not out of conviction, and you also had your intelligence, the way you understood things so quickly. In fact, I remember having told you that many times, Elisa. You were the most intelligent, the most loyal and courageous, and I loved you…"

"Why did you stop loving me, then? Did I change that much?"

Arnau observed her with renewed surprise, and was startled by what he saw in those light, almost transparent eyes.

Chapter 4

My love,

Here, in this sunless patio, while I shiver, wrapped up in a coat and a blanket, I close my eyes and remember you. If I squint just a little I can almost feel your skin against mine, see your blue eyes and hear your voice. I'm not crazy... yet. I suppose that will be the inevitable end if we remain much longer like this. The lawyer assures me they'll release you women first and that comforts me. After all, it's only fair, since you had nothing to say before the tribunal. You all stayed outside of what we husbands were doing. I have to ask you to forgive me for that one more time. For tricking you and for getting you into this situation. I detest myself when I think of you there in Yeserías, away from me and from your family, suffering the horrors of this cold...

It was a sanctioned letter and had the same tone as all the others. Exonerations of penal responsibility, trying to get the judge to believe them after passing through the director's censorship. *As if the judge and the director weren't also familiar with the old game,* she thought, but that wasn't important. She recorded the phrases of love in her memory and repeated them to herself again and again, alone. Arnau wrote so well that sometimes she was envious. On one occasion María laughed at her after she had inappropriately gushed about Arnau.

"As liberated as you pretend to be and look how you adore your husband!"

Elisa blushed despite her contention. The other comrades were also looking at her and laughing. But they did it with affection, with sympathy. It was good that a woman loved and admired her husband, and even better when he was a comrade as important and loyal as Arnau. Elisa decided to stand up for herself.

"He deserves it. I'm not un-liberated because of that. I'm not his slave, and he isn't mine."

Everyone was satisfied and the meeting continued.

Elisa kept reading the letter. She could hear the women on the patio shouting as they played ball, the conversations of those working in the kitchen, the noise of the television from the next room. She wrapped herself up more tightly in the blanket, in a vain attempt to escape from the cold, which was becoming her obsession. But she preferred to freeze in the solitary, empty classroom that had never been used, than to endure the closeness of the dining area, where a hot toaster oven as well as thirty women heated the air noticeably.

I'm also sorry you don't have the company of your girlfriends, the ones we met these few last years. Violeta Mercado and her husband have been arrested in Granada, as you already know. I don't know what they'll be accused of, because poor Violeta was so humble and simple, and it would never have occurred to me that she would ever participate in such complicated matters as clandestine political struggle.

Tiny, sickly María, imprisoned, too! Four married couples arrested in Granada, and the two of them in Madrid because it was a few hours later when they left the house where the meeting was held, before leaving for Málaga. Four wives: Violeta Mercado (alias "María"), Carmen Agudo (alias "Teresa"), Pepita Solares (alias "Pepi"), and Adela Tierno (alias "Lali"), all designated by the party to accompany their respective husbands and take care of them. *Like me*, she thought again angrily, but the others were content. They never understood her frustration. On one occasion Pepi, a daughter and granddaughter of workers, professional housewife, reacted strongly to her constant complaints.

"Look here! Anyone would think you don't appreciate cooking and cleaning. You and your airs. I would much rather clean my own house than someone else's!"

That strange interpretation of her frustration made Elisa uncomfortable. She hadn't expected a classist criticism of her desire to work actively within the party.

"That's not it, Pepi. You don't understand. I think I can do something better for the party than stay at home cooking for Arnau…"

"Well, not me! I'm too stupid and ignorant to know how to do anything other than cook and clean, so it seems fitting to me to be here taking care of Manuel. If he were alone he wouldn't eat, and he'd get sick right away, and that would be as bad for the party as it would be for him. We all struggle in our own way, right?"

Elisa nodded her head and decided not to mention it to them again. She felt more misunderstood than ever. She treated all the women of the party as companions and friends. She didn't want to be excluded from the communion of the faithful. She assured them that she considered herself among equals when they met with the workers and their wives in the shacks in the outskirts of Madrid. She ate the same food they did, sat on the floor, ate with her fingers, laughed at their jokes and wept at their sorrows. Why had Pepi had to make that insulting reference to her bourgeois origins and distinguished education? Perhaps she would never be able to hide the fifteen years of training the nuns had put her through to make her into "a real lady," as they said. *And they achieved it*, she thought bitterly.

Millions of prostrations, rehearsed patiently, unhurriedly, with no sense of how ridiculous it all was, for fifteen years. Keeping strict posture in the ranks, as they called the lines, with arms folded behind their backs, each hand grasping the opposite elbow. Chin high, not too high, head neither slanted nor lowered. Looking straight ahead, feet together, silent. She liked it when Mother Perelló mentioned her for the perfection she managed to achieve at all times: in the ranks, in class, in chapel, at the grade-giving ceremony. She was proud of it, and sincerely repented her sin of vanity. Then she would try to compensate by humbling herself before a less fortunate peer. Elisenda was her best friend and confidante during the first years, in spite of the close watch the nuns kept against particular friendships, and Elisa's own suspicions that her feelings for Elisenda were wicked. Because of that, she decided to distance herself from Elisenda as they were going into puberty. But before that, she had always tried to correct Elisenda's slovenly figure. She turned her feet in, wore her hair untidily gathered and her socks sagging, and never managed to cross her arms in the correct position before the Mother called her attention to it. Of course, Elisenda didn't appreciate Elisa's close attentions. She was much more interested in the tree that bloomed outside the classroom window in spring, in the ants in the garden, and in the theological discussions that preoccupied her at age twelve to the point of declaring herself atheist before turning thirteen, to Elisa's desperation and the nuns' consternation.

Elisa smiled when she remembered her old classmate. Who would have thought at the time that Elisenda was right! Not about everything, of course, because, as Arnau said, Elisenda would never do anything useful in her life. They had found the right path, but that poor girl, lost in a miserable hippy commune in London, where would she end up? The memory of Elisenda brought her back to Arnau and she returned to the letter.

> They're not so badly off. I only knew Jesús Pueyo, who I worked with at the same typewriter wholesaler, as you know, but some fellows here tell me his family, who is going to visit them, also knows their family, and the four couples have the luck of being in a small a prison like Granada's, separated only by some walls, and they can pass letters and packages to each other every day. They also see each other twice a week. Oh, my love! If only I could see you twice a week!…

The mail between the prisons carried news from one end of Spain to the other. The prisoners were frequently moved from place to place for trials, hearings, verdicts, or to serve their sentences. In the jails and prisons they met other men and women prisoners who had a friend or relative in some city or other who had been in prison with the friend, companion, cousin, son, daughter, or brother of someone or other. The news made its way around the secret prisoners' underworld, and the rest of the population never suspected anything.

Lidia Falcón

A young woman had just arrived in Yeserías to serve out her sentence. She had been held years before at Trinidad in Barcelona with the daughter of one of the prisoners who was presently awaiting sentencing in Yeserías. They talked extensively about their experiences. The newcomer's husband was in Torrero, the Zaragoza prison where another woman had a brother. She brought the news that the mother of a girl recently arrested in a university demonstration was in Alcalá… The greetings, the hugs, the talking, and the memories, filled the prisoners' conversation hours. Letters from brothers, husbands, parents and friends brought clandestine news, never published in the normal newspapers. They lived an estranged and unshared life, and their channels of communication were also unlike the usual ones. The telephone, all newspapers except *Ya*, the majority of magazines, an unending list of books, were all prohibited, and only a few entered the prison after being held up by the censors. With no movies, restricted television hours, and visiting limited to twice a week for those who had family who could visit them in Madrid, and contact and correspondence with all who were not immediate family prohibited, the network of letters, books, and clandestine news that stretched from La Coruña to Puerto de Santa María, from Ocaña and El Dueso to Yeserías and Torrero, from Alcalá de Henares to Trinidad, from San Juan de los Reyes to Jaén, Soria, Segovia, Martutene and Figueras, kept the prisoners' curiosity aroused, their hopes alive, their imaginations alert, their resources at the ready, their enthusiasm burning, and their optimism always high.

An enormous network of clandestine communications swarmed there, where the jailers and directors believed that the imprisoned men and women were isolated, disoriented, incommunicado and lacking news of their party, of the fighting in the streets, and of their families' lives. The encoded communications they maintained with their immediate families, the innocent packages of food and knitting, the pastries, the coats, the little boxes of tobacco, the bottles of condensed milk and coffee, the books and shoes, were all liable to inform, encourage, advise, warn or anger the prisoner.

There in Granada, 500 kilometers from Madrid, Violeta, Teresa, Pepi and Lali sent Elisa their regards and told her about their lives, in spite of the bars and the distance separating them.

You could almost say they're living a married life. Except for the basics, of course… But it's better not to mention the absence of what tortures me and what I desire so much… They can pass food from one cell to another. The men even give their dirty clothes to the women to clean and they send them back washed and ironed…

Elisa threw the letter down. And out of habit she glanced at the door in case someone had seen her. Was it possible? Those men were capable of giving their dirty clothes to their wives, even when they were all in jail! When they were out of prison, Elisa furiously discussed that macho behavior with that idiot María, and she responded, with her usual joy, "But I didn't have anything better to do…"

Elisa replied bitterly, "And what did Antonio have to do?" But María wasn't interested in that conversation. Elisa had always been very sensitive. What did it matter?

I would give almost anything to be in Granada and see you twice a week and give you my food and dirty clothes. Life is strange, isn't it? If I had thought a few months ago that I would like to be in prison in Granada, I would have laughed…

"That was the reason, wasn't it? Because I didn't wash your clothes and spoil you like María did Antonio or other married friends of ours…"

Arnau rubbed his hands in a habitual gesture, and tried to smile. He didn't appear to like the turn this conversation was taking.

"We've already discussed that several times, don't you think? Perhaps now is not the right time…"

He spoke cautiously. He couldn't fight with Elisa at that moment. He urgently needed a clear, unambiguous response to his question from her, and in the hour he had been there he hadn't even been able to explain what the business he had brought her was about. But he could not get impatient. She wanted to talk about their relationship, which was over. Why, exactly?

"I never understood before like I do now. Or like I think I do now. Back then we talked about it a lot, but we got sidetracked. Deep ideological questions, political disagreement, my separation from the party, my departure from the party line and methods, the changes in my life, my feminist work… everything was an excuse for you to fall out of love with me. Everything, except that you wanted me to cook for you and wash your clothes… even in prison."

Arnau raised his head in surprise. "What are you talking about now?"

"I was thinking of María and Pepi and Lali and Teresa, washing their husbands' clothes in prison in Granada. And I decided they were such good wives…"

"Antonio separated from María even before we did…"

Elisa stared at Arnau for a few seconds and then began to laugh. "You're right. There's no hope."

Arnau relaxed. Elisa's look said many things he had to understand if he wanted to convince her to help, and for that he needed time. He realized the visit was going to take longer than he had expected. He sat back in the chair and decided to butter a slice of toast. He had to reflect cautiously, like when he organized a complicated strategy in clandestine times. Observe, prick up his ears, be quiet, wait. The enemy will fall. Like the Indians, Antonio used to laugh, and he smiled in agreement, even though he had learned that tactic from the priests at school.

"Of course there's hope. Not in gods or kings or tribunals," — both smiled — "but in ourselves…"

"Relying on our own strengths, right?"

"Obviously. It always gets results."

"It seems that now you people need some help…"

Arnau breathed deeply, but continued savoring his toast. At last he could explain the matter. He swallowed the mouthful and spoke slowly, as if what he was saying didn't really matter.

"Yes, it's true. We shouldn't forget solidarity, should we? The problem, as I was saying, has to do with Cherta…"

"Alias Ramiro."

Arnau took a moment to remember. "Yes, that's right."

"The one who sent me to Madrid to cook for you…"

Arnau looked at her very hard. He replied slowly. "Ah! So that's it…"

"What do you mean?" Elisa looked at him with distrust.

"That's why you don't want to help us. You're still holding a grudge…"

Elisa felt her cheeks redden in anger. Her voice measured, but very tense, she answered, "That isn't what I said. I still have to find out what kind of help you're talking about. You're the one holding a grudge."

"About what, if you please?"

Elisa raised her voice for the first time. She had long since lost that capacity for total control in the face of aggression. It was her age, she had told herself a few months before. When she was twelve she could respond to the most serious provocations with sweetness. Like when Elisenda dared her to prove the existence of God, whose existence she claimed she didn't believe in, or when she could accept, without even knitting her brow, that they gave her a black mark for something she hadn't done and which kept her from being the girl who crowned the Virgin, as she was accustomed to meriting every term. *But today, at thirty-eight, I've lost the endless patience I had and which the nuns so efficiently drummed into me.*

"To be a nun? No, that's not what I sent you to school for."

And her mother looked at her indignantly, reproachfully. The Sacred Heart specialized in educating the wives of the leading members of society. Its clients were aristocrats, upper bourgeoisie, and they expected the school to deliver a refined, classist, perfect education for organizing homes with large families, where ministers would dine every evening.

"No, I didn't send you to school so you could become a nun," repeated her mother. "I sent you to be educated, as they educated me, and my mother, and my grandmother, nothing more. You should be a good girl, religious and obedient, so you can marry well. Like all of us. Now, why would you ever want to become a nun? And why haven't you said anything before?"

For more than a year, Elisa had kept a hermetic silence about her intentions. No one, not even Elisenda, whom she was already quite distant from, knew why she visited the headmistress so often. She could hide it because she had come of age, passed into the fourth year of high school, which required a final examination. Officially adolescents, the girls were kept under the strictest surveillance. Living in the large dormitory, they visited the headmistress once a week, were tested to find out their abilities, and had long moral conversations about their futures. Elisa trusted only the headmistress's advice, and kept her secret with a martyr's pride.

That June afternoon, five months after her sixteenth birthday, having finished high school with unsurpassable grades, she was letting her family know her intention to join the novices.

"And you have to go to Madrid, to Chamartín, to do the novitiate. You're leaving us, your parents, your brothers!"

"That's what's expected of someone who wants to serve God."

Elisa didn't point out that for almost fifteen years her parents had sent her away to school without regret, because it wasn't the role of a saint to respond impolitely to her parents.

Elisa remembered the heat of that brilliant spring, endured in the dark school uniforms and the thick cotton stockings, which she never took off now, not even during vacations. The reform in uniforms and habits instituted by Vatican II hadn't yet been introduced, although the work had started two years before. She and Arnau enthusiastically lived out the reforms a short time later, within the organizations of a church that was undergoing profound changes.

It wasn't necessary for her family to insist for her to abandon the idea of taking vows. Only a few weeks after that conversation Arnau stopped her on her Sunday walk with her friends, and soon she decided that God was equally well served by the secular organizations of the Church and from within the bosom of matrimony. The headmistress herself contributed enormously to the decision, and received her doubts with understanding and perhaps even with relief. It wasn't the order's style to proselytize among its students. On the contrary, they constantly discouraged them from following the example of the sisters.

The expression on their faces seemed to say at all times, "You'd best give up reaching for the extreme of perfection required to join the order."

From the time they enrolled in the school, the nuns indicated that surely none of them would merit being admitted into the narrow circle of those elected to be married to Christ. It would be sufficient if they could meet the standard expected of pupils. With it they would be able to complete their education and enter into a Christian marriage. Beyond these small and human ambitions, sainthood could be found, represented by the mothers, and only a select few would ever achieve it. In seven years Elisa had seen only one student enter the convent. And in spite of Arnau's love, for a long time Elisa felt the pangs of dissatisfaction, thinking of what she considered her failure. After fourteen years of preparing for sainthood, she had had to resign herself to a modest devotion. She realized that the nuns were right when they mistrusted the constancy and virtues of the girls.

Perhaps that was why Arnau meant so much to her. To get him she had had to sacrifice the pride of knowing herself to be different, let go of her greater destiny as a bride of God. Arnau had to make up for all of it. And he did. The memory of Arnau's large, angular, soft hands as they ran slowly along her body in the endless hours they spent making love, before and after marriage, made her shrink as if she had been punched in the gut. That was the same Arnau as the one who looked at her today with distrust, afraid to explain what he had come to ask, and who, twenty years after that golden afternoon in June when he separated her forever from her friends and prayers, had some grey hair and wrinkles in his handsome face.

That Arnau who had looked at her with so much passion, with a wonder he never tried to hide, who had continuously praised her in front of her family, comrades, friends, always insisting on pointing out her privileged intelligence, her best quality, her responsibility and conscientiousness in her work, and her courage and loyalty in the party's struggle. *Too much,* she suddenly thought, annoyed. *It was too much love and too much admiration and too many words of praise. I should have realized how fake it all was. I wasn't as smart as he supposed or as I thought I was. I never noticed the signs of him falling out of love before the separation. I tricked myself or he tricked me. Or he changed.*

For no reason. But his conduct was irrational. She never understood it and neither did she want to understand it. It was better that way. In matters of love, nothing was logical.

"What are you saying?" Arnau looked at her with increased surprise.

"Oh, I don't know. I was mumbling."

"Daydreaming, like always…"

It was a reproach. And yet, before, he had been the only one who excused her lapses and forgetfulness. He assured everyone that they were her greatest charm, without which Elisa would not be herself, and Elisa, proud and encouraged by him, made no effort to concentrate. But she did it when necessary, when she herself saw the need for it. That was enough for her, Arnau would say.

"I have to explain the reason for my visit. It's not very interesting to you, is it?"

His tone was biting and weary at the same time. He seemed on the verge of losing hope. Elisa didn't contradict him. She didn't even respond. Now she looked out the window at the sunlight on the pine branches and she wanted to flee from Arnau's presence, from his insistent pleas for help, from the prospect of listening to a long political speech on subjects that didn't interest her and to accept a surely ridiculous role in she knew not what stupid assignment like those from before.

"If now is a bad time, I'll come back after vacation. We can wait… What are you going to do?"

"I don't know. Maybe we'll go to the beach for a few days…"

He didn't ask with whom. He knew. Like everyone else. And Elisa felt the sharp pain of realizing that he didn't care.

Chapter 5

"Well, she's really taking advantage. She has a good job, her parents are well off, and even though she has three kids, she does nothing but ask Pere for money, and it's not fair. It's really old-fashioned of her, not feminist at all."

Elisa stopped speaking when Isabel Fortuny began to laugh. And she frowned, waiting for her friend to explain the outburst.

"Just look where your feminism shows up!"

"What are you talking about?"

"Now it seems you think Pere's wife is exploiting him, because she wants him to pay the food allowance they agreed on in court."

"But I already told you, she earns as much as he does."

"And the three children, do they also have good jobs?"

"What?"

Isabel shook the crumbs out of her apron and began clearing the table with a gesture of annoyance. "If I didn't already know you, today you'd have me convinced you're a fool. Don't Mr. Pere Ferrer's three children eat, wear clothes, go to school? Are they plastic dolls? And besides, who takes care of them, and puts up with them, cleans up after them and all that? How old is the youngest?"

"Nuria's three."

"The perfect age to start earning a living, huh?"

"Well, but Pere isn't rich. It's that simple."

"Then he shouldn't have gotten married and had three kids. Even simpler."

"You're talking nonsense…"

But Isabel was already on her way to the kitchen loaded down with dirty dishes and paid her no attention. Elisa sat back, sulking, in the wicker chair beside the window and pretended to be interested in the stupid movie the television was offering to its unfortunate after lunch viewers.

Nothing was good enough for Isabel. She was full of Catholic morality of the pre-Council kind. Just like the kind Elisa used to wear on her sleeve in those Tridentine moments the unusual Polish pope had made fashionable again. If not, why was Isabel upset and critical that Elisa should be involved with Pere? He had been separated from his wife for almost a year, and his wife had her own life. Elisa recognized that she knew nothing about Pere's wife's love life. But in the end, everyone had a right to be happy, didn't they? As sexually liberated as they were, and now it turned out that only Elisa Vilaró had no right to have a sexual relationship with a man who wasn't her husband, because he had married another woman before he ever met her.

"Hey, simmer down, will you? Nobody's telling you you can't go to bed with whoever you please. Besides, even if I don't think it's okay, I keep my mouth shut. But today you were lecturing me that you thought it was an outrage that Pere's wife is asking him to pay the money they both agreed on so she and the children could eat, and it seemed like you were losing your common sense, that's all. After taking poor Lluïsa's husband away, you also want to leave her penniless…"

"I didn't take her husband."

The protest sounded lame. It only made Isabel indignant about the obvious lie, and she shouted at Elisa about the way she had zeroed in on Pere as soon as she started working at the school, even though he was married and the couple got along well. In the end, Elisa opted for keeping quiet and pretending she could not hear her friend, and Isabel went to her room and didn't come out all afternoon.

Elisa told herself she didn't care that her friend was annoyed, but she knew it was a lie. Isabel's approval was essential to her. After all, she had no other reliable friend, and this thought pained her so much that tears came to her eyes. She was her only family, because Isabel didn't have anyone else, either. They had gone to the same school, though

Isabel was older, both had left their home towns, and neither of them stayed in touch with their families more than the expected minimum. And also Elisa had lost Arnau, whom one of the brats at the newspaper had carried off right under her nose.

"But that doesn't give you the right to do the same thing to another woman," Isabel vigorously protested whenever the subject came up, which was all the time, since Pere showed up almost every day at the house the two had shared since Elisa left the one she had set up with Arnau. Isabel had said it was about time to move out, after two years of separation. She received Pere with frank dislike.

"But why not? Pere is well educated, practically a guru in linguistics, and treats you with respect and care, plus he's good-looking."

"The town heartthrob. I don't like men who give women children and then go off with other ones."

That was why she didn't have her own man, Elisa reasoned. If she was going to be so choosy, she was destined to be alone, as her mother and the nuns taught. The proof of the wisdom of the maternal advice was Isabel herself, so beautiful and well-educated, who at forty-two had been married only five years, and for fifteen years had been living the notorious life of an old maid, sharing her house with a friend, working at the same office for twenty years and at home alone almost every Sunday. Elisa was different. Elisa knew that men needed to be understood, taken care of, followed…

"Obeyed, right?" Isabel added sardonically. Yes, in the end she had learned why she had lost Arnau. "You didn't understand him or take care of him enough, eh?" Now she had Pere and wasn't willing to lose him. "Even though you have to take on his wife, too? Have you already forgotten what Arnau's separation did to you?"

Elisa didn't want to listen to her. She shouldn't let her friend's words wound her as they were doing. Arnau was different, completely different. They had been together fifteen years, they had been active in the party, struggled, suffered, always together. They were united by ideals that far transcended the routine of the selfish daily life of other couples. "And Pere and Lluïsa also have a life in common you know nothing about, as well as some expensive children."

"Always money! As if it were the most important thing. I'm talking about love and everybody comes out with money. Lluïsa, you…"

"If it's not important, why do you care if Pere gives it to his wife?"

Elisa would have cried, but she had forbidden herself from crying almost two years before. She had cried enough for her whole lifetime in the days of Arnau's leaving. But she needed to unburden herself, to rage against that presumptuous know-it-all Isabel, who always did everything right, and was always giving lectures.

"So, the only alternative is to be alone like you, more embittered and moody every day?"

She wasn't sorry to have said it, even though Isabel blanched, because she showed no other sign of being affected by the attack, and she even exaggerated the calmness of her expression and the neutral tone of her voice when she replied.

"No, by no means. I'm not an example to anyone. Everyone should follow her own path — yes, as the nuns said," she hurriedly added before Elisa could do so with a twisted smile, "but it's still true. Naturally, the problem is knowing what we want, what will make us happy, how much guilt we can live with in peace. The other day I was talking about this with Elisenda and told her the same thing."

"Elisenda? You've seen her?"

"She's back in Barcelona. I saw her a few days ago. She's been traveling around Belgium and France for ten years, after she got out of the hospital from practically killing herself with heroin, you know. She's done a lot of work in the Feminist Movement. She joined after attending the Forum of Crimes against Women, in March of 1976. Now she wants to organize groups of women here to fight for abortion and things like that."

"How is she?"

Elisa surprised herself with her sudden interest in that long-lost companion from adolescence. For many years, Elisenda had been to her a tall blonde schoolgirl with a prominent nose and snotty remarks, someone she had been fond of during their early years. After her expulsion from school, Elisenda remained shrouded in mystery. If the town gossips hadn't kept her informed about Elisenda's strange adventures during those years as a hippy in London, a vagabond in Paris and a drug addict in Barcelona, maybe Elisa would have forgotten her forever. The only near contact she had with her was the enormous bouquet of flowers that arrived at her house in March 1976, a few days before Elisenda was to leave for Brussels and two months after Elisa had been released. On the card Elisenda had written "Forgive me!" in her enormous rounded handwriting. Elisa never knew what she was supposed to forgive her for.

"When did she get back? What does she do? Where does she live?"

"A few months ago, in the fall, during the Hogares Mundet Feminists conference. She got really upset with those women who did those abortions in public and filmed them for television. She said they were stupid girls who did it just for shock value."

"She's become awfully responsible."

It was a tentative comment. Elisa didn't remember Elisenda well. The only time she had known her at all had been the years of their youth, when their characters were half formed. The memory brought Elisa scenes of Elisenda's rebellion, her disruptions in class, her angry retorts to the nuns, her theological doubts that so scandalized them. None of it could make Elisa think Elisenda was irresponsible, and yet she had that impression. Isabel agreed.

"Yes, she's changed a lot in some ways, and not so much in others. Elisenda was always looking for a way to help others. She took longer to find it than you did, that was all."

Neither of them added that Elisenda hadn't found an Arnau to tell her what she had to do. Or perhaps she never let any man tell her what to do.

Elisa wanted to dispel the image of the young girl in love she had been twenty years before, because now she could not understand why she had devoted ten of those years to political militancy. Sometimes she talked about it with Pere and he smiled, saying that all young university students in the sixties and seventies had a bout with that particular disease. Elisa accepted the commonplace because it calmed her to be sharing the same fate with her entire generation of educated petty bourgeois. At the same time it explained why she had recently abandoned all involvement with politics and social activism and had devoted herself to writing her doctoral thesis, to discussing promotions, changes and competition among the faculty at the college, and used her free time to make love with Pere, visit her parents and go swimming at the beach.

"When are you coming back?"

"The day before classes start. I think it's Monday, April seventh."

Arnau agreed. "Well, then we can see each other that day. I'll be leaving for Israel the next day."

Elisa panicked at what seemed like a goodbye.

"But you're not leaving now, like this, without telling me anything…"

"It's a long story, and you don't seem very interested. Since you stopped being involved in politics…"

The comment was a reproach and Elisa picked up on it indignantly.

"That's not true," she lied. "You all think anything that isn't sympathetic with your party is outside of politics."

"Don't get upset, please. I didn't mean it as a reproach, though I know that's what it seemed like."

He couldn't fight with her, but the session was becoming so tedious that he didn't know how much longer he could stand it. He probed the terrain again.

"I've already explained that it's about invalidating another accusation of terrorism. Since we requested legalization we've completely abandoned those methods, but the police are always trying to implicate us in those kinds of attacks. So now they've arrested Cherta. You'll remember they also tried to attribute the 1974 Correo Street bombing to us, the one ETA did and then denied."

"But then the next spring, we started doing it…"

Photos of the dead man in the street appeared on the pages of *ABC*, accompanied by a thorough report, declarations from ministers and police, editorials, articles, pages and pages of printed letters that were published every day. Even the television was offering reports on the subject. Until they came up with a few dead bodies, the activists of the PC-ML didn't attract any attention from the media, despite the twelve years they had already spent in the struggle.

"There are other factors, but that's why it's really essential to make the move to armed struggle now. It's the only thing that scares the regime. They know we're at the final countdown. We've just signed their death sentence."

Everyone listened to Juana in silence, their gazes fixed on the floor or the newspaper. No one dared to contradict her, and there were no discussions at that meeting.

Later, in their cell, Octubre fatalistically commented, "This will be the end of your party, not of the regime. You know it, though you don't dare say it. I don't understand how anyone can be so fanatic and obsessive as to get into terrorism. In 1975, in the midst of good times, when, whether at home or in exile, the only thing the main political forces are trying to do is come to an agreement for establishing democracy..."

Elisa didn't answer. She felt too tired. She undressed while her room mate kept making prudent comments and she didn't bother to reply. She would not have had any arguments other than the ones Juana had used hours before. The words had no meaning for her any more, and she was afraid Juana was the only they meant something to. She lay down and put her head on the pillow with such relief that she had to sigh. It was the first night she was able to fall right to sleep.

The next morning the headlines of *ABC* named the FRAP activists who had been arrested for having something to do with the attacks. Among those names, they found the one that made Marisa scream: Adalberto Rodríguez Linares. In his hands he held Marisa's happiness, and everyone knew she was about to lose it.

"We paid for it dearly. We learned from it."

Pere was saying that no one ever learned anything. He was talking about his students.

"I'd say that if a student learns it's because he already knew everything beforehand. No, I couldn't explain it, but I'm absolutely sure I'm right. Some day parapsychology or spiritualism or something will explain why it happens this way, but the reality is that the student who learns gives the impression that he always knew what you're explaining to him, that all he's doing is remembering it. Taking it out of a box in the back of his head where he had it tucked away. While if a student doesn't learn, though you lose your voice repeating it, it's because he never had anything recorded in his brain cells to begin with, and won't ever be able to record it. Experience is the only thing that teaches sometimes."

Elisa listened with interest to that original dissertation, a product of the linguist Pere Ferrer, but until that morning in March of 1986, seated at the kitchen table in front of Arnau, she hadn't connected it with the traumatic experience of the FRAP activists in the spring of 1975. Especially the women imprisoned in Yeserías, because that was where Marisa Cuéllar was, the companion of the kid who bore the pretentious name Adalberto Rodríguez Linares, and who was destined to be the victim of the party's delirious plans.

The poor photograph, even more poorly reproduced, showed a coarse face with stubble, dark eyes and a square chin that could have belonged to any peasant from his land. A man with an expressionless face, despite the conditions in which the photograph had been taken. A man Marisa couldn't reach, as she looked at him with a pale face and wide eyes. No one said anything. On that printed paper an entire man was summarized — his chronological life, his ideological beliefs, his terrorist activities — for the police who had arrested him, for the journalists who presented him to the public, for the readers who would admire or despise him, for the judges who would condemn him.

Only Marisa knew what the man was really made of. Only Marisa had touched him, talked with him, made love with him, slept by his side and made his food. Together they ran through the streets after placing the bombs, together they studied Marx and Lenin, and together they worked on projects to make the isolation of the squalid rented apartments where they lived weeks and even months, surrounded by hostile, gossipy neighbors, more bearable.

Only Marisa knew the feel of his skin and that beard that looked as alive as a prickly thicket. Only Marisa knew that his heart beat like everyone else's, with loud rhythmic throbs that moved the chest on which she placed her hands, that its hair was sweaty after lovemaking and that the veins of his arms beat when she pressed them under her thumbs. And Marisa now had to identify her man, his large body, with its warm, vibrant limbs formed of muscle, in that dull photograph which tried to show the world with a few black and white dots what Adalberto Rodríguez Linares had been.

Elisa said nothing. She let the others try to comfort Marisa, futilely. Elisa didn't want to see her, didn't want to think about her, didn't want to imagine the blood flowing through her brain, through her veins, her heartbeat, the functioning of her digestive system. She didn't want to continue identifying with Marisa because she looked like she was about to faint. All afternoon she sought out a place to hide from Marisa's gaze, which followed her through the halls, the cells, the dining hall, the TV room, the classroom. She fled and fled, taking turns around the patios, going up to the infirmary only to leave immediately. She ran through the sports field when the officials opened it, surprised to see her in an activity that had never attracted her before, and she got into bed, exhausted, before dinner, so she would not have to feel the presence of that woman who carried her man's dead body on her back.

"No, that's not true. You never learn more than you already know."

Arnau looked at her in surprise. "What are you talking about?"

Elisa was tense, distracted, staring out the window with her brow furrowed. She stubbornly repeated, "No one learns any more than what they already know. It's like free will. You have it, but the only thing that happens is what God had always foreseen."

Arnau didn't laugh. He asked, half annoyed and half worried, "What does that have to do with anything? Now you're using Catholic dogma to explain human behavior."

The headmistress looked at her chillingly, no longer with the accustomed warm gaze. She seemed taller, more rigid, and was making a gesture with her hands and whole torso as if she wanted to keep her distance for fear of contagion.

"Are you sure?"

Elisa nodded. She was afraid of the nun's attitude, but she didn't hesitate. She was sure of what she wanted. Up to then she had been suffering from an illusion. The illusion of sainthood.

"The Lord's grace has abandoned you." she said with disdain.

"The Lord has guided me on the path I had to follow."

"What do you mean?"

"That he always knew what my fate was and I couldn't remove myself from it."

"You are analyzing important theological questions you know nothing about, and your ignorance could lead you into heresy. There must be free will. Otherwise, no one would be saved or condemned."

"The Lord also knows who must be condemned and who must be saved. And it's not heresy to think I can save myself in marriage and might have condemned myself in the convent."

The headmistress didn't respond. She motioned for her to kiss the cross hanging around her neck and considered the consultation over. Elisa's reasoning would have been correct if it hadn't been for that suggestion of protestant heresy about predestination. It was preferable not to continue arguing if it didn't seem possible to change her mind. Once again, the high mission of the convent proved itself to be out of the reach of just about everyone. Even Elisa Vilaró, in whom she had placed all her hopes. She meditated on her knees for an hour in the chapel after the rosary to ask the Sacred Heart for the peace she needed.

Who could Marisa ask for peace? Elisa didn't want to see her surrounded at all hours by the inmates who thought it was their duty to console her with stock phrases, compassionate looks, repeating once and again, "You must endure it with your whole self, you should be proud of him, he fell in the struggle, he's a hero and we won't forget him."

They already considered him dead, Elisa thought with a jump, and remembered that, on the contrary, Carles and Gemma and her friends at work explained that everyone on the outside thought they would be reprieved. That was why they didn't do anything. *Because of that and because they were cowards*, she thought angrily, but even then it wasn't worth the effort to fight with them.

"In jail everyone gave him up for dead beforehand, and the rest, too. They gave up on everyone. As if they wanted it, as if they had been hoping for it for a long time. They needed martyrs, like the ancient Christians."

"You're the ancient one today, you know?" Arnau pushed away his dirty plate, stood up and walked around the room, huffing with rage, as he lit a cigarette.

"Rodríguez Linares's memory is haunting you. You have to leave the dead in peace. We've all changed nowadays, so why bring this ghost who has no Hamlet to revenge him back from the frozen regions beyond the tomb?"

Octubre looked at her with a strange, bitter expression that Elisa hadn't seen in her until then. With Arnau recently out of prison, Elisa refused to speak of the old, painful times, there, at the Porvenir Street apartment in Barcelona, where she and Arnau had found each other after his four-year sentence, and where their love could come to fruition in a very different way from how they had had to live up to then, hiding from persecution. She had thrown off the burden of party activism, letting Arnau carry it all, since it pleased him so much. She buried the memories of her two years in prison, of the visits afterward to Carabanchel to see Arnau, of the family reproaches and economic consequences that troubled her until she found a job at the school, and now, with Arnau recently freed by the second nationwide amnesty, she didn't want to hold on to any memory. She would be reborn from the pain and build her Shangri-La with Arnau, surrendering to the amnesia that would free her from suffering. And yet, there was Octubre, poorly dressed, with a wasted, gloomy face, digging her black gaze into Elisa as a continuous reproach for some faults that didn't deserve to be forgiven or forgotten.

"I haven't forgotten, and I never will," said Elisa. "Someone more intelligent than me said that if you forget history, you're destined to repeat it."

"Now the party has completely renounced violence, you know it. There's no reason to think the old mistakes will be made again."

"Adalberto didn't get a chance to learn."

Arnau puffed at his cigarette angrily. He didn't understand Elisa's interest in that old story.

"I repeat: I don't forget because I want to learn from my mistakes and from others'. But I don't see that same desire in your party members. Or the other parties, either. That's the tragedy of this country. That's why the Left is destined to repeat the same history, but the second time, in the form of a farce. The farce of this Spain I have to play out, and which I can't even laugh at."

Octubre loosened her long black hair, which she hadn't washed, and shook out her hands, which were tipped with black nails. Not even in jail had Elisa seen her looking so neglected. Her entire appearance had degenerated like someone on the brink of life and death. Octubre indifferently replied to her friend's question.

"I'm out of work and it's been days since I paid the landlady. If this keeps up I'll have to go to Madrid to live with my mother. But I don't want to, because she already lives poorly on what my father left her. But that's not important. The terrible thing is that the revolutionary parties are dead, my girl."

Elisa didn't want to get into that kind of discussion. It had been months since she had given any thought to the subject, since she had stopped listening to Arnau when he passed on the party news, since she had even read the newspapers or watched the TV news. And Arnau no longer required the activism he had demanded of her in earlier times. Suddenly she found that her greatest pleasure was living a routine life. Attending her classes, keeping her house, that house she lamented not having had before, and preparing lunch for Arnau certain he would come home in time to eat it hot, now that he no longer had to cross mountain passes or line the upholstery of cars with illegal pamphlets. She never remembered that for years she had borne a grudge against Ramiro for having sent her to Madrid just to take care of her husband, ruining her political promotion in and outside of the party.

"You can behave like that because you've decided to dedicate yourself to your husband, your work and your house. But I have no husband, no work, and no house, and I would certainly not even want any of those things if it weren't that without work I can't eat. But most of all, because I continue suffering from the ignorance and the buried pain of this homeland no one wants. I've looked the reactionary forces in the face, and your party, too. I've trembled in the State Security Headquarters and also in Paris talking with your leaders. And that occasion was even more painful. And I tell you that they won't ever change, because they can't learn anything. Their heads have been squashed."

It was like what Pere said. Octubre had explained it before with different words. Was there nothing to be done, then?

"We're doing some good work among the masses. We participate in new neighborhood organizations, we've worked hard and well in the campaign against NATO, and our party has come out strengthened by it, and we aren't isolated any more, not like during the transition, after the executions."

"Then, what's the problem today?"

"They arrested Cherta three weeks ago."

"You said that before."

"They're accusing him of the latest terrorist attacks by GRAPO."

Elisa looked at him blankly.

"But, does Cherta belong to GRAPO? Why is the party worried about him, then?"

"No, you see, that's exactly the problem. Cherta is on the executive committee of our party, naturally, as always. But the police are doing their best to get us mixed up with terrorism."

"And it's not true?"

Arnau shook his head, disgusted with the half smile twisting Elisa's face.

"You have no right to ask that. You know very well that our party renounced terrorism and even armed struggle when we began seeking legalization seven years ago."

"Well, that's what they always say…"

"Don't you believe it?"

"It could be a tactic. The end justifies the means, right?"

"You're making fun of me. You're holding a lot against us, much more than I ever imagined. You never explained it clearly. Not even when you left the party all those years ago. Why don't you believe what I tell you?"

"That you've stopped using terrorism? Oh, sure, why not? If that's what you say…"

"The situation has changed. It's not 1975 anymore."

"Of course."

Chapter 6

"Are you sure?"

Elisa looked at the newcomer with wide eyes. Marisa was brunette with black, grown-together eyebrows, a hearty complexion and a peasant look, and must have been robust before she went through the State Security Headquarters. Juana Parroto was also looking at her with the concern her situation deserved.

"Pretty sure. When I was arrested I was two weeks late and was going to go to a doctor. Then, at the police station, I thought it would come because I was afraid, and because of the beatings, but maybe that's why it didn't..."

"How long were you at the station?"

"Three weeks."

"That long?" Elisa's face was tense. "Then you've skipped more than once, haven't you?"

Marisa nodded her head. It was a square head covered with a thick mat of hair she wore tied back with a string at her nape.

"We'll have to fix it," Juana declared with no trace of doubt, and Marisa looked at her, relieved.

Elisa turned to her without understanding. "What do you mean?"

"She'll have to have an abortion."

"Here? How?" She was nearly shouting.

Juana looked annoyed and warned, "Don't yell, okay? I don't know how, but it'll have to be done. Marisa can't have a baby now, least of all in prison. We'll find a way. Relying on our own strengths, as Mao said."

Elisa didn't insist, but she thought Mao had never had to have an abortion. Least of all in a Spanish prison.

"We'll just have to ask someone's family for an abortive. Let's see, Pilar Laborde's sister is a nurse. She'll help us."

And Juana quickly left the classroom where they had been talking to carry out her plan. Marisa looked meekly at Elisa. In her eyes, there was a plea for forgiveness. She was begging pardon for bothering the more important and higher-up comrades with a problem which was hers alone and was getting in the way of the party's work. *Like a beaten mule,* Elisa thought, but she was immediately sorry. The thought was obviously classist.

The education she received from the nuns had never disappeared, and she saw Mother Perelló, standing up straight, enveloped by her habit, her face framed by the curved white cap that kept her from looking to her sides, repeating with her beautiful pink lips, "Poor people are very susceptible, so we must treat them with courtesy. Without allowing them to overstep themselves, but letting them know we respect them as the children of God we all are."

But we were superior, Elisa told herself angrily, *in a pyramid, structured from the beginning of time to the end of Creation, in which after Christ and the Virgin came first, Mother Perelló, and then the girls at the boarding school, and much further down, a dark and tattered multitude, which had to be "treated with courtesy."*

So she was surprised when she heard Octubre scream at Marisa, "Idiot! Worse than idiot! You only wish you were stupid and ignorant!" Her own rage choked her as she linked together a series of insults, all related to Marisa's mental capacity. Marisa took the sharp rebuke with her head down, saying nothing. The same way she must have endured her father's scolding. Elisa observed the scene and didn't understand how Octubre could dare to insult a worker that way, when she was struggling so bravely, to the point of putting her own life in danger. Octubre was scornful when Elisa made this observation that night in their cell.

"So what? She's a worker and obedient to her party. As if that were a guarantee of intelligence! Aren't you turning out to be a fanatic. No one could be more foolish than Marisa. First she gets together with a boy and gets pregnant, and then she goes and throws Molotov cocktails at the Legion recruitment center, just to wound a few unfortunate souls who go there because they have no other place to fall down dead, and then she gets herself caught. And here she is now with a terrorism charge and a full belly. Perfect! And on top of it all she isn't even married!"

"It was better that way, so we couldn't be identified. The party told us we should never tell them we lived together. To cover your tracks it's better if they don't find you with someone…"

Octubre and Elisa looked at Marisa silently for a few seconds. All the parties recommended marriage for their activists, not for moral reasons, but so as not to call attention to themselves. It wasn't the time to make free love a question of principle. But in Marisa and Adalberto's case it was different. If they were to be entrusted with armed struggle, they should not have partners, or a permanent address, or a private life. If one fell, he should not be identified by his relationship with another.

"In that case a person shouldn't get pregnant."

"I know. But I really didn't know how to prevent it. He would pull out, beforehand, you know, but sometimes that doesn't work."

"You didn't take contraceptives? The pill?" Elisa added, seeing the confusion in Marisa's face.

"No, there wasn't anyone to prescribe it for me. We lived hand to mouth, with no permanent address, and since I was using an assumed name, I didn't have a social security card, either. I didn't know of any pharmacy…"

Elisa was distressed by that accumulation of impossibilities and ignorance. She had never seen a more unlucky being, more crushed by adverse conditions.

Octubre once described her past for Elisa. "It's obvious you've never been poor. If you'd lived in El Pozo del Tío Raimundo, in a shack with no running water, no electricity, no toilet… the water coming down on your head when it rained, boiling hot in the summer, smelling the crap that ran liquid in the streets, with the barefoot, half-naked kids splashing around in the filthy water… Ten years ago in the factory where I worked ten hours a day, I made five thousand pesetas a month, and the rent for that shack cost me a thousand…"

Elisa knew these and other, more chilling facts. Before she was active in the party, the Catholic groups and charity organizations of the Church had publicized these scenes of poverty. A few times she had even gone to the huts of Torre Baró or the Bamba neighborhood around Barcelona, to give money or packs of food to the poorest families, and the image of misery and powerlessness had always shaken her. But Marisa gave her a different impression. She was a worker involved in the struggle, so her attitude didn't reflect the meekness and demoralization so widespread among the hopelessly marginalized. She was a young woman, twenty-two years old, who had a man at her side who loved her and who devoted himself to the same struggle. Their economic situation wasn't so desperate, either. When they were not in jail, they both collected a salary from the party they could just about live on, as well as the amount they received for the expenses of the activities they carried out. That wasn't the problem. What shocked Elisa was precisely that a woman in such conditions could have that meekness, that irreversible fatalism about her own fate that so contradicted the activity she was undertaking and the ideology that supported it.

"And your man, didn't he know how to use a condom, either? They sell them in the shops in Chinatown and a man knows where to get them with no problems."

"He didn't like them. He said it didn't feel the same."

Her voice trailed off into a murmur at the end. Shame kept her from looking at her comrades, from explaining the cause of her problem in detail. Elisa tried to draw some conclusion from Marisa's story.

"Were you living in Madrid?" she ventured to ask after a few minutes.

"Yes, for two years."

"And before that?"

"We're Galician. The party sent us here to take a leadership course. We were studying the works of Mao and Lenin."

Elisa stared at her and didn't reply. It was Octubre who had the audacity to shout without noticing how disrespectful it was to Marisa.

"Whoa, plenty of leadership courses and books by Lenin and Mao, and not enough knowing how to stick it in without doing any damage. What ignorance, Lord! Your party would've spent its time better teaching you how to deal with the facts of life."

Elisa didn't have to defend her party, which at the moment meant nothing to her. It was Marisa who reacted immediately. With an energy no one would have suspected a few moments before, she straightened up — and in that moment she seemed to increase in size and volume — and arrogantly answered that her party had more important things to do. Giving courses on pills and other stupid things like that was fine for petty bourgeois women's organizations, but they were called upon to carry out the revolution, in which everything would have a place.

"Well, if you rely on that, your kid will be old and crotchety before you finally learn to take the pill."

Elisa removed herself from the general argument that followed Octubre's insulting remark. She only paid attention to Marisa's aggressiveness, since moments before she had seemed like a timid peasant girl. "The power of the ideology," Arnau would have recited. "With it we will fell giants and raise mountains."

"Or the innkeepers will beat us up, and the galley slaves will stone us."

"Oh, what an unbeliever is this girl of mine! And what have I done to deserve this? I'll have to denounce you to the committee head for your ideological vacillations."

And they would both laugh, a moment before Arnau brought it to an end with his kisses, and the squeezes that pushed her toward the bed or the living room couch, or even the carpet, a threadbare, faded rag where they had made love so many times in the tumbledown apartment in the Vallecas neighborhood of Madrid.

Elisa tried to drive off the memories by rubbing her eyes compulsively. She should not let herself think of those scenes, when she found herself in a situation in which it was so impossible to make them come true. She concentrated hard to drive out the image of Arnau naked before her, slowly moving downward until his mouth reached her sex to pay it homage, while he held her waist with both hands, softly pressing her against the wall.

"Don't rub your eyes like that. You'll give yourself an infection."

Elisa smiled and nodded. Arnau was looking at her suspiciously.

"What are you thinking about?"

"That you're right, that times have changed. They don't send ignorant pregnant young things to throw Molotov cocktails into the Legion recruitment center anymore."

Arnau's anger flared up again. "I don't know how you can say that. We were the first to regret that, Adalberto more than anyone, as the entire world knows."

"Of course. I didn't mean to offend anyone, least of all Adalberto's memory. I was just remembering that the one having an abortion in prison was Marisa. Not you, not the other male comrades, not even me, who would have been more sensible…"

The drug took two weeks to arrive, after all the barriers that separated normal life from prison life had been overcome, and had no effect. It didn't even cause the light bleeding it should have.

"Strong and healthy, like a Galician peasant. That baby is stuck in you like a parasite…"

But now Octubre wasn't hurling insults or shouting. Worry had eaten away at everyone who knew about the problem: Juana Parroto, Octubre, Elisa, and Pilar Laborde, who had been the contact in obtaining the abortive. With her brow furrowed and a resolute expression, Octubre decided.

"We'll have to use a cotton catheter. Your sister has to get us several."

They separated silent and troubled. Marisa had said nothing. She had accepted the decisions of the others, recognizing their better judgment, but everyone knew they were facing a serious problem. The women, who had retained their dignity through the arrest, the torture, and several months or years of prison, were terrified by the unforeseen situation. Only Octubre had witnessed an illegal abortion in a shack in her neighborhood, but she hadn't been the one to carry it out. What she didn't say was that she herself had been the patient, and that, after using catheters for two weeks, with a neighbor changing them for her once in a while, she only survived the infection thanks to her physical tenacity and the penicillin a doctor friend prescribed for her when she was already trembling with fever in bed. Now she looked with growing worry at Marisa, and, like the others, was afraid of being discovered. If Marisa became ill, besides the physical risk she would run, an abortion would be added to the list of their crimes. As if they all didn't have enough complications already.

Elisa stopped Octubre in the hallway and asked her, "Do you think it will be safe?"

"I have no idea. I guess we'll be able to give her an abortion, but who knows what may happen afterward."

Octubre observed Elisa's face as the color left it, her trembling lips and hands, and was surprised. She took her by the shoulders and tried to make light of the situation.

"You've got to be more brave, girl! No one would ever know you're an activist in the PC-ML and that you've been through General Security and in jail for a year and a half!"

"Maybe that's why."

And Elisa quickly turned toward the staircase leading to the infirmary. Octubre didn't know whether she was referring to the fear of another arrest or to the way the party would be discredited if Marisa's story became known. Elisa didn't want to clarify her enigmatic phrase. She was too afraid of everything all at once.

The cotton catheters arrived within a week. It was the first time Elisa had seen those narrow strips of white cloth, rolled up inside a sterilized plastic bag. She watched the procedure, hypnotized. Octubre handled the catheters with inexpert but steady hands, and Marisa let herself be manipulated with resignation. Juana and Elisa looked on without doing anything. She didn't think of holding Marisa's hand or comforting her in some other way that would show her affection and solidarity. She stared at Octubre's hands, which probed without skill to introduce the catheter into the dark space of Marisa's insides.

"Well, I think that's it. Now we have to wait."

"That's it? But then…" Elisa said.

"Yes, we have to wait for her to dilate. What did you think?"

"Well, I thought you were going to do the abortion all at once."

"With a fabric strip? Oh, dear, aren't you an expert in the ways of the world. Don't you have any idea how this works?"

Elisa shook her head and saw out of the corner of her eye the interest with which Marisa listened to Octubre's explanations while she got dressed. *She doesn't know, either,* she thought.

"Well, this is older than walking upright," grunted Octubre. "The catheter swells up with the heat and moisture of the vagina, and then, to expel it, the womb will start to contract and will expel the embryo with it."

"How long does that take?"

"It depends. A few hours or a few days."

"Days!"

Elisa's surprise was shared by Marisa, though she said nothing.

"Yes, sometimes two weeks."

"With the catheter inside the whole time?"

"Yes, of course. The Holy Ghost helps in giving birth, but not in having abortions," she joked while she washed her hands in the sink.

"But it will get dirty…" She didn't know how to express her doubts and scruples. She had never had a conversation like that with anyone, much less in front of the concerned party.

"That's the problem, my friend. That's why there are so many infections. If it takes a long time we'll change her catheter, but it shouldn't be handled a lot because the infection is in there waiting. Anyway, we shouldn't be talking like this because we'll scare Marisa. Thank God for penicillin. Don't worry, my girl. We won't let anything bad happen to you. Before that we'll go to the prison doctor."

"Oh, no!" Marisa shouted. "Not that, ever! Promise me!"

"Well, it wouldn't be pleasant, but if there's no other way it's better to have one more charge against us — we already have so many — than to let something bad happen to you."

"No! No way! That would be terrible for my party!"

Octubre looked at her seriously. "Do you really mean that in order to not compromise your party, you don't want us to call a doctor, no matter what?"

"Of course I mean it." Marisa's face bore witness to it.

"You're ready to die, rather than inconvenience your party?"

"I've always been willing to die for my party." And this time Marisa had transformed. When she stood up she had grown, and her dedication made her beautiful.

"Fine, but keep in mind that if you die the whole story will be discovered, and your party will be screwed, anyway, and we'll get that many more years behind bars, so, I can't promise you anything, girl. Besides, I've always been against such useless heroism. By the way, where's your man?"

Marisa had begun to sulk. She had to consider Octubre's objection. She would have answered rudely if Elisa hadn't made a gesture for her to keep quiet.

"I don't know."

"No, and I don't want to know, either. I just thought you could tell him what's happening, if you can get in contact with him."

"No, I can't and I wouldn't even if I could. I shouldn't worry him with my problems now. He's fighting in a very dangerous position and needs peace. What's happening to me is stupid, and he's risking his life."

"You're risking your life, too. And this stupid mess concerns him more than anyone." With the last word, Octubre went back to her cell.

"I think it will be better if we go to bed and try to sleep. If anything happens to you, call me right away."

Elisa lay down with the feeling that she would not sleep. For the first few minutes she anxiously watched Marisa's motionless form in the next bed. The lamp on the nightstand was on and she didn't dare to turn it off. The entire dormitory was asleep. They had waited until two in the morning, when even the night owls had gone to bed, to carry out the procedure, and they posted Juana in the hallway that connected the dormitory with the iron and glass door that led into the first floor foyer of the political prisoner unit, to warn them in case an official came by.

It wasn't likely. The attendants only wanted their shifts to pass by as quietly as possible, and even more so with regard to the politicals. They only came to the politicals' section at night if they were called, and then with a long delay. The fear of finding themselves with a riot made them ignore the first calls: they always seemed to harbor the hope that the caller would forget about it. Now, in the silence of the dormitory, contemplating Marisa, who seemed to be sleeping in spite of it all, Elisa felt dizzy, confused. For the first time in a year and a half she felt the oppression of prison. She was overcome by a weight on her sternum that didn't let her breathe, a headache, an intense desire to cry, which they all knew as "prisonitis." How would it all end up?

"I don't know why you're talking to me like that. It wasn't my fault what happened to Marisa, or the party, or… I don't know, Elisa, you're acting strange this morning. Remembering things that happened so long ago…"

Arnau drummed his fingers on the table, which still had the remains of breakfast on it.

"You reminded me of it all with your even stranger visit. You're talking to me about the party, and it takes me back to those times, the last years I was in the party. And talking about terrorism, I couldn't help but think of Marisa."

"So you did throw the Molotov cocktail."

"Yes, I had two in my purse, but they didn't give me time to throw them. The guys had already thrown theirs and a lot of smoke was starting to come out the window. You could see the soldiers inside choking and they couldn't get out because there were bars on the window. The soldiers started coming out the door, just a few, but they were running way behind us, and then I threw the one cocktail I had ready really hard, and I let the other one go as I ran. They were faster than me, and they caught me right away."

"And the other comrades?"

"They escaped. The soldiers were busy with me, and they were ahead of me, and got lost at a crossroads right away."

Marisa was satisfied to have contributed to her comrade's escape. Elisa didn't know if her boyfriend was among them, because Marisa didn't say and those things could not be asked, but she understood that the satisfaction was the same whether or not Adalberto was one of the ones saved.

One of them always typed on Octubre's typewriter while they spoke in order to prevent a clear recording in case the microphones they feared really existed.

"May I ask you why you chose the Legion recruitment center for the attack?"

Octubre clearly disagreed, and Marisa became tense. She didn't want to talk about party activity with someone who didn't belong to it, and only because of the great confidence Octubre inspired and which Elisa showed toward her had Marisa told her the best known part of the story. But she wasn't willing to argue with her about strategic decisions, which were only for the leaders.

"The party decided it," she replied neutrally, and was surprised when Elisa intervened.

"You can tell her why that decision was made." Elisa added apologetically, "Maybe you can convince her."

Marisa understood. It was a question of ideological propaganda. Resigned, and even happy, she replied, "The Legion recruitment center is one of the places where the army's power is concentrated, and so it's the most fascist. It was the army that had the most important role in the repression during and after the Civil War. It's one of our objectives in the people's war."

Octubre watched her without losing patience. She seemed to feel tenderness for the peasant girl who recited political orders with so much confidence.

"The young men there had nothing to do with the Civil War, and at the recruitment center there are no more than six of the most unlucky soldiers. They enter the Legion because they have nowhere else to fall down dead: lumpen, nothing more than lumpen. Unemployed, ex-delinquents, reformatory and brothel boys. That's who you directed military action against. Why didn't you go kill the general?"

Marisa was confounded. It was probably the first time anyone had told her the Legion soldiers were lumpen. It also would have been the first time anyone had called into question the fairness of the military objective of the party in her presence. She was speechless. She turned to Elisa, looking for help, but found her in a similar state of mind. Octubre looked at the two of them darkly, and for a few minutes there was only a great silence.

But that was before they gave Marisa the abortion and long before she began to bleed. She had just come to the prison and still hadn't been to the infirmary to be treated for the beating she had gotten during her detention.

Marisa began to bleed in the early morning of the same night, and called to Elisa in terror. Elisa looked at the stained sheets, paralyzed. Octubre immediately woke up and told them that it was normal and she supposed it meant it was going well. She gave her a sanitary napkin and they all began to wait again, this time without sleeping. But the end didn't come. The bleeding was slight, and Marisa felt only some small tugs in her womb. The whole day went by that way, and at night Octubre decided to change the catheter. That time the procedure took longer. The blood kept her from seeing the right place to insert the strip of fabric, and Marisa's face contracted as she tried to keep back her moans.

The second night Elisa noticed Marisa was stirring in bed, unable to sleep. In the morning she had a fever. After a brief secret meeting, the women involved decided to go to the infirmary to ask for a dose of penicillin or sulphamide, with some excuse. Octubre obtained two pills, because the nurse respected only her enough to give it to her without a prescription. They felt more and more powerless. One dose was only the beginning. They would have to give one every three hours if the fever persisted. Marisa was lucid, though somewhat groggy, but the others didn't want to weigh her down with their worries. They gave her the pills and told her to sleep. Octubre wondered whether it would be more effective for her to get up and walk, but the cold convinced them to keep her in bed. She might complicate her fever catching cold.

Elisa remembered the three days of Marisa's abortion as an episode inserted into her life like a movie described by someone else who'd seen it. Marisa's fever rose higher, and she became delirious. The other prisoners showed their concern that her comrades didn't tell the doctor. Thanks to the common clandestine procedures, however, it was easy to convince them that they could not let the officials know, and beg them to keep the secret. Several offered to get penicillin from the nurse, and five or six took turns to avoid the authorities' suspicion. Elisa stayed beside Marisa's bed throughout the three days because she didn't know what else to do. It was impossible for her to think of anything else. She felt suffocated by fear, by a palpable and more and more anguished fear that Marisa was dying. When she reflected on it, much later, she could never say whether it was natural compassion for another human being, solidarity for a party comrade or an acute selfishness in the face of the new problems that would arise if they finally had to tell the prison doctor.

The third night Marisa soaked the mattress with blood, while she sweated oceans under the cold cloths Octubre's charitable hand placed on her forehead. And suddenly, when they thought everything was lost, Marisa seemed to get better. Her fever went down. The hemorrhage continued, but she felt more alert. The abortion was finished. For a few days, they were able to provide her with some more doses of penicillin. Then, her strong peasant constitution did the rest.

Arnau looked hardly able to control his impatience. He removed the cups and stacked them into each other, heaped up the crumbs on the tablecloth and crossed his legs compulsively.

"So then, do you intend to help us, or will memories of the past keep you from it? In the end, Elisa, you too went along with terrorism in its moment. Besides, remember that we called it 'the people's revolutionary war.' During the dictatorship, things were different. That's why we've changed our strategy now. After Franco's death, armed struggle didn't make sense. We already talked about that, back then."

"Yes, it's true, I went along with armed struggle." She stared at Arnau for a few seconds and, as if remembering something very far away in time, she added, "If the party had ordered me to, I would have taken a weapon and killed anyone."

CHAPTER 7

"Would you have done it?"

To the other person's amazement, Elisa answered smiling, "If the party had ordered me to, yes."

"You would've gone into the street with a gun to kill someone, and then you would've aimed at that person's head and fired?"

Elisa hesitated a moment. She wanted to be absolutely honest in her response. When she said she would have followed party orders, she meant it, but she had never imagined the act in such detail. It meant accepting the weapon, learning to use it, and going out one morning with it in her purse to look for a victim. And that victim, chosen at random, a guard at the entrance to a bank, an inattentive soldier waiting for someone in the street, would be a human being who was alive a few minutes before she pulled the trigger. Would she really have pulled it?

"Yes, I think so."

When she talked to Carles about it, she understood his surprise. It was the same as that of her friends at work, and of her siblings. One afternoon at school, Maruja Serra discussed Elisa's surprising answer with the other teachers for several hours.

"Listen to this! Guess what Vilaró told me. If her party had ordered her to, she would've gone through the streets killing people. What do you think of that! The lovely maiden with the blue eyes and that angel face, such a little thing… We'd all better watch out!"

Elisa felt very sick while the joke lasted. Several coworkers pretended they were afraid of her, and all of them began to look at her as though she were some strange beast. Elisa just laughed, and at last most of them considered the joke worn out. She never expressed her doubts to anyone.

"You see? Objective, material conditions are what determine the level of consciousness…"

Arnau interrupted himself when he realized Elisa wasn't listening.

"The truth is that now I don't know what I would've done. I always said that, and I certainly believed it at the time, but the situation never presented itself, and I don't know what I would've done in the moment of truth. I would've been really scared."

"We were all scared and we still are when we have to carry out an order, but courage forces us to overcome it."

Elisa didn't feel courageous. She never even tried to be. She hadn't talked at the State Security Headquarters because she knew almost nothing, and the police got their information from the other arrests. But she was sure she could not have withstood torture. She, who had so longed for martyrdom throughout her childhood. Where were her fantasies about the sainthood she would attain by sacrificing her life for the faith, now? When she was given the chance, she no longer had any faith, and wasn't ready to die for it. Not even for her party.

"Don't you feel the same enthusiasm as Marisa?"

Elisa shook her head. Petra looked at her with interest. For a few seconds they were quiet, then Petra asked, "So what are you going to do?"

Elisa looked at her in surprise. "Do? About what?"

"Aren't you going to consult your party about your doubts?"

"No."

She hadn't even thought about it. It had been many years since she had felt duty-bound to confess her most serious doubts to her spiritual director, to spend her nights examining her conscience, and to pray for hours on end, until she had calluses on her knees, for the Lord to enlighten her and enable her to obey the Mother Superior without thinking. No later annoyance or frustration would ever disappoint her as much as the loss of that single point that deprived her of crowning the Virgin one year, after four consecutive years of being chosen as the girl with no demerits in the month of Mary. And when Isabel Fortuny went forward to the altar, haughty as a queen in her formal uniform, in front of the entire school, and up the steps that led up to the image, and placed the crown of white roses she had patiently been putting together all morning on its head, the pain Elisa felt could not be compared with any other disappointment.

Not the lack of promotion in the party, nor her resentment against Ramiro for his scorn and the lowly role he allotted to her in Madrid as Arnau's servant, nor the indifference that was overcoming her in all her dealings with the party, slowly anesthetizing her, ever hurt as much as the humiliation she suffered at the Sacred Heart. *They desensitized me,* she thought. *I have to thank them for that.*

Elisenda looked at her with a teasing smile and said, "You actually want to do that?"

"What do you mean?" Elisa was already quick to get upset at her friend.

"That ridiculous ceremony. Why would you want to make a fool of yourself like that, at our age?"

"You're always trying to make me mad. The cult of Mary is a lifelong devotion. How old you are doesn't matter, duh!"

"But that ludicrous sight of going to the altar with a flower crown and everyone else looking on like idiots and the droning and the incense and all that, it's fine for little girls, but now that we're fifteen, I'd be embarrassed!"

Elisa got angry with Elisenda, but they were already about to go their separate ways. Elisenda was expelled from the school for bad behavior and soon ran away from her next school, where they tried to tame her, while Elisa patiently, tenaciously followed the path to sainthood, from which only Arnau diverted her.

Only he had caused her the deepest pain of her life. *They didn't desensitize me from that.*

"But when you got here you seemed to have found God in your party…"

Elisa wasn't aware of having changed so much since coming to prison. Looking for God? Did she give the impression she was looking for God in every corner?

"Well, yes, you did. With that saintly face and that silly expression you put on so much and the way you get sidetracked. Half the time you don't even seem to be here. I don't know what's going on in your head."

Elisa didn't know, either. Mental lapses, absences, lack of contact with reality, she had always suffered from them. At school they began as a result of the spiritual exercises, of the long hours of prayer, meditation, silence. The annulment of the will in the fusion with God. For a long time, she believed it was a sign of divine grace, but now she didn't know what to attribute it to. Although, if the nuns heard her, they would say that divine grace cannot be disposed of at will. And why would she want to lose it? She only wanted to be able to concentrate when she needed to.

"It's a characteristic of the students of the Sacred Heart," Isabel Fortuny told her one day when they ran into each other in town, after she was married. "Haven't you noticed that we all seem stupefied, detached from this world, made foolish with so much praying and so much silence? Just look at our classmates. We all have a screw loose."

Isabel had even stopped going to mass after having been pink band, green band, and blue band throughout her school years. *Because there were no more bands and no more colors,* thought Elisa. She was the one who had deprived Elisa of that coronation when she was fifteen, and now they both understood each other, so many years later, when Isabel had separated from her husband and was living alone in Barcelona.

"So, what are you going to do?"

"Nothing. Why do I have to do anything?"

Octubre looked at her with curiosity. It wasn't obvious to Elisa that she should share her ideological doubts with the party. Elisa didn't feel that committed to the party.

"So leave it."

Elisa looked at Octubre, amazed. She had no reason to make such an important decision now, either. She needed time to think. She didn't add, "And to talk to Arnau," because she guessed Octubre would not have liked that. The same way she didn't like what she considered the hypocrisy of Elisa's behavior.

"You might have to think, but in the meantime, you should discuss your crisis with your comrades. You should be more honest with Juana than with me, for instance."

"With Juana?"

Octubre smiled at Elisa's surprise. "It's hard to talk to Juana, you don't have to tell me. But honey, she's from your party and I'm not. You must have had a reason for choosing that party and not some other. Because I suppose there must be a lot of other comrades like Juana, aren't there?"

To be honest, Elisa would have had to reply that there were, but the subject hadn't been important to her. She chose the party because Arnau had chosen it. He had explained very carefully how the Communist Party of Spain had betrayed the revolutionary ideals of the working class. One afternoon in June, exactly like the one which had brought them together two years before, he gave her a complete run-down on the revisionism of Carrillo and the Communist Party, which they always considered a splinter group. Agents of the oligarchy introduced into the bosom of the working class, as Lenin had already described them so long ago. And the obligation of a conscientious Marxist-Leninist was to unmask them so they could not keep doing so much harm to the proletariat with their bourgeois discourses on national reconciliation, the union of the forces of labor and culture, and the renunciation of class struggle. Carrillo, their leader, was much more dangerous than the fascists. In the end, they were not fooling anyone. Therefore, their struggle, their energies, their work, should be directed fundamentally against the followers of Carrillo's splinter group. They never called it anything else, they never considered him anything other than a traitor, a revisionist and an agent of Yankee imperialism.

"It was fashionable at the time," Elisa excused herself, blushing at Carles, while he laughed heartily, waiting for coffee at the breakfast table. The same table where Arnau was now waiting for something more than coffee from her.

"It was fashionable at the time, naturally," she mimicked herself and smiled.

Arnau seemed more peaceful. With a smile, he replied, "Of course. And you always knew I didn't agree with him about everything. Do you remember how we didn't know what to do when we went to the Assembly of Catalonia? Since *The Worker's Vanguard* was insulting everyone like that, there was no kind of dialogue with any other party, even though a lot of parties were interested in us."

"Oh, yes! Do you remember when they called Tierno Galván 'an agent of the oligarchy'?"

They were overcome with a fit of laughter that calmed her nerves. Finally, Elisa had to dry her tears.

"How could we bear it?"

Elisa looked tenderly at Arnau and didn't perceive his change of attitude. To hide his annoyance, he lit a cigarette. Then, smiling, he replied patiently, "I think we did what we had to. I'm not sorry."

Elisa looked at him now as if he were someone she had just met.

"Oh, how silly of me! You're still in the same line. Sorry."

"No, you don't have to say you're sorry. You've changed, but I haven't. Back then a lot of things were justified, even mistakes. It seems ridiculous to call Tierno an agent of the oligarchy today, but in all honesty it was true. What politics is the socialist government pursuing now? Simply following the bourgeoisie and at the same time dismantling the Worker's Movement. Before the dictatorship was even over, the party predicted what we're going through now. The trouble was that we didn't know how to avoid it."

He didn't realize that she wasn't paying attention. She was fascinated by his hands, the way he held the cigarette, flicked off the ash. She looked at him with surprise and tenderness at the same time. Not because of what he said. It was his tone of voice, that voice which had kept her awake so many nights crying, obsessed with the loss of his love.

"You still love him, don't you?"

Carles looked at her, at the same time bitter and understanding. She roundly denied it, but he didn't believe her. No one believed Elisa was over Arnau. Everyone who knew her agreed that if Arnau made the slightest sign she would go back to him immediately, asking for forgiveness besides. Her mother, her sisters, her coworkers, with their reproaches or their jokes, led her to understand that they knew all about that passion she could not control.

"He was your first love, perhaps the only one?"

She denied it again, but it was a lie. That good boy Manel, the schoolmate with whom she had consoled herself during the fifteen interminable months during which Arnau purged his rebelliousness in military service in Sidi Ifni, was never her love, although he motivated the first serious rift between Arnau and herself. Arnau couldn't bear the jealousy when he found out, and much less when she tried to prolong the friendship with Manel when Arnau came back, with an obvious desire to provoke him. Then, he was very much in love with her and the separation didn't last longer than a month. A tormented and melodramatic month during which all the commonplaces of ill-fated lovers were voiced.

In the nights of insomnia and tears that followed the final separation, Elisa tortured herself, tirelessly wondering what could have made Arnau fall out of love with her after fifteen years of shared life, faithfulness, shared dangers and goals. Arnau, who had seemed more in love with her than she with him, who everyone said was bewitched by that insignificant goody-two-shoes with the angelic face, when with his looks he could have had Sofia Loren. Arnau, who had waited until she awoke from her mystic dream to win her over patiently when all the girls in town would have fought for the privilege of his embraces. Arnau, who tolerated her adventure with Manel, not even seeking consolation in another's arms, who understood her better than anyone else and even loved her absent-mindedness, her memory losses, her incomprehensible lapses. Arnau, who suddenly one day, fifteen years later, when the dictatorship was over, free from prison, when they were beginning to get settled professionally and had already been able to rent a decent house and furnish it tastefully, decided he was in love with a coworker and was leaving with her. That was all.

"Nothing more, right?"

Carles looked at her with a hostile, mocking smile.

"I never knew anything more had happened."

"Because you never figure anything out. But Arnau must have been tired of you for a while. These things don't happen in one day, and it doesn't make that much difference meeting someone else. When a relationship breaks up there's more to it than another lover. No matter what they say, it's not true. They say it in order not to upset anyone."

Carles expressed himself brutally. The persistence of Elisa's love for Arnau bothered him, and he wanted to hurt her. He didn't like her distractedness. He didn't make excuses for it or allow himself to be entertained by it the way Arnau had. He was continually reproaching her for her forgetfulness and mental lapses. "I think you're subnormal," he told her once, and only apologized when she began to sob uncontrollably. But whenever it happened again, he again complained and rudely criticized her. Sometimes Isabel, who visited them often, reproached her for putting up with Carles's scolding and urged her to leave him, but only Elisa knew how much she needed someone's company, even if it was Carles.

"And why exactly Carles?"

But that was exactly it. Carles and no one else. At least, not immediately after being separated from Arnau. In spite of the difference in personality, behavior, and temperament of the two men, in spite of her mother's indignation and the astonishment of Arnau's family, in spite of Isabel's thoughts, it had to be Arnau's brother Carles and no one else who took Arnau's place in the conjugal bed.

She wasn't ashamed or modest in the beginning. It seemed the most natural thing to her when she found herself defeated and acutely depressed after closing the door after Arnau. Only once was she confused, and a sensation close to shame came over her when she heard several coworkers at school saying, "That one sure does get around! Take one out of the bed and she puts another one in without noticing the difference."

Their guffaws made Elisa uncomfortable. She hadn't thought until that moment that anyone could criticize her conduct. Arnau was the one who abandoned her...

"But that doesn't mean you have to throw yourself into Carles's arms the same night Arnau left..."

"I was sad and alone… I would've killed myself if Carles hadn't kept me company."

Isabel jumped. "Come on, Elisa, don't get dramatic. I don't believe a woman like you, who chose the most adventuresome life of all, could say things only an undeveloped character from a romance novel would say."

"It was true. Carles saved my life."

"Well, I didn't know that. Was that why he cashed in?"

"Don't be crude, Isabel. I'm talking about the most serious situation of my life. Don't make fun of me. I don't talk about these things to anyone. Just you."

"You could've called me that night. I would've kept you company and saved your life, too, without asking anything in return."

"Why are you talking like that? It sounds like you hate Carles."

"I can't sympathize with him. So many years as a priest, so much devotion and piety and all that, just to end up in bed with you."

"It had to be someone."

"But, what a coincidence it was you! And just when you were your most vulnerable."

"He was lost, too. He hadn't decided to go secular yet, and he was confused, uncomfortable, and I needed him…"

"Why? Why him, exactly?"

Arnau looked at her and waited, resignedly, for her to return to the present and answer him.

"Sorry, what did you say?"

"I was asking you why you rejected Cherta so much. I already know he was the one who transmitted the leaders' instructions to move to Madrid to take care of me, but there were other comrades who agreed with him, who made the same decision, who had even more power than him within the party, but you aren't bitter toward them."

"Oh, yes, of course. Only I didn't see them, and didn't have to deal with them afterward. In the end, you aren't coming in their names to ask me a favor."

She didn't know if she was more bitter toward Cherta than the rest, but she didn't care any more, either. She felt trapped by Arnau's interrogation. Her back hurt from sitting in the same position, the cigarette smoke was bothering her, she had slept little, and ahead of her lay yet another sleepless night correcting exams before she could start her vacation. Why was he trying so hard to ask her, to cajole she knew not what answers about distant subjects? Why did everyone always try to get her to choose a party — and always that word ruling her life, controlling her actions, her thoughts, mortgaging her past and preventing her future?

"What's your decision, once and for all?"

Juana Parroto was tired of trying unsuccessfully to get an express declaration from Elisa.

"I don't know, I'm not sure…"

"We can't wait any more. I know you realize that. We have a serious question before us, all the parties represented here have already taken a position, and the other prisoners have already made up a communiqué. We're the only ones left, and we're the ones who have the most responsibility."

"That's exactly why I don't want to make a snap decision."

"Elisa, you'll have to define your stance. You're the highest in rank, but I venture to say that you're doubtful, and I'll communicate it that way to the party executive."

Marisa watched them with wide eyes. She had lost several pounds since the abortion five months before, and despite their sitting in the sun every day in the courtyard during the torrid July in Madrid, she seemed pale. She hadn't regained the vitality that had been apparent when she arrived at the prison, despite the torture and long solitary confinement. Her usual reserve and awkwardness seemed exaggerated. She almost never spoke, and didn't participate in the meetings except to agree with Juana's proposals, and all she did was walk around the courtyard and do unending needlework that she ultimately sent back home.

Now she felt lost. The argument between her two superiors seemed inconceivable. If the leadership wasn't united and monolithic, who would be? As surprised as she was, the part of the executive branch within the prison needed a swift response. The prisoners from the PC-ML came to fifteen, the most numerous group from a single party inside the prison. The rest of the base was waiting for the meeting to end to find out whether the decision was adopted. At last, Pilar Laborde, who was usually very cautious, intervened.

"But come on, now, Elisa, how can we not accept the executive decisions, if they've already been made anyway?"

Everyone looked toward Pilar with approval. It was obvious that disagreeing would be senseless and would do no one any good. But Elisa felt burdened by such a decision. She timidly dared to disagree, "If we send them a critique maybe they'll think it over…"

"Oh, stop it!" Juana almost shoved her as she answered bitterly, "The party leaders have done all the thinking they need to do, they don't need us going and giving them advice. We only need to know if you're signing this document or not, and if not I guess you'll remove yourself from the meeting until we can make a decision about you."

"Well, we don't have to let things get out of hand, either. Elisa has reservations because she's been here a long time and isn't familiar with developments on the outside."

"I've been here as long as she has and I understand perfectly that our party has made a decision to declare the people's revolutionary war! We've been preparing for it for the last two years, and they know when the moment arrived…" Juana was beside herself, shouting.

Pilar wore a displeased expression and Marisa looked at everyone with an open mouth. Finally, one of the others quieted everyone's murmurs and imposed order.

"Come on, let's finish with all this noise and arguing. Elisa, do you agree to support the executive decision and sign the communiqué we've written? It's getting late and the meeting with all the others has to begin after the consensus. It's time to make a fair copy of the document."

Elisa accepted, and everyone breathed again. Afterward she told herself that the people's revolutionary war wasn't the same as terrorism, and it seemed to her that that way she could still have her remorse.

"You're too hard on yourself. You can't feel responsible for everyone all the time, my girl. Go on, say a Hail Mary for your intentions."

The spiritual counselor assured Elisa that she was saint material because she always felt responsible for the world's problems, but she couldn't see herself that way. She could mortify herself continually, fast, squeeze the hair shirt until she made herself bleed, walk on rocks and pray on her knees for hours on end, but she didn't feel responsible for the pains of the world. She didn't know them, and she didn't want to know them.

She wasn't impressed by the stories the Mother Superior sometimes told about the little black children dying of hunger in Africa, and later, when she took packages to the shacks in the outlying neighborhoods, the sight of their poverty didn't especially impress her.

On one occasion when they were arguing, Arnau asked her maliciously, "Is there anything that matters more to you than yourself?" He didn't give her time to answer before he added, "If you love me it's because it gratifies you."

Elisa had never heard that reproach before, but she was unable to ask exactly what he meant by it because the argument took another course. Later she forgot Arnau's accusation. Only in the last days before the separation did he tell her again, "Your problem is you love yourself too much," but everything was lost already and she didn't need to understand why Arnau thought such a thing.

She was more impressed by the lives of the saints, and by the mystics in particular, than by the common life of mere mortals. She should love everyone in order to deserve divine grace, but the feelings she felt for the inhabitants of the shacks in La Bomba or Somorrostro was so mixed up she never dared to call it love.

She always felt incomplete in that way, and that was what she told her counselor, and for exactly that he had made the diagnosis about Elisa's rigidity. She always tried to escape her remorse by concentrating on a vision of Jesus. She reached toward him, searching for the ecstasy Saint Teresa and Saint John of the Cross had felt, but it was denied to her. To her, faith was always more important than charity. The faith which precisely at that moment she lacked.

Marisa waited for her at the door of the TV room where they held the meeting, to ask her, "I don't understand. Why were you so hesitant? Aren't you in favor of armed struggle?"

Elisa didn't bother to answer her with a similar question. Marisa was ready to give her life for the party, and if she was released, she would go back to throwing Molotov cocktails without hesitation.

"I don't think the country is ready, that's all. The people don't want war. Wars arise in places where social and economic conditions are different. I think a people's war, like the one in China, would be impossible in Spain, a country so different in size, culture, socio-economic situation. Perhaps in twenty more years…"

"Comrade Elisa, what you're saying is revisionism and Trotskyism and I'm warning you…"

At that time, Elisa didn't wait to hear Juana's threats. Neither did she understand an accusation of Trotskyism based on those hesitant opinions, but she preferred not to figure it out. With a snort, she ran toward the stairs in response to the bells that called them to be counted for the night.

"But you said that if the party had ordered it, you would have taken a pistol and gone out to kill anybody, didn't you? So what are all these scruples for now?"

Arnau was beginning to show his anger and annoyance. He abruptly extinguished the cigarette butt in the ashtray and stood up.

"Well, it seems I'm wasting my time. If you don't want to help me, tell me once and for all and don't keep me here longer. We have many serious problems and I can't allow myself the luxury of sitting here discussing matters from ten years ago with you."

Elisa was startled. Those words meant that in a few minutes Arnau would be in the street, far from her, forever, all hope of ever seeing him again lost if she refused to help him now.

"I still haven't said I don't want to help you. You're the one accusing me of who knows what…"

Arnau hesitated a moment and then decided to sit down again.

"It seems that both of us are accusing each other of who knows what mistakes made a long time ago. Because you also signed the document agreeing to armed struggle from prison, and you always knew we were preparing for the people's war. That was one of the most debated subjects in the party, and if both of us joined it, it was precisely because it proposed seizing power by force and the dictatorship of the proletariat, against Carrillo's projects of pacts and reconciliation. Or don't you remember our own history any more?"

Elisa agreed, and tried to do it enthusiastically.

"I'm going to make more coffee," she added, "and I'll bring some sandwiches, because sitting here talking, it's gotten late and you must be hungry."

She didn't wait for him to reply and went quickly into the kitchen. He would have tried to end the conversation. She felt pressed again, forced to define herself, to make decisions she didn't want. She no longer knew why she had joined the party, why she signed the document and wasn't even sure that arrogant claim, about taking up arms if the party had ordered it, was true. If Arnau wanted to talk with her about her former life, that life they both lived, concealed from the party that always saw everything, hidden away in poor tumbledown apartments, shivering in the winter, with no couch to sit on or a shelf to put books on, so they were piled on the floor… But Arnau didn't seem to want to talk about the only thing that interested her.

He came into the kitchen, and while he helped her, he insisted, "You went along with the party line at the time, you should remember, and now we've changed the strategy with the social change our country has gone through and we find ourselves on the vanguard of the workers' and citizens' movement. We're participating in all the core movements, we connect perfectly with the demands and needs of the people. The proof is that diverse political groups claim us so that we can join with them in the elections. You have no reason to reproach us…"

Again, Elisa agreed, smiling.

Chapter 8

Elisa followed hesitantly as Octubre made her way through the crowd with the confidence of someone who has always moved in such surroundings. The assembly had already begun and most of the seats were taken. A good number of people even remained standing, blocking the door. Elisa wanted to tell Octubre they should leave. She had accompanied her friend against her will, and now the prospect of standing for several hours, sweating and being pushed around, wasn't at all attractive to her. But Octubre was already too far ahead to talk to, and surprisingly, she was able to supply Elisa with a chair and was herself sitting two rows in front. Elisa sat down, trying not to draw attention to herself, but no one seemed interested in watching her. An older woman dressed in black, who seemed to be one of the hostesses of the conference, held out some sheets of paper to her. Elisa looked at the woman, disconcerted, and then she saw that everyone had the same paper in their hands and was concentrating on it. She attempted to read the pages, but she could not understand them. She occupied herself looking around for a familiar face.

The majority of the people gathered there were men. There were only five women, besides Octubre and herself, including the hostess who had given her the document, and they were all over forty. *Actually,* she thought, *there's no one here younger than thirty.* She recognized a few university professors, union leaders, participants in the Movement for Peace, and leaders of the communist parties, including the one which was no longer her own. Soon the whispering, throat-clearing, and hushed conversations indicated that the attendees had finished reading the document. Those seated at the president's table, who had patiently waited for the attendees to read, decided to begin the session.

Elisa thought no one could understand a twenty-page document in a superficial reading of fifteen minutes, and some of them must have been familiar with it already, and others must have done the same thing she had, given up on reading it and hoping the discussion would better inform them.

Seven gentlemen were seated at the president's table, each one representing a leftist party. *The leftist pact*, she thought, and smiled. The pact the communists had been longing for over fifty years, out of nostalgia for the short-lived Popular Front. The only ones missing from the table were Carrillo, and, of course, the PSOE. It was a new front in keeping with the times, since one representative from an ecological group and another from a pacifist association were sitting in the presidency.

Elisa was startled when the president, a member of the PCE leadership, opened the discussion and called on the first person asking for the floor. Surprisingly for Elisa, who had gone many years without participating in that kind of meeting, the first speaker identified himself as an independent, but asked for some amendments in the draft that demonstrated his political training for that type of declaration. Even more surprising to her was that he referred to women's issues and asked for something about them to be included in the text. A woman seated in the front row spoke on the same subject. Elisa didn't know her, and would have liked to ask someone who she was, but Octubre was far away and she didn't want to broadcast her ignorance. *She's younger than me*, she thought, observing the speaker, and a strange nostalgia overcame her. The times of the Assembly of Catalonia were no more.

At that moment, one of the old leaders of the unionist movement asked for the floor. Elisa didn't know him, because during her first stage of public activism he had been in prison. She was very interested in hearing him in person and she leaned forward to see him. It was impossible because he was in the front row and she was in the last, and besides, the acoustics were bad in the crowded room. After a few moments some bolder voices shouted that they couldn't hear. The speaker showed his satisfaction at the audience's interest and started over in a louder voice, but he didn't stand up and couldn't be seen.

"I only want a few minutes to make a few observations that seem very important right now in reference to the document we have to approve this afternoon." The table smiled and nodded understandingly. "It doesn't make sufficient reference to the role the Spanish bourgeoisie should have in the transformation of the country, because, as Vicens Vives says, the bourgeois revolution hasn't taken place in Spain, and that's still true, because, friends, the bourgeoisie governing today is the same one that had to abandon the colonies at the end of the last century, and wanting to function the same in the metropolis as it had in the colonies, it allied itself with the landholding and financing bourgeoisie…"

Elisa stopped listening. She looked around, observing the faces of the attendees. Everyone seemed to be familiar with the speaker's discourse except her. A few beside her began to talk quietly. Two older women on the other side of the aisle laughed unabashed. Elisa was completely mystified. She could not comprehend that in March of 1986, a very prestigious union leader could be talking for a quarter of an hour about the bourgeoisie of the last century and its revolution to an assembly of people older than thirty, almost all involved with the university. No one seemed willing to protest. The minutes went by as the orator continued commenting on the circumstances of the bourgeois alliances and the audience members talked amongst themselves. Elisa attempted to communicate with Octubre by making discrete signals, until she got her to turn around and look at her. With her brow furrowed, she gave a shrug that meant, "There's nothing to be done with someone like that."

At last, the union leader finished his long-winded speech. A general sigh of relief ran through the meeting. Next, an old, trembling, man, who turned out to be a socialist dissident from the general party line, asked permission to speak. The presidency honorably gave him the floor. Everyone waited patiently for him to clear his throat, stammer, and blow his nose before beginning his speech. The words came out so slowly that Elisa's attention wandered in the meantime. She thought she would ask Octubre afterward what he had said but it got so long that she was afraid Octubre wouldn't know, either. *He must be a survivor of the war and the resistance*, she thought, because of the general respect and admiration he received. The slow preamble concluded with a plea that they not criticize his party, in spite of the numerous infidelities it had committed over the course of its years in power, given that at the core there were thousands of members who disagreed with the politics of its leaders.

When Elisa thought the platform would respond to him, the floor was given to another known party leader, a university professor. With an aplomb he must have learned while participating in hundreds of parliamentary debates, and delivering thousands of lectures, and from being trained to head meetings, he held a very marked-up copy of the assembly document and began to make a purely academic correction of its style. He indicated page numbers and paragraphs and read the rewritten text. He spoke so quickly that almost no one could follow him. There were protests from the audience, and he replied that he would be offering a clean corrected copy to the table, and someone bad-natured answered that no one else would have a copy, but no one supported him and the speaker paid no attention. The presiding members looked at him, but none of the participants seemed to be listening.

Elisa very quickly got tired of the procession of corrected paragraphs, epigraphs, Arabic numerals, Roman numerals, Greek letters and Latin letters with which the professor classified the different sections of the document. Elisa could tell that the laborious correction effort involved no fundamental criticism of the text, anyway. When his exposition was complete, the speaker submitted a copy of the corrected document to the presidency and sat down triumphantly. Elisa heard Octubre mutter quite clearly, "And the rest of us can go to Hell!" but no one seconded her.

The hands kept going up, and the commentary promised to be endless. Members of the pacifist groups, collectives which had worked in the campaign against NATO, many of them members of the same organization, repeated each other's observations. It seemed to Elisa that everyone agreed about the text, except the old socialist. One woman raised her hand insistently and seemed annoyed by the delay in giving her the floor. The platform explained to her that the list was very long and Elisa lost hope. She didn't know what she was doing there and she didn't understand Octubre's interest in sitting through all that babble.

As drowsiness began to overcome her, she felt as though she were in the school chapel listening to the monotonous prayers that moved in hypnotizing waves of tone and rhythm. Elisa answered mechanically while she tried to communicate with the Lord. She always had doubts about whether her mental lapses were really mystical ecstasies, a sign of divine grace, in spite of the assurances the Mother Superior and her spiritual director gave her. She felt brusquely shaken when, lining up to leave the chapel, Elisenda whispered in her ear, "Religion is the opiate of the masses." She could not nor did she wish to reply, because that would be breaking the rule, but after finishing with their study, Elisenda approached her again and, with the malicious expression she always put on when she wanted to scandalize her friend, she whispered, "Religion is the opiate of the masses, did you know?"

"Where are you getting that?" She was more interested than scandalized.

"They told us this morning in philosophy class," Elisenda replied, charmed by the success her revelation had with her devout friend.

"I didn't hear it."

"Because they'd called you for rehearsal. Mother Perelló told us."

"Well, go on. It must have some symbolic meaning."

"Symbolic! Horsefeathers! It's so boring with so many masses and prayers and the thousands of hours we're in the chapel, practically in the dark… Naturally, I'd rather be in an opium den."

Elisa was disappointed that the enigmatic phrase was nothing more than one of her friend's sarcastic jokes.

"Oh, leave me alone. We're getting too old for this stuff."

"Hey, don't be a fool. Mother Perelló really told us that the communists say religion is the opiate of the masses. It's right here in the book if you want to see…"

"Oh, whatever." Elisa felt calmer now, but disappointed without knowing why.

"Whatever my foot! I totally agree with them. There's nothing more suffocating and boring than so many religious rituals. I tell you the communists are right!" she shouted through the hallway, while Elisa moved away from her toward the sinks and tried to disassociate herself from her friend's extemporaneous heresy.

The unwanted feeling of approval she had experienced upon hearing the metaphorical definition of religion stayed deep inside her. *I must surely have already been tired of so many services and so much praying,* she thought. *Maybe that's when my transformation began.*

The livelier tone of one of the speakers brought her out of her reverie. She recognized the style of the sermons her spiritual director regaled her with every Sunday, and realized that neither then nor now did she understand what they said.

Octubre used to grumble that everyone was like a priest because they had all been educated at the skirts of a confessor.

Elisa didn't think of all the leftist party leaders as overprivileged Catholics, much less the workers who had participated actively in the Worker's Movement against the dictatorship.

"They're even worse, lady. They've also been educated among priests. Who in Spain today can say that he wasn't raised between the skirts of priests and nuns and under the principles of the National Movement?"

Elisa kept quiet to avoid having to hear for the thousandth time that only she, Octubre, and four others who hadn't been exiled, were educated in a progressive, democratic way.

Was that why the pacifist leader now seemed to be giving them his blessing, or why that old socialist was using an unbearably paternalistic tone when he made recommendations to a younger member of his group?

"No, dear, that's because they're former reactionaries." Octubre laughed her head off, remembering the language that stuck with them both at the congresses they participated in with a bunch of youngsters after 1976.

"Do you remember Gina, Brunhilda, and Bertha? It would have served those pests right if one of them had stood up to tell them that it was all an unbearable bore and that none of the youth of today were willing to sit there and take it…"

Elisenda would have been perfect for that, thought Elisa, but she didn't say it. They were having coffee after the conference, and Octubre was venting about everything she had seen and heard. At that moment, Elisa was weary of speeches, didn't know what she was doing there and didn't understand Octubre's interest in continuing to undergo that punishment.

She and Elisa had met up in Madrid at a teacher's conference given by the school where Elisa had gotten Octubre a job, too, when her friend enthusiastically explained at a lunch date that they had just had the convocation of an assembly of diverse groups which had worked together against NATO. According to her, it was a unique opportunity to rebuild the left.

"But, you said years ago that the parties were dead and that after that it's only gotten worse…"

"Look, Elisa, as we all know, things change. The NATO referendum has mobilized millions of people all over the country to fight the government's proposals, and it has to be taken advantage of. A victory like this…"

"But we lost the referendum…"

Octubre stopped and looked at her thoughtfully. Then, to her friend's surprise, she began to laugh. After a few seconds she replied, "You're right. Just look, even I'm talking with the same old slogans. What a disaster. It's contagious, and I don't know if there's a cure. But even so, I think it's worth the trouble to rebuild the forces to the left of the PSOE. After so many years asking for it, we aren't going to turn up our noses at the opportunity, are we?"

"What are those forces?"

"Well, all the communist parties and left wing socialists and above all, the social movements that have arisen in the last ten years: feminist, pacifist, ecological… Like in Italy, or Germany and Holland. This is the challenge of our time. If the parties don't understand it, they're done for. The pacifist movement has to be taken into account, of course, since on this occasion it has shown itself to be quite effective, above all with the women. It's time for us to be taken into account as a force unto ourselves, don't you think?"

Octubre was standing up at that moment saying exactly that. She furiously brandished the document and protested the absence of all reference to feminism and wondered whether the assembly would really come together in an electoral platform, and if so, where was the program and the conclusions that affected women? She wanted to participate in their name. Her speech was very brief and had a strange impact on the meeting. The ironic tone she had used at the beginning wasn't understood except by two or three men. The rest, including the women, seemed surprised by Octubre's vitality and her critical energy, and as her speech hadn't lasted longer than three minutes, they seemed unable to recover when she finished.

Elisa waited for some response, even an angry one, from the president, but she was surprised again by the indifference of all the members of the platform, who continued undaunted, giving the floor to audience members without making any reference to Octubre's petitions. The men in the audience continued making corrections to the document's style in accordance with their own little groups. When the woman who had been asking for the floor so insistently finally got her turn, to Elisa's surprise, she gave it up, saying that another participant had already said the same thing. The men kept standing up and each one spoke for a long time. Another woman also gave up her turn. When it seemed to Elisa that she was going to fall out of her chair with sheer boredom, the presiding members began to offer their responses from the platform.

The leader of the left fraction of the PSOE bitterly responded to the old activist who had asked for moderation in criticizing the party. The principal leaders were not the only ones responsible for the state of things; the committees and middle executives, the activists who voted for the leaders' proposals, were all responsible, he energetically affirmed. "Let's not fall into the trap of believing that only two or three dictators keep the party in this state, like under Franco when it seemed no one was pro-Franco except the dictator." When Elisa thought the matter was settled, the old socialist stood up again to repeat the same arguments he had used in his first turn. The argument showed no sign of ending, until the communist member of the platform proposed a new version of the paragraph and the two opponents seemed equally displeased.

When Elisa thought she had endured enough, not just for a day but for her entire life, her interest was again revived when she heard the ecologist sourly reply to Octubre's comments. He said that if all those present at the assembly representing diverse sectors of the population asked for their demands to be explicitly written out, the document would be endless. The question now was to quickly approve that text, because the next day at one in the afternoon they had to present it at a press conference, and later each party, each collective and each group would work with its people.

The communist leader tried to calm Octubre's obvious indignation, assuring her that they would make some necessary corrections on the question of women, as two of the speakers had already proposed, and considered the matter settled. Elisa feared Octubre's reaction, but, when she saw that she wasn't going to react in spite of her furrowed brow, she decided to leave. She stood up slowly, trying to take her leave of her friend, when another speech by the union leader interrupted her plan. The unionist, clearly amused, addressed Octubre and said that he was very happy to hear young and new contributions — later Octubre would comment that she should always be grateful for the part about "young" — but that, aside from the demands of some marginal sectors of society, most worthy of consideration, the important weight of the country fell on the shoulders of the workers…

Elisa deduced that with his spiel he was claiming the leading role for his clients in the document, but the unionist was never able to make his point because, out of the place where Octubre was sitting, at the back of the audience, the shout sounded out like thunder.

"And the women workers!"

The amazement that was reflected in the male faces, the aborted laughter of three of the women, while the other two kept calm although clearly annoyed, and the mute humiliation of the union leader, all seemed exaggerated to Elisa. She had witnessed similar incidents many times at political or feminist assemblies, and they had never occasioned that kind of astonishment. At last, the president of the table made the observation to Octubre that "workers" was the generic term, and she, much more incensed, shouted back that if they wanted to change society, language was one of the places they should start, and that, besides, she was talking about women's participation in society, because there were more working women than men. At that point, the assembly came apart as if it were evaporating. And every time Octubre told the anecdote, laughing, she repeated that metaphor, which Elisa recognized as quite correct, because in a few minutes the audience was emptied out and the assistants divided themselves between the lobby, the hallways, and the staircase, which they went down with all speed.

Elisa stood up, aching from hours of sitting in the same position, deafened by the speeches and suffocated by the tobacco smoke. She stretched painfully and went out to the lobby to look for her friend, whom she found vigorously arguing with the platform president, the youngest of the communist leaders at the assembly, who was trying to convince her that she had been unfair with the union leader.

"I tell you, Octubre, you were really unfair. You crushed him. He's precisely the one who recognizes women's contributions the most, he always says 'union men and women' and all that…"

"Words, words, words," snorted Octubre, but he didn't understand the quotation.

He merely repeated, "You crushed him."

"I'm so important," Octubre said sarcastically. "The bourgeois of the last century and of this one, the police, even Carrillo, haven't been able to crush him, and I, in one second…"

The people who were crowded around them decided to leave. Only two young men looked at Octubre with admiration mixed with fear and repulsion. In the stairwell they found Margarita, the only woman on the leadership of the PCE. She showed some understanding toward Octubre, and, overexcited, she shouted back, "Give up, woman! There's no hope! There's nothing to be done with them. You'll be as old as me, and you won't get anything. They have chauvinism in their bone marrow. They'll have nothing to do with the youth or with women. They're mummified!"

"And is the PC-ML here?"

"Yes, the boy and girl in the second row…"

"What role does your party intend to play in the leftist pact proposed by the PCE?"

Arnau found himself very distant from the subject. He was tired of the conversation, of the widely divergent topics Elisa kept bringing up. The fatigue of the last nights, sleepless on account of Reagan and Qadafi, not to mention Antonio Cherta's arrest, left him heavy, indifferent. He saw that Elisa had circles under her eyes, too, and remembered her mentioning something about correcting exams. He thought that if they were sensible people, they would stop remembering and arguing about nonsense and both go to sleep. For a moment, the idea of sleeping together jolted him as something unexpected, but perhaps desirable.

Elisa, on the other hand, now seemed divorced from her feelings, interested only in finding out the party's plans, as if she were affected by them.

"A week ago Octubre took me to a meeting in Madrid with almost all the leftist parties and groups." She smiled again before adding, "Octubre never stops."

Arnau had no interest in Octubre's activities, but felt slightly motivated by the topic.

"I didn't pay that much attention. It's not exactly an electoral platform, because they don't want it to be. More of a kind of coordinating committee, the way the Feminist Coalition was here, remember? But I don't know how they're going to operate, and the document was too long to read in a few minutes. The conclusions weren't very definite, either, and there was still no regulation of functions."

Arnau tried to joke about Elisa's habitual distractedness and she acknowledged it, but was still sure it wasn't all her fault.

"And I would have liked to have known whether your party was there and who participated..."

"I don't know, that all has to do with Madrid. An alliance like that wouldn't be possible here. In Catalonia the lines are much more firmly drawn, and the antagonism is vicious. You know, any kind of agreement between the PSUC and the PCC is impossible, and we're thinking of supporting a republican candidate..."

"Republican?"

Her amazement was so visible that Arnau smiled. He enjoyed throwing people off with that news. Condescendingly, he asked in turn, "You do remember what the Republic is, or have you forgotten?"

Elisa recovered her composure and it seemed to her that a reply was required. "I can't remember it because I've never lived in a republic, but I think most people would react the way I am. Do you think it can succeed at all?"

Arnau's face darkened, and he limited his reply to a murmured "We'll see." Elisa thought he must enjoy the theoretical and playful aspect of politics. There must have been quite an uproar within the party before making such a decision. She comforted herself thinking that there were still a few months before the elections and they could still change strategies.

"We have to be prepared for the future. Tomorrow, Spain will be a Republic, you can be sure of it."

Elisa sighed with weariness. The leader's style wore her out. Ramiro had just concluded his last harangue with that phrase. He had bored the entire local committee, and Elisa, who hadn't eaten for many hours and had to go to Málaga that same night, thought it was completely absurd to keep them all there in some comrade's minuscule and derelict attic on Olmo Street in the middle of Madrid where the sun oppressed them, to toss encouraging speeches at them. *As if it were 1936,* she thought, and the idea that it was actually the month of July, 1973, disheartened her. She could not even convince herself that the Republic was an interesting goal to the majority of the Spanish people.

Just as well that everyone showed their desire for the meeting to end, and she and Arnau quickly left the house, after receiving Ramiro's too-familiar instructions. *Which did no good at all,* she thought with melancholy, because right there at the door of that house, where the narrow street was blocked by three enormous private cars, three fanatics, pistols in hand, jumped them, to the surprise of the neighbors who came to their balconies, roofs and doorways. Besides all the shoving she received, Elisa was driven to the State Security Headquarters with grief in her heart at seeing how they pistol-whipped Arnau and how all the comrades, one after the other, were captured as they came out of the house. The only one who got away was the owner himself, because for reasons of security and rank he was obliged to wait on the stair landing for the meeting to end. When he heard the uproar, he was able to hide in the toilet in the hallway he shared with the other tenants of the rest of the attic rooms.

"One more of Ramiro's brilliant schemes…"

"What? The Republic?"

Arnau was frivolous and amused. He knew that comment went with some deep thought Elisa was lost in, very far from the subject at hand.

Elisa smiled before answering.

"No… well, that, too. I was remembering the last meeting we had in Madrid, when they arrested us all. If Ramiro hadn't insisted on seeing us before the trip to give us our final instructions… And it wasn't even instructions, just more of those speeches he was such a big fan of…"

"They would've caught us somewhere else. We had an informer inside for several months, remember."

"Maybe someone could've gotten away. You never know. It would've been harder if we'd been spread out. There we all were…"

"Oh, no," he denied with conviction. "Just a few of the executives. If they'd followed us to Málaga the whole organization would have fallen. Maybe it was better that way…"

Elisa observed him at length. Did he want to convince her of Ramiro's intelligence so she would help him, or did he need to convince himself in order to stay in an organization that consumed all his energy?

"So you think it's not worth the trouble to do anything?"

She jumped abruptly because she had thought she'd actually said what she was thinking. She looked at Arnau, embarrassed, waiting to find in his eyes the reproach implied in the question, but he seemed calm, taking her response for granted. Elisa shivered, remembering that he had the same attitude in the months before the separation. The same calm at Elisa's leaving the party, at the indifference she showed toward the political activities that took up the greater part of his life. Was that the real reason he left her? But the image of Roser, with those silly brown eyes and that enormous chest, made her indignant. Roser had never been involved in politics and never would be in her life. He was the one who had changed, not her.

"You changed, too. First you stopped being active when you got out of prison, remember."

"I had to think about him, still there in Carabanchel, and we didn't have a dime…"

Isabel looked impatient.

"Yes, I know. But then, when he was back with you and got to organizing the party again, you didn't follow…"

"He didn't ask me to." Now Elisa calmly thought it over. It was true. He had seemed content to see her fulfill her role as housewife. He made no sign that he was interested in her taking part in the work of the party, he didn't press her to do it, he didn't even make allusions that could have had a double meaning when he was talking about the depoliticization of the people or about the opportunism and nepotism of his former friends.

"He wanted you at home, then, waiting for him. He always wanted a good wife."

Elisa looked with astonishment at Isabel, who seemed unaware of the effect her words had while she unpacked the boxes they had just moved to the new house.

"But he was the one who put me in HOAC and then in the party…"

"A good wife should do what her husband says."

"And in the party…"

"But weren't you really upset when you found out the party had sent you to Madrid to cook for him?"

"But he was against it, too."

"Are you sure? Did he really defend you?"

"We were clandestine. Orders couldn't be challenged…"

It was useless, and she knew it. She endured Isabel's ironic look and the "Well, there you are" which was her only commentary, without responding.

Only a few minutes later she asked, with a helpless expression, "So, you think he left me because of that? If he wanted me at home…"

Again Isabel stopped working to look at her with tenderness and pity.

"You know the answer."

"I really don't know. It's been a while since I thought about it, but it doesn't seem like the Republic has many supporters today…"

Arnau made a gesture of comprehension, and replied with a sad expression.

"I know what you think. But you were witness to the fact that it was widely accepted at the beginning of the transition."

Chapter 9

Arnau stopped arguing and sat down at the typewriter. He and Elisa had shared a knowing glance a moment before, and without saying a word, she handed him the sheets and the carbon paper. The others continued the unending discussion, which had been going on since five o'clock that afternoon, when the first fireworks of the festival of Saint John could already be heard. Later, Elisa couldn't recall the particulars of the disagreements. The everlasting problem of coalitions, Octubre explained, is to combine ideological differences with enough flexibility to leave room for options that were disparate in many ways, but have a common link. That was what Arnau tried to convince Antonio Cherta of after the meeting.

"But we can't just relinquish our principles," Cherta stubbornly repeated, and Arnau began to feel very tired. It was two in the morning. The meeting had ended at midnight, after the Saint John bonfires on the street corners of Barcelona had gone out, and the document Arnau had tried to draft was still unsigned.

"Look, Ramiro, the problem is that everyone else thinks the same thing. If we can't agree on the basics, the whole thing goes to hell, understand? There's no other way the people from ORT, Judges for Democracy, Esquerra Republicana, teachers' collectives, organizations out of FRAP and our party can ever agree, because we're separated by very different conceptions of society…"

"But we're all pledged to the same struggle to restore the Republic."

"Of course, that's what it's all about, and that's what I've been saying for seven hours. What made it so hard was that everyone got involved in sterile arguments about Leninism, democracy, and even feminism."

Elisa listened without interrupting, dead on her feet, waiting for those two obsessed men to decide that the moment had come to put an end to politics for the day, which was quickly becoming two. She had also been a mute witness to the meeting held that afternoon in their brand new apartment in the Gracia neighborhood, scarcely two months after Arnau had gotten out of prison. And she had observed with boredom how all the people gathered there kept repeating the same old mottoes. A miniature replica of the Assembly of Catalonia, or worse, because at least that assembly had the end of the dictatorship as its founding ideal.

"And the Unió de Republicans de Catalunya proposes ending the monarchy," Arnau had explained at the end of the brief commentary with which he began the meeting.

The members would have seemed unanimous in their purpose, if it hadn't been that, when Arnau was just beginning to elaborate the constitution of the Unió, the representative from ORT interrupted, saying it was essential to indicate that it was a people's democratic union. The representatives of the Artist's Union and UCO, two FRAP organizations, instantly seconded the demand, to Arnau's despair. Without hiding the oppression they felt, those who were there for Esquerra Republicana and Judges for Democracy immediately interrupted Arnau to make known their repulsion and indignation with respect to the Marxist organizations' manipulation of the Republican movement throughout the history of Spain. When tempers were dangerously high, and the history and prehistory of the Civil War were threatening to be discussed, Arnau brought a little order to the proceedings by requiring the organizations incorporated in FRAP to withdraw the word "people's."

They agreed, acknowledging his superior status as a member of the Central Committee of the PC-ML. But the man from ORT, who had just arrived from Navarra and embodied the rural, clerical stereotype of his organization and his place of birth, insisted on keeping his republic the "people's." When he understood that he held his position alone, he became increasingly agitated. In the end, he resigned himself to the majority's agreement, but the distrust that had been aroused in the representatives of the petty bourgeois organizations didn't go away.

For Arnau, it was Octubre who delivered the coup de grâce, demanding that there be an express declaration recognizing women's rights, at which the ORT representative first showed amazement and then rejected. In that matter, which he classified as "hogwash," to Octubre's outrage, he found sufficient reason to reject the final document, using it as an excuse to avenge his previous defeat.

"You're being unfair, Arnau," Elisa interjected, suddenly interested in the subject. "Octubre's proposal was accepted immediately without discussion by all the members, who were already expecting it, because they knew she was coming, and besides, nowadays it's necessary to take the Feminist Movement into account. The man from ORT is still living in the sticks, he just came down from the mountains of Navarra. It seems to me that it will be very difficult to come to any agreement with ORT. I find them small-minded and sectarian and they all act like priests."

Cherta said, "Well, it seems fitting to me that we should make it clear in the constitution that we want a people's republic. That precisely defines the regime we're fighting for, and in the end we're the majority in number of organizations and active members in the Unió de Republicans de Catalunya."

Arnau had given up arguing for the night. He took little sips of the last cognac of the day, and seemed not to be listening to his comrade. Elisa tried to share a look of understanding with him but his gaze was lost in the patterns in the wallpaper. He finally got Antonio to leave, after promising to come back to continue the discussion, and Arnau went to bed that night without saying another word.

"They'll never agree, Elisa, I tell you. Men are unreasonable and obtuse."

"Arnau blames you for the failure to come to an agreement the other night…"

"Great. Now they have a woman for their scapegoat, what more can they ask for? What did I do now?" Octubre snorted through her cigarette, the last of the first pack of the day, and awaited Elisa's explanation with a sardonic smile.

"You wanted to mention women's rights in the document, and the guy from ORT didn't…"

"Everyone else agreed with me!"

"That's what I told him."

Octubre began to laugh. Her dark eyes gleamed with indignation, excitement, and two cups of coffee.

"Look here, what's happening is that men can't bear the explosion in the Feminist Movement. They always thought they were the center of the universe, the kings of creation, the politicians and leaders by divine right, and they're finding themselves pushed out of the leading roles by women, by these political upstarts, and many of them are no more than twenty-five years old besides… They won't be able to stand it, you'll see."

"That could be, but if the Unió fails, that won't be the only reason."

"Oh, of course not. Men know how to fight among themselves quite well. They've been doing it for all of history and some of prehistory."

Octubre had suddenly joined the feminists, who, in the spring of 1976, were reorganizing after the general experiment of 1975, which the United Nations had declared the International Year of the Woman. It was a pleasant surprise for Elisa when she got out of prison, to get reacquainted with her country. The inward looking place she had been taken from two years before, trembling with fear, obscurantist and backward, was now transformed into a vital place, aggressive, full of hope, casting off the shackles of forty years. Especially the women, those anonymous, invisible beings, whom she remembered only as sitting at the breakfast table repeating well-known complaints that no one listened to. At most, women accounted for a single word in her party's documents, always followed by the qualifier "workers." Other women, the majority, allowed their lives to slip by among silks and furs as the luxury prostitutes of the bourgeoisie, and didn't deserve anything other than the scorn of the conscious proletariat. Those same women had gone out into the streets, decked out in clothes that vaguely recalled hippy gear, and with an aggressiveness that no one ever suspected of them, held meetings in public places, wrote letters to the press, advertised colloquia and consciousness-raising groups, where, still more contrary to the custom, they discussed their lives, in the most risqué detail, with no holding back.

In those first months of the spring of 1976, the Catalan Conference on Women was being organized, following up on the conference in Madrid in December of the previous year, which had been still somewhat clandestine. At first Elisa didn't participate in the meetings. Upon her release from prison, she had tacitly given up on political activism. She had been in Barcelona only six months, and was convinced that the business with Arnau's lawyer, the visits to Carabanchel, for which she needed one free week out of every month, and her job search occupied every minute of her life.

It was quite true that besides her family, whom she visited in town on the weekends, she had no other confidante for her plans and problems than Isabel Fortuny, whom she had rediscovered living alone in Barcelona. None of the comrades who were still free made any effort to contact her, and when on one occasion she thought she recognized someone at the entrance to the movie theatre, she lost him immediately, and suspected that he had avoided her. When Octubre landed in her house with the feminist news, it was impossible for Elisa to assimilate all the information quickly. Nevertheless, she soon understood that her party had never seriously considered the possibility that one of its activists should dedicate her precious time to the women's meetings, and that, if she did it more on her own account than by higher orders, her activity would be looked down upon as a fringe amusement.

"Because they're old-fashioned, I tell you. I've always been saying it, haven't I? Well, now we aren't going to ask their permission to work on what matters to us. Our dumb women's problems like sexuality, motherhood, work for women, non-sexist education, etc. And we're going to discuss them in public, scream about them if necessary. And we're going to get organized to fight for our interests, not for theirs like we have up to now, and now we won't have to worry about our leaders, or fathers, or bosses. It's all over, damn it! We're going to have the revolution our way! Especially since they don't intend to have one at all."

Elisa soon began to share Octubre's enthusiasm and allowed herself to be taken to the meetings, commissions and committees created that spring in order to organize the Catalan Conference. Men were also admitted, but with no right to speak or vote. It later became famous in the history of Spanish feminism, mainly because the political parties, which had participated so little in the work and shown so little enthusiasm, threw themselves into the convocation. Not only did they give instructions for their activists and sympathizers to attend, filling the university auditorium to the brim, but also, during the final days, even the main party leaders of all persuasions formally attended in order to legitimize the work of their women subordinates.

Octubre went along informing Elisa of all the ins and outs of the groups and parties which made up the Feminist Movement at that moment, because although Elisa went to several days of the Conference, she found it impossible to make contact with the leaders in the huge crowd that packed the auditorium. The bad sound system and the heat sometimes kept her from following the topics being discussed, and the last afternoon before the end of the Conference, she decided to go home and rest after so much activity. A moment before leaving, she thought she saw Pilar Laborde on the stage getting ready to speak, but she didn't feel excited about seeing her again.

"Well, you really missed something. Pilar, you know what kind of ovaries she puts into the struggle, she stood firm up there in front of four thousand people from all the parties, but mostly socialists and the PCE, of course, and she let loose a republican speech, and my girl, when it was over, everyone went crazy with applause, and it made some of the PSUC and Christian Democrat women so mad that they jumped up and started calling her a troublemaker, but she went on unperturbed, saying that they were the only troublemakers, because when she had spoken everyone had applauded her, and since it was true, they had to shut up." Octubre paused, and then added thoughtfully, "Maybe it really is possible to get a republican movement going before this monarchy crushes us all with its throne and its crown."

Elisa didn't understand what connection there might be between feminism and the Republic, but she didn't try to, either. At least not while Arnau was still in prison. Because a few weeks after he got out, he contacted his friends in the leadership and began actively working in the Unió de Republicans de Catalunya, federated with the Republican

Convention, and she soon got up to speed with the objectives of the PCE-ML on that question. It was much more difficult for her to discuss the latest events in feminism with him.

"And Arnau, you know, is one of the most progressive members of the party..."

"That doesn't mean anything," grumbled Octubre. Elisa looked at her with a mixture of interest and discomfort. She didn't completely understand Octubre's synthesis of the revolutionary proposals and feminism, women and class struggle, and though she argued with Arnau in defense of her friend, she lacked Octubre's deep conviction.

"In any case, we're the ones who have to do the work, you know? That's one of the most important things feminism has discovered. Because although you and Arnau and many others in your party and other parties don't know it, Augusto Bebel warned already at the end of the last century that women shouldn't count on men's help to work out their problems. What we should thank men for, in the words of Mrs. Pankhurst, is that they've shown us the joy of the struggle. And it's true, now I feel happier than ever."

Elisa observed, with surprise, that her passionate and temperamental friend wasn't the only one discovering new horizons and going out to conquer them with the energy, vitality, and joy of adolescence.

"Since feminism, we must take part in politics, in all kinds of politics. I don't agree with those who would shut themselves up in a feminist ghetto. I want to compete with men and win in the same arena. That's why I'm trying to get us into the Unió de Republicans de Catalunya. It's a young movement that could be decisively important for future events, and we don't have to stay in the margins, you see?" Elisa agreed with her friend's plans with vague enthusiasm, and she carried them out, taking part for the first time in an activism in which she had neither bosses nor subordinates.

Arnau foresaw the inevitable failure of the Unió before it was a reality. After the last meeting, which concluded with a watered-down document that meant almost nothing and was really underwritten only by FRAP, PCE-ML, and Judges for Democracy, and then only because the judge who went to all the meetings was Arnau's friend, as he confessed to Elisa.

"The Unió de Republicans was born dead. It has no future. The party executive is doing all he can to keep it alive, but it's a lie. All we have are the FRAP organizations and my friend the judge. We're not going to get anywhere like this."

Elisa noticed her husband's dejection, so unusual in him, and wanted to console him.

"This is only the beginning. Franco's only been dead seven months and we still have to strengthen and deepen the Unió..."

Arnau shook his head, to her surprise.

"No, it's now, now or never, that we have to put together a strong republican movement. Look, now the government is weak, it's feeling out the terrain, it still hasn't legalized the PCE because it doesn't know how much influence it has, it still has to call elections, establish the form of state. Now there's a lot of confusion, now is the moment to organize and infiltrate the people. Later the bourgeois will catch on, and again take up the weapons it has — I hope at least it won't be literally! And it will put us all into tidy rows. For now, the PCE is willing to accept the monarchy. All the other parties will follow. You'll see..."

"You were right, I realized it some time ago, but that's exactly why I don't understand your resurrecting such an old idea... ten years later!"

Arnau sighed with weariness. He had no words for arguing the matter.

"You never get what you don't fight for..."

"Fighting for what the people don't demand is arbitrary."

We sound like the Marxist-Leninist catechism, thought Elisa, suddenly bored with the conversation. Like a ringing bell, her memory brought back abstruse classes in apologetics which the headmistress presented them once a week. When she was fourteen years old, the arguments in defense of the faith were more elaborate than the crude threats of the catechism.

"Do you believe all that stuff about if you touch the Host with your teeth, even if it's just a little scrape, you'll be struck down dead?"

Elisenda whispered to her with her head on the partition that separated the girls' sleeping areas. Elisa did believe it. At seven years of age, on the eve of celebrating her first communion, she already felt called upon by divine grace to be a saint, and she knew that the main condition for it was to accept everything the headmistress told her, unquestioningly.

"Anyway, you'd have to be pretty dumb not to know how to swallow the Host without it touching your teeth, so the first ones struck down by a thunderbolt will be Rosita Méndez and Laura Sotés. I'm going to make a list of the stupidest and ugliest ones and see if they keel over in the middle of mass..."

"What are you laughing at?"

Arnau was surprised and annoyed at the hilarity with which Elisa's distraction had concluded.

"I was remembering some of the jokes Elisenda used to make in school. She was so clever..."

"Did you associate that with the joke of trying to reclaim the Republic now?"

Elisa made an ambiguous gesture. She didn't want to annoy Arnau, who seemed so suspicious.

He smiled and added, "You can tell me the truth, Elisa, I won't be offended. I'm aware of the difficulty of trying to resurrect the republican ideal in Spain right now, but I also think that, from the ethical point of view, it's essential. The continual turncoatism of the leftist parties with the bourgeois has brought the country to its present degenerate state, loss of revolutionary objectives, everything you know and what everyone is talking about. Maybe we'll take longer, but I'm sure that, if we hadn't lost those ten precious years, today we'd have a strong republican movement. The constant propaganda the successive governments have bombarded the people with has made them see the monarchy as an indispensable institution for guaranteeing democracy in Spain, and the royal family as adorable..."

Elisa didn't know how the PC-ML intended to compete with the propaganda of the government and the other parties, but she decided to let Arnau have his dream world. In the end she didn't really care about the subject, and the only thing she wanted was for his visit, which seemed to have lost its initial objective, to prolong itself interminably. And she could not even say what she hoped for from it. She constantly feared that Arnau would get up and leave, above all when he had achieved the goal that had brought him there: to get a her to promise to help Cherta out of the mess he was in. So, not completely consciously, she delayed and delayed the moment when she would have to give him a definite response.

What would Isabel say about her behavior? She would call her a hypocrite, and Octubre would shout that it was typical of the student of nuns she continued to be at heart. What about your dignity? And the feminism you so defended?

"None of that is left to you anymore, otherwise you wouldn't have come between Lluïsa and Pere."

"A whole bunch of feminists slept with their friends' husbands, contributed to the number of divorces and illegitimate children, and defended trilateral relationships in practice."

"And that seems all right to you? I mean, correct from the feminist point of view?"

Isabel was twisting her mouth in a typical look of disgust as she gave the finishing touches to the rooms she was going to occupy in the little house in Valldoreix. Elisa accused her of being critical just because she didn't like Pere and had to put up with him there so often. Isabel almost lost her usual reserve.

"Then why have you come to live with me? You and Pere could have rented an apartment and lived together, what the heck! Now you've left Arnau's house and gotten me tangled up in renting this one, which costs an arm and a leg, so you can keep Pere here all day. Look, Elisa, I don't believe in communal living, you know? I don't adapt to others very well, but I'm going to try with you because I've known you a long time and we're two single women. After all, it's been fifteen years since my separation and I haven't lived with anyone since. But with Pere here all the time it's going to be a mess. Think about it, the same way you ought to think about whether you feel very good about causing the discord between Lluïsa and Pere, trying to take away the money she and her children need every month."

And then she continued to grumble that she didn't understand those revolutionary women who continued to behave the same way as the worst shrews of the past century. Like Elisenda, who in fleeing from a traditional marriage had ended up selling her body for the entrance to a rock festival.

"I remember the last time I saw her in the hospital, she was with Gina, and I found out that both of them went to bed with the first dirty drunk they found for a hamburger or a bed for the night, and I told them what ideological firmness they had, that for all that they were better off getting married. More food and less screwing."

"I've already been married."

The evenness in Elisa's tone seemed to surprise Isabel, who stared at her for a few moments. Then, she nodded and answered, "I thought it was all about changing the world, not repeating it."

"Only feminism can make the qualitative leap necessary to change the world. The paradigm of our times, now that all the socialisms and communisms are dead..."

Octubre became inflamed every time she spoke, and Elisa was captivated by her friend's emotion.

"You're not listening again. We're wasting time. Besides, why do you care what the party's doing now? I'm not here to indoctrinate you. I'm here to ask you a favor. If you don't want to do it for me, tell me once and for all, but don't keep me here begging all morning. We've already suffered too much, don't you know that?"

Arnau was somewhere between threatening and pathetic. Elisa shook her head and powerlessly searched for the words that would show her solidarity.

"We're condemned to the ghetto, to impotence. They don't deserve compassion. I've known them all my life and I'm telling you. They live in another world, another time. The people will get beyond them, I assure you. Women are starting to do it now, young men have been laughing at their little battles for long time, and next it will be the workers. At this very moment, look at the tales they're telling the jobless... My father once told me that a comrade came to him, very excited, and told him that someone, I don't know who, someone that interested them, would not be convinced, and said, 'It's no use, his cranium is squashed.' And my father was outraged, and yelled at him, 'Well, blast the squashed craniums!' The people will set them on fire with their scorn… I tell you, I've known them all my life. For you and me, for all women, feminism is the only option. They'll figure it out and leave all the parties without any female members, and the rest can get along by themselves."

Octubre's eyes were on fire, and she continually moved her thin hands as she stretched out her stained, threadbare sweater, with its several stains. Elisa recognized that she could convince her listeners. She was sorry to juxtapose that image with the pathetic one Arnau presented at that moment. What else had Octubre told her?

"Leave them, have no pity for them. They're pathological masochists. Like those nutcases now in GRAPO, the only thing they really want is martyrdom. They were definitely taught to admire the first Christians, who were eaten by the lions. I tell you, they get a lot of pleasure from living marginalized, clandestine, running from the police, feeling like heroes…"

Elisa could not accept that she was entirely right. She remembered Marisa's bruised face when she came to Yeserías from the State Security Headquarters, and the skeletal limbs of Juana Parroto and Pilar Laborde, and…

"No, Elisa, those were other times. I'm talking about now, about when we have to work and struggle in another way…"

Elisa shook her head again, and managed to say, "Oh, of course. I don't mean you any harm. Besides, times have changed…"

Arnau made a gesture that was a yes and a no at the same time.

Chapter 10

Elisa stood up with her hand raised and waited for the president to point to her. She began, her expression serious.

"We're all here to agree to collaborate, to unite and facilitate our struggle against the dictatorship. But this will be impossible and any strategy we adopt will be inadequate if there isn't respect for each of our ideologies. I ask that the repeated insults against Comrade Stalin be withdrawn. I value his memory, and the revolutionary vision he brought to the Soviet Union…"

Whistles and murmurs drowned out the end of the sentence. Elisa reddened with rage at the various sounds the assembly received her plea with. She stood and waited silently for the uproar to end, and continued with renewed force.

"I'm not asking anyone to agree with me, but I don't share the ideology of many present here, and yet listen quietly to all kinds of praises of the Pope, the King, the encyclicals, and other such ideological manifestations, with which I find myself in complete disagreement. In the same way, I would like the rest of you to respect me. It's the only way to show that the Assembly is as democratic as it claims to be. Otherwise, I'll think it's only democratic when the speakers are saying exactly what the rest want hear. That's a dictatorship. Democracy consists precisely of defending the right of others to say things one doesn't necessarily agree with."

A storm of applause put a flourish on the end of Elisa's words, and she sat down, her cheeks burning with satisfaction. At the end of the Assembly several participants came up to congratulate her. Even the Christian Democrats, who didn't want to be identified with the portrait of dictatorship she had so opportunely painted. Outside in the street, Arnau hugged her effusively.

"You were magnificent!" he exclaimed. "No one could've guessed how much power there is under that good-girl façade. Wow!"

Elisa was also pleased. Arnau's hug encouraged her, but it wasn't essential. Before talking with him, even before the Assembly's applause, she was sure of herself, ready to shout her truth and defend it scratching and biting. She was sick of so many petty bourgeois hypocrites, drones converted to democracy at the last minute, when the dictatorship no longer seemed like a profitable prospect. That was who they were, naturally, and she knew them well. She had spent her entire childhood and youth dealing with them, and had seen them dismiss the field workers, throwing them out of their shacks with all their junk and their children, grandmothers and pregnant wives, and then send their own wives to take a basket of food to the shanty town… only to get indignant at her defense of Stalin, in the name of freedom and good intentions. Scared, that was what they were! No, panicked! That one day the red guards would have the revolution and she and some others would come to take away their business, their profits obtained through corruption and exploiting workers, and the hunger and sickness and death of so many men and working children.

Arnau ended his exaltation, kissing her repeatedly on the mouth. Then, laughing, he confirmed, "You're amazing, you always are, and you're getting more eloquent every day. I myself am amazed at how well you can argue and relate facts and situations… but, my love, don't scream those things in the street. We haven't established the dictatorship of the proletariat yet, we don't even have a bourgeois democracy. We're still under the same fascist dictatorship as always…"

"They just get on my nerves, you know? I know them so well. They screwed my life over until I was twenty and I know full well what they want. They've put on sheep's clothing now and intend to fool the people with all their democratic talk, really just so they won't lose the least bit of their power. When this is over they want to keep ruling, nothing more. It makes me so mad…"

Arnau laughed. "From the passion you put into your diatribe one would think you're a convert…"

But not even his friendly jokes were able to calm her down for quite some time after they got home.

"When did you start to feel so doubtful?"

Elisa tried to remember. It was getting more and more difficult. *Prison is eating away at my energy, my memory, my life,* she told herself. It was common. The food lacked vitamins and salts, and had too much fat and starch. Elisa, unlike the majority, had lost weight because she could hardly swallow the usual grub. Octubre looked at her curiously. For some time, she had been observing the changes in Elisa, who had arrived in prison showing off her revolutionary steadfastness and indestructible loyalty to her party. Elisa shrugged.

"I don't know. I don't even know if I ever felt as sure as you say."

"That's what you say now, but when you came here you were very different, you just had to listen to yourself. And other comrades who were at the Democratic Assembly of Catalonia tell me you were quite a rabble rouser. Especially asking for the rehabilitation of comrade Stalin, who had been insulted…"

Elisa smiled as she remembered, nostalgically.

"Yeah, I guess back then I was sure about what I was saying. Though I think I was more upset with the bourgeoisie who made up the majority of the Assembly and with those I knew so well because they were like my father's associates and my uncles' associates and Arnau's parents, than I was excited about Stalin. I repeated party instructions and exploded with rage facing those hypocrites. I still hate them just the same today, believe me. Maybe what's happening is, I feel more mature, less… like a convert, hell, just like Arnau told me I was then, and at the same time, my party's pamphlets convince me less. Most of all after tonight's assembly…"

The assembly had taken place after the meeting in which the executive committee of the PC-ML in Yeserías prison approved the plans devised by those members of the party leadership who were still free. In Yeserías, at that time, they lived in Department Three, for the politicals, thirty-four women who represented practically all the parties and tendencies of the communist left, as well as one woman from ETA, who only stayed a week before her sentencing.

Elisa didn't expect the activists from the PCE, ORT, MCE, PCI, PTE, the Young Red Guard, and LCR to agree with the strategy of armed struggle the PC-ML had just initiated through its popular front, FRAP, when the majority of those parties had asked to be admitted into the Democratic Union, which Carrillo was the main proponent of. So the aggressive tone Juana used to respond to the criticism the PCE leader made seemed completely out of place, especially when Juana called the PCE "Carrillo's splinter group," which provoked her opponent.

"My party is called the Communist Party of Spain, PCE, understand? So please be good enough to call it by its name."

Juana became disconcerted when she looked at Elisa, and Octubre intervened, saying simply, "She's right, Juana."

And Elisa nodded timidly. After the incident, that assembly followed the path of so many others and concluded that an agreement was impossible. To Elisa's thinking, an agreement hadn't even been pursued, convinced as they were that the latest events had made it unfeasible. Every month, *The Worker's Vanguard* published the harshest criticisms of the politics of pact and consensus that Carrillo advocated, and, except for the LCR, all the other parties were at the door of the Democratic Union, begging to be let in, convinced that the regime was in its death throes. How could they accept, or even understand, that the PC-ML had put its resources into suicidal terrorist activity, precisely now? Elisa was certain that only Carrillo's desire to eliminate competitors would keep those parties out of the Union, which neither the Christians, nor the liberals, nor the socialists opposed. But, for the PC-ML, in the storm of Carrillo insults, a more measured and accurate analysis was lost.

She noticed, without surprise, that she didn't care what her leaders decided, though Juana threatened her with writing a denouncement to the executive committee about her uncertain posture that was contrary to the party line, and she would have to answer the accusations from prison, without being able to draw on any support. Her stomach shrank when she thought of Arnau. What would he say? How would he bear the situation in Carabanchel, surrounded by the members of the executive committee, who would make him responsible for his wife's indifference? If she could talk with him beforehand… She didn't know when they would allow another visit to Carabanchel to see her husband, but the prison visiting room, where all the conversations were recorded in a very obvious way, was no place to have a conversation of that kind.

Elisa felt discouraged. The question Octubre repeated drew her out of her reverie.

"So, what are you going to do?"

It was useless to stall by asking, "About what?" She knew she had to make a decision, but she didn't feel she had the strength. She could no longer consult with her spiritual director, or Arnau. What could she possibly decide by herself? Octubre tried to understand her and talk it out with her, but Elisa had a feeling that, despite her distance from the PCE and her harsh criticisms of it, she was taking advantage of the situation to proselytize to her. As if a person could become pro-Carrillo after ten years of piling all the Marxist-Leninist invective of the PC-ML on Carrillo.

She remembered an anecdote about Unamuno. The rector of Salamanca was visited by Jehovah's Witnesses, who wanted to attract him to their cult. He responded, "If I don't believe in Catholicism, which is the one true faith, how can I convert to yours?" Jaime Bonavía, the university English professor, who was also an English teacher at a distinguished girl's school, enjoyed reciting this anecdote, to add a long sidebar about his own agnosticism. Sometimes he did it in the bar, where he found Elisa and other students, and always ended up wanting to drive one of them home. And those who had accepted commented later with disgust that the professor was much more of a dirty old man than he seemed. Isabel was the one who informed her that Elisenda had fallen into his womanizing trap in London, and Elisa thought that one day she would ask her why.

"All right, could we concentrate on what I've come to tell you about?"

They were at the table in front of the sandwiches, and Arnau seemed more relaxed. Elisa had already accepted that for ten years she had been a confident activist in his party, and agreed with him about not bringing up reproaches from the past.

"Antonio Cherta was arrested two weeks ago. All the circumstances made it easy for the police. They were justified by the latest bombings in Madrid and they applied the antiterrorism law to him. We couldn't find out what he was accused of until after he was in Carabanchel. Since we were legalized, we haven't had any serious incidents with the police. But now they've accused him of illegal association as well as terrorism. Just think of it, ten years after the dictatorship… Well, the case is that they're accusing him of perpetrating some terrorist acts that look like they were done by GRAPO, but the police, the judge, the public prosecutor, or someone, finds it convenient to say GRAPO and FRAP are the same thing, or that they collaborate, or that GRAPO is the terrorist arm of the PC-ML. A little of everything. I still haven't had a chance to read the indictment, but in few days the lawyer will get it to us. We're looking for reliable witnesses to say that GRAPO was never the terrorist arm of the PC-ML, which we never had, of course, and to say when we finished with FRAP, and to explain that our party resolved to end armed struggle a long time ago, and that they know Cherta, and that he is incapable of disobeying the party's orders…"

Elisa couldn't help but laugh, and Arnau looked at her with a patient annoyance, like someone who expects everything and can't do anything but put up with it. Elisa quickly interrupted herself.

"Sorry, I know it's not a pleasant situation, but imagining Cherta making war all by himself, without counting on the party's approval, it's too unreal…"

"Well, that's the idea, for you to say that in court. You shouldn't be afraid, there's no danger for people who belonged to any communist party before democracy. We'll be as little trouble as possible. You can even do it on one of your days off for Easter Week. I don't know if you're going somewhere…"

The sentence hung in the air, and Elisa didn't know whether Arnau expected a definite answer in order to schedule her testimony, or for his own personal interest. Elisa didn't want to tell him she had planned her vacation with Pere.

They had never talked about it, and her feelings about it were confused. She didn't want to be interrogated by Arnau about her relationship choices, but she didn't stop feeling the itch his silence caused her, that attitude of visible indifference toward her personal life, so different from the anxiety he showed about Cherta's problems. He pressed her a little more.

"Of course, if now isn't a good time for you, you can testify after the vacation. Let's not wait for them to give him probation in a few months… if even that…"

"I don't know. I'd planned to leave for the beach tomorrow."

"With Isabel?"

He immediately appeared sorry to have asked the question. Elisa looked at him, biting her lip, and hesitated to answer, as he frantically looked for a way to dodge it. But before he could, she made up her mind.

"No, Pere and I had planned to go to Cadaqués."

It was said. For the first time since the separation, she had dared to mention her new companion to him. He seemed to hesitate before responding, with the same voice as always, "Oh. All right." She could have talked about something else, finally answering the question he had asked so many times, ending the long morning interview with a formal promise to go to court when the lawyer told her to, and graciously saying goodbye. But Elisa needed to know many things that were still confusing between them. And the occasion wasn't going to repeat itself.

In a challenging voice, she asked him, "What do you think? I think this would be a good time to talk it over."

He responded stubbornly. He tried to avoid the question, pretending he didn't understand, but it was a mistake.

"Talk what over?"

"Pere, of course. We've never talked about it, and I think we should."

Arnau seemed to be finding it hard to breathe. For a few moments Elisa thought he would not answer, or that he would start to cry. So she was the more surprised by his response, apparently serene, although a little more serious.

"I don't believe I have to give an opinion. It's your life."

"You and Roser is your life, and we've talked about it a lot."

"It had something to do with our separation. Roser came into my life when I was with you, while Pere has only been your partner for a year…" He interrupted himself. "Or more?"

Elisa thought he would probably be happy to know that she had gotten together with Pere before breaking up with Carles, and it made her angry. She answered with obvious sarcasm.

"Oh, no. Sorry!"

"Then it's all very simple. I leave with Roser and you find Pere later. I don't have anything to say about it."

Rage overtook Elisa. Drawing closer to him, she replied, "You don't have anything to say because you don't care, or because you care too much?"

Arnau paled. He had seldom seen Elisa losing her habitual, unalterable composure. He tried to respond calmly, but the words would not come out.

"I care, of course I care. I don't know… It wasn't a pleasant topic. Don't get upset, please."

"It's easy to tell me that! I've been putting up with this situation for two years and I can't do it any more!"

She unleashed a convulsion of tears. Arnau was visibly surprised. He failed to understand the turn the conversation had taken. For several days he had been preparing for the interview, anticipating Elisa's reproaches against the party's chauvinism, her exclusion from the leadership positions, the sectarianism of its activists, or the terrorist strategy that developed ten years before, but he never expected that the crisis would come as a result of a discussion of their private lives. The scene seemed especially out of place to him. He didn't know what to make of the outburst. It must be motivated by his reaction to Elisa's love life, which he always thought was respectful. What should he have done, then? Plan fights, stage scenes of jealousy he didn't feel?

Elisa looked at him, taking advantage of a pause in the sobbing. In a concentrated and resentful tone, she asked, "Didn't you ever feel… weren't you ever jealous of us?"

"Of you? Do you mean both of you at the same time?"

Arnau again had the feeling he was dealing with some unknown being, whose language he didn't understand. It had happened to him many other times in his life with Elisa. For a time he told himself she had an introverted and difficult character, aggravated by the repressive education she had received, but his friends, and most of all the comrades in the party, had convinced him that all women were unpredictable. Capricious, unstable, forgetful and given to whims. They formed a population apart from men. The dark continent, he remembered vaguely, while he watched Elisa crying, not knowing what to do. She was usually more stable. He didn't understand what had happened.

Elisa replied, enraged, "You never know what's happening to me when I'm hurt. Only a man could be so insensitive!"

The accusation surprised Arnau even more, precisely when he was thinking she was the unintelligible one.

"But do you really mean you thought I would be jealous of both you and Pere?"

"Why not of me?" Elisa became aggressive to hide her shame and doubt. She was immediately sorry when she heard Arnau reply with spontaneous honesty.

"Because I didn't love you."

Elisa pretended she had expected such an answer. She told herself she already knew it, but the sound of those words ricocheted in her brain like a volley of stones.

Without showing her dejection or her doubt, she immediately asked, "And you didn't love Carles, either?"

"What are you talking about?"

Arnau felt more and more confused and tired. The unforeseen conversation was beginning to seem like something out of Kafka.

"What I said, damn it! Didn't you love Carles, either?"

"Of course I love my brother, but I don't know what the devil you're getting at. Aren't we talking about Pere? Isn't that who you're going on vacation with?"

An infantile desire to contradict him, to provoke him, to disconcert him, pushed her to say absurd things.

"Oh, definitely not. I only said that to see how you'd react. I can stay here over the break and go to court if you ask me to."

"No, it's not necessary. I already told you that, unfortunately, we can wait a few days. I don't even think the judge will be in court these days."

"If you ask me to, I'll go tomorrow."

Arnau saw the trap. He needed time to think and he didn't have it. Why was she acting so aggressive and affected now? What did she mean "if you ask me to"? Was she insinuating? Did she still love him, as all his friends said?

He didn't know how to choose the most important of so many questions that were jumbled together in his mind. In the end, he asked the last one.

"But, aren't you in love with Pere?"

Chapter 11

She needed to hold Arnau's lean, almost hairless body close to her. She felt a physical necessity localized in her fingertips, the palms of her hands, her breasts, and her nipples, which became erect, aching for the touch when she remembered that embrace. Her memory brought back the countless times she held her man's muscular and tanned torso in her arms, and cursed a thousand times the carelessness that allowed her to lose him, and angrily regretted the times when she was tired or distracted and rejected an opportunity to love him.

"You still think about Arnau, don't you?"

Pere looked at her darkly. He had sat up in bed and was smoking a cigarette, intense and annoyed. Elisa didn't know how to answer. Searching for the words, she pronounced the least appropriate ones.

"How can you tell?"

"Bah! Your entire being says it at all hours. A second ago you called me Arnau again. I really don't know how the other men who've been with you could stand it. It's impossible to compete with an invisible rival." Pere got up and began to get dressed while he spoke. Leaning over his socks, he argued, "You remind me of Scarlett O'Hara. In love with Ashley all her life, married to other men, longing for sex with him while she went to bed with Rhett Butler, you're the living image of the old lady. A nineteenth century lady like Scarlett, or, more accurately, a Greek woman from heroic times. A Penelope, but worse. Because Penelope was always certain Ulysses loved her, while you know for a fact that Arnau doesn't love you any more."

Elisa kept quiet, not daring to reply curtly the way she wanted to: "What do you know?" But Pere understood her as clearly as if she had said the words, as if his ear were connected to her brain.

"Unless you still believe that deep down he still loves you and Roser has him trapped."

The mocking expression Pere showed through his smile made her blush. She didn't have to answer, because he continued talking while he buttoned his shirt.

"Your constancy in love is worthy of an elegy. It's a constancy you haven't had in political or feminist activism. Your whole life summarized by one love. As sweet as a romance novel, or the teachings of your nuns. You didn't marry God, but you will love the man who substituted for him eternally. Perfect, Elisa, perfect, for a nineteenth century novel, 'Letter from a Woman,' or 'Diary of a Woman,' right? The romantic apotheosis. You live in the margins of life, Elisa. When it's not your activism in the most sectarian of parties, and there was a reason you were active in that one and not some other, it's your faithfulness to one man… I know, I know you've been to bed with others. You've been doing it for a year with me, but are you really unfaithful to Arnau? As Rhett says to Scarlett, 'You give me your body but not your soul.' How long are you going to live in that unreasonable fantasy? Your whole life, like the crazy woman in Dickens's *Great Expectations*? When will you wake up from this dream? It's worse than your mystical mental lapses from the time when you were a saint-in-training. Because, in the end, sainthood is a definite goal, though difficult, but now you have no goal, other than that of worshipping Arnau, who doesn't even love you. This role of the romantic Victorian virgin very much contradicts your former feminist activism. Did your companions teach you so little during those months? Is all you have what you learned as a child? Are the prayers and religious counsel the only thing that stuck in your brain cells? Did all the other activity glide over you like a shower without leaving a trace? Political instructions, high-sounding declarations of principles, arrests, prison, and even terrorism did nothing for you. You were ready to kill for the revolution, and now you behave toward the man you love like a Japanese geisha."

When the front door slammed as Pere took his leave, shouting that when she was cured of that morbid passion, she should call him, Elisa sat down in the front room, alone. She wanted to think about the accusations Pere had so cruelly hurled at her. She was alienated, removed from the world of normal human beings. She always had been.

"We're human beings, too, you know."

Elisa sat down on the bathroom floor and squeezed her legs hard against her chin, holding them between her hands. She should have covered her ears, but she didn't want to. Through the walls she could still hear the panting, and she wanted to be breathing like that, while her whole body shouted for some masculine hands to touch it.

She didn't understand how Pilar Laborde and Juana Parroto hadn't managed to stop the newcomer from engaging in that activity which must have seemed inappropriate for a PCE-ML militant, but Mercedes González didn't seem willing to accept the prohibitions of her political superiors. Elisa was sure Juana and Pilar could not resist the magnetic influence Mercedes held over everyone, with her almost infantile face and innocent smile. The same one she had used that afternoon when, the week of her arrival in Yeserías, she approached Elisa and said in her sweetest tone, "Want to make love with me?"

Years later Elisa was still ashamed of her frightened face, her scandalized gestures, her aggressive response, to which Mercedes responded with a simple shrug, still smiling.

"That's what the feminist movement has been so good for. It's made us abandon all our spineless prejudices, fears, scandals over nothing. Do you remember Mercedes and Nieves?"

It wasn't Elisa's refusal that threw Mercedes into Nieves Argaraizábal's arms. Nieves was a college girl who identified with the ETA Sixth Assembly, or with any of the other complicated organizations that operated in the Basque Country, and who everyone supposed was studying in Madrid in order to escape larger responsibilities. Nieves was a lesbian, but not everyone knew it or how to tell. Only Mercedes had the intuition to guess. Elisa had never imagined it, and it wasn't a matter of knowing what to make of Nieves, whom she hardly ever spoke with, but of accepting, or more accurately, of expecting, that lesbian relationships would arise among women in that sterile and prolonged incarceration. Because, although Elisa had felt needy and depressed almost constantly, she had never considered the possibility of making love with her companions, as feverish and solitary as she was.

"You don't masturbate?"

The question made Elisa jump and immediately called the attention of her companions. Mercedes could not understand their curiosity and scandal.

"Please! This is 1975, my friends!"

Elisa didn't know whether the other prisoners shared her puritanical attitude, but she well knew the atmosphere in which her comrades lived, and understood their prudish response to Mercedes's simple question. Elisa didn't masturbate, she never had, and was almost sure the others hadn't, either. She had some doubt about Octubre, but she would not have dared show it. In any case, if Octubre had undertaken that activity in prison, it must doubtless have been in the early morning hours, when all the women she shared the dormitory with were asleep. She would not have dared to give them a public demonstration of the procedure, as Mercedes had proposed to them that afternoon.

That same night, the class was organized in the general barracks, where thirty beds were lined up along the two walls. And neither Juana Parroto nor Pilar Laborde protested, but stayed there, hypnotized by Mercedes's manipulations. Elisa hadn't been able to bear it. Without attracting attention — no one worried about what she was doing — she left the dormitory, but didn't go to her own, where Octubre was reading in bed, not interested, she said, in seeing what everyone knew. Elisa went into the bathroom and sat on the floor, next to the adjacent wall, where she could clearly hear Mercedes' panting, and the silence of the rest, hypnotized by their comrade's performance.

Mercedes didn't have much experience. The movements were rushed, repetitive, and the innocence of her twenty years was obvious in the slow contortions of her body, her closed mouth and the brief panting. The experience lasted less than five minutes, but it left an indelible mark on all the students. *Even on me*, thought Elisa, *though I didn't witness it.* Was that why, years later…?

When Elisa tried to criticize her comrades for attending the spectacle, Octubre laughed at her. Leaving her book, she teasingly replied, "Forget your bourgeois prejudices. We all need to fulfill our sexuality. We're human beings, too, you know. Not only men masturbate and stick it in each other's ass when there's no woman around. In jails, in convents, women pair off, make love, keep each other company, and masturbate together. Didn't you know that, my little saint?"

Elisa firmly denied it. She never knew about such activities at her school. She had never even heard a rumor about anything like it in the fifteen consecutive years she lived with the nuns and girls at school. It would have been such a serious scandal that it couldn't have gone unnoticed by anyone, not even by her, as oblivious as she was. She had heard stories of not-very-orthodox caresses the teachers gave the boys in the priests' schools. Several of her schoolmate's brothers talked about it years later. She remembered with great detail how one of Elisenda's brothers explained how the priest made appointments at his house with the handsomest students, and sat them on his knees while pretending to give them lessons. But nothing of the kind had ever happened among the girls. And she roundly denied it, shaking her head repeatedly.

"You're just like Queen Victoria when she failed to include lesbianism in her laws against homosexuality because she refused to believe it could exist between women. In prudish England, homosexuality was illegal, but not lesbianism."

"I don't know what Queen Victoria did, and naturally by this time I know that women can have sexual relations with each other," — she didn't add that she actually didn't know how this would be done — "but I maintain that it never happened at my school."

"Fine, lady, it doesn't matter if it never happened or if you just never found out. What's obvious is that women can love each other and that they do so whenever the situation that encourages it, like now. Didn't you ever think that it's really more logical for women to love each other than men? The tenderness they share make the relationship much more pleasant than masculine violence and aggression. Didn't you ever want to try it?"

Elisa shook her head. She didn't share her friend's theories. She so strongly desired Arnau's presence that she was unable to appreciate the substitute Mercedes or any of her comrades could offer her.

Octubre laughed boomingly. "If the lesbians heard you call them substitutes…"

At that moment Elisa could not understand the explanations Octubre offered her. Several years would have to pass before she did.

"I need you with my entire being," she had written Arnau in her last letter. Elisa thought Arnau would be living in prison given over to political arguments, in that "Komintern" that was the political prisoners' barracks in Carabanchel. In her memory, which faded and became distorted with the passing of the months, Arnau's body got taller and more robust. She closed her eyes and could smell his skin, feel the hair on his chest, and she embraced his torso in her arms. She thought she could remember that she came up to his chin, and when she raised her head, his chin scratched her forehead.

Her hands went down his sides, along his ribs, down the ridge of his waist, and arrived at his lean hips. There they hesitated, delaying his pleasure. She could feel his impatience in the vibrations he sent her. His sex was so hard she thought it would hurt him if she touched it, and when she took it between her hands, his trembling seemed like suffering. If she hadn't had so much experience, she would have let go for fear of hurting him.

She rubbed that beloved member with both hands, more and more quickly, but teasingly didn't let him achieve his desires. She took a few seconds to abandon herself to his embrace, and when she did, Arnau fell onto the bed and pulled her on top of him. She felt his erect penis necessary and deep inside her, the brushing of his hands that softly and without respite caressed her nipples, and began to cry.

Sitting there, on the prison floor, noting the throbbing and warmth of her own vulva, her nipples, the swelling of her breasts, and that ache in her lower stomach, she cried until all sensation dulled.

"We masturbated regularly. As you can imagine. Single men, locked up in threes, for years. There were a lot of homosexual pairs, but not between the politicals. The revolution forbade it." And he laughed as he sat up in bed to light a cigarette.

Elisa didn't tire of looking at him, for hours on end, now that she finally had him back, almost three years later, and could live out with him all the daydreams that had tormented her in prison. The men masturbated regularly, and she smiled at the innocence that made her think of him as a monk in prison.

"But, where did you do it? And how?"

"Like always, little one." And now Arnau kissed her earlobe while he talked. "Such innocence! In bed, with our hands, of course. What did you think?"

"In bed? In the dormitory? What about the others who slept next to you?"

"Oh, no one cared. The others did it, too, at the same time, or they read or they slept. Just like when we used the toilet. You get used to it, my little moralist."

Elisa quieted down, slightly embarrassed of her innocence. As she ran her fingers through the hair on Arnau's chest, and smelled the cigarette smoke, she saw Mercedes, naked in bed with her knees slightly bent, panting slowly, as her right hand made little circles in her pubic hair. Pilar, Juana, Marisa, Mari Carmen and Nieves all looked at her hypnotized. That had been the second session, which Elisa hadn't been able to escape from. With wonder and fright at the same time, she contemplated Mercedes' light maneuverings. When Mercedes returned to reality, blushing and happy, and asked who wanted to imitate her, it was a sudden revelation to hear Mari Carmen volunteer. Mari Carmen didn't undress, and even used the sheet to partially hide herself from her comrades' gaze, but the movement of her hand, her panting, her moist, parted lips, her closed eyes, and the slight moan with which she ended the task, was later known as a feat that ranked forever among the heroic acts carried out in prison.

Octubre looked at Elisa's swollen face and left the book she was reading on the bed. That night Elisa needed to talk to her, to relieve some of the anguish of the memories provoked by Mercedes' exhibition.

"How can they…"

The laughter in the adjacent room seeped into Octubre and Elisa's dormitory.

"Religious prejudices?"

Elisa got angry at Octubre's ironic smile.

"You judge everything by that! You're the one who has prejudices against me…"

Octubre stopped smiling. She didn't want to hurt her friend, who was in such need of advice that night.

"Maybe you're right… Sorry. What's wrong?"

"It hurts. It hurts! I can't joke about so much desire!"

Octubre looked at her a moment without understanding.

"I need Arnau. I need his body and his hands and his kisses…" She started sobbing.

"Lucky you."

Elisa didn't hear the words until Octubre repeated them, and then she thought her friend was accusing her of something.

"I mean that the majority of them have never enjoyed that impatience, that excitement you feel."

"That can't be. Marisa has a lover. Pilar is married and I wouldn't guess Juana is a virgin."

"It doesn't matter. You don't know women."

Elisa didn't understand why Octubre said it as a reproach.

"Juana is probably not a virgin, but, if you bothered to talk to her about it, she'll ask you the oddest questions, like where's her clitoris, a word she heard for the first time in jail, from Mercedes' lips, whose arrival, then, has been most fortunate."

At Elisa's surprise, Octubre nodded repeatedly.

"But, that's the same as saying…"

"No, Elisa. That's exactly the question she asked me a few days ago, in all seriousness."

"But, then…"

"You want to know if she hasn't had sex until now, and of course she has, but to satisfy a man a woman doesn't have to feel pleasure in return."

Elisa remembered that conversation whenever she listened to the women who came to the feminist group, years later, demanding help for their petty miseries. The stories of life for women that got sorted out one afternoon after another in the Feminist Coordinator's office showed her an underworld unknown to her until that point, and it was full of frustrations, ignorance, and aggression.

"Because they always kept us in the most helpless ignorance of sexual matters. I'd guess your mother lived at your father's side for forty years without ever knowing what an orgasm was. That's how it was at the time, and, unfortunately, in our time, too, for the most part."

After every session, Octubre angrily commented on the alienation women suffered. Until one night, after the meeting, having ingested two rum-and-Cokes, she explained to Elisa that she, too, had been married to a guy who threw himself onto her every night and fell asleep afterward, without her ever knowing what had happened.

"And he was an activist in the PCE! Imagine! Lots of talk about the liberation of the proletariat, but for him women existed in the world just to be fucked."

As she spoke, her beautiful light brown eyes transmitted the frustration she had accumulated over several years of being treated like a prostitute.

"Do you understand now why feminism goes beyond socialism? Except for a few of the anarchists, revolutionary men have never worried about sexual oppression. Only we women can end this problem, as old as the world, because we're the victims."

She paused, immersed in memories Elisa could not share. Then she smiled, and as if guessing what Elisa was thinking, said, "It's curious that such a pious girl, educated according to the oldest models of Catholic repression, should be so well informed about sex and not have had those problems with her husband."

Elisa blushed violently. Talking about sexual matters had always intimidated her, especially her own experience, but she didn't want to act so prudishly with her friend. With obvious effort, she replied, "Arnau taught me. I was fifteen when he asked me to be his girlfriend, and before a year was over he had gotten me to go to bed with him."

"But you wouldn't have known anything."

Elisa agreed, a little relieved at the normal tone the conversation was taking on.

"No, of course not. And it was very hard for me to overcome my scruples. I still confessed after the first few times, to the scandal of the priest, who had known me all my life. But I loved Arnau too much to deny him anything. Then, I wouldn't have cared if I'd gotten pregnant, or about any of the risks that we were warned about so many times at home and at school."

"The power of love…" Elisa thought she noticed a tinge of mockery in Octubre's voice, but she was speaking in all seriousness. "It's good, very good and important, because love helps a lot. There's no doubt Arnau is a great guy. He knew how to win you over, seduce you, and give you pleasure as well. A rare jewel. How many would envy you, used to suffering brutal and ignorant males, who never knew how to make a woman happy, and then beat them because of stupid jealousy!"

Elisa didn't answer. She understood that Octubre was speaking from experience and she didn't want to seem nosy or impertinent, especially when her friend seemed to need to confide in her. But that night the conversation didn't continue, and now Elisa remembered with a stab of pain the last thing she had said, after a few moments of silence.

"Take care of Arnau. Don't let them take him away from you. Men like him are rare."

Now, ten years later, those prophetic words anguished her. The regrets for so many stupid things she had done, the precautions she hadn't known how to take, her blindness, her ignorance… Anger made her clench her jaw and her eyes filled with tears.

"If you really love Arnau that much, I don't understand how you could let yourself get tangled up with Octubre like that."

Isabel looked at her, playful and curious, while trying to distract her from her constant regrets.

"If Carles was your salvation, as you just said, what was Octubre, eh? Arnau was still with you then. There was no reason for something like that. On the contrary, I'm sure that was what made him…"

Elisa almost screamed, "I know! I know what you think. You've told me a thousand times! And you're probably right, but I'm sick of hearing about it, of feeling guilty about it, of feeling desperate about it, and about Carles, and even about Pere, who you're constantly rejecting. I'm always at the center of everyone's anger, all the contradictions, and I don't know how to do anything right… I don't know!"

Isabel, with her calm elegance, and her simple words, stopped the attack of sobs Elisa had wanted to surrender to.

"That happens to everyone."

"No, I'm not in love with Pere, and you know it. I like him, he's a good friend and all that."

Arnau waited fearfully for the confession that still hadn't been spoken yet in the course of the morning, but the sentence remained suddenly cut off on Elisa's pursed lips.

They didn't know what else to say. Arnau perceived that turning the conversation to the topic that interested him at the moment would make Elisa reject him. Following it along the path she had drawn meant entering a dead end. Unless she promised, or implied that she promised he might have to… Arnau continued to rebel against that tactic. He had never had to use it and he especially didn't want to with Elisa. But telling her he was indifferent to her wouldn't have been the truth, either. His objection to starting a new romantic relationship with her was provoked more by his desire to behave loyally than by any displeasure it would cause him. Not even the memory of Roser kept him from it. In the end, without this reproach ever having come up between them, Arnau was aware that she had been the first to break the sacred trust of the relationship. His love for Roser wasn't so overpowering or so passionate that it would keep him from going to bed with Elisa.

"What are you thinking about?"

The question guillotined his reflections. "The feelings you describe can be more solid than a passionate love that quickly dies. In any case, Elisa, you've chosen it yourself."

Elisa didn't want to respond. She didn't want to hear what Arnau was ready to tell her. She wasn't even sure, yet, that he was wrong. But she clung to the convictions of her whole life. Only a deep and passionate love could build something solid between people. Only the love she felt for Arnau had allowed her to undergo deprivations, loneliness, torture, prison. And that feeling had nothing to do with what she felt for Pere. Her activism wasn't based on ideological convictions allowing her to look death in the face. If it hadn't been for Arnau, she would never have started down that path, she couldn't have endured that period of her life in prison, she would not have been able to maintain herself with as much dignity as she had. She was also sure, now, that Marisa, Raquel, Milagros, and Juana had worked in the same way, for all the pamphlet-like harangues they unleashed every day about the ideological firmness of a revolutionary. If not, how could they bear it?

Chapter 12

"FRAP put out of action by Madrid police. Among the fourteen terrorists arrested were the presumed perpetrators of the murder of Officer Lucio Rodríguez."

Elisa stared at the headlines while Marisa held up the *ABC*, trembling. That Thursday, July 24, 1975, the nightmare began.

"On the fourteenth of the present month, Officer Lucio Rodríguez Martínez was murdered while on duty at the Iberia Airlines Scheduling Center, on Alenza Street."

Elisa didn't know whether she had read the murder report, or whether they had associated it with a FRAP attack at the time. She only remembered the report from July 11, about the arrest of seventeen FRAP activists and the fall of the organization's safe houses in Madrid. And now, more arrests.

"The Secretary of the FRAP Provincial Committee was a reporter. The terrorists had a 'safe house' in the town of Leganés at their disposal. Two of them were arrested in Paris, where the Spanish Communist Party had entrusted them to proceed with 'executions.'"

The usual contamination of information the police supplied to the newspaper ended up getting the Communist Party of Spain, which they called "Spanish" to add insult to injury, confused with the PCE-ML. For a moment, Elisa was distracted thinking of how angry Carrillo would be about seeing himself implicated in terrorist attacks.

"They confess to the murder of a police officer. Therefore they murdered the policeman on Alenza Street. The head of the armed group was arrested."

Octubre read monotonously to control her emotion. Marisa said nothing, unable to move, even to breathe. Even Juana stayed quiet, with her brow furrowed.

"He admitted to being the perpetrator of the murder. On arrest, he was carrying two boxes of ammunition."

A good photograph of Adalberto crowned the report. The newspaper headlined the news of Adalberto's arrest as "Murderer arrested." It explained that in his declaration, Adalberto had confessed to murdering Officer Rodríguez and wounding Officer Fernández. For a few moments Elisa felt as if she were outside of her body, levitating in a space outside of time where nothing could hurt her, beyond the prison dormitory where the PCE-ML members gathered to speak without witnesses, amid the constant clacking of Octubre's typewriter, which Juana keyed at listlessly with the sole object of preventing the conversation's being recorded.

It wasn't Marisa, but Elisa, who fainted as Octubre read the ominous report. When, a few moments later, she regained consciousness, laid out on the bed by her companions, while Octubre fanned her with the very newspaper that brought the fatal information, she had to admit that her friend was right to scold her.

"Is it possible? Like a nineteenth-century lady. It wasn't Marisa who fainted, but you… That damned nun's education!"

Elisa thought Octubre repeated herself too often, continuously reminding Elisa of her religious education to make her feel guilty for all her own defects, but she wasn't strong enough to protest. She looked for Marisa and was ashamed. Marisa was at the window reading the page on which her personal tragedy was announced.

"It must have been the heat…" Elisa interrupted. Then she asked, "How many were there?"

"Seventeen."

"How did they arrest them?"

Octubre looked quickly over the report and shook her head. "It doesn't say. Professional secret."

"But, so many…?"

Elisa remembered her own arrest, hunted down like rabbits in that roasting attic on Olmo Street, one year and three months earlier, and cursed the activists and the party leaders for learning nothing from it. At that moment, she thought she could physically feel the weight of the hand of the policeman who had stopped her on the street, grabbing her arm so hard that she had a purple band for weeks. She heard his shouts and smelled his breath, stinking of tobacco. Two women were among those arrested. Their pictures stood out. Two girls younger than 25, thin, weak, with dark eyes, and with a look as assured as it was naive. Could it really be that they had thrown Molotov cocktails, participated in hijackings, car bombings, knifings, arson attempts on several buildings, including the newspaper *Ya,* and attacks with commercial inflammatory devices, as the police accused them?

She closed her eyes and lost herself in the rays of light that filtered through her eyelashes. It was stupid to be surprised that Milagros and Raquel were accused of terrorism. There beside her, Marisa, whose eyes were dilated with fear, thinner every day and with deeper bags under her eyes, was wasting away in that grimy prison for having thrown some Molotov cocktails at the Legion recruiting center more slowly than her comrades. And didn't Elisa herself often repeat that if the party had ordered it, she would have fired on any policeman? Octubre and Marisa whispered near the window in order not to bother her. She felt a pinch of shame when she thought of her fainting spell and then, with no transition, she fell asleep.

"You need to get your blood pressure checked. It must be really low. That's the only explanation for the fainting and exhaustion."

Octubre kept her company, sitting beside the bed that long summer evening. The heat had tired her and her face was sweaty and pale, as she never sunbathed. Her greasy hair stuck to her temples. Elisa again suffered the anguish from which sleep had freed her.

"How's Marisa?"

"She's in shock. I don't know if she comprehends."

Comprehend what? Elisa looked at Octubre in fear, and didn't want to understand what those words meant. It was just a few arrests, added to so many others the party had suffered. Unfortunate, terrible, as they all were, but no different. Why would they be different? What could be special in the case of those comrades whose faces, with furious expressions, appeared on page 53 of the newspaper? Terrorism? Marisa and more than one of the others also found themselves there for committing terrorist acts. Was that not the charge that weighed upon those accused of participating in the Correo Street bombing? Weren't they being tried under an article of the Military Justice Code that could result in a sentence of thirty years in prison or the death penalty? And the accomplices of the ETA members? Weren't they all there, waiting for the sentencing and hopeful all the while for a freedom that glinted on the horizon?

Octubre looked at Elisa with a furrowed brow.

"You could be right, all the facts are pointing in that direction… and yet I have the feeling that this mess will get worse. The women implicated in the attack on Correo Street have strong support from the international movement that's come together in their favor, and we can't forget, either, that the majority of them really had nothing to do with the attack. While those comrades of yours…"

She didn't finish the sentence. It wasn't easy to say that those young men and women had no support. That the majority belonged to a poor and anonymous proletariat, and that the international community, presided over by the most prestigious European writers and politicians, would not come together to help them. And above all, wasn't it true that they had committed the murders? Elisa looked away from Octubre. She remembered Juana's happy expression when she got the news of the FRAP attacks, the jokes about the victims, the threats against those who didn't understand the strategy, which would condemn many other enemies to death, her promises of triumph and the sentences with double meanings, accompanied by laughter, with which most of the women comrades alluded to armed attacks carried out by their party, compared to the tepid collaborationist politics of the other parties.

"You're not being fair, Elisa. Your comrades got the strength to resist torture, prison, even death, from their profound convictions. Remember Marisa when they released her, Juana and her silence. That conduct doesn't only result from love for a man."

Elisa didn't respond. She wasn't sure Marisa's, Nieves's, Raquel's, Juana's, Concepción's, and María Jesús's heroism didn't really correspond to a desire to make their men admire them, to fulfill the expectations they had placed on them.

"You say that because that was the case for you, right?"

Octubre looked at her with a mocking smile as she finished dressing. The conversation about love always implicated Elisa in an unflattering way. And why only her? Didn't everybody do stupid things, make mistakes, and even commit crimes, for love? Why did everyone reproach her, or mock her about her relationships? Had they been that ridiculous or strange?

"In fact, you couldn't say that, strictly speaking, about a woman who's loved the same man for years and years…"

And Octubre closed the conversation with that sentence, going into the bathroom, adding a new reproach to those already expressed. Years later Elisa would remember this commentary when Pere bombarded her with his reproaches, and she thought that lovers were always inappropriately jealous, even of past relationships.

"Do you mean to say that for you there was an absolute separation between love and your political activity?"

"Not exactly, not as you put it. Obviously, I wouldn't have been able to live with a woman from the right, as I've already said, but it's also obvious that my relationship with the party wasn't conditioned entirely by yours."

Elisa didn't want to keep asking, at least not at that moment, in order to avoid a topic she detested. On the other hand, how would he explain his current relationship with Roser, that stupid middle class señorita? But that demonstrated to her, at the same time, the separation Arnau could maintain between his affections and political commitments. And couldn't she? Were men and women really so different? Was that what made her so politically dependent, first on Arnau and then on Octubre? Was that why Marisa, Juana, and Raquel marched like zombies to the beat their husbands marked for them, while the men freely decided their political commitment?

"Like zombies? You're still being unfair."

Arnau's reproachful expression made her blush. His contempt enraged her, and at the same time, she could not pull herself away from the desire to belittle her women comrades, to minimize their efforts in those years past, to reduce them to a stupid and passive role in that submissive obedience they showed so long for their men and their party.

"Because you think that was your role, because you feel profoundly disgusted with yourself, especially now that you've abandoned your feminist work on account of Arnau. But I don't think you have a right to deny the merits of your former comrades just because you don't feel right about the role you've adopted as obedient wife."

After such a severe censure, Octubre left Elisa's house and their relationship changed forever.

Elisa felt trapped between the old criticism put forth by her friend and the annoyance she perceived in that new Arnau, who now looked at her contemptuously, in a way she wasn't familiar with, in silence, as if words were not enough to show the disgust Elisa's statements had caused him. When he finally spoke, he was more weary than angry.

"I don't know how you can talk like that. You don't seem to realize how much times have changed. The behavior of our men and women comrades was heroic ten years ago. Then it had a moral justification, though it's debatable whether it was a political mistake. But you seem to be forgetting the destruction the dictatorship caused for forty years. What we're discussing today is that with the socio-political conditions of the country so changed, the strategy of armed struggle has to change, too. That's the terrible mistake ETA is making."

Elisa stirred in her chair wearily. She didn't want to undergo the oft-repeated analyses of strategy and the socio-political reality of the country. She remembered with deep disgust the interminable political sessions she had to sit through in the eternal afternoons in jail, the boring and repetitive meetings of Juana, who always said the same thing.

"Basically, as always, your true love is the party."

Arnau again appeared disconcerted.

"How can you say that? Anyway, it would be the struggle, the revolution…"

Now Elisa laughed heartily, freeing up the anguish that had been accumulating since she heard the clanging on her entrance grate that morning. And she smiled about so many times she had had to sit quietly listening with a reserved and apparently concentrated air to the interminable disquisitions of the party leaders, and then voted yes to she knew not what proposition that was always approved unanimously. She never found out whether the other members had been as distracted as she was or had really understood what had been discussed.

"Oh, Arnau, please, so much has happened. We know each other well, and you're made of the same stuff as the rest. Obsessive paranoiacs, as Octubre called you."

"Have you noticed that all the leaders suffer from the illness that Marx called 'parliamentary cretinism'?"

That morning, in the middle of July 1975, many important things had to happen in the lives of the two women now seated on the floor of the courtyard of Yeserías prison sunbathing in minuscule bikinis, and also for the entire country, which was preparing to live through one more upheaval of the many it had already undergone, and would have yet to suffer in its ruptured history. But in those moments, Octubre was smiling peacefully with her eyes closed against the light, while Elisa drowsed lying face down on the towel she had carefully laid out on the cement.

"He said that it was an illness that made parliament members believe and act as if the life of the country took place only between parliamentary benches, while the real people, those who moved and worked and ate and loved in the streets, outside of that cretins' enclosure, functioned at the margins and in ignorance of what they all did in there…"

"Where did he write that?"

Elisa shook off her sleepiness, interested in the words of a Marx she didn't know.

"In *Revolution and Counterrevolution*, when he writes about the Frankfurt Assembly, in the midst of the 1848 revolution in Germany and Hungary. While the people were killing each other in the streets those cretins continued meeting in the parliament trying to control the country's fate."

"Really?"

"Haven't you read it?" Octubre opened her eyes to look at Elisa curiously.

"No… I actually haven't read Marx… other than the *Manifesto* and a few articles — well, parts of articles, quotes, that they print in *The Worker's Vanguard*."

"A strong theoretical background," Octubre joked.

In the party there was no theoretical background, or very little. Some had been in Albania or China, but she suspected they had done more sightseeing than anything else. There had been a leadership course Arnau himself had given, and she had benefitted from, until she felt she knew it already and what he explained bored her. Little additional effort was spent on the theoretical preparation of the activists.

"Almost everything I know I learned at the university, and, surprisingly, from the courses we took in JOC and HOAC. It's odd, really."

She surprised herself by looking at the problem with so much distance. It was probably the sun, the sleepiness, the serene cadence of Octubre's voice that kept her from getting upset, or even worrying about her friend's criticism of the real state of affairs within the party.

"Everyone knows the Church has had very good doctors."

"Yes, but only those of absolute faith. Neither the lower nor the middle management ever participated in the Church doctrine. Only an elite could study and have opinions. Remember that for centuries studying the Bible was prohibited. That was why Fray Luis de León went to prison."

Elisenda looked at her sulkily, while she tried to make her friend understand that they should follow the Mother Superior's and father confessor's orders.

"Well, I don't get it, understand? I don't get it! And until I do, no one will convince me, not even you. All this about saying yes to everything because those old priests and nuns say so, is for the birds, and you, you're so smart and studious, you could show it by using your own head a little. Why should you play the pivot, eh? With your slow reflexes and everything. And why do you have to go, you don't care about the team or the sport or the championship. To annoy me, that's why. Just to annoy me! You're a scab, consorting with the enemy."

"You don't understand, Elisenda. You must tame your vanity, keep your soul from becoming conceited with qualities that have no merit in the eyes of God and that only relax the spirit and leave it vulnerable to the devil's temptations."

"What nonsense! The devil and demons! Only you could believe all that about the devil. It's not like you're a little girl. I don't know how you can keep from laughing about that bloody nonsense at your age."

"Please don't swear!"

But Elisenda was already carried away and her friend's exclamations and exaggerated horror made no difference to her, just as they didn't stop her from explaining in great detail the latest theological problems that had been worrying her. Hell included in its sufferings the greatest one of all: the absence of God. But that Hell with all the fire, eternal tortures, abode of the hopeless, was impossible to accept. It was insane to think that a good, just, and merciful God could send his creations, those weak and sinful creatures, who, to make matters worse, He himself had made that way, to burn in the infernal cauldrons. And, if it was dogma that Hell existed, it wasn't dogma that there was anyone in it, but in that case it was a farfetched idiocy to invent Hell and then not send anyone to it. She could not believe that God was such a practical joker as to put together a scheme like that. And in such a case, if Hell didn't exist, and Elisenda felt more and more inclined to accept that such a monstrous thing was purely the invention of monks and nuns as twisted as the ones she knew, then Hell obviously meant the absence of God, because if the devil didn't exist, neither did God. At that point in Elisenda's commentary, Elisa was so terrorized that she fled, running to the cloister to say six Hail Marys for the salvation of her friend's soul, which was at the door of immediate condemnation.

"What are you laughing about?"

Octubre sat up to look at her, surprised by the sudden laughter Elisa had let loose in the middle of silence.

"I was remembering an argument with a friend at school about Hell and God. And I was laughing when I remembered how scared I was of Elisenda's heresy. We were so young!"

Arnau looked at her without understanding.

"We were so young when we believed in the infallibility of the Pope, and then in the secretary general of the party."

"Ah…" He didn't dare go on. He saw himself slipping into that tricky mess Elisa had gotten him into, and now he doubted that she had done it as innocently as she pretended.

"But not now, Arnau. Now, to try and keep believing the same dogma just looks ridiculous."

"What dogma? Could you be less cryptic, please?"

"It doesn't matter what you call it. Parliamentary cretinism, anyway. Being sure that everything the party does is fine, and if the people don't follow the instructions they're given within the judgment of the line drawn by the Central Committee, it's the people who are wrong, isn't it? In the end, working and struggling just for the party's existence, as an end in itself, not as an instrument. Like savages who find a radio part in the middle of the jungle."

"Well, I don't know what your point is, other than to call us savages."

Elisa overcame another bout of hilarity, and responded seriously. "Your pomposity when you talk to me about the struggle and the revolution. You don't seem to have changed at all. I guess almost none of the party leaders have changed." She wanted to laugh again when she remembered the names used by the PC-ML to judge the other political forces.

"At the time of arrest he had a briefcase containing two boxes of ammunition of 50 Super Speed brand cartridges each, fourteen bullets of the same caliber in a matchbox, two copies of *The Worker's Vanguard*, one of *Action*, and a pamphlet entitled *The Democratic Junta: Amalgam of Traitors, Monarchists, and Socio-Fascists*."

Elisa wasn't familiar with her party's documents about the Democratic Junta and she jumped when she read the pamphlet title. Marisa didn't bat an eye. Juana continued reading. Elisa suddenly felt enormously alone.

"Things have changed, and you all have changed a lot, too. I remember when you considered the Democratic Junta an 'amalgam of traitors, monarchists, and socio-fascists.'"

Arnau looked at her with a strange expression, which she could not interpret until he answered.

"That's what they were…"

"Arnau, please…"

"Do you think that's stupid or unfair? Think about it a little bit, in light of what happened. Among the members of the famous Junta, Carrillo was first on the list and principal mover, right? Well, it's him and no other who his own party is calling a traitor every day. Look, if they'd paid attention to us back then… In general, today, all the Left, except his little group, agrees that the ex-secretary general has ruined the party. That must be for some reason. The other illustrious component of the famous Junta was García Trevijano, who ended up a common criminal after they discovered what he embezzled in Guinea, and the third founder, Calvo Serer, who defended his membership in Opus Dei on television a few months ago. What are we supposed to think of these people?"

"Oh, I don't know. And besides, what happened to them doesn't matter now. But Arnau, remember how you left the party fed up with sectarianism, and one of the main things you couldn't bear was precisely the relationship with the Communist Party."

Arnau hesitated a few seconds before smiling and nodding.

"Is it true?"

Elisa looked in surprise at her husband, who on returning from one of his party meetings, told her the most shocking news of her life. He smiled then with the same playful and amused expression that he had at that moment, but that morning a deep, though repressed anger had shown up in his expression and words.

"I'm fed up, you know? Completely fed up. Nothing can be done with them. They have sectarianism in their bone marrow, in their grey cells, their craniums are made of stone."

What had Octubre once said in jail about squashed craniums?

"They think they're still living clandestine, in the first years of the dictatorship, because in the last years they were also doing thousands of absurd things that ended the lives of many activists. But now, in 1981, when they've even asked for legalization, they keep operating like paranoiacs. Their lives are conspiracies, and they won't change… I'm wearing myself out with them, trying to show them what political work with the masses is, and I'm not getting anywhere."

Elisa felt victorious for the first time in her relationship with Arnau, and could hardly hide her satisfaction. *I didn't know just how little that feeling would last,* she thought with despair. Those were the times when Octubre had dragged her into the Feminist Movement, and Elisa once again occupied her nights with politics after five years of inactivity.

"That's why Arnau left you. He wanted you at home, as a good and industrious wife."

After their breakup it was very hard for Elisa to contradict Octubre and Isabel when they both wanted to attribute Arnau's romantic detour to her feminist activism. Was it possible that all he really wanted was a loyal wife dedicated to looking after him, after having dragged her through that party of guerrillas for ten years? Was it possible that, because she attended a weekly meeting at the Feminist Coordinator's and sporadically showed up at some conferences, Arnau could feel passed over, abandoned?

"That wasn't exactly your only activity. You went to Madrid, Granada, Gerona, Santiago de Compostela to conferences, big functions. And above all, you went around repeating the feminist teachings of the time, which made men green. And those weren't the only activities that bothered him, as you well know."

Elisa didn't pick up on the allusion. She stubbornly exclaimed, "But he agreed!"

"Did he?"

At least he said he did. He even seemed so interested in the feminist phenomenon that he made everyone who heard him think it was the wave of the future. That was the time when the meetings were held in his home, but now the participants who filled the space had curly hair, fringed shawls, faded jeans, booming laughter, shouts and songs, so different from those other party meetings Elisa was familiar with, made up mainly of male characters with serious, worried faces, who talked deliberately, pompously, always satisfied about the importance of their mission, which was nothing less than saving humanity.

"Because women are only trying to save themselves, they express themselves more simply, they show their insecurity without trying to hide it, speak about everyday things with a common language everyone understands. That's why the Movement will succeed, you see. Because it speaks to women about their daily problems in a comprehensible way, without pretensions of universal redemption, in the abstract idiom of our political leaders."

Elisa had to admit that Octubre was right, remembering with scorn the interminably tedious meetings of the party's executive committee, where she was the only woman, where they only discussed matters of high strategy and tactics, which none of the members understood, anyway. The majority of the party leaders were workers, or mid-level employees, and they proudly held it as an example of the representativeness of the working class, compared to the other communist parties, in which more intellectuals were active than workers. And they showed their ignorance in submissively accepting all the orders transmitted by the political bureau, whose members lived in Switzerland. Arnau and Elisa were the only discordant voices, and they never found support in the surprised expressions of their comrades.

"So I'm leaving. Because there, I'm the voice that cries out in the wilderness. If they continue with this sectarian politics they're getting ready for suicide."

"And nevertheless, notice that almost six years later you're still with them and getting ready to defend the republic in the next elections."

Arnau didn't take the reproach with antagonism. He seemed suddenly docile.

"I wouldn't know what to do. Political struggle is an addiction."

"There are other parties."

"So what? Have you seen them? Our party is small, marginal, sectarian, but honorable. After seeing the catastrophe of the PCE and PSUC, so much the more reason to continue with the PC-ML! At least we don't lose elections."

"But you know you're condemning yourself to marginality forever."

Arnau's face darkened before he answered. "All the communist options are condemned to marginality in Europe. There is no path for revolution in developed countries. Capitalism has made the people rotten, made everyone bourgeois. Not only the middle class, the plague of the West, as Agnes Heller defined it, but even the workers and the beggars. In Spain today the only thing the workers want is to have a car, a TV and a VCR. Politics and culture don't interest them."

Elisa answered him with mockery colored by tenderness. "Is that what you say in the executive meetings?"

"Yes, every day."

With a gesture of surprise, Elisa asked, "And what happens?"

"Nothing, of course. Times really have changed a great deal. My state of mind has caught on with some, and the rest don't dare to kick me out."

"Defeatism has won."

"No, by no means. If that were the case we'd dissolve the party. We're conscious of the difficulty of our work, but we also know it's indispensable in the context of our country. There have to be some ethical options against so much political and electoral opportunism. The spectacle Carrillo and his people made fighting against PCE and PCPE in Galicia over one percent of the votes is regrettable because on top of it all they had no other message than a few promised reforms exactly the same as the socialists and Esquerda Galega and other leftist groups that could be adopted by any social democratic party. If the socialists didn't represent a liberal right and nothing more, if they really became a social democracy on the Swedish model, the demands of the Spanish left would be taken care of so quickly that they would leave it with no reason to exist."

"That's why feminism is indispensable, I tell you. Men have already completed their revolutionary cycle. The transformations of the feminist revolution are the deepest. They'll change the world, you'll see. And all the programs called Marxist-Leninist, sectarian and dogmatic will get old very fast, surpassed by feminism's proposals."

Elisa wanted to believe it. She could not feel as enthusiastic as Octubre about the new message, but recognized that compared to the ancient parties' instructions, compared to the tapped out esthetic the political leaders were presenting, confined in their discourses as much as they were in their jackets, the women had a vital, rejuvenating air, and their words sounded alive while the men's stank of death.

But at home she found an Arnau dispossessed of the reason for his whole life, waiting for her after work, feigning interest in some household chores, and studying the dry courses for a career in journalism that had never interested him. For several months, Elisa felt insecure, unable to accept the new situation as normal.

"You felt guilty about participating in a political activity he didn't participate in, while on the other hand, it seemed fine to you when he was the party leader who hardly had time for dinner at home on weekends."

Elisa couldn't find a solution. In the end she decided to stop working so actively in feminism, but when she disappointed her companions by announcing her retirement from the group, Arnau had just reconciled with the party, and that afternoon she could not respond to Octubre's shouting.

"Can't you see? Can't you see, you idiot? Did you think Arnau depended on you? Not even when you were at home waiting into the morning hours for him to get back from his endless meetings, and not now when he stayed home while you were with us. In the first case, it never bothered him to leave you alone and keep you in a secondary place under his political passion, and then he was only preparing for his return to the nest. He must not have even noticed your absence. He must've been writing a very long report, both an analysis of the present situation and a self-critique, to go back with honors into the leadership of his worshipped party."

Octubre's reasoning didn't work for Elisa. She didn't feel motivated to go back to feminist activism any more. She still participated in some of the events that were organized for the right to abortion, but all her companions saw her listlessness.

"And meanwhile, Arnau was preparing for his escape."

Isabel had always insisted that his disaffection began with Elisa's feminist militancy, and although she argued in her favor that he abandoned her as soon as it seemed the activity was disruptive to her relationship with him, Elisa herself showed very little conviction in her weak defense.

Was that what he wanted, after all? A good girl who would obey him? But she had always done that. Even when she worked in feminism, she was always dependent on Arnau, attentive, continually vigilant to please him. She would have abandoned any activity if he had asked her to, but he never had, and that was the worst part. The hypocrisy with which he pretended to good-naturedly accept Elisa's activities, her new group of friends, Octubre's inflamed feminist discourses, the rowdy meetings of young women that took over the house every Wednesday night —and he served the tea, parodying the role of housewife — all that pantomime went toward nothing more than masking his displeasure, or, worse, his indifference. Because by then he must have already stopped loving her.

Arnau appeared surprised by her tears. When he opened his mouth, she anticipated and responded, "I was remembering Marisa and Adalberto when they arrested and tried him."

"Why?"

Elisa could not explain the association of ideas that had brought her to that memory. Arnau's disaffection had no similarity to the passionate love Marisa showed for her man and that she claimed he felt for her, though she never personally saw any proof of such affection. But that afternoon so many years back, when Elisa was recovering from her fainting spell in the prison dormitory and observed Marisa standing beside the window and reading the ominous report, she wondered what Arnau's absence would mean to her. She could not know then the little time that separated Marisa from that terrible loss.

"Those were horrible times." But it seemed to Elisa that Arnau was saying it conventionally. There was no trace of emotion in his voice and his look was distracted. "That's why we have to avoid continuing to live out the consequences. We must clarify our present activity once and for all. You must say everything you know about our work, in the past and now, to acquit Cherta, as well as the whole party, once and for all. Will you do it?"

Irritated by Arnau's indifference toward the memories that still deeply pained her, Elisa reacted violently to the request.

"And why me? Why? Why don't you ask any of the others who've left the party? Any of them could help you. Why does it have to be me?"

Arnau looked fed up with the never-ending argument. He didn't know if, in fact, Elisa was right and it would have been better to ask anyone else. If only that weren't impossible.

"And why not? Why someone else and not you?" he interrupted her arrogantly. "I thought I could propose it to you, that's all. I thought our relationship was honest enough for me to ask you a favor. If that's not the case, tell me and that's enough. Besides, you know perfectly well that you were on the Central Committee in the end, and you know things about the organization and central functioning of the party that the others don't. I'll have to look for other Central Committee members but I don't even know where they live any more. I didn't even learn some of their real names. Have you forgotten what it was like to be clandestine?"

"Quite the role I played on the Central Committee! Especially in Madrid, where I was nothing more than your servant."

"Yes, that's true, Elisa. But it's over now. We talked about it and there was nothing to be done. Now the matter at hand is helping a comrade, who is innocent of the charges against him. And now it's not like in those times when they tried and sentenced people in military trials that lasted all of two days."

Chapter 13

Violence had a presence there, all-powerful, dominating the atmosphere of the prison where three hundred women lived poorly for months or even years. Elisa heard the screaming from where she was in the dormitory. It came in through the open window and suffocated her like the humidity of that hot and endless summer's afternoon. The insults were always the same, but so brazen that when she first arrived at the prison it seemed impossible to her that women were capable of speaking like that. That morning, after more than a year of hearing them, she was indifferent to them. But the screaming bothered her, because it meant that the women were becoming physically aggressive. The screaming was now so shrill that she could not help going to the window to see what was happening in the patio.

An official was standing between the two contenders, who had scratches on their faces, long tears in their grey prison smocks, and locks of hair in their hands. Suddenly, the aggression tipped against the official. The two women threw themselves onto her, and in a whirlwind of incomprehensible screams, five or six more prisoners came from the Department of Common Criminals to help their companions. The official had fallen to the ground and could not call out or blow her whistle. It seemed that she would not be saved, because none of the other prisoners, who observed the scene from the windows and doorways of the departments that looked out into the patio, seemed willing to intervene, or even go for help.

Elisa fought her impulse to alert the guards. Distrust, fear, and the familiar question of who the enemy was, held her back. But the blood she saw staining the prisoners' hands repulsed her so much that she felt the acid rise to her throat. In the end, the other officials arrived — it was always a mystery who had alerted them — and the fight lasted only a few seconds. The first fighters were quickly dragged away by several jailers and the official who was wounded on the ground had to be helped to walk. The other women who had taken part in the melee tried to escape detention. Some were able, getting lost in the dormitories, but three were held down and taken to the interior patio of the Commons.

The women who caused the incident were locked up in solitary confinement. The tiny rooms contained a narrow iron bed, a nightstand and a chair. A barred window and a door covered with iron faced the interior patio which the political prisoners' windows and eating area also faced. The woman in solitary had no rights except to daily rations and to go to the toilet. No paper, no newspaper, no books, not even cigarettes, in a place where nicotine was the only drug. María ended up there, with her dress torn and her hair half pulled out, without medical attention or a comb with which to clean up the disaster a little. It wasn't really necessary, anyway, since no mirror would allow her to look at herself. María was twenty years old and had already spent one of them in jail. No one knew exactly why she was there. The confused and long-winded explanations the other prisoners passed along said that police persecution, the dislike of a judge from her town, indifference, corruption, the laziness of the Madrid tribunals, all kept her imprisoned without cause. She found herself in a state of juridical uncertainty, medieval in nature, in which the Law of Public Endangerment buried its prisoners. Without a fixed limit on time in prison, the judge received a report from the prison directors and decided at his own discretion to keep her interned, without allowing her to guess how much longer her sentence would last.

María's situation became a torture that wore away at her psychologically. Most of all because six months before she had given birth to a sickly little boy, and had been at death's door when the midwife at the Penitentiary Hospital brutally yanked the child out. Then, María's breast milk was pure water mixed with poison, as the prisoners said, and the child was at serious risk of dying, especially when the other prisoners, trying to help her, gave him bottles of condensed milk with unboiled tap water, and the little one protested such a diet with horrible green diarrhea that made the dormitory stink for days.

María also had bleeding cracks in her nipples after attempting to nurse the baby for the first few days, and some occasional bleeding, which no one tried to stop, and which weakened her even more. The weakness caused by her illness, the postnatal exhaustion with no medical attention, the repulsion of that stinking creature, the heat of that September, after the burning July and August, the heaping together of women and children, six by six in the dormitories, all sharpened the aggressiveness those women could not direct anywhere except against each other. The arrival of the official had provided them an adequate victim. Now María was locked up all day long in punishment cell number one, but the thin partition and bars let the prisoner's voice, laments and obsessive pleading pass through. Sometimes an official's voice was mixed in with María's, telling her to shut up. Once Elisa was afraid she had heard a slap or a kick, followed by strident crying. Elisa thought she had heard it, but she denied it, trying to hide from the problem. A week later it was obvious that no one could stay out of it. Because in Department Three, the political prisoners' department, María's laments could be heard distinctly all night, demanding medical attention for her injuries, asking for water, cursing her torturers, threatening to commit suicide.

It became necessary for the politicals to assemble to decide what action to take in solidarity with María. They had to demand medical attention for her, and an appointment with a psychiatrist. The public had to be alerted about the treatment given to women in solitary confinement. The unending laments of the punished woman were a background to the assembly meeting in the dining commons.

"She has a very small child besides. He's only a few months old, he was born in prison, and now they leave him all alone in the cell, except three times a day when they bring him for nursing."

Elisa remembered that human creature, skinny, covered with strange purple spots, with skeletal legs that appeared below a threadbare woolen shawl his mother covered him with, even in that torrid September. On a strange whim his mother had started to call him Israel, but the priest refused to baptize him. She did it by herself and at her own risk, with the name of Luis, although the prisoners continued to call him Israel.

As the name suggested, now the little boy was abandoned and alone, locked in the common criminals' dormitory for hours on end, he himself also serving out the sentence imposed on his mother.

"We must mobilize soon. If we don't, that girl will go crazy. She already whispers more than she talks, and only talks nonsense. The baby will get sick, too."

Enthusiasm spread among the politicals, united for the first time by a common cause. They all wrote petitions, new ones every week, that ended up on the director's desk. They asked the director for private interviews, and soon clandestine correspondence brought the news to family members on the outside who should alert the media.

Meanwhile — and this parenthesis lasted a long time — the punished woman kept screaming and crying, singing, whispering to herself, and her voice became the punishment of everyone in the wing of the prison that led into the same patio as María's cell, while the boy wasted away from colitis. No one knew whether it was caused by the isolation, loneliness, and abandonment, or his mother's milk, rotten from her nerves, unable to withstand the prolonged torture.

"And while we write petitions to the director and demand María's freedom, no one does anything for our comrades on trial…"

Juana's voice indicated her weariness for the first time. Not even she had illusions about the help they could expect in saving their companions. Since the news of their arrest on July 24, the PC-ML activists had become quiet and anti-social. They knew that the promises of freedom and mass solidarity fighting published in the party pamphlets, which got to them more regularly then, were useless. No one could base their confidence on the triumphant declarations of their party about the masses' support of the correct party line. For some time, Juana had limited her meetings to a brief and incomplete exposition of the situation. Everyone felt inhibited and anxious in the presence of Marisa, Raquel, Nieves, and Milagros, whose partners were accused of several fatal attacks, and more with Concepción and María Jesús, who were both to be tried in the same case.

One morning Elisa woke up more tired and confused than usual. María's laments, which now seemed like howls, had given her several nightmares when exhaustion overcame her anxiety and she had fallen asleep. She dreamed she was running from a pack of barking hounds that had the faces of the policemen who had interrogated her, while she held María's baby boy in her arms. He was dead, but suddenly turned into Adalberto, who smiled at her while he told her he was also dead. "Death is stalking us," she murmured as she got up, and she shivered with cold on that hot September 12. After breakfast the newspaper arrived with the "late-breaking" news.

"The Military Tribunal against five FRAP activists for the murder of an armed officer has begun and will continue this morning." The report, unusually long for the brief late-breaking section, abounded with details of the trial, which had been postponed and begun again because of the lawyers' appeals. They were desperately trying to prolong the trial.

"The appeal has been resolved and the legal proceedings have been annulled, the judges' challenge has been determined and the Military Tribunal has been reactivated, all in five hours. They're determined to get to the end and no one's going to stop them."

Octubre spoke slowly while they walked around the patio. The sun set in the premature September evening, and Elisa realized that it was the second autumn she was spending in prison. To the rhythm of their steps, María interminably repeated her disconsolate laments.

"I don't know what we'll be able to do. There's no solidarity. It seems to have run out with the Correo Street bombing. Six of the accused in that trial, out of twenty or twenty-one, have already been released on ridiculous bail. The terrorism charges have even been dropped and now they're under TOP jurisdiction. The rest are here, not knowing when they'll go to court, while your comrades, who were arrested at the beginning of July, are already on trial. You could say the regime still wants to demonstrate its power. It needs to recover from the Correo Street trial, which got out of its control after all that publicity."

"Oh, shut up, Octubre, just shut up, please! I can't take it any more, I won't listen to anything else about the Military Tribunal! It's torture, just torture, to always be talking about the same things and always end up saying the same thing: They're going to kill them, they're going to kill them! It's horrible. Horrible!"

Octubre fell silent. Perhaps Elisa was right and those thoughts were just destructive masochism. The profile of a Civil Guard's three-cornered hat, his cape, his rifle, and the sentry box were silhouetted on the purple horizon. Night was falling and that figure against the pale sky looked like an illustration of a García Lorca poem. Several prisoners claimed that some prostitutes went up to the wall at night to cheer up the soldier's watch. Elisa didn't want to believe it, but she didn't watch from the dormitory windows, either, as her companions invited her to do several times. She was afraid it was true. Now she was more afraid than anyone that Octubre's reasoning was true. What would become of them, especially Concepción and María Jesús, who were on trial at the same time as their comrades? What would happen if they sentenced them all to…

On September 13, twenty-four hours after the Military Tribunal began, three of the accused, Adalberto among them, were sentenced to death. The three compulsory days for putting in appeals against the sentence before the Supreme Council of Military Justice had passed, when a new Military Tribunal began on September 18, for the death of Civil Guard lieutenant Pose. The public prosecutor asked for the maximum punishment for the five defendants, among whom were two women, Concepción and María Jesús, both pregnant. Twenty-four hours later the tribunal condemned all five FRAP activists to death.

On September 19 the very brief Military Tribunal took place against Juan Paredes Manot, alias Txiki, in Barcelona, for his possible implication in the death of First Corporal of the armed police Don Ovidio Díaz López on the preceding sixth of June, during a holdup of a branch of the Bank of Santander in the city. For such acts, the juridical-military public prosecutor requested the death penalty. At the same time, in Burgos, Ángel Otaegui Echeverría, alias Scorch Face, and Jose Antonio Garmendía Artola, alias El Tupa, were on trial for their implication in the murder of First Corporal of the Civil Guard José Posadas Zurrón April 3, 1974 in Azpeitia. Both were activists of the ETA Fifth Assembly, and had been arrested August 27, 1974. El Tupa had been implicated in the Correo Street bombing as well.

"Are they going to kill them all?" Elisa asked Octubre with wide eyes.

Octubre had no response. In a corner of the patio, under the tepid sun of that September 20, Concepción and María Jesús sat on the ground resting. They stayed together most of the time, as though only they could understand each other. Concepción's belly was beginning to get round with the visible signs of that expectancy which had been so much discussed during the trial. Her companion, on the other hand, seemed to have grown thinner in spite of her condition, and the pale color of her face, the deep black circles under her eyes, and her trembling hands didn't forecast a happy end to that pregnancy. Elisa imagined another abortion in the prison, and while she feared for the lives of the sentenced men and women, she imagined a new female death in that uninterrupted reproductive labor, which not even the filthy conditions of the prison stopped.

"In all the jails of the world, women with children get sick, die, live poorly, and add seeing their children suffer and die to the rest of their punishment. And now it's an honor. When my mother was in Ventas, there were mothers who collected as many as six. Yes, Elisa, don't look at me like that, the untold history of our resistant people and especially of women would be good for at least the party activists to know. When they sent a mother to the firing squad — oh yes my friend, they shot a lot of them even pregnant! Just like they do now in Iran or Chile. When they shot one, the other women took charge of her children. One of my mother's friends promised another comrade that when they killed her she would take care of her children, and she rounded up three, two from the friend and one of her own, but then they condemned her, too, and, the last night when she was waiting for execution, isolated in a cell where she couldn't communicate with her companions, she shouted out, asking someone to take care of the children. The rest of the prisoners, shouting, kicking the bars, throwing the chairs, got the jailer to let one of them visit the condemned woman to calm her down and explain that they would all take care of her children. The poor woman went to the wall very comforted. My mother took charge of one of those creatures then, a three-year-old girl, and then she sent her to my grandmother and I, so she would be a little better off, but she died soon after. I don't know what of. Cold and hunger, and all that. You should know that we were living in a basement on Doctor Esquerdo Street, which was two floors underground. The moisture ate through the walls. We never saw the light of day, and we slept and ate all three of us within 20 square meters, and the toilet was in the stairwell. When I started going to school, the doctor told my grandmother that I had to study in the daylight for a few hours because I was losing my sight, and then we both went to Retiro Park, and there, in the winter, dying of cold, I did my homework."

Elisa shivered in the warm September afternoon, while her friend spoke as if she didn't realize the effect her tale was having. There were still more sacrificed victims than the men who were executed during the era of hardest oppression. They were those women whose murder killed two beings, or whose death abandoned their young children to the terrible orphanhood of the prison.

While Octubre and Elisa talked, observing the intimate dialogue between Concepción and María Jesús under the twilight that was wrapping around them, María's moaning went on without rest. Sometimes an exasperated official opened the cell and scolded her, sometimes one took her out to walk around the patio outside of regimented hours, trying to calm her down. But it was useless, because María moaned mechanically, tirelessly. Disheveled, with deep purple circles around her eyes, she was unrecognizable to those who remembered that robust brunette girl who laughed and talked in a loud voice at all hours. With her mouth open, drooling, she emitted a monotonous sound like the crying of a dog. She no longer spoke to anyone, and even the official who brought her food and took her out for walks was startled by María's psychological deterioration.

"What does the director say?"

The prisoner who had spoken with the director sighed wearily. "Nothing, he said nothing. Or next to nothing. He told me I shouldn't get mixed up in it, and María's fine and she's a faker who's fooling everyone. He says she needs a severe punishment because she's always causing trouble, and she's really hardly suffering at all. We, us politicals, are just being too sensitive, imagining María's being tortured when really she's enjoying bothering us."

All the political prisoners at the meeting felt discouraged. It was useless for Juana Parroto, with her usual optimism, to try to incite hope in the others. The shadow of María's skeletal body projected on the patio seemed like a bad omen every afternoon at five o'clock, the hour of her walk. When they brought the boy to be nursed at noon, four, and eight o'clock, his cries combined with his mother's moans, and Elisa thought she had never heard such mournful sounds. In a little while, she thought, the cries of two more babies will be heard in the prison, combined with the cries of the widows of the men condemned to death. She wondered with alarm whether she would be able to bear it, and was afraid she would be defeated more easily than those directly involved.

She never wanted to go into the maternity ward, where several mothers and their children stewed in their own smells, with wet diapers hanging on the backs of chairs, full chamber pots under the beds and bottles of sour milk on the tables. More than once she had wondered whether she wanted to have a child, but she always implicitly left the decision to Arnau. She felt attracted and at the same time frightened by the mysterious process of gestation and birth. She was afraid of physical suffering, but she wanted to know the experience. Now the animal confusion that reigned in the maternity ward of Yeserías repulsed her.

Those children were not like the ones she had known in her family or seen on the street. They looked deformed, most of them skeletal, though a few were abnormally fat, soft as if they had no bones, more like larva than human offspring. María's little boy had been covered in purple pustules that made Elisa retch. She had never wanted to take him in her arms, and if it was normal for her to feel a general difficulty in relating to children, with the children in the prison the difficulty became impossibility. Who could love those little monsters, like the defective beings fed on goat milk in that experimental hospice in Paris, in Daudet's *The Nabob?* No one, no one could love them, not even their mothers. That was why most of them abandoned their babies long hours in the room without paying any attention when they cried, or gave them bottles of tap water with the secret hope that the green diarrhea would save them the many troubles that had engendered them. The memory of those children wasn't far from the hesitant decision she made when Arnau no longer wanted to make it for her.

Some years after Elisa got out of prison, a mother suffocated her son in his cradle in the maternity ward in Yeserías. The prisoner was there for having murdered another child before. When Elisa read the news in the paper, she felt tremendously tired. So much useless suffering. So many beings produced by wombs cursed with fertility, who only knew a few weeks or months of suffering as their entire life experience. Condemned to die before they were born, with no one saving them the inexorable voyage of gestation, birth, and the slow death that would be the end of them.

Adalberto, Bravo, and Sánchez, whose death sentences had just been published in the press, also lived out the inexorable destiny reserved for their children. Their wives had to mourn the loss of husband and child at the same time.

"The Military Tribunal against members of FRAP implicated in the death of an armed officer last July 14 in Madrid ended yesterday at 9:30 a.m. The tribunal, in an uninterrupted private session, has passed a verdict in which they impose the following punishments: death penalty for Adalberto Rodríguez, Manuel Sánchez, Francisco Bravo; thirty years maximum security for [...]. Rodríguez, Sánchez, and Bravo are also sentenced to five months imprisonment for use of a stolen vehicle..."

Elisa thought they were making fun of her when Octubre read that part of the report.

The press also stated that the accused had been interrupted several times when they claimed they were innocent of the charges against them. "They're going to kill them, and they won't even let them speak." Elisa went to the sink to vomit once again.

"Yes, it's not like those times any more... Now they don't kill anyone."

"Well, it's not like that... In Spain we have countless violent deaths for many reasons, but it's better not to get into that. What's important is not to go backwards, not to live off the ruins of the past."

Elisa was surprised by Arnau's impatience. She had to excuse herself, but she wanted to keep talking about that topic she had carried locked in her brain so many years.

"I'm sorry, this conversation brings me back to the past, to those months that were the worst of my life. I'm the first one who wouldn't want to remember them."

That September was always associated with María's moaning, Israel's pustules and diarrhea, the maternity ward of Yeserías, and at the same time, with the faces of those five men who died before she had ever met them. After so many years, why should she remember with so much clarity María's punishment and the anecdotes of the children's lives in the maternity ward, when they had no importance beyond themselves? Perhaps because they were directly connected to life and death and the two extreme circumstances were present every minute of those months in prison. Perhaps because the prisoners' violence unleashed the wave of punishments, laments, of absurd nightmares and María's endless moaning that tortured her days and nights.

María served her sentence, hour by hour, for two months, and the negotiations of the prisoners and the committees that worked in the streets didn't save her a single hour. All sentences were served in the last days of the regime, which was also serving out its destiny, day by day.

"Sorry, it's my fault for talking to you again about the party's problems."

Arnau calmed down. He didn't want to set her against him at the last minute, precisely when it seemed he was about to convince her. His worry about convincing her was transparent.

Elisa gravely shook her head.

"No, that's unfair. It wasn't your fault they executed five men on September 27, 1975."

Chapter 14

"They're moving her! They're moving her!"

Elisa woke suddenly from the daydream into which she had escaped. For some time, she hadn't been paying attention to the book she had sat down in a corner of the study with, nor did she realize who was in the same room with her. She could not have said what she was thinking about, either. Perhaps she saw herself in her town's square, strolling around the old plaza on Arnau's arm, a young and happy Arnau in Sunday dress, who exhibited her with satisfaction, though everyone knew it was she who was bursting with pride. She didn't understand why everyone was crowding into the dining commons around Juana Parroto, who was orating loudly beside a surprised and tearful Marisa.

"They're moving her! We can't allow it! We must stop it! We have to resist with violence if necessary!"

Octubre pulled on Juana's sleeve, and with an unmistakable gesture, she pointed to the rest of the prisoners, who were trying to escape the dining area.

"If you give that order, no one will follow you. Let's see what they're taking her out for…"

"Who? Who's going where?"

Octubre stopped the downpour of reproaches Juana was getting ready to pile onto Elisa for her ignorance and quickly replied, "Marisa, to the State Security Headquarters."

"Why?"

"That's exactly what we have to find out. That's what I was saying to Juana…"

Marisa looked like a frightened deer. She cringed so much that her middle had contracted. In spite of the months that had passed, she hadn't recovered from the weakness caused by the abortion, and her fear made her tremble as if she had a fever.

Back to the State Security Headquarters. Elisa shivered, too. The feared move, the worst of all threats. Only Juana Parroto still had a voice to keep making loud speeches. The rest of the women, being members of her own party, could not say a word. It was obvious to all of them how useless it was to disobey such an order. The prisoners could not even try to organize a violent protest. Marisa was a physical manifestation of fatality, and in a few minutes she was bodily carried off by two officials to the sentry box of the guard corps, to be placed in the car that awaited her in the parking lot. Elisa kept looking at the bars of the entrance gate which had closed behind her while the red September twilight fell over the prison and María's laments created a mournful musical background, like they did every afternoon.

Three days later, Elisa could not take her eyes from the wounds that festered on Marisa's shoulders and feet, black, purple, yellow, swollen until they lost their identity, those hands which had been strong, with black nails and blood clots in the quick. She hated herself for her oversensitivity and blushed with shame under Juana's disapproving look.

"And you were the one who would've killed if your party ordered you to?" Carles looked at her in commiseration.

Elisa repeated, "I couldn't stand it, you don't understand, you don't understand… No one who wasn't there, who didn't see her and touch her and talk to her, can ever understand. And she didn't identify him, you see? She didn't identify him… She was there in front of him and he looked at her and didn't make any sign of recognition, and she denied it over and over…"

Adalberto's eyes were smaller, hardly visible in the masses of swollen violet flesh that were his cheeks. Marisa might have truly believed that she didn't know him, that she had never seen him before, if it hadn't been for those large, coarse hands and for the shape of that body she knew so well. Now she needed to touch and kiss and smell that body, and heal its wounds with her caresses, with her kisses, with her whole body as a cover that screamed out its right to hold him, to lay down next to him, to sleep at his side for endless hours while rest and love did their healing work. The effort of looking at him without moving filled her eyes with tears, and she thought she could also see tears in the purple slits his eyes had become.

And while she felt her blood stream become paralyzed, and first her arms and then her hands froze, and her legs became stiff and useless, those beings with masculine appearance moved around the two of them, rolling up the sleeves of their sweat-soaked shirts, with greasy hairs stuck to their skulls or their necks, with sunken or pop-eyes, with twisted mouths and noses, shouting furiously.

"Identify him. Identify him! This is your man, your pimp, whore! You slept with him, you rolled around like pigs in the same sty! Look at him, how handsome we've made him! Look what a pretty little mouth for kissing! Go on, slut, get closer! Give him a kiss now that you have him close! What? Does it make you sick to see him like this? Have you given him up for dead? Don't you want anything to do with him? Go on, tell him you're going to look for another as soon as he's fried! Tell him! Tell him something, you sickening pig, you piece of shit! Hug him, go on!"

The push threw Marisa against the man, who remained rigid, motionless, his emotions hidden behind the beaten skin on his face. Marisa pushed herself up lightly on his torso, where his shirt stuck to his skin in a mess of moisture and blood, and she smelled the man's sweat and fear. For an instant her mind recovered the salty taste of that skin, and her cheeks and hands reconstructed the touch of that rough, hair-covered chest she loved so much.

She stood up and shook her head again.

"I don't recognize him. I've never seen him before. I don't know who he is."

One of the police officers sat down at the table with the typewriter and rubbed his head.

"It's useless, I tell you, useless. This kind of whore doesn't give in, I tell you. There's nothing to be done with a communist. You can always tell which ones they are. Even if you pull out all their hair they don't recognize even the most obvious evidence. Leave her alone, I'm fed up. Besides, who cares whether she identifies him or not? He's been sentenced. Her ID wouldn't add anything."

A tall, blond, blue-eyed, elegant officer who was famous among the politicals punched Marisa in the jaw and she fell to the floor.

"God damn this pig! She's been wasting our time for three days. I don't feel like letting her out of this so easily. I have to know she's mixed up with him, damn it! We all know they've been sleeping together for five years, pieces of shit! And together they've been making Molotov cocktails and shooting at Civil Guards. And she's going to tell me, she is!"

"You didn't identify him? Ever?"

Elisa looked wide-eyed at Marisa. She was so pale Octubre was afraid she would faint. With her swollen lips, Marisa attempted a smile that made her moan, and repeatedly shook her head. Her pride was evident in the groaning sound that was her voice when she said, "No, I never identified him, and neither did he. They couldn't get me to say I knew him."

"But it didn't mean anything to him. You couldn't hurt him. Only you could have gotten mixed up..." She stopped talking, in order to avoid the fatal words.

Juana Parroto interrupted the emotional silence.

"It's not a question of what could hurt him or not. An activist does not weaken in front of the police. Marisa has done her duty and so has Adalberto. Congratulations to you both. The party congratulates you and the people will always remember. Our enemies have had another lesson about the way revolutionaries behave."

To see him there, to look at him and pretend she didn't feel any emotion. To force her pupils to stay indifferent, force her hands down so that they would not frantically reach for him, immobilize all her limbs that must have jumped when she saw him, overcome the reactions of her stomach, her liver, her heart, which would beat and secrete bile and acids until they dissolved themselves, while her vocal chords would scream until they wore themselves out: "It's him, and I love him, I love him, I love him!" without her being able to avoid it. Elisa wept uncontrollably, sitting on the floor in a corner of the patio, hiding her head between her knees, tightly pressed by her hands. She hiccuped and her nose ran and she moaned without taking care that anyone should hear, though she was alone and night was beginning to fall, and the outline of the sentry-box guard's patent leather was the only thing that stood out against the crimson sky.

"It couldn't happen now…"

"Now there's torture every day, Elisa." Arnau spoke with the hard tone he used when he was very angry. "I don't know if I have to remind you of Arregui, the guys from Almería, Agustín Rueda, and three months ago, Zabalza. They've hit Cherta more than once… Amnesty International has published in its annual report that in Spain, torture is still being practiced at police stations."

"But they don't execute…"

"Oh, no? Then Arregui, Rueda, the boys from Almería, and Zabalza, what are they, asleep?"

The sharp irony wounded Elisa, who could do nothing more than lower her head. She knew Arnau understood what she meant but he would not recognize it, and his examples were irrefutable. They could not continue the discussion down these paths.

Silence swooped upon them while Arnau nervously walked the length of the dining room. Adalberto's unknown face filled Elisa's imagination. She saw him with the square chin and dark beard and luminous dark eyes and a mustache with fallen ends like Pancho Villa, as Marisa had described him when she was arrested, and in his look was written the unbreakable resolve never to give up. Not even in the presence of love.

"She never saw him again. The farewell before an eternity they didn't believe in was that last contact, when the policeman pushed her against him and she smelled his sweat and blood a few seconds, before saying that she didn't know him…"

Octubre wept soundlessly as she listened to the story her friend told about the grave events that followed her release from prison, without squinting her eyes or sniffling. The tears simply slid down her cheeks and nose and neck in an uncontained stream without her doing anything to dry them. Elisa had already cried all she could, and she felt exhausted. She could not cry any more, or speak, or keep repeating the words that explained that infernal September of 1975 to Octubre, now that it was all over, buried in silence and oblivion within a few weeks.

"We won't forget, no, we won't forget. We'll always remember our martyrs, they did it for the causes of freedom and democracy. Don't you forget, either."

Why did those words, spoken in a strange, quiet tone, sound like a threat, while Arnau stared at her especially hard?

"I never doubted it, really," she stammered, not knowing exactly what he wanted her to say. "That's why I was a member of that party during those times."

"And today, too, we're fighting for democracy and freedom... for the people, not for their exploiters and hangmen. It's in the name of the people that I ask for your help, if they still matter to you at all."

"True friends of the people...
You fell in the fatal struggle!"

The voices were serious and sustained. Not even their being off-key detracted from the ceremony. The women wore dark expressions, looks of hatred. Some closed their eyes, most squeezed their fists. They sang unhurriedly, each standing behind her chair in the ramshackle eating area. The funeral march rose in volume during the most tragic moments, slowed down at the arpeggios, deepened at the ends of the lines. Tears slid down many faces. No official dared to go into the dining area, and no one was in the patio toward which its windows faced. Beyond it, sheltered behind the large doors of the infirmary hallway, which faced the police officers' department, several dozens of the common prisoners crowded together in silence. They looked with respect and wonder at the dignity of those thirty women, who had filled the prison with fear by singing a song no one knew, off-key.

Sentences carried out. Three condemned prisoners were executed in Madrid, one in Barcelona, and one in Burgos. According to a report by the General Captaincy of the First Region, at 10:15 yesterday morning, the death sentence given to three FRAP militants was carried out. The execution took place in Hoyo de Manzanares, at the firing range of Matalagraja, and was overseen by the armed police force and Civil Guard.

The police forces had begun to arrive at Carabanchel Prison at about 5:30 a.m. Minutes later, three trucks with horses arrived and the riders entered the prison. At 7:00, Bravo's defense lawyer arrived with the condemned man's father and brother, who left in another car with Bravo's wife soon after. Bravo's wife was sent back to Yeserías Prison. Finally, at 7:20, Bravo's mother, brother and sister left the prison, and a dramatic scene developed at the door.

At about eight o'clock in the morning, the retinue composed of fourteen Jeeps of the armed police and several of the Civil Guard's cars left the prison. A caravan with the condemned traveled a trajectory safely escorted by the Civil Guard for its entire length until its arrival in Hoyo de Manzanares. At the end of a five km gravel road, the place of the execution had been marked.

There, Rodríguez and Sánchez were executed facing forward by a squad of the armed police; another squad of the Civil Guard carried out Bravo's sentence. The squads were made up of ten men with a sergeant and an official.

The bodies were buried in the cemetery at Hoyo de Manzanares, where it seems they will remain, though Rodríguez's father has expressed a desire to move the body to Vigo, and Bravo's corpse will definitely be cremated in Murcia. Sánchez had no parents or siblings and no one has claimed the body.

Juan Paredes Manot, alias Txiki, was executed by firing squad at 8:30 in Sardañola. After having waited for the execution all night accompanied by his brother Miguel, who stated that their mother, who was in Zaragoza, didn't want to travel at that

time, as she wanted to remember her son as she saw
him on the day of the Military Tribunal.

Burgos, 27 (summary). The press office of the
General Captaincy of the Sixth Military Region
provides the following notice:

All requirements ordered by law carried out.
Today the sentence of capital punishment imposed on
the terrorist Ángel Otaegui Echeverría, alias
Scorchface, accomplice to the murder of the first
corporal of the Civil Guard don José Posadas Zurrón
on April 3, 1974 in Azpeitia, has been carried out.
The condemned prisoner has been executed by firing
squad, in accordance with military legislation, and
was accompanied by his immediate family.

Marisa wasn't among Adalberto's immediate family. Marisa had
said goodbye to her partner two weeks before at the State Security
Headquarters with a single embrace of the blood-soaked body of that
man who was being buried in Hoyo de Manzanares that morning.

Sánchez had no parents or siblings: the last night of his life began
the total solitude that would accompany him into eternity. No one
claimed her right to console him as girlfriend, companion, or wife,
either. Only those thirty women who repeated the chorus of the hymn
of solidarity in the dining commons of Yeserías Prison remembered
him.

"True friends of the people…
you lived in frozen prisons…
You fell in the fatal struggle!"

Elisa moaned softly, falteringly, as she stammered the lines of the
funeral march. She could not look at Marisa: she stared at Octubre's
empty chair. Octubre had been released a few days before. Without her,
and with Marisa's terrible ghostly presence, Elisa felt truly alone for the
first time in two years.

Five minutes of silence followed the end of the funeral hymn. Five
eternal minutes, like the eternity that had already welcomed the five
men. Juana kept her gaze fixed forward, her mouth contracted and her

cheeks tense. *She looks beautiful,* thought Elisa, as beautiful as the struggle for justice and liberty for which those men, now martyrs of the people, had fallen. Juana thundered an epitaph, and at the end, she began to sob convulsively.

With wide eyes, Elisa watched the catharsis of the woman who had been up to that moment Juana Parroto, and who now moaned, screamed, and hiccuped while from her mouth there came an incoherent speech no one understood, until they heard her stammer the name of Jesús Sánchez and the unexpected declaration: "He was my lover, my companion," which astonished all the prisoners.

Juana wept for the first time over her murdered love, the love she had kept hidden for the two years she had been in prison. That love she had never let anyone suspect, from whom she never received a letter, message or package. That love more clandestine than her communist activity, more unknown than her private life. That love for the man who had fallen machine-gunned that morning in the Burgos countryside, without having pronounced a word about his companion, who had been interned since two years before in the Madrid Provisional Women's Prison, at Juan de Mena Street, number 10, commonly known as Yeserías.

They looked at her in amazement, Marisa Cuéllar, who in the same prison had lost Adalberto Rodríguez Linares's child, and Concepción López, who carried José Bravo's child in her womb. The three men had fallen dead in the same minute of the same day, and they left their women widowed, locked up in the prison, but only Juana Parroto had so effectively hidden her relationship with Jesús Sánchez that no one, not even those of her comrades who belonged to the party leadership, had known the emotional ties that bound her to him. That man who had died alone, with no friendly presence in the cell where he waited, with no family member at the prison door, and who left his love locked up in Yeserías in her own silence, without a note to say goodbye to her before that eternity in which neither of them believed.

Juana had lived through two years of prison in silence, in the unshared secret of that love that maintained itself with the very strength of its feeling, because no letter and no news arrived to nourish it. She lived through three months since they arrested her love and everyone knew they were condemned, seeing Marisa and Concepción and María Jesús suffer, and generously offering the consolation all the prisoners gave them, without receiving any herself. On the contrary, Elisa knew all her companions avoided Juana's company because she wore everyone out. For the first time, Elisa wondered whether the constant and tedious arguments about revolutionary ethics, party discipline, courage for the struggle and other repetitive topics she overwhelmed her comrades with, were not directed at herself. Whether they were a constant self-therapy with which Juana maintained that iron integrity that had sustained her during that long and lonely imprisonment and which only at that moment had collapsed.

"But why? How could it have hurt Jesús if his relationship with Juana was known? It probably wouldn't have hurt her, either, since when they began the terrorism she'd already been in prison a long time. Why did she have to hide it and torture herself like that?"

Elisa looked at Carles and furrowed her brow. She made a great effort to find the answer he was asking for and which she also needed.

"It's a question of principles. It didn't matter whether it hurt them or not, or even the party. They had made a commitment not to tell anyone about their relationship and they kept it. A question of revolutionary ethics, can you understand that?"

Carles looked at her a few moments and the two understood each other. They had been educated to obey principles no one had asked their opinions about and which, reaching adulthood, they saw were irrational. How to understand that the people who defended ideas as disparate as those which formed her spiritual nourishment for years were capable of showing more courage and integrity than they were?

"Do you believe one of us would've been capable of acting like that, even when we were good believers?" Elisa formed the question Carles was about to ask, and they looked at each other, perplexed.

"All revolutionary activity requires ethics. Anyone who doesn't feel how necessary it is, who makes opportunism the ideology of his life, out of comfort and corruption, has nothing to do for the future, has no place among us, you see?"

Arnau was speaking with the barely controlled emotion of those painful times in which they both shared the suffering for the arrest of the comrades, for the tortured people, for the hungry and exploited of the entire world, when they lived in the ramshackle apartment in the Vallecas neighborhood of Madrid.

Elisa folded the newspaper and was surprised to see that Arnau was crying. With some low, repressed sobs, and some tiny tears that didn't dare roll down, ashamed of their weakness. He looked at her and excused himself for his momentary lack of spirit with a smile. He pointed to the newspaper and added, "Daniel has fallen." And he explained, for Elisa's lack of comprehension, "That was his code name. Look, there he is, Juan Menéndez Ortega. I found out his real name when I got to the secretariat of the organization. He was the one who brought me into the party and was responsible for my cell for several years. An excellent man. His body never seemed to need to eat or sleep or rest. He'd been in the Civil War at fifteen, and then he lived through all the wanderings of the resistance. First Argelès, and then a guerrilla in the Pyrenees. Luckily he didn't fall into the hands of the Nazis. But in the end, the Civil Guard located him and shot him, and he still survived wounded in the mountains, hiding in a cave during the day and going down at night to the river where he washed his legs, which were completely raw from the shrapnel. He ate roots he dug up with his own hands. When weakness overcame him, some peasants found him, picked him up and turned him in to the Civil Guard."

Elisa suppressed a cry of distress, and Arnau agreed.

"You know that what matters isn't belonging to a class, but having consciousness of it. The poorest are often the most reactionary."

Elisa nodded gravely. She was so overcome she could not speak. Of course she would help them. She was still faithful to some of the principles required by revolutionary ethics.

Arnau understood, and in a sudden outburst of joy, he came close and kissed her cheeks, but she didn't receive the pleasure she had been expecting all morning. She shivered, and he asked her affectionately, holding her arm, "Are you cold? Do you feel sick?"

Yes, she was sick. Sick with pain, weariness, hopelessness. She could not ask for help, because Juana needed it all. She was the one the others were attending to with great care and who they now carried to bed between three of them, while she cried and screamed spasmodically. They had to give her a tranquilizer injection, and there was no more singing in the dining area, where a few prisoners were eating silently. Elisa didn't have Octubre at her side, since she had abandoned them one day after Marisa's transfer to the State Security Headquarters, after which the final chapter of the nightmare would begin with the new arrival of Concepción and María Jesús, pregnant and tortured. They were so bad that the prison director would not admit them, the doctor himself said he would make a report against the police, and when they came back from the hospital, hardly a week after going in, the infamous Military Tribunal had already started, and in a few days that seemed only minutes, everything was over. And now Elisa felt more victimized than anyone, stuck there for two years, powerless and alone, while silence and death took control of the prison.

It's our destiny, she thought, suddenly frightened by the idea. "We're all dead, all of us who've fought to change the world are dead. We live in a world of shadows in which the body can't understand that it no longer exists. We're simply a pious memory for the scholars in the libraries."

"That's not true, you know it's not true. The executions caused the most serious crisis the regime had suffered up to then. Even more serious than the time of the Military Tribunal in Burgos in 1970. Remember, a lot of countries cut off relations with the regime. Olaf Palme walked through the streets of Stockholm begging for money with a box hanging around his neck, for the Spanish antifascists…"

On September 28, the Spanish papers could not hide the reactions from all over Europe to the executions of the previous day. *ABC* had to dedicate several pages just to report summarily on the incidents. The report from two days before had had a large headline: "CLEMENCY AND JUSTICE." It could not be forgotten that six of the eleven sentenced to death had been pardoned, among them the two pregnant women, the Basque crippled by head wounds he received in the shooting skirmish with the Civil Guard when he was arrested, and the reporter.

LIDIA FALCÓN

Thousands of people demonstrated against Spain in Paris. They destroyed several sites and wounded eleven policemen around the embassy. There were also protests in Marseilles, Bayonne, Hendaye, Rouen, Bordeaux, Nantes, Strasbourg, Grenoble, Rennes, Limoges, Clermont Ferrand, Toulouse, Narbonne, Pau, Lyons, Carcassone, Tours, Dijon, Le Havre, Nimes, Nice, Quinper, Lille, Troyec, Saint Jean de Luz, Nevers [...]

At the Spanish Consulate in London this morning, several threats were received upon the notice of the execution of the five condemned men. Yesterday Ambassador Manuel Fraga Iribarne received a delegation of the Trade Unions, who went to see him to give him a letter of protest. Before that, 250 people had protested at the door of the embassy.

In several cities in the Federal Republic of Germany last night, anti-Spanish demonstrations occurred.

Thousands of demonstrations in Sweden. Several thousand people demonstrated today in the center of the capital carrying red flags and banners with aggressive messages against Spain. The demonstration had been organized by a communist group who called themselves "Action Committee," formed the previous night.

Havoc in the Spanish Embassy in Copenhagen. Some 300 people congregated today before the Spanish Embassy in the capital. The building's windows were broken with stones amid shouting against Spain. Later the protesters directed themselves at the ambassador's residence, where they also caused damage to the windows.

The ambassadors of the Federal Republic of Germany, Denmark, Holland, Britain, and Norway, were called back by their governments.

Destructive entrance of protesters into the Spanish Embassy in Lisbon. Countless works of art, signature antique furniture, seventeenth-century tapestries, important paintings, which form part of our history and part of the world's spiritual heritage, burned easily because of a lack of protection, which is what characterized the event. The flames were visible from very far away. The incendiary assailants had hours of freedom to proceed at will. Finally, when the military forces arrived, they were dispersed with machine gun fire in the air. But the catastrophe has been committed... The very beautiful seat of our embassy in Lisbon was assaulted yesterday morning, burned, and practically destroyed by the communist hordes, with the passiveness and indifference of the authorities and public forces of the new Portuguese government.

The relations between Spain and the EEC will suffer a serious setback, a high official of the European Commission declared today in Brussels. Numerous acts of protest throughout the Benelux territory must be pointed out, with particular violence in Brussels, where harsh encounters took place last night between the police and young Spanish emigrants. In Holland and Luxembourg, the protests in the street and attacks on official and private centers have been reproduced, though with less violence than in Belgium, where the liberal press has harshly criticized the intervention of the police against the Spaniards, calling them "brutal and inappropriate."

"It doesn't matter, Arnau, it doesn't matter. The dictatorship only ended with the dictator, and we, all of us, including our party, which declared the people's revolutionary war, were unable to finish him, or even speed up his end. You just told me yourself that communism in Spain is condemned to marginalization. You see! So many dead, so much suffering, so many hopes, in the gutter, like so much sewage. No one wants to talk about that struggle or those hopes nowadays. A few homages, timid and ashamed like the one in Valencia, where they've prohibited the republican flag, this year that's the fiftieth anniversary of the Civil War, and, in a few months, nothing. That's what the demonstrations of support and the destruction of the Spanish Embassy in Lisbon were good for: so that today everyone wants to forget and move on."

In the solitude of the dining commons, which everyone had abandoned in order to close themselves up in the dormitories, Elisa shivered with cold again. Silence and death took control of the prison.

She remembered some lines Octubre had written a few days before being released. She tried to remember them exactly, and she repeated them in a whisper:

"We will be exemplary trunks
of a centenary forest,
memory and vanity
of a trembling people,
beings and legend as one.
We will have smiles for our dried up voices,
for our eyes that can hardly see,
for the memories that jab our wounds,
for the included mercies…"

Elisa pointed out the depressing tone of the poem, and Octubre was surprised by her interpretation.

"Well, I was trying to write a kind of elegy to our heroes. I don't know why you say it's demoralizing."

Elisa didn't want to insist, but seeing Octubre so honestly worried about the meaning of her poem, which had eluded her until then, she carefully reread the lines.

"You see, all that about 'beings and legend as one,' and 'our dried up voices,' not to mention the terrible finale: 'And will we be body and soul/ and mind and life/ in vague displays of grandeur,/ and foolish honors of heroism?'"

Octubre reread the words Elisa's finger pointed to, and shook her head in doubt.

"Maybe you're right… It's actually not finished yet. I wanted to compare the heroism of some with the opportunism of others. I was going to end with something like this: 'which they award to notorious thugs'…" She began to laugh at Elisa's disturbed look. "I haven't quite got it, I see. I'll try to make it better."

But she didn't finish, because her orders for release arrived before she could, and at the moment they said goodbye, both of them drowning in tears, Elisa reminded her of her disappointment with the poem and Octubre insisted she would compose an epic ode to all the martyrs of the Spanish revolution.

Sitting in her corner of the patio, while the evening fell prematurely on that September 29, Elisa told herself that it wasn't necessary to compose odes to the martyrs anymore because no one wanted to hear them. Those five dead men who brought the summer of 1975 to an end would be as quickly forgotten as they were buried. And, for the first time, she was sure that none of them would be remembered, either. *Probably not even we want to remember this time. Those of us who survive will frantically try to escape from this past.*

While she watched Arnau gesticulate without hearing his words, she told herself that she had never been so right as she had been on that horrible afternoon of September 27, 1975, sitting on the cement floor of the patio of the politicals of Yeserías, while Juana Parroto shouted out the hidden love that had so tortured her during her two years of prison, and the other comrades tried to calm her down and put her in her bed, and Octubre's cursed verses repeated themselves over and over in her memory:

> "And will we be body and soul
> and mind and life
> in vague displays of grandeur
> and foolish honors of heroism?"

"I must thank you in the names of our heroes and martyrs..."

And that time the so often-repeated formula didn't sound like hollow pomposity. In her ears the rhythm of the funeral march still echoed:

> "True friends of the people...
> You fell in the fatal struggle!"

Chapter 15

Octubre carefully observed the sidewalk in front of her, where chairs and tables were lined up on the café terrace and the first customers were beginning to arrive. The sun wasn't very warm yet, in spite of its being midday, in that severe Parisian climate at the beginning of September. Her appointment didn't seem to be there yet, but she didn't think the security measures would require her to wait standing on the sidewalk. Paris wasn't Spain. She crossed the street and sat at a table. It was pleasant to savor a pastry on the terrace of a Parisian boulevard while the companions she had left only one week before, would be in formation beside the prison's dining room tables to be counted by the guard officials. The memory of them, and especially of Elisa, pinched her heart. She was there for their sake, she told herself, and then she realized that it wasn't only for the women. It was for all of them: for Adalberto, Jesús, José, Begoña, Txiki, Otaegui, and for the struggle, why not? And she shook her head to sign and seal her thought.

They made the appointment with her the night before and left her alone in the apartment, and she had spent the morning wandering the boulevards, enjoying the weather and the spectacle of so many different people busy and free in the streets of Paris. She had had breakfast in a *tabac* and started her diary in a small notebook she felt confident about hiding deep in the lining of her purse. *If I were in the party, they'd sanction me for recklessness*, she thought, and smiled, happy about not having to obey any orders. She felt really good after having rested. She had left from Barcelona in the car of those two friendly girls in the afternoon two days before, and they crossed the border without problems, even though Octubre used her legal passport because, with the rush, they hadn't been able to supply her another one. But at the frontier at La Junquera during the summer they didn't watch anything closely, as she assured the worried kid who looked at her in terror when she explained the problem, and so it was. They found themselves having dinner in Perpignan as if they were three carefree tourists, and at ten that night they took the train for Paris. She wasn't comfortable in the berth, and all night long she dreamed of oppression and prisons to the rhythm of the unstoppable rattling of the train. Fortunately the day went quite well, despite the nuisance of the afternoon meeting in the apartment where she was staying, to report to her contact about the news from prison, and at night that magnificent bed had been her delight.

"May I sit with you?"

The man looked at her with hard, cold, but alert eyes, and waited for her gesture of agreement. To Octubre, the gimmick seemed naive at first, but she realized that all the tables had in fact been occupied while she was writing in her diary.

"Are you all right? Have you rested? Do you need anything?"

He was accustomed to speaking with French formality. Later, when he was used to Castilian, he switched to an informal manner. He was slim, but not skinny, and had a pleasant face despite the hardness Octubre noted under every feature, the same material every bone and muscle in his body was made of. He explained that Octubre's meeting would be in the afternoon after eating — the Gallicisms were inevitable, Octubre thought; how long must he have been there? — and that he would keep her company until that time.

Octubre was sure they were treating her with so much care and respect because she wasn't a member of the party. *If I were, they'd drag me off by the hair, they wouldn't even say hello.* But she felt optimistic about the stupendous gift of freedom and that trip that seemed like a vacation, despite the mission she was responsible for.

It was a mission that she had assigned herself, and which, to her surprise, had been immediately taken up by the contact. But at her official interview, when she was sitting across from that small, hard-as-nails woman, who looked at her smiling, with beautiful frozen blue eyes, she understood that only a mistake could have gotten her the appointment.

"Are you set up alright? In a few days we'll try to find you a permanent place, though it might not be as nice."

"Permanent? I'm leaving the day after tomorrow."

The two women looked at each other in confusion. Finally, Lina asked, "But, haven't you come to stay?"

Octubre shook her head. She was going back to Spain right away, the struggle was there, as everyone knew. She had only asked for an appointment to bring her a message from her companions and Lina's comrades, who were in prison, and also explain her own opinion concerning the struggle. She didn't understand the mistake.

"They told me you needed to go into exile, that you had a harsh sentence coming up and that you wanted to join FRAP in Paris…"

Her initial politeness was gone, and Octubre noticed a tension in the muscles of her face and limbs that indicated impatience. *She thinks I'm wasting her time,* Octubre told herself, and she was upset about the result of the interview.

"FRAP? Álvarez del Vayo died a few months ago, didn't he?" she asked stupidly, to gain time.

Lina nodded, and added ironically, "Yes, here we are without a president. Perhaps you'll want to apply."

Octubre laughed as if it were an inside joke, but she had the feeling that it was a serious offer.

"I asked for this interview to report what's happening in Spain and ask you to stop engaging in terrorism…"

The woman's hostile look immediately indicated to Octubre the measure of her failure. It was useless to look for the most persuasive words that would give the story the touch of truth it needed. The passion Octubre put into them fell apart on their way from her mouth to her listener's ears, who listened in silence and apparently in no hurry. Sitting in a spot in the dark away from the halo of light from the lamp on the table, Octubre's first contact in France listened motionless and silent, but Octubre perceived in his whole body the same censure that showed clearly through his boss's attitude.

The repression had worsened in a brutal way as a result of the latest attacks. The incessant arrests intensified at the beginning of March when a FRAP group was broken up in Toledo. The unusualness of installing FRAP in a city so small and removed from subversive activity was a surprise to the public and to the prisoners themselves. That March was so full of overt action that even newspapers like *ABC* and *Ya* had to publish some of the attacks and demonstrations. On March fifth a device exploded next to the monument to the fallen in Madrid. The photo showed the damage to the monument and to some nearby buildings, and the women who gathered around Juana Parroto, who triumphantly held out the *ABC*, felt encouraged by their comrades' activity. On March eleventh a Molotov cocktail was thrown at the rector of La Laguna's car, and two days later another device exploded at the university of the same town. No newspaper attributed it to any specific organization, but all the FRAP and PC-ML activists, who were one and the same, believed they had moral authority to confirm that it was their organizations which had done them. This granted them an indubitable prestige among the rest of the prisoners — though it bothered them at the same time — because of their ability to organize a terrorist group in a city as isolated from the peninsula and its problems as La Laguna.

The postponement of a sentencing that should have taken place at the Tribunal of Public Order was attributed to these activities. Their comrades Jesús and Jorge Díaz Gómez, José Luis Fernández, Enrique Aguilar Benítez and his wife Virginia Fernández Paragón were accused of participating in the attack on the police in the demonstration of May first, 1973, in Madrid, where one policeman was knifed to death and eleven were injured. They had already been in prison two years awaiting sentencing, which made Elisa suspect that the postponement wasn't exactly beneficial to them. But when Octubre expressed the same doubt, Juana Parroto so aggressively affirmed that it would be precisely the people's struggle that would get FRAP and their party's activists out of prison and precisely not the fascist tribunal members, that they all changed the subject right away.

But in spite of March, April and most of all May having been especially active months for terrorist attacks, with Molotov cocktails hurled into all kinds of establishments, and even the burning of a hotel in Mallorca on behalf of FRAP, as well as the constant activity of ETA, the repression had never before come down with the violence of that terrible August. It was aimed against activists, sympathizers, workers' assemblies, the press, priests, neighbors' meetings, and simple citizens who had shown their solidarity at some time with the antifascist movement. Dozens of activists fled Madrid to the provinces, especially Barcelona, asking for shelter from friends and sympathizers against the relentless persecution the police had unleashed since the latest deaths caused by FRAP activists.

The rage of the forces of public order, especially the Socio-Political Brigade, centered on FRAP, because there was more news about that kind of terrorist attack which ETA had become master of, and new problems came to be added to the familiar ones. Especially after one of the prisoners escaped Yeserías on April 12. She was accused of perpetrating, with help, the knifing death of a police officer during the May first, 1973, demonstration. One morning in spring she disappeared from the prison.

"Bam, just like that. She evaporated. Mari Carmen didn't say goodbye to anyone and no one knows how she got out, but it was wonderful. No one realized, not the officials, nobody, until lunchtime. I myself was one of the ones who called her to lunch thinking she must be asleep in her dormitory…"

Anxiety began to extend throughout her party comrades when, at one in the afternoon, Mari Carmen didn't present herself to be counted, although a PCE member prisoner said she thought she was talking in the visitation room, and the very young official believed her. But half an hour later, there was no one at her plate of grub, and Juana Parroto muttered something about undisciplined members, though Mari Carmen was practically untouchable because of her status as party heroine. Elisa simply wanted no complications, and they began to worry about finding her before sanctions fell.

"And we even had the interior patio floor that led into the dining hall all torn up then, up to the dormitory windows, and all the raw sewage was piling up there for days, making us sick with the smell. And, well, it turned out that the easiest way to call her was to open the window, stick our heads out and shout towards the dormitory windows, which were above, but no one wanted to do it because the stench was unbearable. Then I go, I open the window and stick my head out to yell at her... But, what do you expect!" And Octubre could not hold back her laughter, which was sincerely echoed now by Lina. "She'd already gone, truly, just as if she'd disappeared."

The search for Mari Carmen ended with shouting and shoving by the officials, and later lockups, first in the dormitories and then in the eating area, interrogations in the director's office of the prisoners who had seen her last, and the suspension of all visits and packages, and much more that they were all willing to bear. It didn't diminish one bit the happiness, enthusiasm, and rejoicing that seized all the prisoners, even the common ones, who spent the entire afternoon singing and dancing. Each time one of the officials or the director showed discomfort or displeasure, an explosion of contentment among the prisoners inevitably followed, "As you can imagine." And Lina understood, and shared her happiness.

But precisely because of the success of Mari Carmen's escape, because of the increase in violent attacks by FRAP, almost supplanting ETA in momentary fame, the police had come unleashed. Carrillo had aroused interest with his presentation of the Democratic Junta in Paris on April 13th of that year, formed by Calvo Serer, José Vidal Beneyto and Carrillo himself, as the only majority opposition to Franco, but no one paid attention to his efforts any longer. Socialists, Christians, and diverse progressive groups immediately formed the Democratic Platform, and the whole world was already fed up with the news of one or the other, and the fusion of the two, which was called the Platajunta, although neither seemed to have any future. FRAP's armed offensive and ETA's continued terrorism were highlighted on the front pages of all the papers, on the television news, and the radio, with the same fury the Carrero Blanco and Correo Street bombings had been publicized with. That was why, the previous April 26, a State of Emergency had been decreed again in Guipúzcoa and Vizcaya. Arias Navarro's speech on February 12 had such a special charisma that, ever after, any similar speech was called "the spirit of February 12," and it had seemed to espouse the politics of peace and reconciliation, but it had only caused mass arrests in Madrid. In the Political Science department alone they dragged away several dozens of young men accused of belonging to FRAP, LCR and ETA Sixth Assembly. On May first, police fire killed a man in Vigo, and dozens were arrested all over Spain, with sporadic demonstrations and a standstill until further notice in the Economics Department in Málaga, where, in spite of the fall of Antonio Cherta and of Violeta and their comrades, it was obvious that that party wasn't as completely broken up as the newspapers reported. They had no other option than to publish the events that followed that agitated May first, with seventy people arrested in Madrid, assemblies and demonstrations in Barcelona, people wounded in Santa Coloma de Gramanet, fifteen FRAP activists in Madrid who threw four Molotov cocktails inside a Triumph automobile dealership, shootings in the streets of Bilbao, four dead in Guernica, and the Guipúzcoa police searching for the ETA Fifth Assembly commando Wilson, who had fallen in Barcelona in July. Tensions in Spain was at a dangerous point…

"Thank you for your report, Rosario, but our archives work quite well, and we've known these and other facts since the moment they happened. I don't know what you're trying to tell me…"

Octubre's train of thought suddenly derailed. Of course, it made sense that the party leaders would know the facts she had compiled in her report, based solely on the scarce press releases and the news from other prisons, but she wasn't trying to give Elena Odena, Secretary General of the PC-ML, exhaustive facts about the struggle in Spain, and much less the activities of her own party. Octubre was trying to use those and other events, the most recent ones, precisely the most important ones, in order to explain why the repression was dangerously sifting through the antifascist resistance in Spain.

"We won't be able to go on like this. They're arresting hundreds of people from all the organizations. They've destroyed entire work sectors, as many unionized as neighborhood organizations, and associations it took years to put together. They've even crushed outside support. In Madrid or Barcelona it's impossible to find a friend who'll hide someone in their home, not even for one night. Especially since

Wilson's arrest. He's informed against everyone who ever helped him, from Huertas Clavería, the journalist who talked to him for five minutes, to the priest of the parish who took care of him, to the nuns who hid him in their convent, and the doctor who treated him…"

"And what do you want us to do?"

Lina left no room for doubt, but Octubre knew she had to carry out the mission she had assigned herself to the end.

"The attacks must be stopped. It's impossible to continue with terrorism—"

"Armed struggle: don't get confused, my friend."

"What?"

"Armed struggle, not terrorism. Terrorism is something very different, Rosario. ETA practices terrorism, killing one police officer here, another there. That's why it won't get them anywhere. We've declared the people's revolutionary war in Spain today, and that's the essential step in taking power."

Octubre looked at Lina's face carefully. Young, thin, beautiful, with those attractive eyes, so clear, so sparkling, intelligent, and she was sure she was speaking seriously, but she could not hold her own opinion back.

"You've declared the people's war in Spain, you? On who? Who are you? Who have you declared war on?"

"On the fascist regime, of course, and we are the Marxist-Leninist Communist Party and FRAP, and all the people's organizations that follow us."

When she saw the tranquility Lina answered with, Octubre got angry.

"What are you saying? What do you mean you've declared war? As if it were that simple. Mayor Móstoles did that to Napoleon, too. The important thing about wars is not declaring them, but winning them! What army will you fight with, eh?"

"And with the same expression as always, and a sarcastic smile, you know the sort, she replied, 'With the people's army,' and then she assured me that the time for the popular uprising against Franco had come, that they were just the vanguard of the fight, but that right away the revolutionary masses would follow them, since they were impatient to take up arms to put an end to fascism, and establish a democratic republic like China and Albania. They had a very complete and in-depth report on the armed uprisings that were being prepared in all the Spanish provinces, where the plain people were already asking their party for arms… And all this, which lasted more than an hour, she told me with an ironic smile at my ignorance and incredulity, and with her gaze lost in far regions only she could see, which must have been somewhere beyond the mountains of Albania. I suppose Enver Hoxha himself was dictating those phrases to her, and she took them directly from his lips as he pronounced them from the balcony of his palace…"

Octubre paused, drank the beer she had in front of her in one swallow, and awkwardly dried her tears.

"I was totally disappointed. I didn't even have any indignation left. In spite of all the fanatics I've known in my life, and how obtuse, stubborn, obstinate and dimwitted I consider the leaders of my ex-party, the truth is that I'd never seen or heard anything like that. She also had the appearance of a modern young woman, well-dressed, beautiful, with a clear complexion, educated, elegant. I tried several times to answer back to her, but I couldn't interrupt that hallucinatory discourse. It took me forever to get a word in, and when she finally had to pause for breath, I warned her, 'They're going to kill us all!'

"I was desperate, remembering the week before. On no sleep at all, I had feverishly looked for shelter, money, and passports every day, for several boys who'd shown up at my house, sent by companions who'd known me in prison, asking me to hide them from the police persecution at their heels. Several of them had to sleep on benches in the plazas, if you can call it sleeping, anxiously watching and waiting for some policeman to ask for their papers. They'd run out of friends, there were no more sympathetic people with houses, no one had any money any more. All my acquaintances ran away from me when I started explaining that I needed help for someone in the antifascist struggle. The dictatorship was starting to seem like a better option than the demented struggle the PC-ML patriots had unleashed.

"And Lina, with the same imperturbable smile, with her gaze fixed far away and perhaps with a special delight in the words, said back me, 'There are casualties in all wars!'"

Elisa could not keep listening. She felt very ill. She had been having palpitations, dizzy spells, she vomited every morning. The doctor said it was her body adapting to freedom, with all its ramifications, from the different food, to the different sleeping habits, to relating to people. But she knew that the cause of all those alterations in her health was disgust, the enormous disgust that invaded her after attending the funeral they held in Yeserías for the five executed men, knowing Juana's terrible secret, and having to face freedom exactly five days after the executions. She had left Marisa behind in prison, a speechless specter, and Concepción, five months pregnant and condemned to life in prison after waiting two weeks for the pardon of the death sentence she and María Jesús had taken away from the Military Tribunal. María Jesús was in the penitentiary hospital, where she arrived in time to be saved from the hemorrhage caused by her miscarriage. Elisa had always known María Jesús would not have that child which refused to grow in her womb and which she didn't want to see growing up in a prison.

And now, hardly a month after taking her first teetering steps on the streets of Madrid, she was listening to Octubre tell that surreal tale about her interview with the main person responsible for all that suffering.

"That woman has the life and death of others in the palm of her hand, and the other guys in the executive committee stroll around Paris or live in Geneva, or wherever the fuck it is, while our Marisas and Adalbertos let themselves be killed in Madrid and Burgos, convinced they're fighting the last battle against Franco…"

Elisa didn't want to listen to Octubre saying the same thing she was thinking. Later, when Arnau told her that in all wars the generals stay in the rear guard because, if they didn't, the army would lose its leaders right away, she got so upset at him that she screamed hysterically and they didn't speak to one another again for several days.

Was it impossible to find balance anywhere? Not in gods, kings or tribunals, but even less in the human beings she had known. They were all trying to elevate themselves to the status of kings and gods. They had the time, the work, the effort, the energy, the health, the love, and even the lives of everyone else at their disposal, all entrusted to them to fulfill she knew not what insane dreams of power and glory their pathological minds invented.

"I don't agree! I already told you back then." Arnau got up from the chair and walked furiously around the room. He needed to move, to combat the paralysis he was feeling after so many hours sitting in the same position, and at the same time, to release the anger the conversation was causing him. "You always have to judge others' actions according to your experience with the nuns. Revolutionary activists aren't fanatics, trained to kill without knowing who or why. That's exactly what the bourgeois say. That's exactly what the exploiters want the people to think. They're the ones who kill indiscriminately to maintain their power. Look at what's going on in South Africa, or El Salvador, or Nicaragua. With all the mistakes we make, in spite of the limitations of our comrades, when we chose the path of the revolution we weren't stupid fanatics who followed the directives of the leadership like some deluded member of a sect. Marisa and Juana, Concepción and María Jesús and the comrades who died on September 27, were all conscious that they were fighting to bring freedom and democracy to Spain.

"In spite of what Octubre thinks, if our comrades had heard Lina, they would have agreed with her. They died so that in their homeland such things would never happen again. If they were alive today, in a certain way they'd be happy to have contributed to these poor standards of democracy we do have. You should understand, you and all those like you who doubt, that a single person, like Lina, cannot direct several thousands of people who live very far away and have never seen her, as if they were puppets on a string. There is no long-distance hypnotism. All of us, the several thousand who are active in the PC-ML and FRAP acted the way we did because we agreed with the party line, because we connected with a way of life, of thinking, of understanding the struggle, of wanting the revolution that was exactly what the organization offered us. No one forced us to stay with it. No one. It's impossible to force anyone to work on any political option if they don't agree with its line. The same way the Franco regime wasn't just Franco. There were, and unfortunately there are, many pro-Franco people in Spain, and they were the ones who kept the regime going. It's never just one person who maintains a regime, a State, or a party. People only believed that when magical powers were attributed to the king and the emperor, and even then, there were times when the army or the people got rid of the king. Please stop thinking that your comrades, your friends and companions in prison were victims of Lina's cruelty, when they'd never even seen her, besides, and of the influence of their husbands. They were brave women with personalities, with a great faith in the struggle they were carrying on, and in the ideals they defended, though sometimes they might've been wrong about the way they did it…"

"Excuse me. Perhaps you're right. I was very moved by all those events and now remembering them…"

"Would you really say, now, that your ten years of activism were only a monstrous mistake, made out of obedience to your husband?"

Elisa was uncomfortable and frightened of his attitude, dizzy from his continual pacing, intimidated by his questions and hostile gaze. She no longer wanted to ask herself why she had dedicated 20 hours every day to party work since Arnau came back late that day from the HOAC meeting and told her, with an intriguing air, "I met a very nice guy who's a communist. He's going to get me an interview with one of his party leaders." Perhaps she would have lived in a completely different way if she had fallen in love with the son of her hometown grocer, who looked at her with watery eyes and tried to see her whenever he brought up the deliveries to her house, but was never able to say anything to her because Arnau got ahead of everyone?

"It wasn't only love for Adalberto that pushed Marisa to fight the way she did, or Juana or any of the others. They also felt a great love for the people, because you must love the people a great deal to decide to fight in their favor, even when they themselves don't ask for it or want it. Then, under the dictatorship, when every day someone was killed in a demonstration, a strike, or an assembly, it wasn't so clear that a more aggressive, more revolutionary line was a mistake. Remember the reaction against the national reconciliation the pro-Carrillo gang was constantly pushing. And besides, look how much good it's done. Those rains brought this mud. You, too, agreed with the party line, for many years. Precisely the most difficult years, when they sent you to the Assembly of Catalonia with all those privileged petty bourgeois bastards. When you shamelessly declared yourself Stalinist… Don't you remember how you criticized those hypocrites who were just starting to distance themselves from the regime, because it wasn't going so well for them anymore, who pretended to passionately desire democracy? Don't you remember?"

Arnau showed true anxiety while he waited for the response.

Elisa could only nod.

"Are you going to help us, then?"

With an effort, Elisa murmured, "You know I am."

"Thank you. I knew you couldn't forget that you'd been struggling along with us for ten years."

Elisa didn't respond. She didn't want to think about her real motives for agreeing to Arnau's request. It was better to accept his reasoning about faith in the struggle that had sustained her and her comrades in the tragic past. She closed her eyes to muffle the mocking voice that told her inside, *He's got you wrapped round his finger, fool! He always gets everything he wants out of you! Is this your ideological strength, your faith in the struggle, and other odds and ends he's put into his usual political speech?*

"And when I've gone to court and said what you want, I won't see you again, will I?"

Arnau turned around and stopped searching for his wallet, already getting ready to go.

"You heard right. What I've been trying to tell you all morning. You'll use me, like other times, and then you'll leave me, as always."

"But, where's all this coming from?"

She had him trapped. He hadn't been able to free himself from the threat that had been hanging over him for several hours. In the end she had decided to say what she was thinking.

"You don't want to talk about that, like you never want to talk about our relationship. You left me almost without an explanation, and you've never wanted to talk about Pere or Carles. You're afraid to discuss our love."

"Oh, Elisa, please… We've talked about everything this morning. We've been talking for five hours. We've covered all the topics, and our separation is long past now."

"Not so long, not for me. I never found out exactly why you left me alone… like that…"

Arnau detested talking so directly about something he wanted to forget forever. He evaded the core of the question by replying, "You didn't stay alone, exactly. Carles stayed in the house with you."

Elisa stared at him and replied furiously, "Yes, fine, I'd really like to talk about that…"

CHAPTER 16

She was screaming more than crying, with loud howls interrupted by the contractions of her throat. She didn't want to be quiet. She needed to break her liver screaming and tear her vocal cords. It was the first time, but it would be the last. She would not have people feeling sorry for her in silence, she would not permit her case to be looked on by family and neighbors with an ironic or compassionate smile. She wanted to kill him, she had to do it. She was going to do it, and also that disgusting whore, thousand-headed hydra, venomous serpent...

"Elisa, please calm down." And then he said the most ill-timed thing possible: "Everyone's going to hear you."

That was exactly what she wanted, for the whole world to know what an evil creature Arnau was, how disgusting that pig Roser was, a viper in her house. Eating, drinking, wearing her out every day, smiling and praising her, while she developed a hypocritical strategy to take Arnau away from her. After fifteen years of love, after almost four years of prison, after miseries, tortures, pain, pain, pain. Like what she felt now, ripping out her insides. Anesthesia, she needed anesthesia, quick, quick! Morphine, heroin, in big doses, to kill the pain and to kill herself and before that, kill those two. *Anesthesia, now! I'm dying, I'm dying!*

"Elisa, please, pull yourself together, calm down."

Carles looked at her with his most concerned expression. He held onto her convulsing head, and tried to dry the saliva escaping from her half-open mouth. When she looked at him, he had tears in his eyes and that made her burst into tears. She sat up in bed, put her head on Carles's shoulder and cried a long time. In the end she felt drained. It didn't matter at all to her any more, she didn't hear what he was saying.

She didn't even have the strength to hiccup. Carles laid her out on the bed and dried her face with the edge of the sheets.

"What's going on, Elisa? Tell me. Why were you screaming in your sleep? Why did Arnau leave at midnight with a suitcase?"

Elisa breathed deeply. She wanted her tone of voice serene, tranquil, void of emotion. She was sorry Carles had awakened her. Only in dreams was she permitted to scream, insult, and make death threats at Arnau and Roser. Sometimes she would go to bed early so she could dream she was screaming insults at them, hitting them. She hoped to kill them in the next dreams. By biting them to death, and her mouth overflowed with saliva at the thought. She had to spit on the floor and signal to Carles not to bother when he began to look for a container for the vomit he thought was coming.

"He left, for good. He decided to stay at Roser's house."

"Have you been talking about separation for very long?"

"Oh, no. Talking, no. Just for two weeks, when I found out he'd been sleeping with Roser for half a year."

Carles shook his head, with a worried expression.

Like a priest, yes indeed. Exactly like a priest talking with a parishioner about her marital problems. A shake of the head, a click of the tongue, and on to something else. He won't insult them, he won't say he'll kill them, he won't tell me to kill them both, to tear them to shreds, to hang them, to burn them. A click of the tongue, and I'm sorry, this has been a very bad situation. And I can't scream at him or hit him, for being a conciliator, for saying to me in that priest voice, I'm truly sorry, I didn't think Arnau was capable of something like this. And I'll have to answer in a normal voice, no one could've imagined it. But why couldn't we imagine it? Because Arnau was a Marxist-Leninist, or because he's a good guy who doesn't hit me, who doesn't rob or kill and gives me the money he earns? Or because as a young man he was a good Catholic? Or because he's so handsome, so tall, so healthy? Or because he's always so willing to do a favor for a friend or a brother, like now he's brought Carles home to take care of him because he's decided to leave the priesthood? Or because Roser is a stupid, mean bitch, and awful reporter, an idiotic writer, a viper I had in my house for several months so she could ruin my life? Is that why Arnau's a good guy and I can't shout or curse or hit him or kill him?

"Yes, it was a dirty trick, on Roser's part, too. And you didn't know anything was going on?"

She surprised herself by replying in a normal voice, a bit more calm. No, she hadn't known anything because she was stupid, he already knew that, everyone knew it, first Arnau, that was why he dared to bring Roser to the house, on the pretext of the work they were doing together, and he had her eating lunch and dinner there almost every day, and they even went to the movies together, and she, stupid Elisa, absent-minded, with her head always in the clouds, who continually suffered mystical absences, never figured out anything. But, what about him, Carles? Hadn't he realized what was happening, either, right in front of him, right there in the same house where he lived? Hadn't he perceived the scent of sexual desire, the enraptured expressions that accompany love, the secret asides between the two, even when they were with other people, the blushing, the altered breathing, the shining eyes, the senseless sighs, the unprovoked, unbridled laughter, alternated with unjustified sadness and melancholy, and Arnau's boredom when she wasn't with them, the yawning, the fatigue that made him to go to bed at ten o'clock, the tasks that kept him locked up in his office for hours on end, the aggressiveness that led him to provoke unexpected arguments, and then the overwhelming joy when Roser appeared in the doorway, and again the secrets, laughter, sighs, knowing looks of understanding; hadn't he seen any of this, he who didn't suffer from mystic attacks, and who was accustomed to distrusting human nature, as the confession box had taught him? He, Carles, Arnau's only brother, intelligent, astute, conventional, who had no job and spent most of his time at home studying, hadn't found out about the amorous conspiracy that was developing right there, right in front of stupid Elisa's nose?

"Actually, I suspected something, but I couldn't imagine…"

"Why didn't you tell me?"

"What? I didn't know anything, I couldn't put my thoughts into words. It was a feeling more than anything. Intuition, perhaps…"

"The perfume of love…"

"Perhaps… Didn't you smell it?"

Elisa shook her head. "I'm stupid, you already know that."

Carles jumped. With a softer tone of voice he scolded her, "Why do you say that? It's not a matter of intelligence or stupidity. Your naïveté is a sign of trust, goodness, purity of heart…"

Elisa shook, half crying, half laughing. Carles looked at her compassionately, and that made her angry, but she could not stop crying.

"That's what Octubre told me the first day I met her in prison… But it's not true, it's not true. I'm bad and stupid, that's my problem."

Not being sufficiently sharp to assess situations, to smell danger and get ahead of it… Not being prepared to imagine the possibility of betrayal, to see it and think of it as a true, real, inevitable thing… Her usual absentmindedness, her distractions, which Arnau had liked so much, were his best alibi. Hidden behind them, like a protective cape, he conceived and acted out the betrayal, and no one stopped him from carrying it out in front of the distracted blue eyes of his adoring wife. Her enormous stupidity permitted him to carry on both relationships simultaneously, pretend the two loves, even though the one he owed to Elisa, to the unalterable Elisa, was much more than the one he could give to that ignorant upstart, that girl raised at her mother's skirts, whose one skill was taking her friends' husbands away. Elisa's enormous denseness had been her enemy. She wasn't good, she was just dense.

She could be as bad as the next person, or even worse. She could kill both of them. First, Roser, slowly, pulling off her flesh in an unending torture, like the one she felt now and would continue to feel forever. That was why the torture for the two of them had to be eternal also. Eternal like the Hell they had thrown her into. Why shouldn't there be a hell? *Hell must exist; not the symbolic one, or a psychological one, or Sartre's, or mine or anyone else's. Real Hell, the one with the flames, the burning pokers and pots of boiling oil. It's only fair that it should exist for evil people like Arnau and Roser. It's not fair, it's a mockery of all the social and even the natural laws, which call for harmony, justice, and balance, that sinister people like Arnau and Roser can live peacefully and even happily, without feeling even the shadow of remorse, not even a slight stomach irritation after committing the worst of all crimes: the murder of our love.*

After turning her into a rabid rat that needed to bite and scratch the flesh of those pigs and tear them up and infect them with bubonic plague, with the red death: rage. They were living happily, relaxed, showing the world their serene, cheerful faces, which said, "See how we're calm people, deeply in love, who only want to live in peace? The only one who's over-excited and off her hinge is Elisa. Mild-mannered Elisa, look how she's turned out. Screams, tears, insults at all hours. So much talk about feminism and it turns out that when her husband chooses freedom, she behaves like a harpy from times long past. She's turning out to be like a vestige of that Calderonian morality she criticized so much."

They lectured on that theme to anyone who wanted to hear, with a smile on their faces, a glass in one hand, lounging on the couch in Roser's house, where Elisa had been so many times discussing the latest news with them, and always the latest news, because, since they were both reporters, it was the only thing that mattered to them, she realized now, while they never asked about her, what matters were worrying her, what questions kept her awake, what problems was she having at work.

And on that same sofa now they explained to their friends, Antonio Cherta, María, Octubre, even Isabel, the very old motives of the recently-discovered love and the moth-eaten discourse about freedom, accusing Elisa of being reactionary and old-fashioned. They, who had behaved like the most medieval or bourgeois pair of lovers, hiding in doorways, fooling around in the car seat in the park, in Elisa's bedroom when she was working, they had betrayed the best Elisa had given them: her trust, and her friendship. They, who laughed at her stupidity, her naïveté, at her absentmindedness and lapses with the same cruelty with which savages make fun of the mentally deficient and torture them, hitting them, tying cans to their clothes, throwing insects on them, and pouring water over their heads, that was how they made fun of her, lied to her, spat on her, taking advantage of her foolishness, and of her silly surrender to those who she thought loved her. But she could be as bad as the next person, worse even than them. She could tear out their eyes, little by little, and then grind them up in a mortar and serve them to them to eat, and pull off their legs and their fingernails, making sure they didn't die quickly, so she could keep watching them suffer as she suffered. But, with her stupidity she had let them escape alive and happy. And now she was there, writhing with an agony she could not bear without howling, while the educated fool Carles attempted to console her.

"Do you feel better? Do you want me to make you something? Some tea?"

"Yes, I feel better, thank you. There's some tea in the kitchen, I don't know what else there might…"

Console her! How could that pious moron, with the cassock still stuck to his butt, who repeated phrases with the nasal monotony of the matins and routine confessions, console her? How could he console her, when she wanted to burn the house and die in it, or, better, their house, and watch them writhe in the flames? How could he console her with a tea, a ridiculous tea, when all the water in the world should not be enough to cleanse the blood she wanted to shed? How to console her with four pitiful words when she was asking for Hell for the both of them, when she demanded with her screams eternal damnation for their bodies and souls? How could that slick character who retained all the bad habits of twenty years of monastery, console her with his stereotyped words of support, when she wanted the Apocalypse?

"Is it okay? Do you want more sugar?"

"No, thank you, it's fine."

Carles held the plate for her, and she licked at the cup pretending to swallow the sweet, hot liquid. Disgusting liquid that Arnau drank at all hours until she got used to its strange acid smell and bitter taste, and which now repulsed her, made her sick, she wanted to vomit it, spit it out on Carles, to see if he would change his expression of commiseration, his soft manners of a man who knows how to be with a friend in difficult times. She wanted to pour the cup over him and burn his brown eyes, which now had a doglike expression of fidelity, and his delicate hands that had never touched more than white linens, of peerless delicacy, prepared by nuns for their holy touch. And then spit on him and step on him and tear out his hair and stick her heels in his eyes.

"Thank you, I don't want any more… I'm a little nauseous."

"The best thing would be for me to give you a brandy. I don't know why it didn't occur to me before. There's no better medicine."

She drank the brandy, admitting that this time he was right, and when the tears refused to continue gushing from her red eyes any more, they drank whisky, with water and ice, and then without water, and in the morning hours Elisa recognized that the touch of Carles's fine aristocratic hands was pleasant.

"He kept me company. He gave me tenderness and affection, and he very effectively helped me endure the crisis at the time. He was very important to me at that stage of my life."

No more questions? That's all? Don't you need to know how much true love, the kind that keeps you from breathing and eating and sleeping without the beloved, there was in our relationship? Are you satisfied with that response? After two years of not knowing, not asking, never pronouncing Carles's name and looking me in the eye at the same time, is that all you hoped to hear? Or perhaps because you don't want to get deeply into the subject, you'd rather just accept this compromise answer? Are you perhaps afraid I would detail my passion for Carles? Are you really jealous, even though you deny it?

"What do you think?"

Arnau tried to situate himself quickly. The expressions that had passed over Elisa's face and had at first surprised him, and then frightened him, had to be interpreted correctly and turned to his own advantage. Those flashes of anger that gave her light and insignificant eyes a grandeur they never had, the blushing that suddenly stopped only to make her face more pale, the shaking of her hands, the alternated rage and tenderness, was this then love? Did it mean Elisa still loved him? In spite of Carles and Pere, of the two years gone by, and of the firmness with which she assured that she was past the first disappointment of the breakup, the same with which she assured that the only thing she felt for him and Roser now was sincere friendship? Was it true then what Roser, Antonio, and María told him: that Elisa went on as in love with him as ever? How could he not have realized sooner?

"Well, I'm a little upset, you see? I didn't expect the conversation to take this turn."

He had to gain time, he had to quickly think how to position himself. It was all about winning the duel Elisa's provocative eyes had challenged him to.

"You only came to settle the matter having to do with your party, right?"

"Yes, of course. It's been a long time since we talked about anything personal, and, in any case, I wouldn't have done it like this…"

It was best to put up a face, for the moment. He could not surrender so quickly: it would look suspicious. Although Elisa was hardly observant. Or perhaps now she was, perhaps she had subtly changed her usual disconnection to reality. He had to find some terrain where he would have some sure footing, but Elisa didn't let him recover.

"We haven't talked about anything personal since that afternoon I found you both together on the couch."

Arnau made a grimace of displeasure at the memory of that stupid mistake of his that Elisa had reproached him for so many times.

"I know it bothers you to talk about that day, but after you left we never said anything about the two of us again."

"Elisa, please! Everything's been discussed. It happened and I'm sorry, but two years have gone by, it's time to forget it, or at least put it away. You can't spend the rest of your life reproaching me for it. Since our relationship is over, we don't have to render each other accounts of our lives. There's no reason to say anything else about…"

"Not even about Carles?"

Arnau didn't know how to avoid the subject. "Why about Carles?"

"Because he's your brother, damn it! It's pretty unusual for a separated wife to go to bed with her husband's brother…"

Elisa noted with satisfaction that the words bothered Arnau deeply.

"Both you and my brother were adults. I'd been gone for some time. I had no—"

"That same night." At Arnau's confusion, she specified, "We went to bed that same night you went to Roser's for good."

"Why are you telling me this? Why are you telling me these details now? They're not important any more… Elisa, I've been living with Roser two years and we have a twelve-month-old daughter, what else do I have to say to you?"

That you love her, that you passionately love that stupid middle class señorita, a typical representative of the plague of the West — to use a phrase from Agnes Heller, the author you quoted so much — with no ideals, with no other interest than having you in bed, eating well, buying cars, and annoying me. Tell me you love her, that you feel she understands you, that you communicate profoundly on the important topics of life, that you tell her all your plans, that you ask for her advice in your political activity, that you talk every night, discussing the latest in the life of the country that so consumes you. Tell me that and I'll finally understand that I shouldn't hope for anything, that I can't interfere in your life any more! Ah, now you're talking about your daughter! The prefect recourse, the last subtle maneuver to justify your silence, to avoid questions! How weak you've become, that you have to resort to such tricks to avoid facing the truth! You have to inspire pity to get amnesty. You want my amnesty to not think on your own, to not question yourself about the contradictions you're living. Oh, no, I won't let you go like this, peacefully, talking to me about your daughter like some bourgeois father, in exactly the moment you've come to ask me to get involved in one of your party's messes, like in the old days! I won't let you leave until you tell me clearly what you feel for Roser today, what your daughter really means to you, that crying soft baby, more like a larva, who, according to you, like any other middle class chauvinist, justifies all the outrages you commit against women, including the creature's very mother! You have to give me a convincing explanation of why you had a daughter with that ugly, evil shrew Roser, and never wanted one with me! Why? Why?

Suddenly she thought that she hated all children, with their soft pale skin that reminded her of huge worms, damp and crying, constantly sticky, stinking of defecation, covered with pimples and irritations, like those prison babies: Israel, Pedro, Marujita, and Manuel, Concepción's son, who managed to be born in prison while María Jesús's child melted away in an unending hemorrhage in the Penitentiary Hospital. Elisa wasn't there any longer when the one miscarried and the other gave birth. The news came to her, brought by the usual messengers of the prison world.

Concepción dealt with prison well, devoted herself to her son, waited for the pardon or the amnesty, which were foreseeable since the dictator had died and was no longer around to keep alive the memory of his time of repressive splendor, as if the strength he needed to keep living were centered on that unbreakable will to keep killing.

María Jesús and Marisa vegetated, buried in a permanent depression no one even thought of trying to alleviate. Their emaciated faces and the dark circles under their eyes, their lifeless gazes, and the smell of hatred that oozed all over their persons showed that any help would be too late. No pardon or amnesty would bring their dead back to life or give them the will to live.

The months that followed the executions disturbed the life of the prison, in the same way that they changed the life of the country. The routine discipline that had reigned in Yeserías for decades incomprehensibly relaxed after the austere funeral the politicals gave their heroes. The director and the officials tried to move unnoticed through the prisoners' lives. Perhaps they believed a riot was imminent, and expected rebellion or hunger strikes, and preferred to wait out the bad times cowering in their hiding places.

"If they'd known how weak we were they wouldn't have been so afraid. Our party was dismembered, fatally wounded after collecting so many dead bodies. The activists who were still in prison could hardly bear the impatience they felt to distance themselves from the party definitively when they were free. They were fed up with meetings, orders, manifestos, hunger strikes, overconfident declarations that explained nothing about the latest events that had led the party to dismemberment. Many of them would never associate with the other members again. Once I thought I saw a former prison companion in the street, and it seemed like he avoided me. Meanwhile, Carrillo and his followers were organizing the most humiliating surrender operation that's ever been included in the dark history of his final years. Agreeing with Suárez, they accepted the monarchy, the flag, and the anthem Franco had used for forty years as a symbol of the dictatorship, and got involved in pacifying the Worker's Movement and the movement of citizens and associations, to allow Suárez to organize the imperceptible transition we're living through now. All the ideals the Worker's Movement and the Communist Movement had fought for, leaving their best men along the path, this path to freedom that's scattered with dead, tortured, mutilated, savagely executed bodies, without ever giving them a sincere tribute, they've been forgotten, betrayed, without anyone's grief."

Elisa observed the obvious emotion Arnau unloaded in that spontaneous speech. Across from him, the Swedish reporter who was researching a story on the transition in Spain was writing with dedication in his notebook. He showed no emotion, although Elisa was sure Arnau's opinion was the most aggressive of those he must have collected in the days he had been visiting various political celebrities.

"That is to say that the transition, the sweet democratic transition in this Spain which has suffered a forty-year dictatorship, the longest in the Western world, after Portugal, and there they didn't go through a war like ours, was made by the banks, the landholding oligarchy, the Army and the Church, which had secularly governed the country and had been sincere allies to Franco. And here we are. That's why Suárez and now Calvo Sotelo are no more than puppets in the hands of such powers, and the PCE their puppet."

Elisa felt uneasy at Arnau's analysis, which seemed too schematic to her. She dared to step in.

"What you're saying is true, but it gives me the impression we couldn't have done much else. The people were confused and frightened when Franco was dying. There were no mass mobilizations in any sense at the time. We were all too scared."

"The PCE took it upon itself to demobilize the people. PCE, CCOO, UGT, the organizations that could've given directions to fight, constantly gave orders to be calm, to wait. They resorted to conspiracy and salon politics before popular struggle."

Arnau was particularly bitter that afternoon. It was during the time when he had distanced himself from the party and his mood was a reaction to his frustration about that situation. Elisa, nonetheless, dared to contradict him.

"But it would be good to know why, why the PCE accepted such a diminished role, and also why its activists and the CCOO affiliates, for example, so easily accepted those instructions. No man alone has all the power of a country, not even of a class sector…"

The journalist raised his gaze from his notebook and looked at Elisa sympathetically and with interest. In his perfect Spanish, with no trace of a foreign accent, he kindly asked, "And what was the reason for something like that happening, in your opinion?"

Arnau was at first surprised, and then, to Elisa's confusion, visibly annoyed by the attention the reporter was paying to his wife's opinions, and she in turn had been flattered by the Swede's deference, since she wasn't accustomed to it. None of the Spanish reporters paid attention to her when they spoke with Arnau. This motivated her to elaborate on her opinion.

"I think we need to clarify two lines of thought: on one hand, the Spanish people weren't the same as they were in 1936. They didn't want war or revolution. They were living in very different conditions from forty years before, wrapped up in the comforts of modern industrialized capitalism. It was useless to make proclamations about people's war, popular uprising, or revolution, like the minuscule extremist parties constantly did, marginalized as they were from social reality. The leaders and activists of those parties seemed to be living in another world, not wanting to see the radical transformations that were taking place in their country. It was a schizophrenic dynamic, because among the people there didn't exist the least desire to throw themselves into a bloody and suicidal fight, given the militarization of our society, to achieve who knew what utopian objectives. Almost no one had to struggle any more in order not to die of hunger, to have shelter, even if it was bad, and even pay the car bills. And fighting for freedom of expression, of conscience, of the press, et cetera, the Decalogue of bourgeois freedoms in which the longed-for democracy became real, that was exactly what they were busying the leaders of the large democratic parties of the country with, and they left the matter in their hands."

She paused, with the satisfaction of seeing the enormous interest the journalist was taking in her long-winded speech, and without stopping to look at Arnau, whose bad mood she could perceive without looking at him, she continued.

"On the other hand, the leadership of those parties found themselves with the dilemma of opting for marginalization from political life, facing a majority of people who didn't follow their party line, or accepting the pacts offered them. What Arnau said was true, with respect to sharing out power among the eternal dominant classes of the country: the Army, the banks, the Church, the landholders; but they, too, found themselves in an uncertain situation. For a long time, up to the first elections, they didn't know how much power was really behind the PCE and PSOE, the unions, the mass organizations. That's why they also consented to the legalization of the PCE, the CCOO, and all the other parties to their left, which were accepted little by little in the register of political parties, and, finally, the organizing of the Constituent Assembly, free elections, and all the rest, without making a big scene like the one they made last February 23. In short, in spite of the fact that I can't feel content with the situation my country is in, I see in this transition an almost inevitability to the events, that a different attitude of the PCE or PSOE couldn't have changed."

"Right! So, for you, the behavior of the PCE and CCOO is correct? The collaboration with the bankers, the military and the same oligarchies as ever, almost all longtime fascists, seems like appropriate political behavior for a Marxist-Leninist party? If the masses felt confused, afraid, wasn't it time for a Leninist party, if that's what it was, to place itself at the vanguard of the mobilization? Do you really think that in those circumstances, Lenin was giving instructions to wait, delay and stay quiet until the same people as always placed themselves more peacefully than ever in power?"

The Swede found himself more and more interested in the argument that had come up between the spouses, and listened with his gaze fastened on their faces, while taking notes ever more quickly. Elisa understood that Arnau was truly displeased with her intervention. She hesitated before replying.

"It's possible you're right from a theoretical standpoint, but I'm afraid that when it came time to put it into practice, at the end of 1975, it was already too late. Our party denounced Carrillo's politics of abandoning principles way back in 1963 — and now I don't know if we were in time even then — exactly because it clearly saw his collaborationism, which was definitive for the slant things took on. In the end, the hegemonic party in the antifascist struggle was always the PCE, and they made the decision toward this social democratic politics at the beginning of the seventies. In '75 it was already too late... What could we have done?"

"It wasn't too late for the battle for the Republic, we saw for ourselves. The PCE again sterilized our efforts, broke up the organizations, slandered the leaders of the movement..."

"Well," Elisa interrupted impatiently, "they did that, you're right, but the masses, those wide masses who should've demanded the Republic, weren't with us, anyway."

"We were still too weak. Christ, Elisa, remember! We'd just gotten out of prison, the party had fallen apart, the other parties to the left of the PCE hardly had anyone. The entire responsibility for that failure must be attributed to the PCE."

Elisa considered for a moment. She felt the journalist's gaze on her, but now the matters Arnau presented to her unsettled her more than the attraction she held for the foreigner.

"I don't know, I really don't know, but it's often been said that if the PCE hadn't accepted the conditions Suárez imposed, in the name of the powers that be, the coup d'état was ready to go. Just look at what happened February 23..."

"Elisa, please! You can't pay attention to those stories." Arnau's visible impatience was creating a tense atmosphere Elisa hated.

"But it was obvious that on February 23 a coup d'état was organized with many more people involved than the ones who showed up in Parliament or in the media." The journalist had intervened opportunely, he had realized he was the only one who could take the pressure off of what was becoming a bitter dispute between the two of them.

Arnau took control of himself and responded more calmly.

"I maintain the opinion, which I believe the facts support, that the coup of February 23 was a prank more than a serious plot. If a sensible and objective analysis is made of the sectors which could've been involved, and of the interests they should defend, remembering the essential question — who benefits? — we would see that a coup and the subsequent dictatorship, that is to say a repetition of the same events as 1936, was out of place in 1981. The Army, hero of the military uprising, isn't motivated for a coup today. First, the socioeconomic composition of it has changed, several books have been written about that, so that it's no longer made up of aristocratic commanders and peasant soldiers. The chiefs of the Army today belong to the bourgeoisie and even the middle class; besides which they have posts in all the businesses and enjoy infinite advantages, all of which Franco gave them and no one's taken away. They live without working, in the best of worlds, enjoying the perks of the uniform, and everyone knows that when a military dictatorship is established only a few can be ministers and heads of state, the rest continue living as they did before. Why risk themselves in the fight, and who knows, maybe even die, to place Armada and Tejero in the government? That was why the majority of the military captains didn't support the coup, and that's a fact. If not, we'd have had more problems than we did during those twenty hours.

"And on the other hand, the capital, that is, the people who have to pay the expenses on such an enterprise, because no one thinks about the gasoline every tank uses when it starts up, or about the food that has to be rationed to the soldiers so they'll hold out, those gentlemen are doing the same business as always, no one's expropriated the farms or the factories. They haven't imprisoned a March or a Cardinal Segura, and the banks haven't been nationalized. They evade foreign exchange every day with impunity, make trusts with foreign firms, export the capital to other countries they consider more feasible. Why have a coup? In 1936, besides the triumph of the Popular Front, the Republic had begun to reform the Army, the secular school, agrarian reform… that was why the war broke out. There's no other reason. The capital and their allies continue to have all the power in Spain. They don't need a war, which would also put them at risk, to get what they already have."

The tension had relaxed, the journalist attentively wrote what Arnau said and Elisa listened with interest. When he finished his address, only the sound of the pen scratching the paper was heard. Arnau was very satisfied with his analysis and his evident triumph. Elisa waited a few moments before commenting, simply.

"Yes, your analysis is correct. The problem would've come from a radical opposition having developed against those dominant classes you've mentioned. Then they would've had many more reasons to organize a military coup… like in Turkey, for example, to cut off the people's movement for the Republic and other radical transformations."

For a long time, Elisa remembered the radiant look the Swedish journalist gave her, the slight smile with which he silently congratulated her, and first the confusion, and then the fury, with which Arnau replied.

"So, you're content with the situation we live in? Do you think the PCE and CCOO are following the politics they should?"

That night, after the visitor who had so shrewdly provoked the controversy was gone, Arnau was unusually aggressive toward Elisa.

"So maybe you know what we should've done in 1975?"

"No, of course not. I haven't thought about it enough —"

"Then don't pontificate about things you don't know! Especially to make me look ridiculous in front of a foreign journalist interested in PC-ML politics for the first time!"

Arnau was so angry he slept on the dining room couch, in spite of Elisa's sincere repentance. After hearing Elisa's version of the incident, Octubre commented, "He must've been doing good deeds in order to be able to go back to the party with full honors, and you've spoiled an article in the Swedish press for him, where they could've made the PC-ML's thesis public for the first time."

Elisa didn't want to believe her. That was why it was all the more disconcerting that a few weeks later Arnau had decided to reenter the party.

Now Elisa was looking in his face for that Arnau who had been so severe with her when she didn't meet his criteria. Would he require the same thing of Roser? Would he treat her with the same harshness when he thought her comments or behavior were not exactly suited to what he thought was required of the partner of a Marxist-Leninist leader?

In that case, she thought angrily, *he'd have to beat her, because she doesn't know a fig about politics, and since she ignores everything that doesn't have to do directly with her personal comfort, she isn't willing to learn, either. But he puts up with her, and considers her attractive. He's chosen the typical ignorant, doting, submissive wife.* She jumped, remembering that that was Octubre's customary accusation against her. Then, was it true that he had always chosen an obedient little woman for a wife? And how had she not realized that in fifteen years of marriage? This singular visit had to happen before so many unresolved, undiscussed questions presented themselves for the first time. Maybe because Elisa had reached a certain level of maturity, some distance from the facts that so tortured her two years earlier. She observed him with care, and a new wave of fury flooded over her. He was wearing a contrite expression in keeping with the declaration of fatherhood he had just made. Changed from a professional revolutionary who was ready to plant bombs on every corner, into a petty bourgeois father who was deeply concerned about his daughter's well-being.

She felt a furious desire to insult him. She was again experiencing the passion of those days immediately following the separation, when Arnau's image and words obsessively clung to her memory, when she felt herself dangerously descending into the abyss of insanity. Again, she needed — had she ever done it? — to cry and scream and bite and stamp like that night two years ago in which Carles came to console her. She had to hit him, wound him, as he had done to her then, without a shred of compassion. She had to take revenge for every one of those miserable minutes she had spent during the last two years grieving over her lost love. Words were not good for anything when rage welled up with so much violence in her throat. Searching out the best sentence among those that occurred to her, she pronounced the words as if she were spitting them.

"I was pregnant, too."

Chapter 17

The vomit rose into her throat, choking her the way it did every morning. At first, when she thought she was sure, she hid the news while she weighed the possibility of an abortion. Now she hesitated to tell anyone, afraid of the comments it would provoke. She needed to reflect thoughtfully about her desire for that child. She knew that some of her friends would reproach her or make fun of her, and most of all she was afraid of the reaction such news would provoke in her home. Perhaps her mother would be the only one to encourage her to have it, mainly because of her religious opposition to abortion.

"But do you really want to have a baby? Right now?" Isabel looked at her incredulously.

"Why do you always have to doubt my judgment?"

"Well, what do you want, anyone would think that it doesn't make much sense for you to have a baby now that you've just broken off the stable relationship you had with your husband, and find yourself in the middle of your professional development."

"Not 'just'! He left me a year ago…"

"And he's just had a child."

It was Octubre who looked at her with hostility mixed with contempt. It was Octubre who had no excuse for her, who criticized her the most severely, with unrepeatable epithets. And while she yelled at her, Elisa felt the nausea more strongly than ever.

"Of course you're nauseous! But not enough! You should puke until you turn yourself inside out, to see if you can hurl out once and for all, with the food and bile and innards, that stupid love for a man who doesn't love you... who doesn't love you... do you hear? Who probably never loved you! He probably only wanted meekness, obedience, like the kind you always gave him. He used you in his little political adventures until he got tired of you. Nothing more! Get it?"

When Elisa tried to protest, Octubre silenced her with more yelling.

"And it doesn't matter, anyway! If he loved you, great, while it lasted, and then it was over! Get it? Understand? The love ran out, it's that simple and nothing more, and your blind obstinacy goes unheard..."

Elisa became infuriated, and at the same time she started to feel better.

"What does my pregnancy have to do with what you're talking about? The baby isn't even his, Christ! It's been a year since we separated and I have my life and he has his and..."

"And now he's had a baby, exactly! And not with you, that is what's bothering you! That's why you have to get pregnant immediately, and throw up and faint and I don't know what else, to attract attention. As if all the stupid things you do every day don't attract enough attention."

"Millions of women get pregnant and have morning sickness and fainting spells and no one thinks they're stupid or that they have babies to attract attention or to annoy everyone else."

"But you do! You do!"

They were both shouting at the same time, in a frenzy of powerlessness and rage they could not stop. For a long time Elisa was ashamed of that unusual, unrepeatable scene. *The first time in my life*, she thought, *that I really lost my self control.* That difficult control in the exercise of which she had been trained for her first fifteen years with results which had been up to that point satisfactory. But there was Octubre yelling at her, insulting her, getting more hysterical than she was, without Elisa ever understanding what was the purpose of that attack of fury the news of her pregnancy had provoked.

When Octubre fired at her, "You're crazy. That's what it is! You're crazy! If you can't figure out your codependency on Arnau, and the quantity of stupid things you do for his love, you must be crazy, simply put. You're crazy!"

Elisa left Octubre's house, slamming the door, and decided not to see her again.

"Ah!" He was apparently indifferent and distant. "And whose was it?"

Elisa looked at Arnau bitterly. She cursed his serenity, which allowed him to be as distant as someone talking about a subject completely removed from him. She squeezed her jaw in order not to shout.

"Carles's."

It took her a few weeks to admit it to herself. Several weeks of indefinable uneasiness and a pathetic loneliness. She cut off communication with her friends, because, though Isabel didn't show Octubre's kind of aggressiveness, her irony wounded Elisa more than Octubre's rage. She didn't dare tell her mother or siblings the news, while still undecided what she would ultimately do. And at school, she took great care to hide her state, knowing full well the displeasure pregnant teachers caused the director and the faculty, especially when, as in her case, they could not even justify the offense with a stable marriage.

But one afternoon, when she found herself especially depressed, she decided to confide in Carles. He had always been very understanding, she told herself, he had kept her company exactly when she most needed him. But while she tried to find reasons to trust his support, the evidence of the bad relationship they had had for several months made it impossible for her.

Since the autumn, and it was already March, Carles and she had maintained a distant, bored, or irritable attitude toward each other. Elisa was sure it was Carles's fault, for demanding attention from her she could not give him.

"He's jealous," all the people around them told her, "he's jealous, in the worst way, because he's jealous of his own brother." Elisa didn't want to accept that simple explanation, which would oblige her to recognize the evidence that her emotional dependency on Arnau was obvious to everyone.

Carles was sitting in his usual place next to the lamp, reading, when Elisa asked him to listen to her. Elisa never knew whether the news had made him happy or upset. A little of both feelings mixed together in the expression of surprise and the minutes-long silence he received that confession with, the most difficult he had listened to in his long experience as a confessor.

"But, is it… ours?"

Elisa clearly perceived that plural with which he prudently hid the transcendental question, and noticed at the same time how Carles was also convinced that their relationship was secondary for Elisa. She became indignant at the doubt in his words. She was perhaps, and only perhaps, still in love with Arnau, but she wasn't going to play a mean trick of that kind on Carles for that. Or, perhaps as all men were capable of betraying their wives, they always expected similar behavior from them? Or, even worse, did Carles suppose Elisa had chosen him only as a revenge against his brother? That was what Octubre repeatedly told her, with her habitual severe criticism of Elisa's behavior, especially lately, when the relationship between the two women had also seriously deteriorated.

Octubre had been, since some time before, hostile toward Elisa, which made her constantly argue with her friend.

"Nothing I do seems right to her," Elisa complained one day to Isabel.

To Elisa's surprise, she responded, "She's jealous of you, too."

Elisa could have felt flattered by the attention she inspired in her friends if she hadn't been too confused to allow herself the luxury of applying a sense of humor to the situation. She responded with displeasure.

"That's all I needed!"

And Isabel, amused, was the one who expressed the obligatory comment.

"You should be proud of stirring so many passions."

That night, standing before a surprised Carles who remained seated, Elisa saw herself playing out her sessions with the father confessor at her school. Her lover's distrust wounded her more sharply, not only because it had no justification — although she had to admit to a certain sadness at the impossibility that the child was Arnau's — but, above all, because he confronted her instead of providing the support and solace she needed.

"Of course. I thought you knew me, Carles. You don't trust me, but I on the other hand trusted you completely when I explained the problem to you. I'm very concerned. I don't know if I should have it."

And only after so clearly explaining the cause of her anxiety did she understand that such a possibility hadn't entered into any of his calculations. Weeks later, she was in bed, *sine die*, by doctor's prescription, because of the bleeding that had started.

Isabel, who kept her company during some of the long hours of waiting that were predicted for her, commented, "It's impossible for Carles to consider the idea of an abortion. His past weighs too much on him."

"But, do you think he wants this baby?"

"He'll get used to it, I suppose. It must have been a big surprise at first."

She didn't add that for her the important question was whether Elisa wanted it, because Elisa's state of weakness and depression wasn't the best for giving her new doubts to think about.

"And what happened?"

"I lost it."

"I'm sorry."

Elisa could have slapped him, spit on him, bitten him for that expression of commiseration. Again, he was triumphant. He had become a father, with no effort, and she, who by natural design possessed the capacity to produce children, hadn't been able.

"You weren't able?" Isabel asked her sarcastically. "What a mystifying way to say that you didn't want to!"

"That's not true! I was even in bed for more than a month to avoid losing it."

"Lose what? Do you really think you had something to lose? And you're telling this to me?"

Elisa reddened with an unfamiliar embarrassment. Isabel feared for her mental health. Did she really think she could have had a child?

The solution to the problem came quickly, brutally resolving all the doubts, fears, and contradictions that distressed Carles and Elisa. She hadn't been four months along when she had the final hemorrhage, resolving the question definitively.

At the clinic, Isabel heard the surprising news first, from the doctor's lips: Elisa had never been pregnant. She had suffered the retention of an unfertilized egg.

"Was it a hysterical pregnancy?" Isabel exclaimed before the doctor could finish his explanation.

The doctor smiled with a strange expression that indicated his pleasure with Isabel's knowledge on a level with his scorn for Elisa's unbalanced behavior. Hours later, when she awoke after the strong medication they had given her, the two friends agreed not to explain such a bizarre story to her mother or to Carles.

Isabel wanted to tell her seriously to see a psychiatrist, but never dared. Elisa seemed to accept the episode as a normal occurrence, like a tooth ache.

"She doesn't realize anything. She thinks it's normal that she lived four months believing she was pregnant, and even suffered several side effects and hemorrhages with no pregnancy to justify them. I'm worried about her. Her natural absent-mindedness is almost turning into schizophrenia. She doesn't see the reality that surrounds her, and doesn't see herself participating in it."

Isabel was hoping Octubre would give her an answer that would calm her fears. Isabel profoundly admired Octubre, but she couldn't stand her. She always said the passion Octubre put into any topic, even if it was unimportant, wore her out.

Once, Elisa had mockingly retorted, "Since you're so refined, educated in the most exquisite principles of your school, where all exaggeration was proscribed and the ideal of the good señorita was, even more than moderation, stateliness, Octubre must doubtless seem excessive to you. She represents everything those nuns taught us to reject and despise: communism, intensity, sincerity, frankness, accompanied by the simplicity of an education on the streets of the outskirts of Madrid. *Demasié* for an elegant pupil of Sacred Heart."

Isabel accepted the criticism exactly as was expected of an elegant pupil of Sacred Heart. She smiled cordially and told Elisa she was right, but Elisa guessed that the accuracy of her assessment had wounded her friend's sensibility. Octubre soon perceived more warmth in Isabel, that straight-laced señora, as she always called her. On the contrary, Elisa, who had provoked the change, was unable to perceive the good effect her words had had, too absorbed in her anxieties and conflicts to notice her friends.

That afternoon, the initiative to meet with Octubre to talk about Elisa's situation had come from Isabel. Facing her across the table at the café, she carefully observed Octubre's contracted face, the furrowing of her brow, her dark expression.

"I already knew it, but I have hardly any influence over her. She won't listen to me and is very aggressive with me. Most of all when her love for Arnau is showing…"

Isabel and Octubre looked at each other in silence for a few moments. Both were familiar with the origin of the change in the relationship between them, once such good friends, and it wasn't worthwhile to repeat things they already knew. Octubre's last sentence stayed in Isabel's memory as the key to the problem.

"I never should've stopped being her friend. I loved her too much."

Some time later, Isabel repeated it, while commenting on the similar problem of Elisa and Carles and when she asked in surprise, "What do you mean?" Isabel smiled enigmatically before answering.

"That when one loves someone very much one should not stop being their friend, that's all. Octubre said that, and she was right."

And Elisa looked at her, startled, but made no reply.

Elisa's strange behavior made Isabel and Octubre meet more often, and with more pleasure, at the time when Elisa was ostensibly distancing herself from Octubre. Once Isabel dared to mention her new attitude, but Elisa merely replied with disdain.

"Octubre has always been very aggressive and possessive. And you've also changed a lot. Just yesterday she was too poorly educated for you."

Isabel didn't reply. For the last few months, when that strange pregnancy began, or perhaps before that, when Elisa and Octubre's relationship began to disintegrate, Isabel had been observing the strange changes in Elisa. She accepted the belief common among all those who knew her that Elisa was still in love with Arnau. If not, what was the hysterical pregnancy all about? But she doubted it when she heard Octubre claim that Elisa's feelings hadn't changed at all in that year, that she maintained her love for Arnau with more strength than ever. Isabel hesitated to define the feelings Elisa was going back and forth between.

The relationship with Carles ended almost instantly after the simulated miscarriage, and Elisa showed up one afternoon at Isabel's house telling her she was finally leaving the apartment she had put together with Arnau and that she wanted a change of scene. She begged, rather than asked, her to keep her company for a while. The loneliness she felt once the relationship with Carles was over was too much for her.

But when it seemed that this second breakup was going to deepen the wounds she still had from the first, which hadn't scarred over, Elisa introduced Isabel to Pere with a confidence that also seemed artificial to Isabel. As if she were again living disconnected from reality. If not, how could her disregard for Pere's civil status be interpreted, when she saw his wife every day at school? The day Isabel brought up that subject, she was surprised to see that Elisa wasn't at all disturbed by that fact. On the contrary, she continually complained of having to do without Pere on the weekends because he had to be with his wife and daughters. Until one day she triumphantly announced Pere's separation, and received Isabel's observations with greater displeasure.

"Well, so what? I'm sick of all the morals you're always dumping on me. You'll always be the perfect Sacred Heart student, damn it! You presume to be so liberal and free of the school's uptightness, but you're always moralizing."

"I'm not free of anything. I carry all the sermons and rosaries and novenas and confessions from our childhood on my shoulders. What I'm trying to do is carry them with dignity. Nothing more. And it seems odd to me that some alumnae of that school are involved in activities that go against what they've been taught as much as terrorism and sexual libertinism and drugs. No educational project could've failed more miserably."

Elisa replied with ill temper. "Can you really call my relationship with Pere sexual libertinism? You're really getting more and more reactionary!"

Isabel smiled. "No, I wasn't talking about you. Obviously you can't call what you're doing sexual libertinism. It's nothing more than one of those nasty things middle class señoritas, well educated in convent schools, do every day."

Elisa protested angrily at her friend's claim, but she had to remember, at Isabel's insistence, the examples of everyday life within the school, which taught, under the nuns' attentive rod, the path of success through competition.

"Even the way God preferred you, remember?"

The memory of certain experiences they had together ended with unrestrained laughter that alleviated the tension.

"Do you remember that nun who taught French? For her, all the virtues of a señorita were embodied in how well she knew that language. She told us several times that one girl she'd had as a student had been so stupid and lazy that she hadn't wanted to learn the language she so lovingly taught, until she married very well, to an important man. But after a few years the husband returned his wife to her parents saying that, since she didn't know French, she was of no use to him…" The guffaws became more shrill at the example of the teachings they received for so many years.

"No, they weren't stupid, Elisa. They were perfectly programmed to mold, place, and domesticate the girls. Do you remember how the nuns who took care of the littlest ones, especially the kindergartners and the ones from the little boarding school, were the strictest? They didn't have the slightest bit of tenderness or warmth with the children from three to ten years old, the ones who needed it most. The one in charge of the boarding school, I remember her now, that cold Basque, with pursed lips, who never smiled, she would have been too ferocious for a member of the Gestapo. And the girls from seven to ten were in her hands. And the ones who took care of the littlest ones, I'd say they were just odd. Always silent, stiff, as if they hated the little girls. That's surely what they felt. And someone who hates can't transmit anything other than hate. They didn't teach us to love each other, that was the problem. We didn't love ourselves, or our classmates, or anyone at all. We detested the world, the devil, and flesh, without anyone ever teaching us that we ourselves were the devil, the world and the flesh. That's why we failed to ever be loyal — we didn't even know what the word meant. I dedicated myself to taking away several of my classmates' boyfriends for a whole year, and I was very pleased with the success I had among my companions and with the respect that showed through the nuns' apparent indifference. In the end, the only thing that they had trained us conscientiously for was to compete amongst each other. So you and I fought over the May crowning of the Virgin, that year I defeated you, as if we were born enemies…"

Isabel was taking the conversation in the direction that interested her, and Elisa lost the good humor that had caused her to remember those anecdotes. Elisa wasn't willing to be the object of anyone's moral critiques. She felt sure that she had finally achieved the personal peace and stability lost after the serious breakups that had so wounded her, and she didn't want to put them at risk again. She interrupted aggressively.

"And that's why I'm a sexual libertine, right?"

"No, no I already told you I wasn't talking about you. When I said that, I was thinking of Elisenda. I followed her adventures closely all those years."

Elisa was relieved to be able to stop talking about herself.

"Ah! How is Elisenda? Have you heard from her lately?"

"I got a letter a few days ago. She's coming back to Barcelona after eight years."

"Eight years."

Elisa repeated the number several times, as if by doing so she could understand the different meanings it contained. Eight years before, Elisenda had traveled to Brussels to participate in the Tribunal of Crimes Against Women, which thousands of women from all over the world had organized to denounce violence against women, which the United Nations called "the most common covert crime in the world." Recently rescued from death, Elisenda left for it with Gina, her last friend, on the ferry from Dover to Calais. Isabel had told her, on several occasions, the circumstances in which she had found Elisenda in San Pablo Hospital in Barcelona: dangerously intoxicated with heroine, abandoned by the delinquents who had gotten her addicted, seriously ill and very weak after several years of traveling through the hippy communes of Europe and the dumps where the tramps survived. She had saved herself. That was what the letters that came to Isabel every once in a while said, and they profusely thanked her for her help, which had been essential to her survival.

"She's saved herself… It doesn't seem possible, does it? The way you described her, it seemed much more likely she would go back to drugs or die doing something dangerous."

"Yes, she's saved herself. Some do get saved, you know. Feminism is what finally saved her."

"You think?"

Elisa showed all her suspicion in that short question. It seemed unlikely to her that feminism could become such an effective therapy. It hadn't done her much good. In any case, it aggravated her incompatibility with Arnau. She remembered that Octubre had also gone to Brussels, and she came back from the Tribunal amused and upset at the same time.

"I suppose it's good they had the Tribunal. The echoes have reached Spain, but we've wasted a lot of time. Most of all because it was organized on the basis of personal testimony, so we spent hours listening to women's tragedies. Maybe it bored me more than it impressed me because I already know the stories. Maybe the others who attended, although they were more concerned with kissing their companions — yes, my girl, yes, the majority were lesbians — possibly they took something away from it. Well, the proof of it is that Elisenda Verdiell — she approached us as soon as she found out we were

Spanish — was thrilled. She decided to immediately join a self help group on matters of health and sexuality. She seems to have discovered a new world. Above all she was amazed we Spaniards were so well prepared ideologically and that our representation was the most numerous, with thirty-four women from all over the country. Well, if it was useful to her, maybe there were others who'll feel motivated to work in feminism after the Tribunal, too. I would've wanted to establish united strategies for feminist struggle, but it seems like we're still far away from that. There's a lot of divergence in the groups from all over the world."

Elisa listened distractedly. Her interest at that time, March 1976, was centered on the impatient waiting for the amnesty that should release Arnau from prison, while she was anxiously looking for work that would free her from economic dependence on her parents.

"That's what it seems like, doesn't it? She finally found a purpose for her life, after she'd been searching so eagerly since she was a teenager. Elisenda has a great passion to live and be useful to others, and she couldn't develop that in the dull world of her family. Well, like you, right? That must be why you were friends, you found each other so quickly..."

Isabel interrupted herself in confusion because, in that autumn of 1985, the future that wasn't even imaginable ten years before had already been set in motion. Elisa's supposed religious calling, which had transformed into her devotion to political struggle for so many years, was no longer important. It belonged to an irretrievable past. Isabel watched her friend's reaction out of the corner of her eye with a disturbed look, and Elisa, who had understood, blushed violently. The values that had determined her life's path until then and had allowed her to live with the security of someone who knows she has been chosen for missions the majority of her compatriots were rejecting in terror, had been lost, leaving her with a vague feeling of annoyance, the sensation of having squandered the years of her youth. The Elisa sitting in front of Isabel that day didn't seem to hold onto a single trace of that former way of being. Unadulterated, purified of all the ideological duty they had piled onto her for decades, her only objective was to satisfy her immediate desires, and Elisa read this unfavorable opinion in Isabel's face, but didn't know how to protest against it.

"Anyway, life has taken us all far away from our point of departure. Elisenda is now very enthusiastic about the feminist struggle, and she's coming back, with a lot of experience, ready to revitalize it here. She says we're all out of touch. It seems she's going to rock the boat. She can do it, you know her. By the way, she wrote to me asking for your address, she wants to see you right away… I already told you, she was very impressed with your prison time. She considers you a hero."

That observation again grated on Elisa's nerves. She thought all of Isabel's words contained a hidden reproach. She preferred not to respond. It wasn't urgent to see Elisenda.

"I'm sorry," he repeated. "It must've been very painful for you. But you'll be able to have more, I suppose. Well, that is, if you want…"

Arnau felt tremendously annoyed. He spoke with conventional words of condolence, without knowing, and fearing where Elisa wanted to take the conversation.

"Of course," she responded disdainfully.

She kept saying that she wanted children so everyone would believe her. On one occasion she claimed that she had always wanted them, and didn't even blink at her mother's expression of surprise. She didn't want to remember her previous manifestations of displeasure at the possibility that had caused so many arguments in her parents' house. Now she assured them it had been Arnau who had imposed the necessity of doing without them because of their clandestine activity. But her parents had heard their daughter's criticisms about the work of a housewife many times, about the dependence and subordination it meant to raise children, and they doubted Arnau would feel the same rejection of parenthood. When Tamara, Arnau and Roser's daughter, was born, Elisa's explanations didn't convince anyone. Nevertheless, she insisted.

"All women want to have children, it's an experience only we can have, and there's no reason to look down on it."

Sometimes she remembered those ugly, malnourished creatures that were so precariously raised in prison and told herself that under those conditions it was easy to reject motherhood. It wasn't about that. A mother wanted the best for her children, and that wasn't exactly prison. The maternal instinct was so manifest that Marisa Cuéllar had gotten married soon after bring released, and already had a fat, round, bright little boy, who was the delight of his parents. And María Jesús?

"María Jesús is in a psychiatric institution."

Elisa looked at Octubre in astonishment. It was becoming unbearable to catch up on the lives of her comrades in the struggle. She was always afraid the tragedy might have brought them down, as in María Jesús's case. She could suffer no more. She had come to the end of her psychic resistance, she was certain. That was why she needed a quiet, routine life by the side of her husband and children.

Octubre smiled sarcastically. "By the side of which husband? Yours or someone else's?"

That was the last time Elisa spoke with Octubre. It had already been several months since they had seen each other. She was sick of reproaches, she claimed. As she saw it, Octubre was the only one who had behaved so horribly that she should always be apologizing. She wasn't going to stand for any more scolding, as if she were guilty of who knew what tremendous crimes. She was only going to associate with nice, friendly people, who would talk with her about the beautiful things in life and not the sinister ones.

"In sum, you've settled yourself completely into bourgeois life…"

Elisa didn't understand why Isabel thought that was so bad. "It happens to us all," she replied aggressively. "None of the comrades who were living in frozen basements and killing people in the streets is still in the same situation. They've all gotten married, had children, they enjoy comfortable homes and try to earn more money every day. Even Marisa Cuéllar decided to get married after seeing her man executed, and now she has a son and a lovely apartment. I'd really like to know why I have to be the only one who should remain pure, distanced from human necessities. Am I the only one who has to live a permanent tragedy, without enjoying love, economic well-being, children? You know what I think? That Octubre's really brainwashed you. And you couldn't even stand her before."

Isabel momentarily lost the patience that usually didn't fail her.

"And you know what I say? That the person Octubre always brainwashed was you. It was notorious, and that's why you can't see her. And not only are you unhappy with yourself and sorry about that relationship, but I also suspect that deep down you envy her tremendously. Her loyalty to her principles, her life, the inalterability of her convictions, which always put you in an annoying position of contradicting yourself. Besides, and most of all, you blame her for your separation from Arnau, even though you deny it…"

That afternoon the two friends didn't speak again.

Arnau had listened very attentively to Elisa's discourse about the desire for motherhood that she had always felt, and the smile that emerged little by little on his lips began to annoy her deeply.

"What are you laughing at?"

"I'm not laughing, just smiling… I was remembering those times when you didn't seem so enthusiastic about playing the role of mother. When you emphatically pushed your family away and even called having a male partner into question."

Elisa stared open-mouthed without knowing how to answer.

Chapter 18

"That's what the feminist movement has been so good for. It's made us abandon our spineless prejudices and fears. Do you remember Mercedes and Nieves?"

Elisa smiled back at Octubre and nodded.

Octubre added, "Do you remember in prison when you called lesbians 'substitutes'?" And she started to laugh boomingly at Elisa's embarrassed look.

"My education. The same as the rest of them… You must remember the scandal over Mercedes's masturbation. We were absolutely conditioned by a phallocratic heterosexual education. I always thought that, really, the women comrades' heroism responded to nothing more than their wanting their men to admire them, to lining up with the expectations their husbands had placed on them."

"You say that because that was the case for you, right?"

Octubre looked at her with a mocking smile as she finished dressing. The conversation about love always implicated Elisa in a way that was hardly flattering.

"And why always me? Doesn't everyone do stupid things, make mistakes, and even commit crimes for love? Why does everyone criticize me or mock me about my relationships? Have they been that ridiculous or strange?"

"Well, you couldn't strictly say that about a woman who's loved the same man for years and years…"

And Octubre went into the bathroom, closing the conversation with that sentence and adding a new criticism to the old ones. Years later Elisa would remember that comment when Pere bombarded her with his recriminations, and she would think that lovers were always inappropriately jealous, even of past relationships.

Octubre came out of the bathroom and looked with pleasure at Elisa, who was still naked, sitting on the bed. Slowly, with exquisite tenderness, she caressed the small oval of her cheek, the contour of Elisa's shoulders, lowered her fingers down Elisa's arms and put them around her waist. Elisa protested weakly.

"Don't start again, please. It's late."

She had to admit that the caresses of Octubre's fingers excited her more quickly than those of any other lover. She observed, with surprise, the difference that existed between that relationship and those she had with the two men she had known sexually. Touch, sight, and smell brought her sensations different from those she had experienced up to that point. The crudeness of masculine movements contrasted with Octubre's delicacy. At first she even told herself the caresses were too light, and were too small a stimulant for her healthy appetite. Later she began to value the exquisite sensitivity necessary to feel those light brushes, and the sharp howls they provoked in her nerve endings.

The first time was at the end of one of those very long, disorderly and uproarious meetings Octubre's feminist group held every Wednesday. When Elisa first noted Octubre's hands on her shoulders, and immediately, with no transition, the burning lips that kissed her repeatedly on the nape, she felt slow and provincial because of the very fear she felt. Both had drunk plenty of the white wine they usually served at the meetings, and the laughter, songs, and shouting got louder as the night wore on. Because of that, Elisa told herself she wasn't exactly conscious of what was happening.

Without saying a word, she had allowed Octubre to caress her shoulders, her neck, and then she imprisoned Elisa's nipples until she couldn't help but shudder. Elisa knew nothing about lesbian relations and so the sweet masturbation Octubre put her through was unexpected and somewhat dull.

"I must have been the dull one, right? When I had to imitate you…"

Whenever they remembered that first time, Elisa always blushed at her initial clumsiness. But Octubre immediately reassured her and even flattered her, praising her innocence, which was her most attractive feature, and her special sensitivity which soon showed her how to satisfy her friend.

The relationship seemed predestined for perfection, if only Elisa's living with Arnau, which she didn't want to question, hadn't clouded the happiness Octubre thought she had achieved.

"It's the fulfillment of the predictions of feminism, you see? Free from masculine exploitation and brutality, women will find a perfect balance only when they have sexual relationships among themselves."

But Octubre wasn't fooling herself about the polite silence with which Elisa received her habitual displays of enthusiasm. They never mentioned the subject, but Arnau's shadow presided over Octubre's bed during the one or two times a week that the two friends made love. Octubre didn't want to make difficult choices for Elisa, most of all because she was afraid they would probably work against her. Although he didn't seem to behave with as much devotion, she told herself bitterly, confused as he was by the stress his distance from the party was causing him. And this situation complicated Elisa's feelings, and Octubre saw her more on edge every day about Arnau's unusual attitude.

Our relationship had come at a bad time, she told herself. If it had come up when Arnau was spending all his time conspiring with the party, Elisa would have felt justified by the way her husband always passed her over in favor of his political calling. But the physical attraction between the two women developed exactly when Arnau had abandoned his work in the party, and was staying at home for hours on end, when before he had spent them on the same endless meetings as always. And even when Octubre saw it was obvious that he didn't constantly need Elisa's attention, and that he preferred to study, read, write, or simply be alone, surely planning out the new strategy he would follow when he was reintegrated into his beloved party, Elisa didn't arrive at the same conclusions as her friend. She was convinced, with her usual lack of perception, that the love, interest and desire to share all experiences which had closely united them in the recent past continued intact in Arnau.

For that reason, the regrets she had about what she already considered a sinful relationship began to cloud the calm of the initial encounters. It was easy for Octubre to detect the first signs of irreversible deterioration. At the beginning she thought that by pretending to ignore it, by avoiding talking about it, it would be possible to ward off the danger. It was only a matter of having patience, of lavishing patience and understanding, exactly those qualities which made feminine love different from masculine. It soon became impossible to hide the fact that Elisa was more annoyed by Octubre's attentions and affections than by Arnau's lack of consideration.

"You see? The more inattentive and even slighting Arnau is, the more she worries about him, the more afraid she is of bothering him, and that means fewer possibilities for me to be with her. On the other hand, every day she treats me worse. I suppose she wants to make me break up with her, but I can't, I can't… I just can't."

She didn't want to add that it had become a passionate and physical necessity to hold Elisa's thin and still so juvenile body next to her, that her presence, her conversation, her infantile temper, and her absent-mindedness were indispensable to her. It caused her unbearable anguish to imagine the day when she could not have her at her side in bed any more, even if it was only the couple of hours Elisa lent her once in a while, always pressed by impatience and anxiety.

"Could it be possible that one day you'll never see her again?"

The fear reflected in her face touched Isabel Fortuny, who was unexpectedly speaking with her that day. There were no strong ties of friendship between them, and generally the only occasions they had been together were when Elisa brought them together. That afternoon, deeply upset, Octubre had called Isabel and begged to see her, and Isabel could never have imagined the reason was to make her the receiver of that intimate confidence. Isabel hadn't known anything about Elisa's new love affair. In the last months they had seen very little of each other, distanced by Elisa's new feminist activities. *They really were new*, she thought ironically, and Octubre's sincerity, which seemed crude and in bad taste, hadn't endeared her to Isabel. But she was moved by the desperation in Octubre's damp eyes and the sunken corners of her mouth, which said much more than her words.

"I understand. I'm sorry for your sake. But you should've known…" The last sentence came out of her mouth unbidden, spoiling the superficial comfort she had wanted to offer. But even so, Octubre was grateful for her words.

"Yes, you're right. How is it possible that at 42 years old I could think things could turn out any other way? Right? And even more knowing Elisa and her fixation on Arnau. But maybe it's true that love is blind… No, I know it's not, and I can say with all certainty that my love for Elisa has deep and logical reasons, but it's also true that it was condemned beforehand to end badly. And no one can do anything about it."

With that affirmation she took away Isabel's role, and Isabel didn't understand what Octubre's purpose for seeing her had been.

"I had to talk to someone. Someone absolutely discreet, who would never repeat this story. For the first time, I find myself without a friend to confide my troubles to. Also, for the first time, this matter doesn't just concern me and someone free of problems. Elisa is a very vulnerable person, uncomfortable with the new situation, confused by her own reactions and so profoundly subjected to Arnau that she'll give anything to keep him… And I don't know whether she'll be able to, in the end."

This last observation, which they both remembered years later as proof of Octubre's insightfulness, surprised Isabel at the time.

"She's been searching for her identity so long, and has continually lost the ones she got from the nuns, family, social environment, her political activity and even her unconditional love for Arnau. And, as we can see now, it isn't all that unconditional, given that her own instincts prevail, when necessary, over her promises and prejudices. That's another of the things, I think, that have confused her, even if she doesn't want to admit it."

In making this last reflection Octubre let a trace of satisfaction show through. Her vanity was flattered when she thought that only she had been able to get Elisa to break her, up to then, inalterable fidelity to Arnau. Surely that fact would console her for Elisa's inevitable indifference in the end, Isabel thought.

"Tell her I don't want to hurt her. I think she's afraid now that I'll cause a situation so Arnau will find out and force her to choose once and for all. But of course, how could you talk to her about this? Then she would know I've told you, and she'd be very upset… Never mind. Thank you for listening to me."

Nevertheless, the situation Octubre claimed she didn't want presented itself when, at the end of her patience one afternoon, she pressed Elisa to make love at her house after Arnau had left, for once, to meet with some friends. Elisa resisted Octubre's advances, insisting that it didn't seem right to her, but, as she noticed with more and more irritation, it didn't deflect the caresses her lover lavished upon her. On the living room sofa, with adolescent struggles, she got Elisa partly undressed, and had hardly started the rites of love when the sound of keys in the lock frustrated her hopes.

"I wasn't the only one caught making love with another woman." And the malicious smile persisted. Elisa didn't know how to respond.

For some time the women were unsure whether Arnau had really seen it or understood it, because, while they hurried to recompose their appearance, opening the window shades all the way and fluffing the couch pillows, he had gone directly from the entry hall to the bedroom and taken enough time before joining them to find them chatting quietly with two steaming cups of coffee. That afternoon, he was especially friendly, entertaining them with stories about his teachers, his companions, and his possibilities for work, which seemed more remote every day, considering his dangerous resume and the fact that he didn't have a degree. After that, Elisa remembered, they had never clearly spoken about the subject. The incident definitively resolved her relationship with Octubre in the way she had always feared: breaking off all sexual relations.

"We've never talked about this," she was able to babble, her mouth dry.

He mercilessly mocked her. "Well, I'd really like to talk about it."

And suddenly Elisa felt the paralyzing panic disappear. Suddenly free of all fear, with a lightness she never had until that moment, she smiled in turn and said smoothly, "Well, I'm at your service. What do you want to know?"

Her response had the desired effect. Arnau stopped smiling. He had no interest in talking over issues that no longer mattered to him, that he even doubted had ever mattered. Perhaps surprise was the predominant feeling when he understood the nature of the relationship between the two friends, and which took him a long time to accept. So long that he never did decide what his feelings about that new experience were, because soon after, he met Roser and he was no longer interested in clarifying that strange event that had never entered into his calculations. He was surprised because, in spite of his sexual experience, which, if not abundant, was at least more varied than Elisa's, he would never have been able to imagine that his wife, whom he thought he knew perfectly, could have a lesbian relationship. He could hardly explain why such a possibility had been so radically excluded from his mind. Perhaps because of her religious roots, because of the unconditional love she professed for him, and which he was completely secure about, but certainly because for him those relationships had no importance. They could be indulgently attributed to adolescence, normal only during that age when teenagers are exposed to each other in school, in dormitories, at their friends' houses, and play at an undeveloped and immature love, with no consequences, before entering into adulthood, which brought real love with it.

"What did you want to talk about?" Elisa insisted, savoring her triumph, though she nevertheless felt a shred of discomfort mixed in. Arnau's silence disturbed her calm.

"Maybe nothing, you're right. We should've done it then, and now it's out of place."

Arnau's quick surrender threw Elisa off. She had been able to overcome her embarrassment over the topic, and she had to make that effort useful for something. Could it be true that her relationship with Octubre never mattered to him, or, on the contrary, his jealousy and suffering was essential to his decision to separate from her?

For a time, she tortured herself with regrets, obsessive questions and doubts about the influence that episode had had on the end of their marriage. But she never dared to confide in anyone about her ponderings. On one occasion it had been Isabel who had referred to it, and that phrase…

"I don't understand how you let yourself get tangled up with Octubre like that. If Carles was your salvation, what was Octubre, eh? Because Arnau was still with you then, there was no reason for something like that. On the contrary, I'm sure that's what motivated him to leave."

It gave Elisa proof that Isabel knew all about her romantic episode with Octubre, but she didn't ask who had told her. She felt guilty enough to imagine that she had been so stupid as to carry on her relationship with her friend in such an indiscreet way that everyone had realized. She had never wanted to talk about the subject with Octubre, but only acted exasperated and contemptuous toward her. She passed the worst moments of that painful episode of her life by drowning herself in a cyclone of doubts, anxiety, anger, and mean behavior that she didn't know how to avoid and which later anguished her. Not only did she live through the sadness of having been abandoned by Arnau, but she also had to bear the torment of Octubre's jealousy, her own remorse for the unfair way she had behaved toward Octubre, and the worry about what Arnau would think of her unusual behavior without being able to know his opinion. Well, it was time to find out. With more courage than she had ever had, she insisted.

"Oh, no. We should take advantage of this occasion that's suddenly come up. Let's talk about everything, please, once and for all. What did you think of my relationship with Octubre? Was that why you left me?"

Arnau didn't hide his surprise at the last question. He would never have said that that episode had influenced his decision to separate from Elisa. He didn't even think about it then. If he had to be honest, he hadn't thought about anything in those moments. Isabel and Gemma, Elisa's sister, and María were the ones who required a more elaborate response to the question. His standard answer, "Our relationship was in its death throes, the love we had at the beginning no longer existed," was the only one that seemed authentic to him. But he couldn't explain why the love had ended, when it had seemed eternal. Simply because there was nothing eternal, and much less love. All his male friends quietly accepted the superficial report he offered them about his new partner, and no one tried to keep discussing that decision, which in the end was only his business.

But that simple answer, to which Isabel always responded, "That's what all men say," wasn't acceptable to any of the women friends. They expected a more sophisticated and concrete explanation from him that would satisfy their need to deeply analyze a subject which, to Arnau's surprise, continued to interest them after so much time.

"No, no, by no means. I didn't separate from you because of anger at all. Besides, that wasn't so important."

Arnau's smile had that mocking, scornful expression that had offended her at the beginning of the conversation. This minimization of the matter let Elisa, for the first time, understand the value she had placed on the relationship she had with Octubre, and, also for the first time, she was conscious of how superfluous her remorse had been, and how different their assessments of the situation were. She was finally going to understand what had tortured her for two years. To him, her romance with Octubre had always seemed unimportant. Fifteen years of living together hadn't shown Elisa so much about her husband as that response had.

"How different we are!" she suddenly exclaimed, angrily, enviously, relieved, and happy to finally reach the answer.

"Let's see if you can hurl out once and for all, with food and bile and innards, that stupid love for that man who doesn't love you. He doesn't love you, do you hear? Who probably never loved you! He probably only wanted meekness, obedience, like the kind you always gave him. He used you in his little political adventures until he got tired of you. And anyway it doesn't matter! If he loved you, great, while it lasted, and then it was over! Get it? The love ran out, it's that simple and nothing more…"

It seemed that Octubre's voice was echoing in the room. So, was it true, then? Was that all it was, that the love had run out for him the same way the water runs out when you turn off the faucet?

"How different we are…"

She wasn't expecting him to reply, but Arnau felt obliged to comment on the claim she had made twice now.

"Yes, of course, but I suppose it's a good thing. Opposites attract…"

"It's not like that."

He was sorry for being so careless, and again felt that the endless conversation was going nowhere.

"Things aren't as complicated as you make them. It's impossible to live with a person who's always asking the reason for everything. Why you get up, why you shave, why you leave or come back. It's a real torture. In love relationships, things have to be simpler to be pleasant. I'm sick of these tortuous analyses. You looked, you thought, you said. Human beings are more spontaneous than that in personal relationships."

"But not in political ones, right?"

His explosion of bad temper had led Arnau to passionately defend spontaneity and primitivism. He, who analyzed every political event with the meticulousness of a scientist, who met endlessly with his party comrades to go over a thousand times what had already been gone over, who saw the manifestation of class struggle in every human being, and who wanted to explain all human behavior in terms of Marxism and Leninism, all pure speculation with no relation to reality.

"Political matters are more complex, there's no comparison."

His mood was getting worse and worse, as it seemed to him that Elisa was rounding him up, taking advantage of his weakness of always following her lead.

"They have an importance that matters of love don't have, isn't that right?"

"No, it's not that. You must've said it before, that men and women are very different, and what you consider important, we don't. We men relate to each other like friends, like comrades, for the sake of the struggle, for the sake of the work..."

"Yes, I understand, you don't have to repeat it. For the sake of the really important matters. That's why men are much better friends and comrades than husbands and lovers."

"Octubre must've taught you that. She was the one who indoctrinated you in feminism, with the result we've already seen."

Arnau no longer hid his hostility. But Elisa felt much more calm. With a strange smile, she clarified, "No, Octubre never said that to me. Juana Parroto did."

"Juana? Juana Parroto?"

He could not imagine Juana in the role of love counselor to Elisa, and much less with that judgment that was so clearly scornful of men, which he had identified as characteristic only of feminists.

"When did you see her?"

"A little while ago. She got back from Amsterdam a few months ago, and was going to Menorca right away."

"Why?"

Juana had disappeared from the party when she was released. No one would have believed she was going to abandon political life, which had been everything to her for more than ten years. The reaction that followed the revelation of her hidden love, once she recovered from her nervous breakdown, was the one everyone expected. She put herself back together little by little, with her comrades' help, and the vitamins the doctor prescribed her, and at the end of a few months it seemed she had regained some of her original aggressiveness. The satisfaction she got from the recognition of her merits by her party also contributed to her recovery. When the first amnesty set her free at Christmas, she got right back into the struggle.

"Because she's become a hippy..." Elisa smiled, savoring her triumph beforehand. It was surely the only complete triumph she had had over her husband that morning, and perhaps in her whole life.

"A hippy? Juana Parroto is a hippy?"

Arnau's surprise tinged with scandal truly amused Elisa.

"Yes, a hippy... Why are you so surprised?"

"And you're not? Does it seem normal to you that Juana Parroto's become a hippy?"

Elisa took time before responding, without acknowledging Arnau's impatience. "Maybe it is, maybe Juana's choice is the normal thing to do. After what she went through, she had no other choice. She was very close to madness..."

"She's crazy now."

"Some of us became feminists, some, lesbians... We had to find an alternative to a life that had run its course. Hearing your dismissive value judgments, I understand why Juana became a hippy. As bad as her commune companions may treat her, it can't be worse than what you all have done."

CHAPTER 19

"I had no doubts, you know? Sometimes I felt a little tired, but that was all. In any case, when I had doubts I blamed it on my own weakness, after my illness."

It had taken Elisa a while to recognize Juana when, that spring of 1986, she had suddenly met her in the street. Without being beautiful, Juana's face had had regular features, long and thin, with large dark eyes and a small nose and mouth. Her most attractive feature had been the silky black hair that hung almost to her waist. In prison, she had taken care of it meticulously. *Her only vanity*, thought Elisa when she watched her comb her hair at night, and she thought it tenderly because it seemed that that slight narcissism gave her just the human touch Juana needed in order not to be a robot.

Looking at her now, as they exchanged hugs and kisses, Elisa sensed the physical change in her. Was it only physical? She was very thin and her skin was sunburned, even though they were coming out of a long, cold winter. Wrinkles were beginning to mark the corners of her mouth and eyes, and most of all, her hair had lost its vitality. Short, sparse, discolored, with no body, it gave her a completely different look from what Elisa remembered from her prison years.

"Oh, my hair! If it were only that…" Juana answered Elisa's question of why she had cut her hair.

Sitting at a table in a café with Elisa, Juana smoked compulsively, moving her hand in circles. She was blinking her eyes a little too much, and would smile or take on a somber expression with no warning.

"…so I accepted the party's instructions without argument and went to Valladolid, where they assigned me to the reorganization of

FRAP, which had fallen apart. And after two months I was arrested again."

At Elisa's smothered cry Juana smiled again, strangely, artificially, and Elisa didn't know what to make of it.

"Yes, it was predictable. It was simply suicide, as if everyone, the party and I, had gone insane. We no longer had leaders. They were still in prison, or in exile or had fled the party absolutely fed up with the paranoid politics that were pushing us to self-destruction."

Elisa's surprise at the words she was using brought to Juana's face again that smile that seemed lit up with beatific visions.

"It was useless to try to put FRAP back together, it was totally dead and we should've buried it with full honors instead of merely sinking it into oblivion. It made no sense to go to Valladolid, to die of cold in that cursed winter, in an awful dump of a pension, where the landlady looked at me with more distrust every day, to meet a dozen times with three comrades, even more down-and-out than me, survivors of the last raids…"

Elisa remembered one of the periods of her activism. She had just joined the party and was alone in Barcelona, because Arnau was completing his military service in a punishment squad in Sidi Ifni, when the party decided to name her supervisor of the organization in Tarragona and Gerona. She was never able to understand how Antonio Cherta, who sent her to inspect the work of the comrades twice a month, could call her work organizing the party when she went to visit those two strange characters who waited for her on the fifteenth or thirtieth of every month at the train station of each of the two cities.

The first day she got off the train in Tarragona and looked on the platform for someone whose appearance could match that of a comrade she was supposed to call Eusebio, she was disappointed at the evident absence of a friendly face. As she walked down the street, wondering whether to look for a pension or go back to the station to wait for the next train, a wheelchair crossed in front of her in the street. When she stopped and let him go by with a "sorry," the password startled her: "My name is Eusebio, and you?" He was missing both of his legs, and hung the tickets for the lottery benefitting the blind from one shoulder. He looked at her with an amused smile.

Elisa never understood Eusebio's permanent cheer or his simple sense of humor, which sometimes bored her. That unusual comrade's duties consisted of distributing the pamphlets Elisa regularly brought him, hidden in the bottom of her purse. Taking advantage of his mobile job, Eusebio distributed the FRAP and PC-ML publications to customers and friends. Elisa wanted to ask him how he dared to undertake such dangerous work, given the restrictions on his movement.

In such a small and reactionary city like Tarragona, to whom could he give those papers filled with insults and threats not only against the regime but also the opposition, without fear of being betrayed? Security measures prevented such questions. The briefing Eusebio regularly gave her while she strolled next to his wheelchair through a desolate, stinking neighborhood, was limited to some conversations he had had with customers and friends about the population's discontent about diverse measures of the regime that affected the city. When Eusebio had to transmit more important and confidential information, he gave Elisa a message written in code to give to Ramiro.

"It was stupid, since it would always have been easier to hide my position as party supervisor if they didn't find strange papers like that on me, written in a simple code a child could decipher."

For six months, every fifteenth of the month, Elisa went to her appointment with Eusebio and had lunch with him, walked around the outskirts of Tarragona and received the dull news about a city in which nothing was happening. Suddenly she received orders to stop making the trips and she never saw her disabled friend again, and she never knew what had become of him.

In Gerona a retired man was waiting for her, a survivor of three wars, half deaf, asthmatic, and indifferent to the work of the PC-ML or FRAP. Elisa was convinced that Pablo merely wanted to see someone he could talk with about his past adventures. Surely the PCE must have abandoned him for useless and his grandchildren would flatly refuse to listen to him. For the year and a half that the relationship lasted before it was interrupted as suddenly as the one with Eusebio, Elisa never got out of him a single "official" report about the state of the party's struggle in Gerona, the distribution of its propaganda, or the people's opinion about the regime. During each visit, Pablo reluctantly promised to prepare the longed-for report, excusing himself from writing it, offering as grounds his ignorance of writing and syntax, and his news about the present situation in Gerona were vague remarks that weren't good for anything.

The conversations took place in a tavern, always the same one despite Elisa's remonstrance since Pablo was a creature of habit and set no store by security measures. The talks lasted for hours and revolved around the Civil War, his exile, guerilla warfare, his anti-Nazi resistance, the German concentration camp, the clandestine struggle in the interior, and his detention, torture, Military Tribunal and prison time. At the door of the Burgos penitentiary, now fourteen years ago, his story concluded. The second topic, less transcendent, and which he allowed less time for, was the meticulous recounting of the everyday gossip about life in the city, most of all in Pablo's family and neighborhood, full of complaints about his wife's stinginess, his children's ingratitude, the disaffection of his friends, and the cowardice of his former comrades.

Though Elisa didn't stop going to the appointment, she also didn't report to Ramiro about the true nature of her contact in Gerona, and it was because the lessons in recent history that Pablo minutely shelled out explained to Elisa what no one had taught her about the Civil War and the postwar resistance. To justify that waste of time when she should have been carrying out party activity, she told herself that Pablo's gossip about his family and friends was really a chronicle of the city's present social situation, which after all was what she was going there to investigate for her party.

"And if I had understood what Pablo was telling me, instead of considering it an excuse to keep visiting him, I would've realized that his chronicle of daily life in Gerona indicated, better than any other report, the impossibility of establishing our party in that city or even the impossibility of the struggle as we understood it at the time."

"You weren't the only one who fooled herself or let herself be seduced by Ramiro's orders. If it was impossible to agitate the population of Gerona in 1970, it was even more impossible in Valladolid in 1976. The comrades there weren't old or disabled, but they could do nothing but survive in that city dominated by the fascists, gripped by panic after the repression unleashed all over Spain the year before. The weakness of our organization became clear when I saw that there were only three boys participating in the party in the entire city. A Renault worker, a waiter and a student. We were so few and so abandoned that I decided to forego some security measures and meet all together, instead of playing at conspiracy and having partial meetings, where you could pretend the organization was much bigger. No, that wasn't the reason for my arrest, though it's true it happened when I was going to a meeting. The reason was the fall of other comrades in Burgos who informed on one of us. All the police had to do was follow him in the city and hunt me down, because he was able to escape. And then I realized what torture really was.

"They weren't content to just punch me like the first time… It was the spring of the democracy… Lord! The party always said that nothing had changed in the country since Franco's death and I can confirm that at that moment, at least, it was true in the police stations. They applied antiterrorist measures, even though I hadn't done anything more than take part in a few meetings to try to rebuild union activity, and since the police had no record on me because I was there with a fake identity, for two weeks I was absolutely abandoned to their sadism…"

Elisa decided to have a brandy even though it was only noon. While she waited for it, both she and Juana were silent. On the other side of the windows, people were walking down the sunny street, everyone living in peace. No one wanted to bother with the frightening tale of Juana's tortures. But Elisa was sure that the general indifference toward the subject of police repression wasn't due to the ten years that had passed since the events took place. Even at the very moment in which Juana was thrown into the hell of her detention at the police station, the people of Valladolid who crossed through the streets adjacent to the Police Headquarters would not have wanted to hear the screams of the victims.

"Above all, they got sadistic sexually. After they beat me, they stripped me, because I never obeyed the order to get undressed. Maybe that small rebellion, that stubborn refusal to entertain them with a voluntary strip-tease, helped me recover afterward. I kept myself going on that small dignity alone. They tore my clothes off, pushing me and scratching me. They threw me onto a table and looked me over while commenting on the details of my anatomy, and said such charming things as 'I wish you had your period right now so we could see you bleeding between your legs! You'd lick up the blood, bitch!' Sometimes they stood me up and touched me. They exposed themselves and masturbated. Not all of them and not every time. They restrained themselves a lot. Probably it was enough for them just to get excited. That atmosphere of morbid insanity, the stink of tobacco, the locked door, the lights on in the middle of the day, the bare furnishings, it delighted them. They screamed all the time, and they laughed. Once, one of them urinated in the middle of the room, threatening to spray me, and the others laughed so much I thought they were all going to end up peeing on each other.

"I went to prison with my clothes destroyed, my pants zipper broken, and there wasn't a single button left on my blouse. Later they invented something else. One of them entertained himself for a while by pulling out my pubic hair, and when I would scream, they'd all laugh, expose their penises, and threaten to rape me. No, they never did. I never found out if it was because they were afraid of the consequences, like a pregnancy or something like that, or if it was strictly forbidden. After that game they usually dumped a bucket of water over me, and while I was still wet they dressed me, hitting and pushing again. Once, one of them stuck his finger in my vagina, but the others signaled for him to stop… And then the worst part began…

"They took me out of Headquarters, they put me in a car with six or seven of them and took me to a hill on the outskirts of the city, and when we got there, they told me that if I didn't tell who my comrades were, they'd shoot me. They pretended to get ready to do it several times, and I never knew when the real one would be. I'd been locked up, underground or in the office where they tortured me for days and nights. I didn't eat, I couldn't sleep, I was waiting for them to kill me at any moment. And then I started wanting them to. It would've been an end to the beatings and sexual torments. In the last days I was delirious. I talked to myself and laughed. When they stripped me and touched me and laughed, I laughed, too. One morning, after I heard the blanks being fired, I clapped and started laughing out loud. Then they got scared for the first time. They pushed me into the car and I was laughing the whole way back, I couldn't stop. When we got back to Headquarters my laughing might alert someone. They locked me up underground, but first the guards yelled at me to shut up, and then they got scared too and went to ask the inspectors to do something. One came down and shouted at me, in a panic, to shut up, and it seemed so funny to me that I laughed even more. Then they gave me a fist in the chin, a perfect knockout. I woke up in the jail cell in Valladolid. Then I think it was the worst…"

Elisa's eyes hurt, they were staying as dry as if they were full of sand, and she could no longer remember a time when she had had saliva in her throat.

"During the month I was in solitary I thought I was going to go insane. No one visited me, no one remembered me. They'd arrested me with a fake ID and I never revealed my true identity. I had been living in a stinking pension, where the landlady hated me. My comrades couldn't go near the prison, my family didn't know anything about me. There could be no greater solitude. I told myself every day that that was the life I'd chosen. No one forced me to enter the party, though my love for Ernesto had some influence, and when the party sent me to Valladolid, I always could've refused. It was my destiny and I alone had chosen it. I remembered the stories of the Bolsheviks, exiled in Siberia, with no food, fleeing across the tundra in the winter with frozen feet. I thought of the dead comrades, of my poor executed Ernesto, and I told myself that that was the life of a revolutionary, until the final victory… It consoled me a little, but my subconscious told me that our terrible sacrifice had been useless. We would never attain the victory we'd given up everything for.

"I always thought I didn't want any compensation for my struggle. No honors, no homages, no medals, no high posts when we won. But I never thought that we weren't ever going to win, that we'd even become outcasts, worthy of curiosity or pity, and the people would look at us with fear or indifference."

Juana was quiet for a moment, and Elisa began to cry, but Juana didn't seem to notice. She was looking out the window at the people going down the street, the cars that filled the roadway, the shop windows filled with tempting, enormously expensive and superfluous things. Elisa sniffled without trying to hide it. She felt devoid of all social convention. She couldn't use up the last bit of strength she had left in checking herself so as not to disturb the educated people in the café.

"In the prison cell where they held me incommunicado for thirty days, I kept obsessively replaying some scenes from one of Marcelo Mastroiani's films in my mind. The movie takes place in Italy during the 1930's. A school teacher, Mastroiani, comes to an industrial town where the factory workers are living in miserable conditions. He's really a union leader there to organize the workers, agitate them and organize a strike. These people, who live in shacks, practically caves — they're so afraid that they don't dare strike. Mastroiani organizes them, puts together assemblies, meetings, heads the demonstrations, and the repression begins. The police hit them, fire on the crowd, and the first dead fall. Then one of the strike leaders, a brave young kid, gets scared and accuses Marcelo of bringing them to disaster… That scene came to me time and again. I felt like I was watching it. In the cell I had Marcelo Mastroiani, bearded and tired, wrapped up in a threadbare coat and greasy scarf, blowing on his fingers in the cold, and the worker — younger, taller, stronger — and he yelled at him furiously: 'You don't know what you're doing, you're a monster, you only want our destruction! What do you care what we do with our lives? You're crazy!'

"And Mastroiani listened to him until the kid quieted down. Then Mastroiani looked at him with that look he has, adjusted his scarf, and replied meanly, angrily, bitterly, 'You're right, it's true, I'm crazy, I'm nothing like you. Look, you have a house, wife, children, work, school. I have none of that. I only live in freezing pensions where no one knows me, I have no wife, or children, or work, and I'll leave the school this very night. I go from town to town trying to spread my ideas and no one's waiting for me anywhere.' The worker looks at him surprised and stunned, and stammers, 'Then, why do you do it?' Mastroiani waited a few seconds, smiled and answered, 'Because I'm of that race of men who believes in the revolution…' Then the strike gets started and the police pursue Marcelo until they arrest him. When Marcelo is driven to the train between the guards, the worker takes over as the head of the struggle. In a few days, some friends tell him he'd better run, the police are going to arrest him that very night. His wife makes him some provisions, they say goodbye at night and he runs to the station. When he's going to get on the train, another man, a stranger, gets off the train, looks at the worker, goes up to him, and gives him a little piece of paper and tells him, 'Marcelo sent me. Go to X, they'll hide you at this address.' The worker feels moved to see that even from prison, Marcelo is thinking of his safety. He gets on the train and the new leader starts walking down the streets of the town…

"I identified completely with that kind of man. I was willing to go without a home or a job or a husband or children; to live in stinking rented rooms where the landlady looks at you with distrust, watches you through the lock and opens your letters; to eat bread with rancid sausage, sleeping three hours once in a while, with no contact with the people besides the meetings with the comrades once a week, and constantly running from the police. But what I wasn't willing to do, I realize now, was renounce the revolution."

Elisa and Juana were silent for a few moments. While she once again contemplated the people walking down the street, Elisa told herself that none of those people wanted the revolution, and doubted that in the poor neighborhoods the people would feel any more attracted by it. Juana was smiling.

"I saved myself from madness remembering Mastroiani! Amazing, huh? Any of my comrades would've criticized me for it. You should only remember Lenin, Stalin, Mao, Enver Hoxha. For me, during those eternal thirty days, locked up day and night within six square meters, none of my heroes existed. Mastroiani, on the other hand, had a face, a body, he was close to me, slept by my side, ate from my plate, and when I closed my eyes I could even touch his scratchy beard. He was another human being, simply hungry, tired, alone, devastatingly alone, who staked his life on the revolution that would never be. The triumph of Mao and Lenin wasn't helpful to me then, and I've never had use for it since. Only the contact with people like Mastroiani, as alone and insane as me, I suppose, who won't resign themselves to the final defeat. Like Daniel…"

In this new pause, Elisa didn't ask any questions. The tears slid down her face slowly but ceaselessly. She was sure she would not have been able to speak. She both hoped and feared that Juana would continue her tale.

"Finally, after a month, the judge remembered that he had locked me up in a cell incommunicado and no one, not even he, had visited me or asked me anything, and then, with no transition, without ceremony, they let me out of solitary. I think the reason they changed my situation was one of the jailers, who feared for my mental state. It seemed I was talking to myself a lot, but the worst part was that I didn't realize I was doing it, I couldn't remember what I'd said. The official told one of the nuns, and the nun told her not to get involved in things that weren't any of her business, but the woman dared to report the case to the director and finally got him to address the judge, asking him how long I should stay in solitary, and then justice's faithful guardian decided that it wouldn't be a day longer, for the same reason it had been thirty.

"When I got out of the cell and they moved me to the common dormitory, the other prisoners looked at me pop-eyed. I didn't speak, I got dizzy and nauseous, I didn't know how to orient myself in space. So I just sat on the bed and, when I looked up, there was a mirror in front of me. I understood why my companions were afraid. My hair had fallen out in clumps. I had bald spots in some places and in others I still had locks hanging to my shoulders. I had two broken teeth and I'd lost twelve kilos. For a while my companions thought I was 50 years old, and when they found out I'd turned 28 that month they didn't believe it. That same day, they took me to see the doctor, and then they cut my hair… They were good people."

Juana stopped the story and smiled. Her new expression, which had seemed so strange to Elisa, was much more relaxed than the one she had had when Elisa knew her. Her gaze was often lost far away, and a sweet smile gave her a silly expression. *Maybe she's more at peace now*, and Elisa surprised herself thinking that she had definitely liked her more before, when the aggressive gaze of her dark eyes and the challenging jut of her chin gave her her own style, confidence in her own incorruptibility. The confidence women who still believe in the revolution must have. The far off gaze and the dull smile gave her a simple air that made her a stranger. Then the tics came back, and the winking and the movement of her arms made her look odd. *Like a lunatic*, and Elisa decided again that she preferred an aggressive, fanatic Juana, even if she were insane, to that friendly little person she turned into once in a while.

"Finally the party started to get concerned about me, and sent me a lawyer. He convinced me to tell my true identity because, though I was being tried for another reason, the accusations were irrelevant, and besides, things were changing in the country. He notified my parents, my friends, everything was suddenly so easy... and still, it was then that everyone got scared. My parents, when they saw me for the first time in the visiting room, screamed so loud a nun came running. My mother was crying the whole time. My lawyer filed a criminal complaint for torture which the judge dismissed after putting together a parody of an investigation. They showed me a series of police officers I'd never seen and everyone swore they were the ones who interrogated me. I didn't know that one of the most common tricks was to give names of policemen who weren't the ones who'd done the interrogations, so the victims could never identify their torturers.

"And then the second amnesty came along and I went free... My life had changed completely. I didn't have the strength for any more struggles, not even to live. My parents sent me to a psychiatrist, who helped me a little, but he couldn't understand that my breakdown came from the revolution being impossible in Spain."

The pause that followed made Elisa think Juana was expecting some question, but she didn't want to ask any. She understood perfectly what conviction had brought Juana to that devastating conclusion. It was Juana who, turning toward Elisa with a sweet, inquisitive look, asked, "Do you know when I understood that it wasn't possible to continue with our struggle?"

Elisa merely shook her head.

"When I read in the paper that they'd named two of the police who tortured me Superior Chief of Police and Director General of something. Yes, Elisa. Those monsters, with twisted faces, with the smiles of madmen, the very same ones who hit me in the face, in the liver, in the stomach, who laughed when I threw up, who humiliated me with the most outrageous insults, were promoted as soon as democracy began. The constitutional government rewarded them for service rendered during the dictatorship."

"The ones who tortured you in Valladolid?" Elisa's mouth was so dry it hurt.

"No, the ones in Madrid. I suppose they interrogated you, too. Octubre said so."

Elisa vaguely remembered a newspaper article that referred to the promotions. She shook her head doubtfully, and was surprised to see Juana's smile.

"You don't remember, either… What really made me lose heart completely wasn't the indignation I felt when I read the news and saw the pictures of those individuals, who smiled with satisfaction while the official congratulated them. It was seeing that no one responded to such a cynical provocation. Not even those of us who had been their victims… not you… not me. My heart froze when I realized that we fighters had lost strength, enthusiasm, in that long war that'd lasted since 1936. And it didn't matter to anyone else. Because the provocations and mocking continued. Many years later, it must be only a little more than a year ago, they named another known torturer from Zaragoza, Information Commissioner. Then, some of his victims wrote letters to the press, which got the ministry to respond that nothing of the kind was included in the man's file… And that was the end of it. And of us and our utopian love for the revolution. Here, we never had trials against the torturers like in Argentina or Greece. Our dictatorship lasted too long. Too long to survive unharmed. If ten years had gone by, like in those countries, we would still have been able to settle accounts — but forty years! Franco lived on in us."

Juana's face reflected a deep melancholy while she silently contemplated the street. With an earnestness she hadn't had up to that point, and which made her seem more like the party leader Elisa had known, she turned to Elisa.

"We didn't realize, for so many years, that fascism was leveling the country. I woke up from the dream of my ideals many months after leaving prison. When I read the news of the torturers' promotions, I began to link that fact with many others. Then I noticed the dream my neighbors had. They lived in a poor neighborhood and they wanted a second house in the country. I figured out what they spent on gasoline every weekend, I listened to the complaints of book publishers, and found out, for the first time, the fabulous expenses on rock and soccer, and, most of all, after the coup d'état on February 23, 1981, I became convinced that the Spanish people at that moment wouldn't have fought a three-year-long war of extermination to avoid fascism like they did in 1936. I realized how much the Spanish had changed since then, and how slow we'd been, appointing ourselves 'vanguard of the proletariat,' always prophesying the revolution, stuck in the memories of a past that will not return. These people would not only not let themselves be killed to avoid another dictatorship, but they also will not vote for communists. Not even my neighbors, who are out of work and receive miserable retirement pensions. Many of them are longing for Franco. Others, as a big risk, vote for the socialists, and the majority don't vote at all. Revolutionary ideals are not even present in the leftist political elites, who've gone running to ask for a post in the State, knocking each other over in a wild race to get there first. Fascism lived in us, in our flesh and blood and brain waves, during the forty years it reigned. That's too many years, Elisa, too many, for us to come out of it unharmed.

"We're all Franco's children and grandchildren. Do you realize, there hasn't been any other Western country with such a long dictatorship? What kind of education, formation, ideals, were inculcated from the cradle into those men who are now leftist leaders? There was no Free Institution of Teaching or Ferrer Guardia Modern School, where the freethinkers and anarchists who brought Spain the Second Republic were educated and developed. Do you realize that all the country's leaders have been educated in religious schools, which have been formed on the principles of the National Movement, that they were Flechas and Pelayos, and read Maritain as if it were a sin when they were 25 years old, and were much more frightened by the 'Marxist hordes' than by the militarists who attempt coups? In the end, we all know that the Armada was dining with socialist leaders a month before the 1981 coup… To make it short, Elisa, we were blinded by our conspiracies, we didn't realize that Spain wasn't the country we wanted, the one our parents had told a heroic epic about. We continued to believe, for many years, that the people would follow us when we launched armed struggle, and we didn't see that people only wanted to buy things. The ideal to achieve was first a car, then a TV, and now video. And so, people spend more time in front of the TV set than any other place. They're all too rich to start a difficult and bloody struggle in which they wouldn't know what they were going to gain... And our leaders have lost their sense of ethics, the only thing that could've given us the revolutionary impulse we lacked. We, who were the vanguard of the struggle, didn't know how to end the dictatorship. Franco died in his bed, not just old but decayed, and we will pay for that until the end of our days...

"That was what I was telling myself during those months I spent at home, stupefied, definitively defeated, for the first time in my life.

"Marcelo Mastroiani's presence had disappeared and even his memory was fading, and instead of his comforting words, all that was left to me was the grief of being alone. No one could keep me company. My parents and brothers and sisters had never understood me, and I couldn't understand my comrades any more. I even had the courage to go to a halfway clandestine local committee meeting in Madrid, but I didn't understand anything. When it was my turn to give my opinion on what they'd discussed, I said, 'It's impossible, the revolution is impossible. You're all crazy.' That marked my fate. Those comrades who had admired me, and I thought loved me a lot, more than their families or their wives, became wild animals.

"My past merits and present worthlessness weren't of any use for defending me. I had become a police agent. They said that was why I'd been freed. The socially conscious comrades never got out, or were executed. I was a dangerous enemy, an agent of the oligarchy, henchman of the managerial class, etc, etc. At first I wasn't aware of the things they were saying about me because I stayed shut up in my house. Only once did I have any warning. My sister came in from the street and told me with surprise that she had run into a friend of mine who knew her at the bus stop, and he hadn't said hi to her. But it didn't seem like it was because of security measures, because he hadn't pretended not to know her, on the contrary, he'd stared at her and then turned his head away obviously. But I was too depressed to be interested in the incident. Until they came to my house one day to beat me..."

Juana reproduced her dimwitted smile when Elisa gasped.

"I couldn't believe it. When I saw the comrade I had so loved there in the doorway, someone I would've died for, and started to greet him, and he, with this horrible look on his face, a paroxysm of rage, punched me in the chin, what mattered to me most wasn't the pain, but to understand what was going on. I defended myself in vain, and I didn't get a royal thrashing because some neighbors came and he got scared and left. I didn't want to report him, as my family tried to do. It would've been too much for me to go to the police to inform against a comrade. I wasn't angry with him. What continuously tortured me and didn't let me sleep were the regrets. I remembered, so bitterly, the times I'd shown myself to be just as sectarian and paranoid. I was sure I would've voted in favor of beating up an informer like me. Separating myself from that personality as if I were pulling my own head off, was the ultimate torture. I didn't eat or sleep, I would've willingly gone through the arrest all over again. In the end, the police were my enemies, but my comrades…"

Elisa needed a break. Her solar plexus hurt, she was suffocating, and she urgently needed to cry but she could not. She had to remain silent to think, she didn't want to keep listening. Was it preferable for Juana to maintain that defiant expression that gave her an arrogant and secure look if it meant she had to belong to that gang of thugs? Or was it perhaps necessary to suffer from that obsessive paranoia to make the revolution?

As if she had read her thoughts, Juana added, "Most of all I tortured myself wondering whether it was necessary to be an obsessive maniac like them in order to keep a strong faith in the revolution. And right away I would tell myself that I was capable of putting up with them and even defending them, even of becoming their victim with resignation, if they were capable of bringing the revolution about. But Elisa, the most painful thing, as you'll understand, was seeing that none of them was in touch with the reality of our country…"

Elisa suddenly remembered the last demonstration she had attended, asking for Spain to leave NATO. She had gotten Isabel to go with her, in spite of her emphatic dislike of crowds, because of her conviction that belonging to NATO was just another of the tricks being played on them. At the end of the rally the speakers went up on a platform and the crowd wanted to get closer. Some young boys, carrying banners of the PC-ML, made their way pushing and elbowing among the multitude until they found a place in the front row. The brute force of the young arms and legs ran Elisa and Isabel over. Isabel fell onto someone else and Elisa got a kick in the shin that left her gasping. When she turned against the attacking group, she saw in the faces, so young they seemed adolescent, such an aggressive determination that she understood the uselessness of any protest or argument. *For them, this is a stage in the seizing of power,* she understood.

When Isabel, indignantly swearing that she would never participate in such hijinks again, said, "If your ex-comrades took power I'd go into exile on the spot, since it wouldn't take them three days to put me in front of the firing squad," Elisa didn't dare contradict her. The worst part was seeing the lack of respect for others… which is what Juana was saying at that moment.

"The worst part was seeing the lack of respect for others in their behavior, and for the first time I realized my past mistakes and understood that the revolution should serve to help and respect human beings, not to crush them."

After another pause, Juana concluded, "Well, that's the end of the story. My mother decided to get me out of Madrid and take me to Menorca, where she had some friends, because she couldn't stand it anymore, and there I met Daniel, who lived in one of the grottoes on the beach, in a commune, and I decided to try it. It works for now, because I don't love him. We're friends, and so he respects me. Men make much better friends than lovers or husbands…

"I'll never go back to what they call a normal life, I'm not prepared. I know I've signed myself up for individual salvation, but I have no idea how to attain collective salvation."

Elisa was bubbling over with impatience to ask a question. "But, are you happy now?"

Juana didn't respond immediately or adopt that beatific expression that bothered Elisa so much. She furrowed her brow, making herself look more like she had ten years before, and replied.

"No, I'm not even half as happy as I was when we were in Yeserías. Back then, my ideals gave me a strength I don't have anymore. But I'm not as miserable as I was when I got out of Valladolid, either."

"So, that's what you think of us? We comrades are bloodthirsty madmen who've persecuted and beat up those who've left, and none of us is worth anything… Good, you've perfectly assimilated bourgeois ideology. There's no difference between what you think and what ARRIBA says. Don't you even forgive us for all we've suffered and the beautiful ideals we pursued, without expecting anything in return? …I understand why you don't want to help Cherta."

Arnau stood up, irritated and sad, and seemed ready to leave. Elisa got up in fear, wanting to stop him. She still had many things to tell him. No, it wasn't true that she considered them all contemptible sadists. No, it couldn't be that he was leaving her house that day harboring such an opinion of her. She couldn't form an exact opinion, like his. She had to talk about it more, comment on it, reflect. If a person didn't reflect, they made terrible mistakes like the ones they'd been making all those years. That was why it was necessary to talk, to ask for advice, express doubts. No, he shouldn't go now, right now, without her being able to explain as many things as she needed, in spite of her incompetence.

"Don't talk to me like that, you know what you're saying isn't true."

Elisa's voice trembled as she said it, but her weakness irritated him because it seemed like she was manipulating him.

"Oh, yes, it's true! And now I have to regret the time I believed anything else. You've never really stopped being the right-wing señorita educated in a good convent school…"

Elisa looked at him with wide eyes, trying to absorb the string of insults the conversation had become.

"Why are you talking to me like that? You're from a good family, too, and you were educated in a good religious school, and so was Cherta, and many other comrades…"

"Leave them alone, okay? They haven't betrayed the ideals they fought for. And me neither, damn it! A minute ago you were protesting against all struggle, all…"

Elisa felt her pain transforming into anger. She shouted, "If I were a man you wouldn't talk to me like that! You're insulting me because I'm a woman, because I was your wife. If I were a friend or an ex-comrade, now you'd respect my point of view and we'd discuss it calmly…"

"Damn it, there's your cursed feminism again! Those must be the latest teachings of Octubre, right? Men never respect women's political opinions."

"No, this time Octubre hasn't indoctrinated me. Pilar Laborde was the one who made me clearly see the contempt men treat women with in political matters."

"Pilar Laborde?" Arnau made a visible effort to remember that name that meant nothing to him.

"We were in prison together. You never met her, though she was in the leadership. She was the one who got us the cotton catheters for Marisa's abortion."

Arnau showed with a shrug how indifferent he was to that information.

"Pilar took up feminism, too, when she saw how contemptuously the comrades in the leadership treated her. Just like you are now…"

Chapter 20

Octubre made her way through the crowd with difficulty, dragging Elisa along behind her. Elisa followed her reluctantly, as she usually did lately. Finally, they found a spot in the front row, but Elisa felt ashamed of her friend's nerve and tried not to look at any of the women around them, and instead eagerly stared at those who were speaking in the center of the circle of people that had formed at one end of the lobby. The convocation ceremony of the new feminist association being formed in Barcelona had begun, and the speaker, a famous Barcelona writer, was describing the tasks the promoters were proposing to carry out through the new organization.

Elisa soon lost interest in the commonplaces all the presenters of the project lifelessly shelled out. After a few minutes, she dared to look around her, searching for familiar faces. She discovered writers, publishers, municipal officials, regional government officials, prestigious names in that tiny world of Catalan intelligentsia and feminism. *All of Barcelona,* thought Elisa with surprise and gratification at the same time, because in 1985, a year of chronic disappointment, the veterans of old struggles were again meeting to encourage and welcome a new project, and it seemed that the enthusiasm that had awakened feminism ten years before was out-of-date.

The speeches ended and a generous appetizer was served, paid for by the city government, as Octubre whispered to Elisa. Elisa wasn't moved by the information, but she knew Octubre was furious. She had worked from the beginning of the movement in the worst conditions, and was now marginalized from the center of power that managed the money and the influence a few upstarts benefitted from and received such perks as gifts they didn't know how to use properly. Elisa didn't feel like consoling her friend, who on the other hand wasn't paying attention to her, more eager to look for other people she knew than to converse with Elisa.

Elisa began to feel out of place, as she always did at that kind of meeting in recent years, when a voice and a face she remembered without being able to place them approached her.

"Elisa! How good to see you. What are you up to?"

The woman was stouter than when she had known her, but she also seemed more jovial, more content, with an open and at the same time clever gaze, and a happy and cordial tone that Elisa didn't remember.

"Don't you recognize me, Elisa? Elisa Vilaró. Of course, it's been ten years! I'm Pilar Laborde." She began to laugh, amused by Elisa's confusion.

They hadn't seen each other during those ten years because, although they had both participated in the movement, Pilar had gone to Zaragoza when she left prison, since that was her home province, and she worked there in the hospital.

"Thank goodness I was able to go into the hospital when they released me with the first amnesty. But it cost me what I had, mostly because the amnesties were so scarce, it was confusing… they were shitting them as if they were constipated… ha ha! I always say that, don't be offended, some of us are so refined…"

Elisa wasn't offended by the crude manner of her companion, which she didn't remember from prison. Instead she was amused and happy to see Pilar's animation, a rather rare state of mind among the ex-activists of the PC-ML.

"Their problem wasn't finding a substitute for their activism. Since I devoted myself to feminism right away… Before, I never dared to show myself as I really was. It was all repression there, my girl. What with the behavior of a revolutionary on one hand, and the jailers on the other, well, we were really screwed up, good God… I don't know how we didn't go more crazy. I, well, I'd always been that way, happy-go-lucky. Although when I got out the leaders came around, being a real pain. I was supposed to make a self-examination, like everybody, and I didn't know what I had to examine myself about. Imagine! Here I thought they'd make me a monument for all I'd been through at the police station and in Yeserías. Well, look, I said to myself, these guys are some stupid jerks and I'm one more for paying attention to them, and I told them where they could stick it, and that was that."

"What did you have to examine yourself about?"

Elisa suddenly felt interested in Pilar Laborde, though she had hardly noticed her while they were in prison. The memory of those years, so fundamental to her life, attracted her with a force the feminist activities she had spent her time on later had never had. Running into former comrades made her compare the different experiences they had had, and she always hoped to find an example to follow in one of their lives. *In search of the lost path*, she thought in self-mockery, and a strange longing came over her. She couldn't understand the cause of that powerful feeling, which saddened her with the desire for that period of time to never have ended. "They were the worst years of my life," she repeated, but she was no longer so sure.

She remembered what Juana had said. "No, I'm not half as happy as when we were in Yeserías. My ideals gave me a strength I lack now." Was that what it was all about, then? She had lost her ideals and without them she could not be happy. Where was Pilar getting her vitality, that happiness that erupted in shouts and gestures? What ideals had substituted for those of their heroic times that had made her so happy?

"What did I have to examine myself about? Well, just about everything. You could say I'd have to have been tortured to death or something like that in order to be free of all suspicion. They accused me... well, you, too, of course, and almost all the rest, but you didn't show up around there at all, and it's a good thing you didn't, my girl! They accused me of lack of revolutionary coherency and I don't know what all. All the objections you made in jail, remember? And your doubts and all that. Well, they blamed it on all of us except Juana, who was the one who told them, of course. It reminded me of the nuns' reprimands, because they didn't let you answer back. They were so upset I thought they were going to expel us all, and even though they'd assumed command after hundreds of desertions, which came from their punishing practices, it was like divine wrath, girlfriend… they gave me a real dressing down.

"I remember what upset them most of all was that I'd supplied the cotton catheters we used for Marisa's abortion, remember? They said I should've consulted with the party, and with the father! Imagine! He was running from the police like a condemned man, poor guy… But, as you know, they were just lousy with machismo. They never respected me a crumb, in spite of that fact that in the end they named me to the executive committee. I remember the way they praised Arnau and Cherta, even though they hadn't been through anything worse than we had, and certainly they hadn't had to give Marisa an abortion and console poor Juana, who almost went crazy over that mess with her man.

"Well, to me, they were all bad news. Even though I went to a lot of trouble not to show doubts or hesitations in Yeserías, you know. Not like you, you always wanted to discuss and argue. And you were quite right, of course, but since I knew it was really looked down upon, and Juana was always sending reports to the executives. You and we two, Juana and I, were in the executive committee, too, but the truth was that we had no say. Juana checked everything with the guys in Carabanchel and we also understood that they were the ones who gave the orders, and we were the ones who had to obey them… Well, I didn't want to get into any problems, and I knew them, and I always thought they were like my father, very nice and open and affectionate while you weren't contrary to him, but if you were, good God! He'd eat you alive. I always came out ahead doing the same thing: honest and open, but what I didn't like I shut up about and went ahead and did what I wanted later, anyway.

"So when I got out of prison, those pigs came to raise objections about whether we should've consulted with them about this or checked about that, whether Juana's reports showed that the rest of us lacked ideological strength, and since she was the only one they respected and admired, not even poor Marisa got any recognition, after everything she went through. Although she never showed up, either. And all the praise for Juana, making her a good example every day, you know? Like the Virgin. Those guys had the same Catholic symbolism. Like all men, at least Spanish men. You know, the virgin mother or the whore. Now that the Feminist Movement has unveiled so many masculine myths, I understand it better. Then, I couldn't understand it or accept it. I could see clearly that a heroine was convenient for them, virgin and martyr. Like it is for the PCE guys, too, that's why they have Dolores Ibárruri, she's their Virgin Mother for their altars. But there's only one and no other. You only have one mother and there's only one Virgin Mary. And every church worships one and every men's party as well. No other woman can compare, she's the exception that confirms all the rules.

"And so those Marxist-Leninist guys devoted themselves to exalting Juana, until they sent her to Valladolid, to screw her over once and for all, of course. And so they finished her off, and then you must've seen the fury they hunted her down with… Well, but I was telling you about how it was for me. I ended up deciding I had to leave. But with no arguments or shouting or anger, since I was quite reasonably afraid of what they were capable of. About that time I found out they'd gone to give Juana a beating… So I disappeared, the same as I did when I left home, so I wouldn't have to argue with my father, and I beat it to Zaragoza. I've never gone back to Madrid, it had too many bad memories for me."

"And are you living in Barcelona now?"

"No, I'm still in Zaragoza, with my routines, but I come to Barcelona often because I have relatives here, all Aragonese have relatives in Barcelona, and besides I'm in contact with other groups that do family planning. That's what I do now, did you know? We got the autonomous government and the city to give us some money, and a few other women and I put together a small birth control service based out of the hospital. It's grown a lot, now there's twenty-something of us, and the demand is really high. Girl, Marisa's situation must have made more of an impression on me than I thought. I can't stand to see a woman having an abortion like an animal. I think I'm doing something good, you know. More useful, of course, than all that nonsense about the revolution and the people's war they bombarded us with in the party…"

"But you must've believed in them once, didn't you? Otherwise you wouldn't have been there."

Pilar nodded, laughing. "Well, I suppose so, of course. When I went in, but I was very young. I was only eighteen years old, and I was sick of my father, and I wanted more than anything to get out of my family's house, stop putting up with my father's shouting and hitting, and later my brothers. Yes, my girl, in our town it was quite the fashion that the older brothers bossed their sisters around, and besides I found Pedro and he was all mixed up in that boring party…"

Elisa could not avoid cringing a little at these confessions, but Pilar was speaking quickly and loudly and didn't notice. To cut off that torrent of words that left her stunned, Elisa tried to concentrate on the scattered report she was giving her. "And what do you do now?"

"Well, I already told you, sister! You're not listening. I spend my whole day on that birth control business, at the hospital in Zaragoza."

"No, I meant, what do you do for a living?"

"Well, the same thing, silly! They pay me to give pills to the señoras, what did you think?"

Elisa didn't reply that she had been confused. It was no longer the times of free activist labor that usually cost the volunteer money and inconvenience. She understood Octubre better.

"So, girlfriend, what are you up to, eh? I heard you weren't with Arnau any more. Well done, my girl! I finally left Pedro, too. There's not much you can do with those maniacs from the party, I tell you. Because they're chauvinists, besides. Marisa also got married to a kid who has a grocery store in Vigo and quit doing all that boring revolutionary stuff. Look, I saw it clearly after a little while, I tell you, but I had nowhere else to go, and I was living with Pedro, who was receiving a salary from the party, so I didn't dare leave both of them, which turned out horrible for me, of course, because while I was thinking it over we got arrested, and, hello, there I was in Yeserías, rotting for a year and a half. And while I was there, like I told you, I didn't want to cause any problems, since it was already hard enough to survive in that pigsty without adding anything else. But when we got out, and Pedro went back to those obsessions about the struggle, and critiques and self-examinations, I said, forget you! And I went to Zaragoza without saying goodbye. It was over, you know? Now I'm with a good kid who wants me for himself and not for the revolution, and he's a chauvinist, too, of course, like they all are, but I learned life's lesson from my father's thrashings, so I don't fight with him, and we can stand each other. Besides, I'm at the hospital all day long, and that does him a world of good because he's unemployed and getting ready for exams to work for the city. I'm really supporting him, but that's okay because this way he's better behaved, and since he has to study at home all day, perfect. Then, when I come home, I make him dinner and hug and kiss him, and what do you want. If I don't, life is awful. So, what have you heard about the others? I've already seen Octubre here, and I talked to her a few times over the years at feminist events. The one I don't know anything about is Juana. I think she did the same thing as everyone else, she left the party and hooked up with a guy, right?"

"Yes… well, no, not exactly." Elisa didn't know how to tell her that Juana hadn't done the same thing as the others, even if that was what it seemed.

"And what about you, girl? Good heavens, I'm the only one talking, tell me something about your life. Of course, I already know I talk too much, I started after prison, it must be because of how much I repressed myself there."

Elisa briefly explained that she, too, had done the same thing as everyone else. She left the party and her husband, and hooked up with another guy who wasn't involved in politics. When Octubre came up to them, Elisa looked for a way to avoid Pilar's congratulations for having done the right thing. Octubre agreed to leave right away because she had juicy news she wanted to share with Elisa alone. Out in the street, she overcame her laughter to tell her.

"Do you know what those hussies have put together today? Oh, yes, all that about the new association they've formed, or haven't you found out what was happening in there? Well, it turns out they have no place, no money, or anything of the kind. The only thing they got were the two cents for the hors d'oeuvres. Yes, believe it or not! The convocation today was really to encourage those of us who were there to get organized to ask the city government for the locale and the money to keep it going. Have you ever seen anything like it! When did they ever give us money and office space? We had to do everything ourselves, and now we haven't even been mentioned. You have to be a miserable social climber to get any credit around here."

Elisa stopped listening to Octubre's well-known diatribe. She didn't feel interested in the bickering that divided the movement, or in Octubre's frustrations, no matter how right she was. She wasn't interested in anything that wasn't her personal destiny, because of what Pilar had said.

Pilar's story confirmed Elisa's suspicions about the true motivations of the majority of women comrades who become active in the PC-ML. Even in the other parties of the extreme left, she would add. Except for Octubre and Juana, everyone she knew had been brought into the party by their boyfriend or husband. Perhaps because they were too young.

"A simple lack of political preparation, Elisa. Notice that in reality all of them were fulfilling the feminine role they'd been taught from the cradle. Get married, love a man, obey him. They would've been active in a right-wing group just as easily, if their husbands ordered it. And in the end, most of them have preferred a conservative, traditional man, in order to better fulfill the role of wife and mother. It's not an accident, Elisa, that the truly activist women, who've taken up an ideology and have their own objectives, are older than forty or fifty, for the most part. Except for Juana, we're all from those generations which were either formed during the Republic or were raised by political parents. The rest of you fell into this world from the confessional and embroidery rooms."

Was that it, then? Elisa once again listened attentively to Octubre's well-known arguments about the decisive importance education under Franco had had for the generation of women born after the Civil War. Juana had also referred to educational conditioning when she spoke about the impossibility of the revolution, and the way the analyses of two such different women coincided surprised Elisa. But she could not forget the different economic conditions in which the country was developing, that was the fundamental thing, Elisa insisted. She didn't like the self-assured way Octubre blamed all Elisa's defects on what she learned during the first years of her life, no matter how much the most important pedagogues affirmed that it was so. It seemed like a fatalistic determinism hardly appropriate to a Marxist analysis. Because, if that were the case, what could be done to change the family situation and social class a woman had been born into? If everything was already learned before six years of age, and they all suffered the indoctrination of the Church and fascism much longer than that, there was no hope. What to do in order to be a mature, authentic person? How to find that woman who wasn't allowed to develop, weighted down under tons of lies and repression that accumulated on top of her for years and years?

Octubre listened to Elisa's questions. A characteristic wrinkle furrowed her brow. Her friend's objections were not trivial.

"In Brussels Elisenda once had a bitter argument with another Spanish woman who was the daughter of a well-known fascist big shot and was putting on airs of being liberal. A companion had just gone off with another's husband, and the argument about feminist ethics came up in the meetings of both groups. At a given moment, the other one, who was a bourgeois señorita of the worst kind, started to defend the tramp who'd taken advantage of her friend's trust to go to bed with her husband. The señorita spoke of love, and other odds and ends you already know, in order to justify the unacceptable behavior of the other. You know, the typical bourgeois hypocrisy..."

Elisa blushed violently and looked stealthily at Octubre, trying to guess the hidden intentions her friend might have had in using that particular story as an example. But her friend was unaware of the feelings her story aroused in Elisa. She seemed occupied with getting to the answer Elisa wanted.

"At one point in the argument, Elisenda accused that pompous woman of being a petty bourgeois reactionary or something like that, and she defended herself saying that it was the education she'd received. And really, the way she was saying it wasn't an excuse, but a defense of her position and a challenge to any liberal present. And then Elisenda, purple with rage, you know her, screamed that she'd been educated in the same way, but with fascist education you either digested it or spit it back up, and that was what she had to decide. Elisenda was really convincing that time, because she was well acquainted with the suffering it had caused her to let go of all that fascist propaganda they'd forced down her throat."

Elisa tried to overcome the confusion references to love relationships with married men always caused her, and asked with her best imitation of indifference, "Do you mean to say that there is no resignation?"

Octubre looked at her for a few seconds with an ironic smile that Elisa knew well, and which deeply irritated her.

"Yes, exactly, that's what I mean. Resignation doesn't fit into a revolutionary ideology, you know. You always go back to your Christian concepts. You should remember that Lenin said that what you have to see in people is where they're going and not where they're coming from, since there's no doubt they have to go somewhere. And you have to go forward, otherwise you just go eternally backwards. Gramsci wrote that a person is a socialist at twenty years of age, not a revolutionary, you see? At forty a person is a policeman, referring to the conservatism inherent in the age. I don't want anything like that to happen to me. I want to be young all my life, which means I have to keep being a revolutionary."

"And? Is she happy now?"

Elisa jumped. She had almost forgotten Arnau, immersed in that whirlwind of memories and contradictory, unsettling thoughts. He had to repeat the question before she understood he was referring to Pilar, whose activity she had mentioned.

"Yes, it seems like it. She's working at the hospital in Zaragoza, in birth control, and she gets a salary…"

"Oh, very sacrificing, I see! She's really in line for the handouts. Come on…"

Elisa had left the sentence unfinished because she had known it was going to provoke such a response from Arnau, and she understood that it was deserved. But, if she didn't want to continue enduring his comrades' scorn, and the revolution was impossible, what else was there to do?

She didn't speak the question out loud, but Arnau seemed to guess it when, barely hiding his hostility, he inquired, "So, that's your other option? Become an official? Dedicate yourself to social service, to the charity organized by the State in exchange for economic security? Is that what we should all do to avoid being sectarian workers? Is that the advice you're giving us?"

"Arnau, please, I'm not giving advice to anyone…"

Her weariness moved Arnau, but he insisted, anyway. "But you, what do you want to do with your life?"

Elisa shook off the laziness that was overcoming her and got up from the couch she had been sitting on all afternoon. She turned on the light and blinked at the contrast. She stood in the middle of the room, not knowing what to do. Pere had left two hours before, leaving her afternoon empty. They had intended to go to an art exhibit, and to find out at the travel agent what was the best route for them for Easter week. All those plans had been put on hold, perhaps aborted forever, when Pere had his attack of jealousy. What had he said when he left? "When you're cured of that morbid passion…" No, the most important thing was, "and when you know what you want to do with your life…" That's what it was all about. Still, after so many crises, breakups, loves and activism, she didn't know what her purpose in life was.

She sat back down on the couch and decided to reflect on that question, trying to escape the prison memories that addled her thoughts. That was what it was all about, of course. Octubre had said very similar things to what Pere had just shouted at her, and even Isabel, with that educated accent and ironic smile. Everyone agreed, then, that she didn't know what she wanted to do with her life. All of them couldn't be wrong. At that moment she was more surprised by Pere's revelation than bothered by the negative opinion her friends had about her. Mainly because she could not understand why the others thought of her as a person lost in a world she could not understand, with no path, perhaps, when she had already been working seriously at the school for six years, was preparing her dissertation, had a normal life, without giving in to drugs or alcohol. Once she used these arguments on Octubre, to defend herself from her usual accusations, and was surprised to receive a loud guffaw as her only response.

Later Isabel more or less translated the enigmatic answer for her. "Octubre can't place you in the category of people who would be considered balanced and normal, with your life. Your argument is silly. You're talking about a literature teacher working on her dissertation, who earns her living and doesn't drink or do drugs, but we all expect more out of you, and I think you do, too. We especially don't want you to waste your time and your sanity faking pregnancies that don't exist for the love of a man who doesn't love you, you see?"

"Octubre just wants to see me acting like a feminist again, it's her latest thing." She didn't add that where she also wanted to see her was in her bed, because she didn't want to offend Isabel's sensibilities.

"That's possible, yes. That could be one of the reasons Octubre feels frustrated and disappointed with you. But you have to realize that, after knowing you in prison, it's a bit shocking that you have no other hopes and dreams than watching TV at home, holding Pere's hand."

"I just want to be happy! I have that right, like everyone else, don't I?"

"Yes, you've already told me that before. That's all very well. And now answer me honestly, truly honestly, okay? Are you really happy?"

Elisa closed her eyes tightly to concentrate. That was the key question, and at the moment, carried away with anger, she shouted at Isabel, yes, she was very happy, except when someone like her or Octubre lectured her like she was doing right then, something that happened far too often, though Elisa wasn't so sure of that arrogant response after Pere's sermon. Perhaps if she reflected calmly, quietly, all alone, she would achieve it. What did she want in life? Arnau? Was that the only objective in her life? Was that the constant desire whose non-attainability was rotting her soul? And was it smart to spend her whole life desiring a man who no longer wanted to be with her? Could she find other objectives which could pay her back for the frustrations she had suffered? She had to answer that question if she wanted to achieve the balance she lacked.

Courageously, she decided to respond to Arnau's question with the truth.

"I don't know, I still don't know."

Arnau didn't hide his surprise at Elisa's honesty. He was about to leave and he felt frantic from having spent more than five hours on that visit he had thought would take half an hour, without being sure whether she understood what he was asking her or if she would really do it. Instead, he had let himself get tangled up in tortuous conversations about unimportant past events he had almost forgotten, while what concerned him had no meaning for her. He wanted to vent his bad mood by saying something offensive to her, but he wasn't going to be difficult with someone who was going to do him a favor. It was a matter of getting what the party needed, but at that moment he felt tempted to look for help from some other ex-comrade and tell Elisa to go to hell. If he had known how to find one of the guys who were with him and Cherta on the Central Committee at that time, he would already have left, getting away from Elisa and her absurd, exhausting questions for good. But at the last moment, when his question had an explicit accusation of uselessness and bourgeois decadence, she was handing herself over to whatever nasty sarcasm he might come up with, just like that, simply, without defenses, confessing that she was living through the painful identity crisis he already knew she was.

Arnau cautiously observed Elisa, trying to discover some sign of cunning. She had manipulated him so many times during that endless conversation and pushed him into making confessions he very much regretted. But now she seemed honestly bewildered, she showed him her authentic face, the confused adolescent who looked for God in every corner. Arnau realized he could regain lost terrain and decided to take advantage of it. He changed position, left his coat again on the back of the chair, adopted a concerned, paternal air, and with a smooth tone, he commented, "That must be very painful for you…"

Elisa nodded her head. She was grateful that he wasn't taking advantage of his upper hand.

"Yes, of course. It doesn't make me happy to be so doubtful. Sometimes I envy you, because you're always so sure of what you want, and you work to get it with that conviction…"

The need to leave soon, knowing Elisa would keep her promise, pushed Arnau to play the last card. He told himself he could not keep wasting time. He came close to her, put his hands softly on her shoulders, and with his serious tone, the one he used to convince everyone, he suggested, "If you want, I can help you… As always…"

Elisa raised her head until her forehead brushed his chin, and she felt his breath on her skin. She was shaken by a trembling from those depths she didn't know in herself, but where her strongest emotions originated. *As always*, she thought, *not even time or disappointment is enough to stem those dreams or quench that desire.* She leaned on his shoulder and cursed herself for it.

To gain time, she asked, "What do you mean?"

Arnau got anxious. He had acted perhaps too rashly, because he didn't have the next step prepared. Her question was logical, but the only response he could give her meant committing himself to something he wasn't sure he wanted yet. The seconds passing by in silence pressed him to say, "Whatever you want."

Elisa didn't dare to raise her head immediately. She had heard the words but she didn't understand them, she didn't want to understand them. If she was supposed to understand he was telling her they could go back to having a romantic relationship, how had this sudden change come about? Or perhaps it wasn't sudden and in reality, when he came that morning to visit her, he did it more than anything out of the need to see her, the desire to start over, as she had thought at first. But, in that case, what would happen to Roser? Or perhaps they had already broken up and she didn't know? She suddenly felt the truth illuminating her. That was what it was all about, naturally: Arnau and Roser had broken up and he was coming back to her, as she had always known he would, as it had to be from the beginning. She pulled away from his arms suddenly, as they were now all the way around her, and looked anxiously in his eyes.

"Have you and Roser broken up?"

Arnau felt himself getting wrapped up in her anxious gaze, pushed by her trembling lips, the excessive brightness of her eyes. With affection and fear at the same time, he lightly took Elisa's arm and murmured, "No, not exactly."

That's what it was, of course. That's what it was. He didn't admit it because he was very proud and wasn't going to let his arm be twisted right then, when they had been arguing for five hours and he had looked for the excuse of Cherta's trial to come to her house, suddenly, just like that, one morning at the end of March, exactly two years after that horrible night when he told her he was leaving to go to Roser's house for good. And now he was back, surely he was back, just as she had been hoping all that time in spite of the advice and criticism and warnings of her friends, who were really just envious of the love that nothing could break and which they had never known.

Elisa's radiant expression startled Arnau. He decided to explain the situation, before it became irrevocable.

"No, Roser and I haven't broken up. But, naturally we don't watch over each other constantly…"

He interrupted himself at the sound of his own words. Elisa's wide eyes added to his confusion. Finally, she was the one who asked.

"Do you mean we could have an affair without her knowing?"

He nodded, relieved that she had understood quickly.

"The way you two did to me?"

Arnau didn't want to respond. He took a step away, but she came close again and took his arm.

"Is that what you mean? The way you two did to me?"

Gently but firmly he released himself from Elisa's hand. He lit a cigarette and backed away from her until he was leaning against the wall. He tried to make his voice sound calm and cordial.

"Please, Elisa, we didn't do anything to you. The attraction came up and that's all. We've already talked about it more than once. Physical attraction exists, it's there, you can't do anything about it, and you shouldn't even try. That's what liberated people defend, right? What would your feminist friends say, eh? Maybe you have to be constantly repressing yourselves like when you were in religious school? Right now I want you, and if you feel the same, what harm are we doing anyone?"

Elisa held her breath trying to understand Arnau's explanation. What would her feminist friends say? Arnau would rather not know.

"I think what you ought to be asking is what would Roser say, not my friends."

"Roser has nothing to say. This is about my life, not hers. That's what we've always said, that's what has to be understood."

His impatience was beginning to show, and Elisa was surprised.

"What are you annoyed about?"

"About this interrogation, Elisa! Roser wouldn't ask so many questions…"

"Roser didn't ask so many, you mean. Roser went to bed with you, when she liked, without asking anything. And that's what you liked."

"Well, maybe so, Elisa. I already told you before that you ask too many questions of yourself and of me. No one can take this continual psychoanalysis."

Elisa wasn't listening to Arnau's reproaches. As if obsessed, she followed her own train of thought.

"Won't Roser ask you now where you've been and what you've been doing?" She thought a few seconds with a furrowed brow, and suddenly added precipitously, "Oh, no, it's not true! She watches you, she watches you constantly, even if you don't realize it, she's hanging on everything you do, where you've been and where you're going, and tries to never leave you alone. She can't trust you, she knows firsthand what can happen."

Arnau was visibly surprised by what Elisa's said, and most of all by her conviction.

"How do you know? How can you talk about what Roser does, with such certainty, when you haven't seen her for two years?"

"I know almost everything you two do. I've always known. I've been keeping track of your lives."

Arnau did nothing to hide his astonishment, repeating, "How do you know? How do you find out what we do?"

"I have friends at the newspaper, of course. I still see Carles, I made friends with Montserrat Benet, Roser's friend. It was easy, don't look at me like that, I don't have magic powers. I've simply used trust and gossip, as all women do, right? I've been watching you now, but now it's too late. Before, when I might've prevented our separation, I didn't know how to do it. I learned afterward. Roser taught me. I know she works at a desk by your side, she goes out with you everywhere, she even picks you up in the car at meetings. That's what she does, right? So that some other harpy, witch, whore, doesn't take her husband away. This is the way it always has to be, right? I remember, when you went with her, that one of my coworkers, an idiot who was also always stuck to her husband, told the others, 'As intelligent and clever as Elisa thinks she is, and look how she's let her husband get taken away. Anyone would've been afraid it would happen, having Roser at home all day.'

"I'm not clever. I was so stupid that I didn't figure anything out until it was too late. And Roser's not like that. Roser is on the ball, she's one of those who watches all the women who come near, no matter how old they are, because they're all enemies, they're all a threat to the stability of her marriage. And she's not wrong. Those were the lessons they gave us when we were little schoolgirls, and in my home, which I paid no attention to. In the end I was a victim of my own modern, superior pretensions. But not Roser, she doesn't try to be different from the rest, and at the same time she's much more astute, not naive like me. Don't think she'd remain impassive while you and I went back to sleeping together. She'd follow you, she'd search for you, she'd invent a million subtleties to keep you, she'd buy you with what interested you most. She'd surely join the party and start studying Marxism in order to be able to ask you a thousand questions. Anyone can imagine the stereotypical strategy of a bourgeois wife who has to fight against a rival to keep her husband."

Arnau listened in amazement. He didn't even have the strength to refute the accusations Elisa was making against Roser. He was much more impressed by the description Elisa was making of the character of his wife, than he was moved to argue in defense of her revolutionary virtues.

"Oh, yes, Arnau, don't look at me like I'm crazy! Perhaps now you'll start to notice her and you'll realize the strategy she's following. I wouldn't be at all surprised if she showed up here in a few minutes looking for you, surprised by how late you are, right? Or at least she'll go with you every time you say you're coming to visit me. If you want to do it you'll have to lie to her, like you did to me, but worse, because I was very absent-minded, and in the end this will turn into a typical bourgeois triangle, hell, a vaudeville trio. Because having your first wife as your lover is quite entertaining in the theatre. And that seems liberal to you? Does my feminist ideology go with this adultery you're trying to get me involved in, like in some classic comedy of errors? What does your Marxist-Leninist conscience tell you?"

Arnau took a few minutes before answering. He lit another cigarette, and had to clear his throat before responding in a hoarse voice.

"I don't think you have to mix up one with the other. My Marxist-Leninist conscience doesn't reproach me for anything. I'm always willing to give my life for the revolution…"

Elisa's guffaw completely disconcerted him. He looked at her with frightened, almost infantile eyes, and didn't know how to defend himself from her retort.

"Oh, please, Arnau, come on! Less pamphlet talk between us, eh? Always ready to give your life for the revolution and not a single minute for your personal ethics. Your party's moral code says nothing about romantic relationships, right? You still apply bourgeois morals in those cases. I shouldn't be surprised. After all, I've been denouncing the male chauvinism of you communist activists for ten years. What offends me is that on top of it all you want to make it pass for liberated. Is it very revolutionary to have two wives at the same time? Did you learn that from Lenin or from the Quran? Damn!"

His voice was hardly audible when he asked, "So, for you, what is the feminist alternative? Repression? Like in the old teachings? Is that more liberal?"

Elisa showed real concern in responding, "There must be a synthesis, but I don't know what it is. The real feminist ethic has to be discovered. We can go forward only when we find it. Perhaps that's the key to the revolutionary transformations poor Juana was so earnestly looking for. That's what I have to do. It's the only thing that will make me change my life. Now I see."

Arnau had recovered some of his usual calm, and tried to be ironic.

"And might we know what you intend to do to achieve such a level of wisdom?"

Elisa didn't seem to care about Arnau's new aggressiveness. Distracted, as though talking to herself, she murmured, "I have to call Elisenda, right away. Now I really do need to talk to her."

"What do you mean? What do you need her for?"

Elisa turned toward him with a condescending look, as if she made the information available only out of good will.

"I need to know how to change, where to get the strength to spit back up a lifetime of education... to learn to be someone else..."

"And what do you want to learn now?"

Arnau started to sit down again, to continue the interrogation with a mocking smile, but Elisa's response left him paralyzed, leaning against the wall.

"I've got to find a new purpose for my life. But first, I have to learn to stop loving you."

Translator's Acknowledgments and Notes

Lidia Falcón is a force of nature: awe-inspiring and unstoppable. I found her through serendipity when I was browsing the Spanish section of the University of Iowa library in search of texts to translate for workshopping. I appreciated her realistic portrayal of Spanish society and, wanting to be a part of such important work, I proposed her most comprehensive novel to date, *Camino sin retorno*, for my MFA thesis. I met Lidia in Madrid the following summer and understood that there would be no turning back from that decision. Although my workshop companions over the next year felt that the novel was uneven, too political or chaotic, I knew that these characteristics were what made the novel so valuable. Falcón somehow transfers all the confusion, chaos, and polyphony of opinions in Spain during the transition away from the dictatorship into a story that coheres slowly, with the benefit of hindsight, just like history. The reader's hard work to make sense of the narrative parallels the characters' struggles.

I would like to thank the members of the Iowa Translator's Workshop, without whose arguments and support I would never have completed the translation of this momentous book, especially Susan Benner. Immense gratitude goes to Linda Gould Levine and Elvira Siurana, for the countless ways they made this journey possible, and in particular to Dr. Gloria F. Waldman, for her hundreds of useful suggestions for the text, which she made out of her friendship with Lidia Falcón since 1974 and her commitment to Falcón's political ideals. Huge thanks to Victoria Joyner, the proofreader who found the typos that eluded ten other people. Any remaining infelicities are mine.

Most of all, thanks to Lidia Falcón, not only for writing this book but for a lifetime of tireless effort to change the sociopolitical situation of Spain for the better.

The following observations may be of interest to the reader in English:

• Octubre's name means "October" in Spanish. The idea that comes across is that Octubre's parents wished to see the October Revolution take on human form in their daughter. If the reader takes the time to imagine the kind of circumstances that would have caused a mother to call her daughter Octubre, the reader's impression of Octubre will be fleshed out in a vivid way, and her thoughts and actions will make sense even before she tells the stories of her youth.

• I have left the novel's occasional Catalan terms in Catalan. This should serve to emphasize the foreignness the terms have even in the original. Though the words are as transparent to a Spanish reader as any other Romance language words are likely to be, they are not Spanish, and they assert that difference aggressively. I hope they will remind the reader of the different cultures that exist in Spain, some of which were severely repressed during the Franco regime. The Catalanness of some of the characters is highlighted in their names. Arnau, Roser, Carles, Pere, and Lluïsa are all names that mark their heritage as Catalan instead of "Spanish" by subtle but noticeable phonetic differences from their Castilian equivalents.

• The title literally describes a path (a physical road, or the path one takes in the journey through life) without a return, or a way back. I believe it alludes to the way Elisa stays with something, whether Catholic religion, her husband, or communist activism, never wavering, until someone else forces her to let go of it, as though she were imprisoned in her life choices. It is also a reference to the way a person drawn into the communist parties will never be able to entirely extricate her- or himself from them, but will have to follow the path wherever it leads. There is no going back. I have tried to suggest some of these connotations in my translated title "No Turning Back."

• During the course of a conversation I had with Lidia Falcón, when we discussed the translation project and her objectives in writing the novel, she explained to me that the characters in *Camino sin retorno* were not people she particularly liked. They were lost and drifting, with no direction, when they ought to have been putting their energies into furthering the feminist cause. They might even serve as negative examples. I was speechless at this revelation, because I had identified strongly with many of the characters and their quest for meaning in Spain and in their lives. I hope the reader will prove that I am not alone in having sympathized with them in spite of (and perhaps because of) their faults. Even if I am alone in this, then at least Falcón's stated purpose is being served. Either way, I believe that the characters, mainly the women, are complex and compelling. These possibilities of intent and interpretation illustrate the truism that authors can never be aware of the complete impact of their writing. The translator takes up the writing where she thinks it left off, working from her own perceptions of the text, and ends up in the same position as the author, ignorant of the final interpretation.

Jessica Knauss, PhD

About the Author

Lidia Falcón O'Neill was born in Madrid on December 13, 1935, during a time of intense political turmoil. The Spanish Civil War (1936 - 1939) led to the death or exile of all the male members of her family. She and her female relatives were left to survive if they could in a fascist system which promoted discrimination against them not only because they and their male relatives had been devoted anti-fascists before and during the war, but also because they were women.

Falcón obtained her first degrees in Barcelona, in drama, law, and journalism. She began publishing short stories at age 18, and her first full-length book, *Sustituciones y fideicomisos*, appeared in 1962, to be closely followed by more works of social theory and criticism, journalism, fiction, drama, and, most recently, poetry. She has been published in every major Spanish newspaper and journal. All of her work has as a major theme the status of women in Spanish society and the world. In 1972, she was arrested for "crimes of opinion" and spent six months in prison. She served a second prison term, of nine months, after being falsely implicated in a bombing on Correo Street in Madrid in 1974.

She is the founder and president of the Feminist Party, which was recognized as a political party in 1981. From that base, she worked to legalize divorce and abortion in Spain. She also founded the journal

Vindicación feminista, and when this folded in 1979, *Poder y libertad*, which continues publishing on women's issues today. Both of these journals took great risks as they crusaded to bring women's issues to public attention. In 1992, she obtained her doctorate in Philosophy with the thesis *Mujer y poder político*. While maintaining *Poder y libertad* and the publishing house *Vindicación Feminista*, and continuing to publish at an impressive rate, she is also active in women's rights in her work as a lawyer. Her most important theoretical contribution has been *La razón feminista* (1981 - 82, translated as *The Feminist Reason*, 2008), which thoroughly analyzes women's place in society in two volumes.

She is the Spanish representative of the international organization Sisterhood is Global. She has spoken at countless conferences, summits, and on television, chaired organizations and committees, and has been awarded medals of honor and honorary doctorates for her tireless work.

Publications

Books

Sustituciones y fideicomisos. Ensayo. Ed. Nereo. Barcelona, 1962.

Historia del trabajo. Ensayo. Ed. Plaza y Janés. Barcelona, 1963.

Los derechos civiles de la mujer. Ensayo. Ed. Nereo. Barcelona, 1963.

Los derechos laborales de la mujer. Ensayo. Ed. Montecorvo. Madrid, 1964.

Mujer y sociedad. - Análisis de un fenómeno reaccionario. Ensayo. Ed.Fontanella. Barcelona. (3 ediciones) 1969, 1973, 1984.

Cartas a una idiota española. Crónica. Ed. Dirosa. Barcelona, 1974. (10 ediciones, 1974, 1975, 1975, 1976, 1976, 1977, 1978, 1979). Ed. Vindicación Feminista Publicaciones. Madrid, 1989. Ed. Des Femmes. París, 1975. Ed. Gyldendal, Copenaghe, 1977.

Es largo esperar callado. Novela. Ed. Pomaire. Barcelona, 1975. Ed. Hacer-Vindicación. Barcelona, 1984.

En el infierno - Ser mujer en las cárceles de España. Crónica. Ediciones de Feminismo, 1977. (2 ediciones).

Los hijos de los vencidos. Memorias. Ed. Pomaire. Barcelona, 1978. Vinducación Feminista, publicaciones, Madrid. 1989.

LIDIA FALCÓN

La razón feminista. Tomo I. - *La mujer como clase social y económica. El modo de producción doméstico*. Ensayo. Barcelona, 1981.

Viernes y 13 en la calle del Correo. Memorias. Ed. Planeta. Barcelona, 1981.

La razón feminista. Tomo II. - *La reproducción humana*. Ensayo. Ed. Fontanella. Barcelona, 1982.

El juego de la piel. Novela. Ed. Argos Vergara. Barcelona, 1983.

El alboroto español.- Crónica de la transición democrática española. Ed. Fontanella. Barcelona, 1984.

El varón español a la búsqueda de su identidad. Crónica. Ed. Plaza y Janés. Barcelona, 1984.

Rupturas. Novela. Ed. Fontanella. Barcelona. 1985. Ed. El Círculo de Lectores, Barcelona 1985, 1986, 1987. Vindicación Feminista Pub. Madrid, 1992.

Violencia contra la mujer. Ensayo. Ed. El Círculo de Lectores. Barcelona, 1991. 2º edición, Ed. Vindicación Feminista Publicaciones. Madrid, 1991.

Camino sin retorno. Novela. Ed. Anthropos. Barcelona, 1992.

Mujer y poder político. - Fundamentos de la crisis ideológica y de objetivos del Movimiento Feminista. Tesis doctoral "cum laude". Ensayo. Ed. Vindicación Feminista Publicaciones. Madrid, 1992.

Postmodernos. Novela. Ed. Libertarias. Madrid, 1993.

Clara. Novela. Ed. Vindicación Feminista Publicaciones. Madrid, 1993.

Teatro. Teatro. Ed. Vindicación Feminista Publicaciones. Madrid, 1994.

La razón feminista. Edición resumida. Ed. Vindicación Feminista. Madrid, 1994.

Trabajadores del mundo ¡rendíos! Ed. Akal. Madrid, 1996.

Asesinando el pasado. Ed. Vindicación Feminista Publicaciones. Madrid, 1997.

Amor, sexo y aventura en las mujeres del Quijote. Ed. Vindicación Feminista. Madrid, 1997

Mirar adelante y desgarrado. Poesía. Ed. Maite Canal Editora y Vindicación Feminista. Bilbao 2000.

Los nuevos mitos del feminismo. Ensayo. Ed. Kira Edit. y Vindicación Feminista Publicaciones. Madrid, 2001.

La hora más oscura. Emma. Atardeceres. Teatro. Ed. Vindicación Feminista. Madrid, 2001.

Memorias políticas (1951-1981). Ed. Planeta. Barcelona, 1999. 2ª Edición. Vindicación Feminista, Madrid, 2003.

La vida arrebatada. (Memorias) Ed. Anagrama. Barcelona. 2003.

La violencia que no cesa. Ensayo. Vindicación Feminista Publicaciones. Madrid, 2003.

Las nuevas españolas. La Esfera de los Libros. Madrid, 2004.

Al fin estaba sola. Novela. Editorial Montesinos. Mataró (Barcelona) 2007.

The Feminist Reason. (Translation of both volumes of *La razón feminista*) Madrid: Aconagua Publishing, 2008.

Una mujer de nuestro tiempo. Novela. Editorial Montesinos. Mataró (Barcelona) 2009.

Collaborations

La liberación de la mujer año 0. Capítulo III, *"La opresión de la mujer: una incógnita".* Ed. Granica. Barcelona, 1977.

Sisterhood is Global. Chapter *"Spain: Women are the conscience of our country".* Editado por Robin Morgan. Ed. Anchor Press and Doubleday. New York. 1984. Traducido al español *Mujeres del mundo.* Ed. Vindicación Feminista Publicaciones-Hacer. Barcelona, 1982.

Flora Tristan. Peregrinaciones de una paria. Editado por José M. Gómez Tabanera. Ed. Istmo, Colegio Universitario. Madrid, 1986.

Dramaturgas españolas de hoy. - Una introducción. de Patricia W. O'Connor. Publica la obra "No moleste, calle y pague, señora". Ed. Espiral. Madrid, 1988.

Esmeralda. – Publicada en la obra colectiva *"La Confesión".* Ed. Asociación de Autores de Teatro. Madrid, 2001.

Theater

El el futuro. - Barcelona, 1957.

Un poco de nieve blanca. - Barcelona, 1958.

Los que siempre ganan. - Barcelona, 1970.

Con el siglo. - Barcelona, 1982. "Dones i Catalunya", montaje dirigido por Ricart Salvat. Representada en Olite, 1982; en Atenas, 1982, dentro del Festival Internacional de Teatro; en Barcelona, 1983.

Las mujeres caminaron con el fuego del siglo. - Barcelona, 1982. Representada en Atenas 1982, en Barcelona, 1983, 1984. New York, 1983, en San Juan de Puerto Rico, 1983, en Búfalo, 1988. Barcelona. 2000. Vilanova y la Geltrú. 2002. Publicada por Vindicación Feminista, Madrid, 1994.

Calle, pague, y no moleste, señora. - Barcelona, 1983. Representada en Sans (Barcelona); en Móstoles, dentro de la Primera Muestra Internacional de Teatro Feminista. Publicada en la revista "Estreno" de la Universidad de Cincinnati. Publicada por Vindicación Feminista, Madrid, 1994.

Parid, parid, malditas. - Barcelona, 1983. Representada en Barcelona, 1986, 1988. Publicada por Vindicación feminista, Madrid, 1994.

Siempre busqué el amor. - Madrid, 1983. Representada en el Festival de Teatro de Carmona. Sevilla, 1989. Publicada por Vindicación Feminista. Madrid, 1994.

Tres idiotas españolas. - Madrid, 1987. Representada en Madrid, 1987 Circulo de Bellas Artes, dentro de la Primera Muestra Internacional de Teatro Feminista. En San Lorenzo del Escorial, 1987 Teatro Carlos III; En Gijón, 1988; En Valencia, 1990; En Bilbao, 1990, Teatro Arriaga; Madrid, 1994, Teatro Alfil.

Tu único amor. - Madrid, 1990. Entremés a 1 acto. Publicada en la revista "Art Teatral". Valencia, 1991.

Three Spanish Idiots: Monologue in Three Acts. -Traducción al inglés del monólogo en castellano *"Tres idiotas españolas"* representado en Australia. 1995.

¡Vamos a por todas! Ed. Asociación de Autores de Teatro y Consejería de las Artes de la Comunidad de Madrid. Madrid, 2002.

CPSIA information can be obtained at www.ICGtesting.com
Printed in the USA
BVOW07s0824231013

334416BV00002B/26/P